Gelus Hearts

THE OREY GELUS DUET

EBONY OLSON

EBANDMUSE & PUBLICATIONS

EBANDMUSE
PUBLICATIONS

Published 2023

Published by EbandMuse Publications Sydney, Australia

Copyright © 2023 by **Ebony Olson.**

Cover by Frina Art

Editing by Striding Ibis Editing

http://ebonyolson.com/

PART ONE

Orey Witches

The Joint Party

"DO you think eating pussy tastes good?" Tapping her chin with her pen, Mia contemplated the periodic table above the teacher's desk. "I mean, I don't think I taste too bad, so maybe eating pussy would be okay."

Raising my eyebrows as I focused on today's experiment, I kept my eyes on the flask I was decanting. "You're asking me?"

"Have you tasted yourself?" Mia still stared at the periodic table.

"No."

"You should."

I lowered the burner's heat by turning the tap to slow the flow. "I'll pass."

"I'm just curious." Swirling her pen around to indicate the room, Mia huffed. "Why are single-sex schools still even a thing?"

"Probably because some parents want their kids to focus on their studies rather than the opposite sex," I responded dryly before turning everything off.

I'd given up years ago trying to get Mia to help with our science pracs. She let me do it all and then just wrote up my findings. She hated science. Her family were naturalists. They were all about purity and only having what nature intended. My mother's magic was in alchemy, and my father's in casting. We believed in science and technology as long as everything is balanced with nature.

"Pfft, like that happens." Mia turned to look at me. "You know, there's a party tomorrow night. One of the boys from Saint Christopher's is having a parent-free eighteenth birthday party. We could go?"

Checking the flask measurement, I wrote it down in my lab book and started doing the calculations. "You got invited to a Saint Chris's party?"

"It's Elisha's brother. She invited a bunch of girls."

Stopping, I eyed Mia. "And you were one of them?"

Elisha was one of the most popular girls in our year. She was blonde, beautiful, and well-tanned from the tanning lotion she applied the same way I used moisturizer. Elisha was a cheerleader and totally obsessed with fashion. She also hated Mia.

My bestie and fellow Orey seemed to rub Elisha up the wrong way, but I had no idea why. I mean, Mia was tall and naturally slim. She was intelligent—when she could be bothered––and captain of the cheer squad. Which was probably what Elisha hated her for. There might be more to it, but whatever it was, Elisha loved talking shit about Mia behind her back.

"Okay, no. But Elisha invited all the girls from the cheer squad. Since I'm the captain..." Mia waggled her eyebrows. "We should go."

"If I get caught sneaking out––"

"Come on, Sasha. You're nearly eighteen and you've never even kissed a boy. Please, we have to go to this party. I want a home run with some drunk, entitled private school asshole who throws around big dick energy like he has it to spare."

Pursing my lips, I looked around and kept my voice low. "We're Orey. If we go to a Vestigial party, get drunk, and do something, we'll be in trouble."

Orey were witches who lived on the edges of two worlds. Orey literally meant 'edge'. We looked like we existed with humans—Vestigials—but we didn't. We lived very different lives and skirted the fringes of their society. Well, we used to. The cross-over was becoming increasingly blurred for our survival over the generations.

"Come on! When was the last time you lost control? I doubt you were even double digits."

"It's not me I'm worried about. I'm not a naturalist who just throws around their power willy-nilly without channeling it through something. If you drink and decide to show off, I get busted too."

Holding out her little finger, Mia gave me her Bambi eyes. Pale sage bleeding to almost grey irises pleaded from behind night dark lashes. "Pinky-promise that I'll keep myself in check."

"Okay, everyone, it's nearly home time. Let's finish our titrations and start packing up, please," the teacher called from the front of the room.

Returning my focus to my notes, I gave up. "I'll think about it. You're on clean up while I finish writing up."

Huffing, Mia started cleaning while I finished writing up our findings and a conclusion to the paper. As I finished putting our names on the sheet, the bell rang. Packing my stuff up, I took our report to the teacher on my way out the door. At my locker, I dumped what I wouldn't need over the weekend and collected my blazer, pulling it on.

"Sasha, I'm glad I caught you." Elisha smiled, opening her locker next to mine. Despite hating my bestie, Elisha was always keen to be friends with me for some reason. I used to think it was so she could copy my homework or something, but I think she'd given up on ever being academic in middle school. "It's my birthday tomorrow night, and Simon's having a party, of course, and we thought it would be great if it was a joint party since you and Savas turn eighteen on Sunday. Savas already said yes when Simon asked him. I've invited Raisa and Yasmine already, so you'll have other friends there."

Raisa and Yasmine were my other Orey friends. In primary school, Elisha and I were repeatedly forced together with our twin brothers because we were both co-ed twins. The teachers thought it was cute. While our brothers were easy around each other, it always felt like I had to try too hard to find anything in common with Elisha, but we were still friendly.

Taking the notepaper with the details, I shoved it into my pocket. "I'll ask Mum about it."

"It'd be great if you could come. I know your mum can be a bitch about you having a life, but you're about to turn eighteen." Elisha cringed.

"I'll ask."

"You know, Simon hasn't asked anyone to the formal yet. Do you have a partner?"

"Not that anyone has told me about." Stepping away, I pointed to the exit. "I have to go."

"Oh, of course. Hopefully, I'll see you tomorrow."

Giving her a wave, I turned and headed for the doors. Mia caught up to me at the exit. Her family lived in town. But while Mia walked home, I had to walk into town to get the bus that went into the canyon to service the hunter's lodge and numerous hiking trails. I'd ride the ten-seater bus to the small five-shops-total village, then walk across the river and downstream to where our house was nestled into the hillside.

"Milkshakes?" Mia asked.

"Yes!"

Milkshakes were code for stopping at the diner and eating burgers. Mia's family were vegetarians, but Mia loved meat. Since I caught the bus from outside the Milkbar four days a week, I usually sat inside, got a drink, and studied during the hour wait for it to come.

Mia had to walk past the Milkbar every day, so she'd join me on days when she didn't have any other extracurricular commitments.

"Good, I seriously need meat! We haven't got to the diner at all this week." Pushing through the doors for the sports field, we set a course for the side gate, which was a shortcut to the Milkbar.

"So, Elisha made tomorrow a joint party for Savas and me. If you devise a plan to get me away from my parents for the afternoon, we could hit the Milkbar on the way to the party."

Mia did a little hoot for joy. "Wait, I thought it was her brother's birthday?"

"They're twins, Mia. Like Savas and me."

"Oh! I never knew that." Mia didn't move to this area until year ten, so she missed the co-ed twin fun of primary and middle school. "Anyway, sounds like a plan. Why don't we tell our parents we are meeting to work on our English essay tomorrow? We go to the library and get that knocked off, then hit the diner and go to the party. You tell your 'rents that you are hanging out at my place until late, and I'll tell mine that I'm at your place."

"Sounds good up until we become each other's alibi. Raisa and Yasmine are also going to the party, so let's ring them in and create an alibi ring. That way, you tell your parents I'm coming over after study. Then, before we go to the party, you tell your parents we are going to Raisa's. We get Raisa to do the same but say we ended up at Yasmine's, Yasmine says my place, and I'll do the same. If our parents check up on us, it'll take them a bit of calling around to realize we're not where we should be."

"You mean if your mother rings."

"Yes. If my helicopter parent rings." Pushing open the door to the Milkbar, I led the way to the booth free in the back. This diner was on the opposite side of town from Saint Christopher's, so you never got any of the boys here. They had their own cafe to hang at.

"Afternoon, Ladies," Falco greeted as we took our seats. "Be with you in a minute." He finished cleaning up the table near ours and walked away, Mia perving on him as he did.

"Damn, he is fine."

Glancing at Falco, I could concede that for a guy in his twenties, he was handsome, with nice broad shoulders, and he had these weird blue-black eyes which almost seemed predatory. Still, like most of the male species, he did nothing for me. I wasn't into girls either; I'd just never been attracted to anyone. Well, one guy, but it was definitely unrequited.

"You know Yasmine has been screwing him. I'm kind of jealous." Mia sulked. Yasmine and Raisa were almost a year older than me. They'd turned eighteen and started going to parties and banging Vestigials almost immediately. Mia had only turned eighteen six months ago, and dropped her panties slightly less than the others.

"Raisa too."

"Of course she's jealous."

"No, she's also been going back to 'chat' when he takes a break. He took both their virginities. They told me all about it."

Lifting her brow, Mia snickered. "Does Yasmine know?"

Shrugging, I considered the menu. "It's not like they are the only ones. Pretty sure Elisha and co have all been tapping him and his older brother."

Chewing her lip, Mia considered Falco behind the counter. "He is a dish. He must have some skill if they are all jumping on him."

The door pushed open, and my other two childhood friends strutted in. Raisa with her red wavy hair tied back in a braid, her fair skin sporting brightened freckles around her green-grey eyes. Behind her came Yasmine, who was busy popping buttons on her school blouse to show her voluptuous assets. Her milk chocolate curls were tied back in a ponytail, and her grey-hazel eyes were highlighted by thick mascara.

"Hey, chickas," Yasmine greeted, sliding into the booth beside us. "How is Friday afternoon treating us?"

"Great. Sasha has agreed to sneak out to the Vincents' party this weekend." Mia grinned.

"Really? How?" Raisa scoffed. My mother's helicopter parenting was not a secret.

"Well, we are all going to be each other's alibi," Mia schemed, and leaned closer to tell them the plan. Falco was back to take our orders by the time it was sorted out.

Just as he got to me, my phone buzzed in my pocket. Sighing, I took it out of my pocket and looked at the message from my brother.

SAVAS:

> Mum wants us straight home from school today. Where are you? I'll pick you up.

Cursing under my breath, I sent a quick reply. "I can't stay. Savas is picking me up. Apparently, mum wants us home pronto."

Frowning, Mia stomped her foot beneath the table. "Seriously? Why?"

"No idea, but when mum says jump, we don't ask how high in our household." Grabbing up my bag, I slipped out of the booth. "Message me what time to meet you at the library tomorrow."

"See you, Sasha." Falco smiled as I left. Giving him a smile, I waved and walked out to the curb to wait.

Four motorbikes raced towards me from the Saint Christophers' end of the street with only the buzz of an electric bike. "Looks like the entire team is picking me up."

"Us," another female voice bitched next to me. "They're picking us up, Sasha."

Great! "Hey, Calliope."

Her pale blue-grey eyes bulged in indignation, then Calliope swatted her platinum blonde hair off her shoulder. "It's Caly out here."

"Right, sorry."

Calliope was another Orey, but older. Actually, I had no idea how old she actually was. I always thought of her as younger because of her genuine adolescent attitude. She thought she was the shit and strutted everywhere as if the world was her catwalk. I'd take Elisha any day of the week over putting up with Calliope.

"Caly Assion? I have a bone to pick with you," a woman called from the door of the Milkbar.

"Damn!" Caly hissed, then threw me a filthy look before going to talk to whoever it was.

Ignoring the spoilt brat, I moved between the cars to where Savas was waiting. Flicking up his visor, he met my eyes with his matching pale violet-grey ones as he handed me his spare helmet. "Why are you pissed?" Savas asked.

"Why do you think?"

While Savas turned his cold gaze on Calliope, I snatched the helmet he handed me. Pulling my dark hair out of its high ponytail, I changed it to a low pony. Pulling the helmet on, I did up the chin strap, then stepped up on the back wheel peg and threw my leg over the back of the bike.

Thank gods we were still in winter uniform, which allowed the girls to wear slacks, or I'd be doing this ride home in my summer kilt. Typically, I had an advance warning to Savas picking me up, and I'd bring my kevlar jeans to change into. They were as good as wearing motorcycle leathers.

"You good?" Savas asked through the speaker in the helmet.

Grabbing the seat holds, I knocked down the visor. "Yep."

"Barden, you want us to wait for you?" Savas asked.

"No. Go." That was Calliope's brother, Barden. Always monosyllabic, if he spoke at all around me.

It was a pity, because he was hot as all hell and the only guy to ever make me want to kiss a boy—but if I tried talking to him, he'd just sit there looking at me. Occasionally, he grunted like a caveman. Barden's family only moved here a few years ago, or at least, he only started school with Savas two years ago. Yet he quickly became Savas's best friend, so I always tried to be polite. Plus, I felt sorry for him, having Calliope as a sister.

While Barden was just a few months older than Savas and me, Vidal and Nash, Yasmine and Raisa's older brothers, respectfully, were in college already. Still, the boys were a team, so they hung out and patrolled together to protect the ignorant Vestigials from the dangers that lurked in the dark.

As Savas pulled out into the after-school traffic, he took it easy, but as soon as he'd weaved through the minor side streets, he rolled his wrist, and the electric motorbike shot forward.

The Assions

WHEN WE GOT HOME, I jumped off the bike and removed the helmet as I stepped from the adjoining garage into the house. Leaving my helmet on the bench in the boot room, I shrugged off my bag, then my blazer, and hung the blazer in the coat closet.

Savas followed me in and did the same, stopping and pulling out his phone and typing a text. Ignoring him, I headed inside and went to the fridge.

"No food, we are going to the Assions for dinner," my mother called from the room off the kitchen. It was big enough to be another kitchen and doubled as my mother's alchemy lab when she found the time to practice. All our skin care and cleaning products were made in that room. "Go get changed. Wear something nice."

Scowling, I grabbed a flask of cold water from the fridge and headed for the stairs.

"Hey!" Dad called from his den. "What's up your butt?"

Huffing, I stepped into his doorway. Savas and I both looked like our dad. His dark hair, pale skin, and cloud-gray eyes. Mum had a creamed-honey glow to her skin, chestnut curls, and pale indigo-gray eyes, which is probably where the undertones of lavender came from in ours.

"The Assions, seriously?"

"They're our friends." Dad closed the book he was reading and took off his glasses.

"Bully for you. They're not mine."

Rubbing at the scar along his jawline, Dad assessed me. "Since when?"

"Since always. Calliope is a spoilt brat and hates me, and Barden..." *makes me drool* "is even worse."

"How does Barden annoy you?"

"He stares at me as if I totaled his bike or something and refuses to say two words to me. Like, all the time."

Wetting his lips, Dad put the book aside and stood up. "They are our friends."

"Well, you go. I'll stay home. I can work on my English essay. That way, I can go to the joint party with the Vincent twins tomorrow."

"There is not a chance you are going to some Vestigial high school party," my mother called behind me.

"Why?" I turned to face her. "I turn eighteen on Sunday, and Elisha made it a joint party for them and us. Why am I so untrustworthy to be allowed to go to a party with my friends?"

"Because you're not eighteen yet, and even when you are, you'll still be living under my roof, so you won't go to a drunken free-for-all with Vestigials."

"So, Savas won't be allowed to go either?" I accused.

"Savas will be working with the team. A Vestigial teenage party full of alcohol and drugs is where you will find predators. It's different!"

"How? Other than my having tits and vag and Savas swinging a dick?" Watching my mother's mouth fall open, I scoffed. "You know what, don't bother."

"What has got into you today?" My mother gaped.

"You're all so fucking sexist; it's unbelievable." I headed for the stairs.

"Language!" Dad scolded.

Ignoring him, I jogged upstairs. I was so sick of having to do everything I was told. Of not being trusted. Of having to go to the Assions' and pretend to be happy to be there. Any of the other Orey families, I'd happily go to.

Changing out of my uniform into my kevlar jeans and a flowing top, I went into the bathroom, brushed my hair, and left it hanging loose.

Grabbing my satchel, I put the book I was reading, my phone, and EarPods in it. Finishing the flask of water as I skipped down the stairs, I went to the kitchen and refilled my bottle.

"I told you to put on something nice," my mother bitched when she entered the kitchen.

"Well, you ignore my wishes; I figured I'd pay it back and wear something comfortable for the bike ride."

"You're coming in the car with me. Go change."

"Sure, Mum. I'll just put my bag out, ready." Instead, I walked out to the mudroom and grabbed my leather jacket and helmet. In the garage, I hit the door opener, threw a leg over my purple galaxy-painted Zero SR —my sixteenth birthday present—and pressed the start button. The bonus of electric engines. No noise.

Five minutes down the road, my phone rang in my helmet. Hitting the decline button, I leaned into the curves of the canyon roads, following the river's natural flow, a steep drop-off to the side. By the time I crossed the river to ride up the other side of the canyon, I felt a lot less resentful.

I rarely got any time alone outside my room. My mother wouldn't let me leave the house unless it was for school or with an escort. Knowing the roads here like the back of my hand, I picked up speed, the road straighter and ascending up out of the canyon. I turned down a side road just before the apex and descended back towards the river. The route started winding with the river again.

Dusk was just falling as I pulled into the Assion driveway and wound up around the tree-lined drive to reach the front door of their large house. Getting off my bike, I stopped to admire the view. The river was more expansive here, far below us, but it sparkled as the sunset. Across the other side of the canyon and further down the slope, our house was perched amongst the trees.

Smiling at the view, I sighed to have to turn away from it. At the front door, I looked down over my outfit and rolled my eyes at my mother's insistence I wear something nice. Translation, girly. Smirking, I closed my eyes, tapped my shoulders and hips, then clicked my fingers and knocked my ankles together. Upon opening my eyes, I wore a cropped purple peasant top and a dark gray-and-purple pleated tartan skirt that barely reached mid-thigh. If Barden was going to glare at me all night, I'd at least give him something to look at.

Pressing the doorbell, I checked my phone and saw the missed call from my mother. Ringing her back, I got her message bank. "Hey, I'm safely at the Assions'. Don't worry, I got changed like you asked. Found a skirt and a top. See you soon." The door opened as I hung up.

Mr. Assion blinked as he looked me over from head to toe. "Sasha. Where's your family?"

"On the way. I was ready before the rest of them." Stepping inside when he opened the door, I set my helmet on the seat bench with my jacket.

"You rode by yourself?"

"The canyon is such a nice ride, and I needed to wind down after a long week. I'm sure Calliope could use a ride after the mood she was in today."

Mr. Assion straightened. "Mood?"

"She seemed pretty pissy when Savas picked me up today." I shrugged and moved forward into the house. As I did, Barden descended the steps in jeans and a button-down, his feet bare and his dark brown hair a mess like usual. He paused and then proceeded a lot slower when he saw me, his eyes seemingly stuck on my exposed midriff and my legs.

"Barden, did something happen with Calliope today?" Mr. Assion asked behind me, breaking his son's stare away from my body.

Grunting, Barden shrugged, his eyes coming back to me as I moved toward the kitchen. What did I say? Caveman.

Sighing, Mr. Assion started up the stairs. "Where is she?"

"Room."

In the kitchen, Mrs. Assion was busy preparing dinner. Spotting me, she smiled. "Sasha. How are you?"

"Fine, Mrs. Assion. Can I help?"

"That'd be lovely."

Ignoring the cold shiver that Barden's presence behind me caused down my spine, I set my bag aside and started helping. Going around the bench, Barden sat on the other side.

"Nelly?" Barden and Calliope always addressed their parents by their names. Totally weird.

Putting her son to work helping, Mrs. Assion seemed not to notice the way her son glared at me even while he was chopping salad ingredients, but I certainly felt his gaze. Thankfully, Savas arrived shortly after, and they took the meat out to start the barbecue. In comparison to Mia's family, the Assions were carnivores.

When my parents arrived, they looked at my outfit and appeared horrified but held their tongues. At that point, the dads all drifted out to burn the meat, and my mother suggested I go find Calliope to hang with her until dinner was ready.

Eager to escape Barden's glare chilling me through the sliding door, and my mother, I grabbed my satchel and headed upstairs. Not that I bothered Calliope. Instead, I dropped on the couch in the kids' retreat, put my EarPods in, and listened to music while I read my book.

An arm nudged my knee to get my attention. Looking up, Barden stood there glaring down at me. Huh, that's why I was cold all of a sudden. Taking an EarPod out, I lifted a brow. Tilting his head towards the stairs, Barden walked down the hall to Calliope's room. Sighing, I got up and put my stuff back in my bag before heading downstairs.

"It just came out of nowhere," my mother said quietly as I walked towards the kitchen.

"Come on, Delila. She's nearly eighteen. You had to expect it was coming? She's been a surprisingly obedient teenager compared to her friends."

"She says that Barden annoys her because he stares at her."

"Well, it wouldn't hurt him to try talking to her."

As if they had summoned him, I felt the chill on the exposed skin of my spine. Putting my back to the wall, I looked behind me to find Barden. He came closer, standing well over a head taller than me, peering down at me as he came right up on me in the hall. Glancing to the kitchen and our mother's voices, Barden looked back at me, his dark gray-blue eyes delving into the depths of my soul.

For three full breaths, Barden stared into my eyes, our breath mingling, and without words, he posed the question I'd been asking myself for two years. *'Do you want me to stop looking?'*

Wetting my lips, I swallowed. Did I? For years he'd been staring at me whenever we were in the same room. I'd always thought he hated me, but it didn't stop me from imagining him doing more. A tickle on my thigh alerted me to Barden's fingers playing with the hem of my skirt.

Glancing to be sure, I looked back into Barden's face. He cocked a brow. That was it. No smirk, no smile, just an arched brow. His hand firmed against my bare skin, slid to the back of my thigh, and drifted higher.

My mouth filled with spit when he grabbed my ass. Suddenly his gaze was the exact opposite of cold on my skin. When his fingers slipped beneath the edge of my panties to grip my naked rump, I bit my lip to prevent gasping and found I couldn't breathe.

"Mine," Barden whispered.

Thumping above us alerted us to Calliope's approach. Smooth as a shadow, Barden slipped away and into the kitchen.

"Did you get the girls?"

Another grunt, this one with a positive inflection. That's how used to Barden's neanderthal language I was, that I could actually interpret it.

In a rush, my breath escaped, and I had to lean forward to control my body as it flushed with heat belatedly. "Shite!" I whispered.

"What's wrong with you?" Calliope bitched.

"Nothing."

"Right..." Calliope snarked as she walked past.

Standing straight, I followed her to the dining table.

"So, anything exciting happening with you kids?" my dad asked as we ate as if we were a big family.

I answered, not even thinking. "People are starting to organize their partners from Saint Chris' for the formal."

Lifting a brow, our parents looked at each other.

"You don't say?" my father answered.

"Elisha Vincent was talking to me about it today."

"I'm sure she won't have trouble getting a date." Savas snickered.

"Why, are you asking her?"

Both Savas and Barden smirked. "No. I prefer quality over easy."

"Savas!" our mother scolded.

"Have you asked anyone, Savas?" Dad enquired.

"Not yet."

"How about you, Barden?" Dad fished.

A negative grunt.

"Sasha? Have you been asked by anyone?"

"Elisha was hinting that Simon might ask me," I admitted.

Not because I felt like being honest, but because I knew the idea of me dating a Vestigial would go down like a tonne of bricks. As expected, the 'rents and my brother quickly gave their opinions. Barden just watched me across the table, and as if we were back in the hall, I could feel his fingers creeping beneath my panties to cup my naked backside and squeeze.

'Mine!'

Swallowing, I focused on my food and let the conversation move over me.

After dinner, Calliope went back upstairs without helping to clean up. No way that would have happened if she had my mother, so I got up and helped Nelly and my mum clean up. The boys had gone upstairs to play computer games or whatever they did in Barden's room straight after Calliope left.

"Thanks, Sasha. Can you take Calliope's drink bottle to her when you go up?"

Giving Nelly a forced smile, I picked up the water flask. "Sure." Heading upstairs, I dropped my bag on the lounge, then went to Calliope's door. I knocked, but she had the music turned up a fair bit, so I just opened it. Calliope was naked on her bed, and so was my brother —they were going at it hard. Thankfully, they were doing doggy and had their backs to the door, so neither saw me. Putting the flask on the shelf by the door, I stepped out and closed it.

When I turned around, Barden stood down the hall, leaning against the wall. Chewing my lip, I moved closer to him. "Um, your sister is busy."

A hybrid grunt-laugh. Eyeing me, Barden backed me up against the opposite wall, and then his hand was on my butt again as he stared into my eyes. When he cocked his brow and tilted his head a little, I couldn't resist.

Leaning in quickly, I kissed him. Just a peck. Before I could pull away, his other hand was at the back of my neck, holding me there. He didn't kiss me again, just stood there peering into my eyes and holding me tight against him. Slowly, he pressed his mouth to mine and flicked his tongue against the seam of my lips.

Startled, I opened my eyes wide for a second and pulled back. Barden watched me, his hand caressing my jaw.

"Mine."

Throwing my arms around his neck, I met his lips with mine and kissed him after two years of longing for this moment.

Groaning, Barden crouched a little, wrapping one arm around my waist, his other hand still cupping my butt. Securing me in his hold, Barden lifted and carried me out to the lounge, lying me beneath him. Keeping his hands glued to my waist and rump, Barden kissed me fervently. I wasn't so restrained.

Gripping Barden's shoulders, I pulled myself tight against him and enjoyed the feel of his silken hair between my fingers. As I gasped for breath, Barden kissed down the line of my throat, sucking and nibbling across my collarbone. When I moaned his name, Barden grabbed my face and covered my mouth with his again.

A flame licked along my insides, from my navel to my sternum, where it grew larger. The room became brighter and hotter. Pulling back suddenly, Barden looked down. Following his gaze, I saw a small flame hovering between us. "What-?"

"Shh." Barden kept his eyes on the flame as he cupped his hands around it. A shiver raced through my body as he seemed to caress it. "Mine."

Tenderly, Barden pressed the flame against my sternum. Heat flared through my body, making my back arch. Turning his hand so that his fingers were pointing downwards, Barden ran his hand down my midline, the flame following him on the inside.

As Barden slipped his hand beneath the waistband of my skirt, his fingers only inches from my panties, my phone rang in my bag.

Removing his hand from my skin, Barden pulled away. Almost instantly, the flame ebbed and died inside me.

Getting up, I grabbed my phone. "It's Mia."

When I turned around, ready to suggest that I could call her back, Barden was already gone.

The Eighteenth

THE VINCENTS LIVED on an acreage in a gated estate. The party was in full swing when we walked there from the diner. As we walked the drive, you could hear the music before you saw the house.

"How can anyone hear each other over that music?" Yasmine complained. "We'll go home deaf." She wore skinny jeans, ankle boots, and a tight v-neck shirt beneath her jacket. Her milk chocolate curls had caramel highlights, making her pale gray-hazel eyes pop against her bronze skin. Her beautiful Latina curves were perfectly framed in her outfit.

"It probably seems loud out here because everything around us is so quiet," Raisa soothed. "Plus, as we get closer, we'll get accustomed to it." Her red wavy hair was swept up in a high pony, the freckles on her cheeks and nose muted by the foundation on her fair skin. Her red wrap dress was almost hidden beneath a knee-length black duffle coat, and her legs were protected from the chilly early spring wind by black knee-high boots.

It was really the first high school party I'd gone to. While the others were eighteen and less inhibited by their parents, Vestigial parties were still a no-no as far as my parents were concerned. In my mother's words,

'Those parties are all drugs, alcohol, and sex. No Orey girl should be amidst that sort of behavior.'

Mia put her hand on the door handle at the steps and breathed. "We ready?" Her black leather mini skirt hung from her hips and exposed more thigh than I ever had outside a pool. Mia's emerald green v-neck stopped short enough to show that the beautiful black skin of her abs was dusted with some sort of gold sparkly moisturizer.

I wore the same outfit as last night. Only my family and the Assions had seen me in it, so no big deal. My Docs came up to my lower shin, and tonight I'd donned a double-breasted peacoat that covered my bum to keep somewhat warm. My legs were getting killed in the wind chill, though.

"Open the door already. I'm freezing my ass off," the person wearing the jeans complained.

We all looked at Yasmine and laughed, then the door was open, and the music got even louder. Inside the house was hot. They had the gas fires burning in each living area, and the place was packed with most of the senior year of Saint Christopher's plus nearly half as many of our senior year.

"I think the only girls not here are all on the chess team," Raisa whisper-yelled.

"I'm on the chess team." Yasmine scowled.

"Yeah, but you have the assets these boys like," Mia replied. "Elisha's brother probably just looked at our year photo and picked out all the girls he'd happily bang."

"If that was the case, the entire year would be here," I replied dryly. "Simon's not really picky as far as I hear it. Pussy and tits, you're doable."

"Ah, yeah. Ah, Sasha, would your brother let you be here?" Mia asked.

"Probably not. Why?" Following where she was pointing, I spied Savas sitting with Elisha's twin, Simon, and on the other side of him, Barden. As Barden's head swung towards us, I grabbed Mia and yanked her and the girls into the next room. "Shite! Okay, we're cool. They didn't see us. But we all have to avoid them. They know we are meant to be hanging out together tonight. If one of us gets busted, we all get busted."

24

"This just became so much more fun," Raisa snickered. "So, we have fun, flirt, and dance but have to stay off the Orey radar."

"Which also means Simon's radar, 'cause he's sure as shit going to tell Savas you are here," Yasmine worried. We all nodded in agreement.

"Girls!" We all jumped as a loud voice yelled right behind us. Elisha was standing there with her posse, all three of them somewhat into their cups. "I'm so glad you could all make it." Suddenly Elisha was hugging us all, even Mia. "Isn't this party awesome? Now, people are just chillin' in the front rooms. The kitchen has a keg on tap and other assorted refreshments. You have to try the punch; it's to die for. The dining room has nibbles. We had pizza delivered not long ago, so there may still be leftovers. The spa is on the back deck if you feel like getting wet. The dance room is at the end of the hall in the rumpus room. Toilets are halfway down near the games room, and the stoner room is opposite."

All of us were staring at Elisha wide-eyed when she hiccupped and cut off. "Ah, here, happy birthday." I offered the little gift I'd gotten her while I was in town today.

"Oh, you're so sweet, Sash." Tearing it open, she took out a charm bracelet with a little number eighteen charm hanging from it. "OMG! I love it. My other bracelet was full up. I so needed this!" She wrapped me in her arms and hugged me tightly. She was a cheerleader; she had strength.

"I figured when I saw your other one yesterday," I squeaked. Not that I wasn't strong. I was on the swim team at school. A totally accidental sign-up. I went to the pool to chill after a terrible first day at school and just happened to be there during tryouts. The coach signed me up as I got out of the pool before others got in.

"I have to keep socializing. I'll catch up with you all later. Have fun!" Moving on, thankfully in the opposite direction of my brother, Elisha squealed and assaulted someone else.

"Okay, it sounds like the dance room is where we need to be," Mia conspired as soon as we were alone again. "First, we need drinks." Following the tile flooring towards the oversized chef's kitchen, Mia poured us all solo cups of the punch. Taking a whiff, I pulled away, blinking. "I'm pretty sure that's paint thinner. I'll pass." Grabbing another cup, I filled it with orange juice instead.

"God, the pizza smells good!" Yasmine sniffed in the direction of the dining table.

"My brother will be able to see us if we step into that space," I huffed.

"I'll go. I'm short enough to hide behind everyone else." Moving in behind two senior boys, Yasmine reached passed another to grab a box. Giving it a bit of a shake, she reeled it in, lifted the lid to peek inside, then came our way again.

A shiver raced down my spine as a heated gaze passed over me. Freezing, I turned and checked behind me. No one I recognized was lurking. Frowning, I moved to the partition and peeked around the corner. Savas and Simon were still on the sofa, surrounded by their mates from school and a handful of girls. "Shite." Going back to the girls, I kept my eyes peeled. "Barden has left the lounge room."

"Will he bust you?" Mia asked.

"Ah, yeah, like she was his own sister," Raisa answered. "You obviously haven't been to enough gatherings with the Assions. If they are in the same room, Barden never takes his eyes off Sasha. He's got it for her bad."

"He does?" I frowned.

Raisa and Yasmine laughed. "Yeah! Why do you think he watches you like that?"

"I always thought he hated me and fantasized about killing me slowly," I admitted.

"Huh, yeah, I guess he does rock the serial killer vibe. I mean, but he's hot as all hell. If it wasn't for the politics about his family and shit, I'd risk it for a go of him," Raisa considered. "But he's never even looked at me sideways."

"Me too. I'd give anything to have one of the guys obsess over me like he does you, Sasha."

"Okay, but to be safe, we should try to avoid him seeing us just the same." Mia laughed at our friends. "I mean, seven minutes in heaven with Barden Assion isn't worth Sasha's parents turning up and dragging us out of here, is it?" Raisa and Yasmine both thought about it way too long. "That was rhetorical. Let's find the dance floor."

Heading down the hall, we passed the rec room, and after pushing past a handful of heavy petting couples in the hallway, we slipped into the dance room. There weren't many in here, which suited us. If it wasn't the place to be, then it was unlikely my brother and his friends would come in here.

We scoffed the cheese pizza between us, finished our drinks, and started shaking our booties on the dance floor. Every now and then, I'd get the sensation of being watched and checked the room, but Barden was never there.

After a couple of hours and running the gauntlet to get drinks a few times, I needed the bathroom. Heading down the hall, I waited in line, keeping an eye out, then slipped into the bathroom. When I came out, I checked the hallway twice and quickly scooted down it toward the dance floor.

As I passed the rec room, a familiar face stepped out.

"Sasha, hey." Falco smiled, his pupils dilating as he took in my outfit.

"Hey, what are you doing here?"

"Elisha invited me." Sliding his hands into the pockets of his jeans, Falco stepped closer. "I hear this is your party too?"

Tilting my head side to side a little, I shrugged. "Supposedly, but I'm not meant to be here, so not really."

Cocking his head like I'd seen eagles do, Falco narrowed his eyes. "So, it's not your eighteenth birthday?"

"Oh, well, tomorrow, yes."

Some other guys coming out of the rec room stumbled into Falco, causing him to step forward and brace himself against the wall, pinning me between the wall and his body. "Shit, sorry, man," one called as they continued stumbling towards the back door. "Girls are in the hot tub."

Nodding his head as if that were code, Falco turned his attention back to me and straightened himself. "You okay."

"Yeah," I muttered as I found some breathing room. A cold thrill ran up my spine, making me search the hallway.

"Maybe I'll catch up with you later." Falco smiled kindly. "If not" –– he leaned in and pressed a kiss right next to my mouth— "Happy birthday, Sasha."

Surprised by the attention and physical contact, I pressed harder into the wall and bit my lip. Falco was a nice guy. He'd always been polite around me, so I think he was maybe a little drunk or used to most girls fawning for his attention and jumping his bones if he even looked at them. "Thanks."

The side of his mouth twitching, Falco followed the other guys out towards the back deck. Chewing my lip, I rechecked the hallway and made for the dance room.

When I got back, a group of boys had joined my girls and were dancing with them, getting very handsy. Backstepping, I decided I wasn't keen to participate in the action. Biting my lip, I considered I could go and find Elisha and hang with her, but I doubted she'd be great company with how drunk she'd been when we arrived.

Turning around, I stopped as cold shivers passed over me right before liquid heat slithered through my veins. Face to face with a boy's black button-down shirt, I lifted my eyes to see Barden glaring down at me. Gazing over my head towards my friends, he clenched his teeth. Lifting his phone, Barden took a photo of the girls, then put his phone back in his pocket. Grabbing my elbow, he marched me down the hall.

Sure he would march me out to my brother and call our parents; I tried to pull away. "Wait, please don't call my mum. I haven't been drinking, I promise. I just wanted to go to one party. I was being responsible. That's why I didn't go over to dance with those boys."

Before we returned to the front rooms, Barden opened a door, stuck his head in, and then pulled me inside and shut the door. The room was dark except for a small amount of illumination through a high window. Looking around as Barden used my elbow to walk me backward, I recognized we were in a mudroom. My back hit a wall. "Barden–"

His finger pressed against my lips. "Shh."

Heart in my throat, I tried to swallow. Watching me for several seconds, Barden slipped his hands around my waist, smoothing over the bare skin that my top left exposed. Taking out his phone, he set a timer for seven minutes, then his mouth pressed against mine.

Pulling back when we were both breathless, Barden watched me, his hand caressing my jaw. "Heaven." When his hand found my breast, I arched and moaned. My small mound fit perfectly in his palm while his thumb strummed my nipple through my bra.

"Are you wet?" Barden whispered as he kissed my jaw.

Blinking at the question, I whimpered a little when he pinched my hardened nipple and kissed me breathlessly again. Before I could fathom how fast things were moving, Barden had my top hoisted up and scooped my breast out of my bra. Dropping his face, he sucked the stiff peak between his lips.

Cursing, I grasped at his hair, things tightening quickly downstairs. Then Barden was slipping his hand inside my scanties.

"Barden," I gasped as he found my clit. Shite, this was moving quickly. Maybe he thought I'd done this with boys before. "I'm a virgin. Like, completely," I panted.

Lifting his face to mine, Barden stared into my eyes, caressing my jaw with his free hand. "I know."

Double blinking at his response, I gazed into his eyes, getting lost in the gray-blue depths. His eyes were a darker gray than the usual pale Orey eyes. He had canyons of black winding through them like a roulette wheel's dividers. "You do?"

"Yes." Barden dropped a kiss on my lips. "I'm the only one to ever touch you, right?"

Swallowing, I panted as the way he played my clit had me squirming. "Yes."

"Good. You're mine." Kissing me slow and teasingly, Barden shifted his hand, his fingers sliding over my channel to find my very wet opening. His mouth covered mine as he pressed a finger inside, smothering the whimper of discomfort, then his mouth dropped back to my breast, and I was lost in the sensation.

His finger stroked inside me, causing me to gasp as it became impossible to stay quiet. Lifting his head, Barden met my eyes, his thumb finding my clit, his other hand my exposed breast, and the combination of all three was too much. Smashing his mouth to mine, Barden smothered the sound of me coming on his hand. Something I'd only ever done to my own touch.

Kissing me as I calmed, Barden removed his hand and pulled back to suck his finger. Pulling it free of his lips with a pop, he moaned. Biting my lip, I grabbed Barden's waistband and opened his fly. Sliding my hand in his pants, I slipped through the opening of his boxers and took hold of his thickness. Dropping his head, Barden groaned.

Caressing him, I watched his face, liking how his eyes shuttered as I stroked him.

Barden kissed me furiously as he groped my breast and ass. "I want you so badly," he moaned, then the alarm on his phone sounded. "But time's up." Dropping his face, Barden bit my breast as he throbbed in my hand and came.

Wide-eyed, I took my hand out. Stepping back, Barden adjusted, zipped up, and reached for his phone. Silencing his alarm, he started typing into his phone. Going to the sink, I washed my hand, then checked my breast; sure, it should be bleeding. Not sure whether he'd liked that or not, I righted my clothing and tried to figure out how I should act now.

When the sound of a message being sent broke the silence in the room, Barden showed me the phone screen. He'd sent the team the photo of the girls dancing with the boys.

DELTA TEAM - BARDEN

Your sisters are at Simon Vincent's party. Drunk and getting mauled by drunk guys. Bring the team in so we can take them home.

DELTA TEAM - NASH

Seriously? Okay, on our way.

When I blinked up at Barden, unable to see his face past the screen's brightness, he switched it off. "Go home. If we catch you, we tell your Dad."

"Seriously?!" I groaned when he just folded his arms and went for the door.

"Sasha." Opening the door, I turned to look at him. "Was I worth it?"

Scowling, I raced down the hall and into the dance room. The dancing had turned into a make-out session. "We've got to go!" I yelled, grabbing my jacket and pulling it on.

"What? Why?" Mia frowned, pushing the guy away.

"Barden saw you all here and sent your brothers a photo. They're on their way. He will tell my parents if we are still here when they get here, and I'll be busted."

Lots of cursing followed as the girls extricated themselves from their drunk companions. We grabbed our jackets and went for the door. Savas was talking to Barden at the other end of the hall, blocking the exit. "Shit, how do we get out?"

Barden had positioned himself so that Savas had his back to us. "The mudroom," I murmured.

Racing down the hall, I threw the door open. Over my brother's shoulder, I saw the side of Barden's mouth lift. The bastard was playing with us. Escaping out into the backyard, we raced around the side gate and onto the front lawn, running as hard as we could.

The Execrable

"ARGH, I think all that running sobered me up too fast. I feel seedy," Yasmine moaned. We'd made it to town, but we had to get to Yasmine's house before our brothers found us. She lived the closest to town, so we'd made her the end of the ring around.

It wasn't that late yet. Our absence shouldn't have raised any red flags. Unless, of course, Barden had already called the 'rentals.

"I can't believe Barden didn't call our parents to come to get us," Raisa said for the fifth time.

"He was playing with us. He wanted us to run. They are probably hunting us tonight, so we need to keep off the main roads."

"Wait, how did you know he sent a photo of us?" Mia asked.

"He showed me, then told me if they catch us, we get busted."

"So, he busted you first?"

"He busted us all right at the start. He heard you ask if seven minutes in heaven was worth getting busted." Shaking my head, I couldn't help smiling. "He let us go when we were just dancing, but when you let those guys join you, he decided to end our night of freedom."

Turning to walk backward, Mia assessed me. "What is that smile?

33

Oh, and now you are blushing. What else happened? Did you play tonsil hockey with the gorgeous but likely homicidal Barden Assion?"

Mia laughed aloud when I dropped my head and focused on my steps. "Oh my gosh! You totally got it on with Barden. That's why he didn't call the 'rents. He wanted to play with you, and you let stalker boy have his way."

"Shh! The whole town doesn't need to know."

Raisa joined in eagerly. "How far?"

"Was he as good as he looks?" Yasmine turned to face me. They all watched me and teased me for several minutes.

"Okay, okay. It was hot. Barden even put the timer on so it stopped after seven minutes. Then he sent our brothers the message and asked me if it was worth it." My lips tilted at Barden's game.

"So, was it?" Raisa asked.

Smiling, I shrugged. "Ask me tomorrow."

Laughing, the girls all turned forward again. We were just reaching the other side of the park when a guy stepped in front of us and exhaled a lungful of vapor. The smell was of raspberry instead of tobacco.

"Evening, ladies," he greeted from within the dark. "Have you had a good time? You look like you've had a good time."

"It's been okay," Mia answered cheerily.

To our right, I spotted shadows moving. "Not alone," I murmured. The girls looked around us, sobering quickly as we realized there were at least five surrounding us.

"It's early. How about you chill with us a while?" he asked. "Would you like a vape?"

"You know that stuff is worse for you than cigarettes, right?" Yasmine lectured as we huddled closer together. Reaching into my pocket, I thumbed my phone screen, tapped it four times, and swiped right with three fingers.

"Please be Vestigial," Raisa prayed quietly, taking my hand in hers.

Stepping out of the shadow of a tree, the man's golden eyes shined in the moonlight, his sideburns long enough to make Wolverine jealous. Yasmine's breath came out as a sob at the sight of the Execrable —the detestable, the wretched. Or, in human terms, evil beings that crawled out of the underworld to do horrible things to people.

These men were the very creatures Orey hunted and protected innocents from. This was the other world we lived on the edge of. The Underworld or Hell, if you prefer the Christian name for it.

"Sasha, you're the most trained," Mia muttered. And by training, she meant I've watched our brothers train to be a team at our place for years.

"In three beats, backs together, strike as one, then run for Yas's. Stay together and pray our brothers are close."

Yasmine groaned. "More running!"

The Execrable smiled. "Please do. I love the chase."

Two, one. Turning to put our backs together, we drew our powers into our hands and struck out. My guy went down in a ball of flames. Mia's was getting pulled into the earth, opening a significant gap for us. We bolted.

"Orey witches! Get them!"

We were running away from Yas's place because the other three stood in the way. Mia was in front, and I would have been right there with her, but Raisa and Yasmine were not as fit as us. Growls and snarls ripped from the dark behind us. "Shite, keep going."

Slowing, I pulled my power into my hands, blue lights sparking. Electricity was the best I could do while running because my body produced it as I moved. Hurting from pulling the power out of my muscles, I dropped the ball, then picked up speed again as it unrolled along the ground behind us like a trip wire.

Seconds later, the night lit up in blue sparks as the first evil one tripped the trap. The abominable beast screamed as the electricity net wrapped around him. Trying to shut off the acknowledgment of what I'd just seen, I focused on surviving.

"They're catching. Go faster," I yelled at Raisa and Yasmine as I caught them. "Mia, open the ground and take them down when I say!"

Far enough ahead of us, Mia had reached the road. Turning, she put her hands on the grass of the park. Cold chills ran up my spine, followed by liquid heat.

"Finally! Separate and go wide," I told Raisa and Yasmine.

They ran to each side while I kept running straight ahead. Picking up speed, I aimed straight for Mia, the snarling closing in. I could feel them right behind me. A breeze of air by my left leg, as one swiped to trip me but missed.

"Do it!" I screamed.

The ground disappeared from beneath me, and I sunk into the earth.

"Shit!"

I had a moment to realize Mia messed up and took me down instead of the beasts, and then the world closed around me, trying to crush me. With microseconds to react, I pulled up water and pushed it out around me, then down and under the solid earth beneath my feet. Once it was mud, I could use the water to force me back up and above the ground. My head and hand came free, gasping for breath.

"Sasha!" Mia reached for me. Grasping my arm, she pulled me from the mud and onto the sidewalk. "I'm so sorry. Fuck, I'm so sorry."

There was screeching of tires and screaming of the evil things as our brothers arrived, their powers lighting up the night. Gasping for breath and freezing cold from the groundwater, I held to Mia, who hugged me tightly. Then Raisa and Yasmine were there and added their body warmth.

"Not. Worth. It." I gasped out as we all huddled there. The girls started laughing. A snarl in the dark cut them off as the one I'd electro-cuted sprang out of the dark for us.

A bright light swept over our heads, arcing towards the Execrable. It disintegrated mid-air, and the ashes fell into the mud, making it bubble and hiss. Above us, Barden stood holding a sword of light in his hand, and enormous black feathered wings spread wide like the human depiction of angels from his back. I blinked, and the sword, the wings, and the light was gone.

"Sasha." Barden dropped down but couldn't get to me through the body pile.

"She's okay, just has hypothermia," Raisa assured. "We're trying to keep her warm."

"She might also have got a little crushed when she went into the earth. We should take her to the hospital," Mia added.

Our brothers were now joining us.

"Fucking hell, Raisa!" Nash scolded.

"Everyone up." Savas pushed through and reached for me. "There might be more. Three is a lot to have together."

"There were five," Yasmine informed as she and Raisa got out of the way. "Mia and Sasha killed two."

"Fuck!" Barden ran his hand through his hair.

He'd told me to run. He'd been playing a game, and it had gone horribly wrong. The thing was, it would never have happened if we hadn't gone to the party. I also chose to run rather than face my brother and mother if I got busted. This wasn't all on him.

"Let's move. Barden, Mia will need to ride with you. We'll take Sasha to the hospital, then call our parents to come and get the girls. Vidal, call your dad and tell him we encountered five near your place." Savas glared at me as he helped me to his bike. "Tell them we'd just picked up the girls to take them home for the night from your place and got ambushed. You brought Yasmine with you, so she wasn't home alone. That's the story. Everyone remembers it."

"Um, how are we explaining Sasha's injuries?" Nash asked.

Looking me over, Savas grimaced. "She got swiped off the back of my bike by one of the Execrable."

"And their clothes?" Vidal lifted a brow.

Shaking his head, Savas helped me onto his bike. "They can explain that. Makeovers or some shit. Let's just get out of here." Taking off his helmet, Savas put it on me. Then he got on his bike and wrapped my arms tight around him. "Can you hold on?"

"Yes," I stuttered through my shivering. "Love. You."

Shaking his head, Savas started the bike. "Scared the living shit out of me, Sash. I saw you go into the earth. Fucking insane move. I bet you'll think twice about doing that again."

Not that I'd planned to get buried alive, but I didn't have the energy to fight.

After tonight, I was thinking twice about ever leaving my house again. The Execrable transformed into disfigured creatures that even my worst nightmare couldn't have conjured. When my parents taught us about fighting them, they were always in man form.

"Did you know they change?" I shivered and stuttered.

We were riding fast, and without his helmet on, Savas probably couldn't hear me. Huddling against him, I looked to my side where Barden was riding, Mia behind him. Like me, Barden had given Mia his helmet. Barden kept glancing my way. Closing my eyes, I saw those enormous black wings and wondered if the others had seen them too.

"Sasha, open your eyes. Stay awake," Mia called just as a motorbike horn sounded.

Too tired, I drifted. The world stopped moving, there was a loud noise, and I fell.

The Birthday Kiss

SITTING ON MY BED, I fiddled with my phone. All night, I'd dreamed of Barden and his wings. I'd been sent many messages from family and friends wishing me happy birthday. I'm sure Savas had the same.

As if I summoned him, Savas knocked on my door. He was dressed, having just got home from his night patrolling. "Happy Birthday," he said, smiling.

"Happy birthday. How was the rest of your night?"

Lifting his brow, Savas dropped to the end of my bed. "Surprisingly quiet." His eyes came to me. "How are you feeling?"

"Fine. Nervous. Confused." Other than a few badly bruised ribs-- they didn't quite crack but weren't far off--bumps, scrapes, and bruises, the hospital declared me a picture of health. "Barden had wings, right? I didn't imagine that?"

Bowing his head, Savas picked at some lint on his jeans. "I was the same the first time Barden revealed himself to me. I didn't know what to think. But then Dad got me to read his books on the crows, and I stopped fearing Barden and came to really like him. He got me, you know. While Nash and Vidal were wary of my abilities, Barden and his

41

family helped improve my control. They'll do the same for you now that you know too."

"So, his whole family are crows?"

"Yes." Sitting up straight, Savas pressed his hands between his knees. "Don't be scared of them, Sash. They are deadly as all hell, but they pose no threat to any who do not threaten them."

"What's a crow?" I asked, trying to differentiate Barden from the animal.

"Orey isn't the only magic between the worlds," Savas explained. "Orey witches have been around for a long time, but the Gelus have existed since the dawn of man. The crows ferry the souls of living creatures between the worlds. Those dead and those to be born. They are allies to the Orey in this town. Without them, the Orey would probably all be dead by now."

"Why?"

"Over the last few decades, there has been a change in how the Execrable behave in this world. No one knows why, but we've seen many Orey die in other parts of the world. It's why the Racles moved here. Their teams and families were wiped out. They were the only family to survive, but Mia lost her two brothers before they escaped. The crows came to us a few years ago. Barden offered to be our ally. We knew then that the Orey needed their help, so we accepted."

"Are they good?"

Lifting his face to me, my brother raised a brow. "Are we?"

Frowning, I considered him. "Aren't we?"

Sighing, Savas stared out my window. "You can't see the Orey or the Gelus as good or evil, Sasha. We walk the edge between worlds. We don't protect the Vestigials. The Orey send the Execrable back to where they belong. It is the duty given unto them. It has become harder over the years, as our lives have integrated more with the Vestigials, to separate ourselves from caring what happens to them. Our generation uses the word protect, but that's not the Orey's purpose. Thinking like that is why other clans were wiped out. The crows reminded us of that."

"That doesn't answer my question. Are the crows good people?"

Standing up, Savas avoided my eyes. "They are the transporters of souls. They don't judge; they just deliver. They are our allies, so I like to think that they are good to us, but they have their own purpose here, and they have what I would consider serious personality flaws."

"Like what?"

"Well, they have a superiority complex, for sure, and some of their ethics could be considered questionable."

Frowning, part of me wondered why, if they were so crucial to the Orey's survival, I'd never heard of them until now. "Why would soul transporters need to be so powerful, so deadly?"

Smirking, Savas tilted his head to eye me. "I asked the same. Apparently, some creatures in the otherworld love to steal souls, especially the new or returning souls on their way to being born in the Vestigial world. They are charged with protecting their vulnerable packages at all costs. So, they became more deadly to perform their duty."

Heading towards the door, Savas yawned. "I need some sleep. Happy birthday, Sash."

"You too."

Unable to rest, I got up and changed for my run. The first half of the run was fine, but when I got to the bridge to cross the river, I thought about Barden and everything Savas said.

Biting my lip, I considered the track under the bridge or the stairs up to the road. Looking around, I shook my head and took the stairs. Forty minutes later, I pressed the doorbell at the Barden's place and bent over to catch my breath. I'd forgotten how steep the roads were on this side of the canyon, let alone the incline to get to where the Assion mansion nestled in, probably the only flat area high up on this side.

When the door hadn't been answered after a minute, I checked my watch. It was nearly seven. Maybe everyone was still in bed. Chewing my lip, I considered ringing the bell again might not meet with a friendly reception if I woke them up. Shaking my head, I pressed the doorbell again. I'd run all this way; I wanted answers.

It took another minute before the door opened. Barden stood there shirtless in a pair of sweats, his hair and body glistening with perspiration. "Sash?" Lifting my eyes from his naked chest, I swallowed, suddenly lost for words at the sight of him. "Sash, is everything okay?"

Watching Barden's brow crease, his pupils narrowing as he stepped closer, I finally found my voice. "Um, yeah. I was doing my morning run and wanted to see you, so I ran here. Can we talk?"

Lifting his eyebrows high, Barden stepped back, opening the door wider. "I'll get us some water. I was just working out as well." Following Barden to the kitchen, I took the glass he offered me and drank it. Smirking, Barden drank his. Once I was done, Barden came closer. "Are you okay?"

"With the fact you're a crow?" He nodded. Wetting my lips, I considered him. "I have some questions." When Barden leaned on the island bench to meet my eyes, I took that as an opening.

"Can we have kids?" *Why was that the first thing I wanted to know?*
"Yes."
"Will they have wings?"
"Do you?"

Taken back by the question, I grimaced. "No. At least, they've never popped out on me if I do."

Smirking, Barden moved around the bench towards me. "I don't know. I will only make up half of their genes. They may, they may not. What would be worse is if one does and the other does not. Jealousy about such things is not pretty. Even amongst Gelus couples, wings are not always guaranteed."

Tilting my head, I considered Barden. "Does Calliope not have wings?"

Leaning on the bench right in front of me, Barden put his face level with mine. "I never said that," he whispered, and added a wink.

"Ouch! No wonder she's salty."

Leaning forward, Barden kissed the corner of my mouth. "You're salty."

Our breaths mingled, and I stared into his eyes, his pupils growing. "Could I see them? Your wings."

Side of his mouth lifting as he nosed along my cheek to my ear, Barden sucked my ear lobe as he took my hand. "I thought you'd never ask." As he stood up, Barden hesitated. "You are eighteen today, correct. Not later in the week?"

"Today."

Tugging me from the chair, Barden led me towards the stairs. Spinning to face me before the bottom of the stairs, he wheeled me in and kissed my lips. It was short but hot.

"Happy birthday," he murmured against my lips.

Panting against Barden's mouth, I lifted my glazed eyes to meet his. "You better not be distracting me to prevent me from seeing those wings."

Grinning large, Barden brushed my mouth with his lips. "Never. Come on."

Barden's bedroom was surprisingly light and airy and very spacious. "I've never been here before," I whispered, looking around.

Barden hugged me from behind. "Why are you whispering?"

"So, your family don't hear me in here."

Snickering, Barden kissed my pulse point. "They're not here. No one is."

"They're not?"

"We have our jobs to do, Sash. Souls can't cross the veils unaided and unprotected." Exhaling, Barden curved his body around me a little, and his wings stretched like a giant feather blanket. Engulfed in his massive wingspans, I stood in awe. Gaping, really. Hand shaking, I brushed the feathers with my fingertips, a shudder passing through Barden as I fingered his feathers.

"You can feel even this little?"

"The underside is where all the nerves are. Very sensitive and erogenous." Lips pinching down my neck, Barden tightened his arms around me until the hard bulge in his pants was bruising my butt cheek.

Bottom lip trapped between my teeth, I caressed over the feather-covered bone support of the wing. Last night, the wings looked black, but now I could see they had that dark green shine to the feathers as the sun came through the window.

"I want to make you mine, Sasha."

Closing my eyes, I tried to step away from him. "Let me out, please?"

The wings shot out to the side, the feathers shaking viciously as Barden dropped his hands from me. His face fell to the ground, and his shoulders rounded as if he felt let down. Still chewing my lip, I ducked beneath his large, feathered limbs, easily as tall as him from shoulder to knee and with a wingspan twice as long as his six and a half feet. No wonder he needed a large room.

Standing behind Barden, I stood awed again by how the wing attachment melded as part of his back from shoulder to waist. Not just an extra limb hanging from his scapula as so often depicted in bird-man or angelic portrayals. "You're amazing."

Head turning slightly, Barden spoke to his shoulder. "You're beautiful." Pulling his wings in, I watched how they folded in and then shrunk into his back, leaving perfectly unblemished skin. God, the back muscles on him.

Unable to resist, I felt along his back, tracing the hardened definition on either side of his spine. "Is this your wings under the skin?" An affirmative grunt was Barden's response.

Turning to face me, Barden eyed me. "Do you need to ask me anything else?"

Wetting my lips, I turned my gaze to the window. "I'm going away to university. It wouldn't be fair for us to start this without me telling you my plans first. You need to be willing to let me go when fall comes."

When I braved looking at Barden again, his pupils were narrowed on me. "Is it because the university you've chosen has the best program or because it gets you as far away from here as possible?"

Closing my eyes, I was sure he would be angry or feel rejected, and I didn't want to see that. "The latter. I need to get away from my mother. I want to have a life and see the world."

Stepping towards me, Barden reached out and ran his thumb over my lips, tugging gently. "I understand why." Barden lifted his shoulders and moved another step closer. "I'm not going to ask you to stay for me, Sash. That will just make you pull away. I'm going to ask for the rest of this year and hope to convince you I'm worth staying for."

Hovering above me now, Barden swept a kiss across my mouth. Chasing his lips, I pressed myself to him, eager to feel the connection between us bloom into that raging fire of need. Barden was right. Decisions didn't need to be made yet. I'd wait until I saw what offers came my way and make the hard choices at that time.

Breathless, I looked to the ceiling, my hands all over Barden as he kissed down my neck, feeling me through my top. He carefully removed my phone and headphones from around my neck and set them aside on his desk. Then our mouths found each other, and the room got another five degrees warmer.

Pulling back, Barden grabbed my top and yanked it up over my head, freeing my breasts to his hungry mouth, firing electricity through my body. Gasping, I clung to him, my back arching to stay close.

Fingers finding the waistband of my leggings, Barden dragged them down my legs while nibbling at my flesh. Moaning, I used my feet to help get free of the clothing, relieved to have his hands on my naked skin. Letting go of me, Barden shoved his pants from his hips, his back muscles bunching and relaxing, showcasing his strength. Standing up, Barden looked over me, his pupils dilating as he took me in. My lip was caught between my teeth as I took him all in for the first time; his cock was big, thick, and slightly curved as it pointed to the ceiling.

When I met his eyes again, Barden closed the distance. "Don't be scared. I won't ever hurt you."

Our lips collided, then Barden grabbed my butt, where it joined my legs and hoisted me up. With a slight squeal, I wrapped my arms and legs around him, moaning as he walked with me in his arms to the bed.

The Denial

PULLING HIS BLANKETS BACK, Barden lowered me to his bed and laid over me. The kisses were slow and deep, his caress igniting little sparks of want that heated my core. Pulling me tighter to him, Barden groaned when he pressed his thigh between my legs, slowly rocking against me, his cock pressing hard into my hip bone. Closing my eyes, I moaned as his thigh rubbed my clit, making me needy for his touch and kiss, like an insatiable hunger.

"I've needed you for so long, Sash," Barden breathed before dropping his head, sucking and pinching my nipples, making me moan his name. Shifting a little, he slid his hand between us and combed my bush before rubbing circles over my clit. Lifting up when I gasped, Barden watched me writhe as my insides started to coil. In the exact opposite way, his pupils were dilating, swallowing up all the light in his eyes.

Dropping his mouth to mine, Barden kissed me heatedly. Despite his years of cold stares, my body sang to be in his arms, having his body touching and rubbing against me. Reaching his hand lower, Barden cupped my sex, then pressed the ball of his hand to my hood while his finger slid between my lips. Moaning at the sensation, I rocked my hips a little faster.

"That's it," Barden encouraged. He pushed that finger inside me, hooking it and finding the ignition switch I'd been lovingly getting to know well for the last six months. Thrusting to match the need in my hips, Barden watched me, and when I closed my eyes, coming close to the peek, he slowed his attention and added another finger.

"God!" Throwing my head back, I griped the soft sheets, my body twisting with the sudden discomfort. I'd never managed to go beyond one finger, and Barden's fingers were bigger and longer than mine.

"Leave the God shit out of this," Barden growled, lowering his mouth to my breast.

Clutching at his hair, I was too caught up in the fast-building pleasure pushing the discomfort and possibly all sanity from my mind. When I struggled to breathe, Barden removed his fingers, using them to caress my breast and pinch my nipples.

"Last chance to stop this, Sash. If you don't want this, if you don't want to be mine, you need to say so now."

Panting, I stared at Barden, the hunger and concern flashing across his face. Could I bear to have him go back to watching me with cold eyes now that I'd experienced his lust for me? No. I wanted him to always look at me the way he had since he'd kissed me the first time.

"I've never wanted anything more than I want you, Barden." When he started diving for my mouth, I pulled back, my anxiety churning my stomach. "You're not going to change your mind once you have me, are you?"

Shaking his head, Barden brushed his lips along my jaw. "I've been addicted to you for years, Sash. It only got worse when I dared to pursue you, to kiss you and touch you."

He looked like he wanted to say more but clenched his jaw shut. Caressing his jawline, I met Barden's eyes and nodded. "Then I want this." Kissing around my throat, Barden touched me some more. "Barden, you have a condom, right?"

Getting up, Barden went to his drawers and pulled out an unopened box. "How do you prefer to remove a bandaid?" he asked while he put the condom on.

"What do you mean?"

"Do you prefer to ease it off slowly, stopping to rest each time it hurts, or just rip it off and endure the momentary pain?"

"Rip it off. Just get the worst over with and move on. Why?"

Coming back to me, Barden knelt between my legs and leaned forward to caress my cheek. "The first time can hurt, Sash, and you could barely handle my fingers, so..."

Blinking my eyes wide, my gaze drifted down to Barden's well-endowed weapon of virgin destruction. "Oh." Chewing my lip, I slowly lifted my eyes back to his. "Just, ah, rip it off."

Smiling, Barden kissed me deeply, his mouth tender and tongue teasing. Shifting his body, the head of his cock slid easily to my core, and then Barden pushed into me. Cussing at the burning stretch, I gripped his back as he rocked into me. With a mighty shove of his hips, Barden impaled me, then stilled, just rotating his hips. Swallowing my whimpers, Barden kissed me slowly, waiting until the grip I had on him loosened, and then he eased back to meet my watering eyes.

"Okay?"

I bit my lip. The pain had been quick and sharp, turning into an uncomfortable sensation like a bad friction burn or a strained muscle. Meeting Barden's concerned gaze, I nodded. Dropping his mouth to mine, Barden gently rocked forward again. It was nowhere near as bad this time, but I wouldn't say it was the incredible euphoria I'd hoped for after self-servicing for months. Who was I kidding? Fingers are not even on the same scale as a dick. Or at least, my finger certainly felt insignificant in comparison to what was delving into me.

The kisses slowly brought my mind out of the shock of that first invasion. As our lips matched the rhythm of our bodies, the desire and hunger for Barden gradually rekindled in my belly, the heat spreading into my chest. The burning discomfort eased but didn't go away. Still, it was bearable, and as Barden rocked faster, pleasure began coiling in my womb again.

"Fuck, Sash!" Dropping his face to my neck, Barden groaned my name, his body moving faster, thrusting harder. Grabbing my thigh, he pulled it up, holding it wrapped over his hip, tilting my pelvis a little and allowing him to surge deeper. My eyes bugged open as that slight change sent me hurtling into an entirely new level of ecstasy.

Clinging to Barden, I cried out as I shattered into a thousand pieces beneath him. Moaning, Barden thrust harder, then jolted, his body tense and shaking above me as he stopped, his entire being seeming to be in agony. He dropped like a sack of potatoes on top of me.

Lying there, breathing heavily against each other, we stayed that way for several minutes. Slowly, Barden lifted enough to see me, sweeping my hair away from my face; he waited. Slowly, I raised my hand, caressed his face, and then urged him to kiss me again. It was different now. Our hunger sated, the kiss seemed to come from somewhere more profound and a more connected feeling entrenching itself in the fabric of my being as the euphoria leached away.

Easing back, Barden kissed me once more as he withdrew from my body and knelt back, eyes glancing to his sated cock, glistening wet with a dark smear spreading down one side. "Was that...?"

"Yes." With a smile, Barden fell to the side. "Mine."

Clenching my legs together, I cringed at the sensation of being empty. Both relieved and feeling lost without him inside me. Pulling me into his arms, Barden cuddled me to him and kissed my temple. Using his hand to lift my face, he tenderly nipped at my lips. When we pulled back for breath, my eyes spotted the clock beside his bed. "Shite!"

Getting off the bed, I started grabbing my clothes, ready to dress. "It's already eight. My parents will be awake, and my mum will track my phone when I don't turn up for breakfast."

Coming to me, Barden stopped my panicked hands. "Okay, but if they check your phone now, you are busted already, right? So, calm down. Let's have a quick wash because we both smell of sex. Then, we'll dress, go downstairs, and have a cup of tea. When they show up, you tell the truth. You tell them why you came here this morning. They'll either believe you or won't, but you'll have told the truth, which matters with your dad. You can't lie to him. He'll know if you lie."

That was one of my dad's abilities. A really annoying one for Savas growing up because he was always into mischief, but it never bothered me. Nodding my head, I let Barden take me to the shower, and we both quickly washed the sweat off us, then dressed. When the doorbell rang twenty minutes later, we were halfway through our cups of tea. Surprisingly, only my father showed up.

"What's going on?" he asked when Barden showed him into the kitchen.

"I was out on my run and wanted to talk to Barden about last night. To ask about the crows. I was here before I realized where my feet had taken me."

When my dad looked at Barden, Barden smirked. "The wings."

When my dad's gaze returned, I cupped the mug in my hands. "Why didn't you tell me?"

"Your mother didn't want you to know. We are friends with Barden's family because they work with us, but there are others, and they are nowhere near as friendly. Your mother didn't want you thinking they all could be trusted."

"Mum would prefer I didn't think for myself, full stop." Getting up, I grabbed my phone and headphones. "Thanks for talking to me, Barden. I should get home."

"Sasha." Dad grabbed my elbow halfway down the front steps and gently held me back. "You ran further than you intended and over-strained your muscles already today. I'll give you a ride home." Looking over his shoulder, Dad let me go and went to his motorbike.

Turning around, I eyed Barden back at his door. When I opened my mouth to say something, I wasn't sure what was appropriate or safe in front of my dad, so I closed my mouth and turned away. I could feel the strain in my muscles getting on the bike, but I wasn't sure if it was the run or having sex with Barden that caused it.

"You should have a long bath when you get home and soak those muscles, or you won't be able to walk tomorrow," Dad advised.

Nodding my head, I wrapped my arms around my dad and wished my mother could be as easygoing and understanding as he was. "Is Mum having a conniption?"

"No. She doesn't know where you are. She slept in this morning." Starting the bike, Dad eased us around to face the driveway. "Let's not make this a habit, okay?"

"I didn't even plan for it to happen today, Dad. I just wanted to know if I imagined things last night. After Mia buried me alive, I was worried I'd suffered brain damage."

"Mia *what*?"

"It was an accident. I was being chased by one of the Execrable, and she opened the earth to swallow him and got me instead."

"I think you can tell me everything that happened last night when we get home. Because none of the boys mentioned you getting swallowed by the earth."

"Savas was probably more concerned about how many Execrable there were. Five of them, Dad. All together in a hunting pack. They changed into these horrifying beasts to chase me too. It was terrifying." And absolutely an adrenalin rush.

"Still, I want to know exactly what went down. Okay?"

Cringing, I cuddled him tighter. "Okay."

When we got home, I went for that long bath, then avoided my dad for the rest of the morning. In the afternoon, I was busy helping Mum prepare the dinner for our birthday. Just the Assions and Grandma Tormen came over. We asked to invite our friends, but Mum wanted a quiet family celebration.

When Barden arrived, I wasn't sure how to act. Was it just sex? More? He said he wanted me to be his and wouldn't change his mind afterward, but we'd not agreed to be in a relationship or anything.

I shouldn't have worried. Besides greeting me with a cheek kiss and mumbling 'happy birthday', Barden spent the rest of the night with Savas.

Still, I caught him watching me several times. He sat opposite me at dinner and entwined our ankles under the table. He was sweet but did not act any differently in front of my family, for which I was grateful. The same couldn't be said for me.

"If you keep staring at that boy, your mother is going to murder him," Grandma chuckled in my ear during dessert. "And it would be such a shame for you to lose such gorgeous eye candy."

Snapping my eyes away from Barden, I realised my mother was looking between us, so angry that steam was nearly coming out of her ears. Licking my lips, I bowed my head and focused on my slice of cake.

Grandma patted my hand, a naughty smile stuck on her face as she engaged my mother in a conversation about some gala they'd both attended last week.

Scooping a fresh bit of cake onto my fork, I dared looking through my lashes to find Barden openly watching me. Trying not to blush, I put the cake in my mouth and slowly licked it clean, trying to focus on the taste and not on how hot Barden's staring made me.

Savas snatched the fork from my hand and shoved it back on my plate. "Stop staring," he said loud enough that the table went quiet. "They're just wings."

"Sorry. They're the only ones I've ever seen," I murmured totally embarrassed.

"Well, if you've seen one you've seen them all," Savas assured. I totally did not believe that.

Barden grunted an objection.

"Dude!" Savas groaned.

"Ooh, how lucky is my granddaughter," Grandma chuckled. "Getting to see your wings for her eighteenth birthday. Is that the only present you gave her?"

Dad had to cover his mouth as he nearly coughed his cake everywhere. "Mum!"

"What? I'm just letting the boy know some pretty jewelry doesn't go astray. You men always think having big *wings* is enough."

My face was bright red as I tried to hide from what I was hearing.

"Why would Barden get Sasha a present?" my mother interrupted, jaw tight with the forced smile straining her face. "He's Savas' friend." The question hung in the air for a moment. "Did you tell your grandma what you got for your birthday, Sasha?"

"Mum got me some really nice earrings," I told my grandma to appease Mum.

"How lovely." Grandma smiled at me, then turned her eyes to my mother. "Did you get them from a jewelry store, or are they those 'stalker' sets you were telling me about with GPS tracking chips in them?"

"Mum," Dad warned and shook his head while my mother slammed her fork onto her plate.

"Wanting to keep my daughter safe is not a crime."

"There is always a fine line, Delila. Always a point where things go too far," Grandma reminded. With a breath, she smiled again and patted my hand as she pushed her chair back from the table. "Why don't you show me everything you got?"

Thanking my grandma for finding a reason to leave the awkwardness of the table, I followed her out to show her my presents. The heat of Barden's gaze warming my back the entire way.

The Pantry

"WELL, YOU LOOK LIKE SHIT," Mia commented when I got to school on Monday morning.

"Yeah, next time, let's do a sinkhole instead of you burying me alive. And by next time, I mean, let's never do that again."

"Bruised ribs isn't too bad for getting buried alive."

"Tell my swim coach, who lost it this morning, that I got injured coming off a bike two weeks out from state trials."

"So, your parents bought the excuse that you came off the bike?"

"Yes, and no. My dad knows I went into the ground, but I've avoided telling him any details. I'm still grounded for the next two weeks." Stopping at my locker, I dumped what I didn't need for the subsequent two periods.

"Why?"

"Because it didn't excuse the way all of us were dressed. Mum suspects we were up to no good and put Savas through the inquisition to try and get him to trip up his story. How about your dad?"

"He questioned why two were killed in the park and the rest by the street. I told him when we got ambushed, we ran, those two followed, and we took them down. He looked skeptical but let it go. I think he knows."

"Yeah, I think my parents know too. Not about the party, but that we weren't where we were supposed to be. Hence the grounding. I'm to come straight home from school every day. Savas has to pick me up every afternoon, which he's thrilled about. Why I can't just ride my own bike is beyond me."

"Too much freedom for your mother," Mia huffed. "Though, at least she let you have a motorbike. My parents were not moveable on that idea. When I asked to learn to ride, they bought me a pushbike, and that's the closest I've gotten to a motorbike."

"They are naturalists," I reminded her. "Hence why you have to walk everywhere. And my mum was not happy about the motorbike. My dad got it for me because I wouldn't stop nagging about it and always sneaking out to ride Savas's bike since we were kids." Thinking about it, I smiled. "We could convert your pushbike to an electric bike."

"Really?"

"Yeah, you can buy kits. It won't be like a motorbike, but it would make riding hills easier. Then you could ride your bike to school instead of walking."

Grinning, Mia pushed open the door for our first class. "Let's do it!"

"Okay, you can pick up a kit from the bike shop, and I can help you convert it once I finish being grounded."

Grinning, we took our seats in class, Raisa and Yasmine joining us, buzzing about all the gossip of the party on the weekend. Who slept with who, who got so drunk they passed out in the garden, who puked, and so on. The school day flew by, fuelled by the gossip.

At the kiss and drop after school, I wasn't really paying attention to the cars or other students. Mostly, the younger kids got picked up from here, so I walked to the front of the pickup area. I'd changed from my uniform into my kevlar jeans and leather jacket. I was holding my helmet in one hand, my phone in the other as I scrolled social media.

When the motorbike pulled up in front of the lead car, I put my phone away and moved forward, pulling my helmet on. It wasn't until I was throwing a leg over that I realized this wasn't my brother's bike.

"Barden?" I frowned as I buckled my helmet up.

"Ready?"

"Where's Savas?"

"School. Hold on." The bike shot forward. Since I hadn't had time to grab the seat, I grabbed onto Barden and quickly leaned forward so I was pressed against his backpack. He didn't slow down for me to adjust, so I stayed like that the entire twenty-minute ride home. It would have been much longer if we were in a car, but the bikes could get through the town traffic a lot faster.

Pulling through the gates to our driveway, Barden drove up to our garage door instead of the front door. As soon as the wheels stopped, I put my hands on his shoulders and lifted myself off the bike. "Thanks for the lift."

Kicking the stand down on his bike, Barden flicked his visor up as he dismounted. "I'm coming in."

Giving him a smile, my stomach went all giddy. Unbuckling the helmet, I took it off and pulled out my phone to open the garage door. Going into the boot room, I put my helmet in its place, put my bag on the seat, and shrugged off my leather jacket. Hanging it and my school blazer up, I texted my mum to let her know I was home. She'd most likely track my phone to make sure I was here.

Wrapping his arms around me, Barden placed a kiss on my neck. My phone rang a second later, but I was surprised to see Savas on the caller ID.

"Hey, I'm home safe. Thanks for the heads up that Barden was picking me up," I whined as I kicked off my school shoes and put them away. It's not that I was unhappy, but I didn't want Savas to know that.

"Sorry, I was stuck in a class that ran overtime. We were doing exam prep," my brother explained. "Look, Barden and I were meant to hang out this afternoon, so he's going to chill at our place until I get there. Can you be nice and let him in and offer him a drink or something. I've still got another half hour of this exam prep, and then I'll head home."

So, for about an hour, I could hang with the hot guy who was still dropping kisses on my neck and pressing himself against my back. "Sure. I'll see you when you get home." Hanging up, I turned around to face Barden, his jacket open to expose his school shirt. Like me, he'd changed out of his blazer but still wore his school pants. Stepping back, aware my dad was home and most likely awake, I tried to keep things like we were just friends. "Do you want to bring your bike inside?"

"No."

Nodding my head, I grabbed my school bag and entered the kitchen, dumping it by the small meal table. Opening the fridge, I grabbed the juice and filled two glasses. Sliding one across the bench as Barden came in, I put the jug away. "Hungry?"

When I shut the fridge door, Barden was right there. He moved towards me, and I backed up. The side of Barden's lips lifted a little. "Yes."

Biting my lip, I backed up and slid the pantry door open. "Okay, what did you want?"

Looking around the kitchen, Barden took my elbow and pulled me into the pantry. Seconds later, I was pressed against the wall while Barden kissed me senseless. When his hand found my breast, I arched and moaned. My small mound fit perfectly in his palm while his thumb strummed my nipple through my t-shirt bra.

"You," Barden whispered as he kissed my jaw.

Biting my lip, I whimpered a little when he pinched my hardened nipple and kissed me breathless again. Moments later, Barden had the buttons to my blouse and the front clasp of my bra open. Dropping his face, he sucked the stiff peak between his lips.

Cursing, I grasped at his hair, things tightening quickly downstairs. The waistband of my jeans loosened, then Barden slipped his hand inside my scanties. "Barden," I gasped as he found my clit. Shite, this was not how I was expecting my afternoon to go. "My dad's home," I panted.

"I know," he murmured as he pushed my jeans over my hips, scanties and all. "So you need to be quiet."

"He could walk in any minute." Swallowing, I panted at the way he played my clit had me squirming. "Barden."

"Do you want me, Sash?" Kissing me slow and teasingly, Barden shifted his hand, his fingers sliding over my channel to find my very wet opening. His mouth covered mine as he pressed a finger inside, smothering my whimper of need, then his mouth dropped back to my nipple, and I was lost in the sensation.

"God, yes," I gasped as it became impossible to stay quiet.

Lifting his head, Barden met my eyes, his focused and dilated, looking entirely unholy. "Then, shh. And stop bringing God into it. I'm not a fan. Swear instead or something dirty, but don't say 'God'."

Before I could react, his thumb found my clit, his other hand my exposed breast, and the combination of all three was nearly too much. Pulling back, Barden took a condom out of his pocket, then quickly opened his pants and shoved them down. Leaning forward, he kissed me heatedly as he rolled the condom into place, then his hands grabbed where my legs met my butt and lifted me up.

Setting my back against the pantry wall, Barden kissed me while I squirmed around until his hard cock was where we needed it to be, then he pushed into me.

"Fuck!" I panted against his lips. Despite how wet I was, it seemed like an overly tight fit, but it also felt amazing.

Barden kissed me heatedly, giving me a wicked grin, his thrusts just as needy, pinning me to the wall. Our breath seemed so loud in the enclosed pantry, echoing back to my ears, so that's all I could hear. My body tightened as the friction on that wondrous spot built to burst, the pitch of my pants and moans getting higher, Barden's grunts getting deeper.

"Fuck, Sash," Barden whispered, his breath coming out hard, his face scrunching up as his grip on my butt tightened.

Wrapping my arms tighter around him as that feeling reached breaking point, I pressed my mouth hard to Barden's as I shattered. My orgasm passed through my entire body like the vibrations of a cymbal. Grabbing my jaw, Barden grunted against my mouth as he thrust hard once more, then pinned me to the wall as he trembled in my arms.

Easing his grip on me, Barden shifted our mouths from a position of muting each other into a slow, passionate kiss. The climax dissolved when we were both still, and my body relaxed against him.

Slowly, Barden pulled back. "You okay?"

"Yeah." I swallowed.

Barden separated from me, easing me down, causing us both to gasp. Stepping back, he considered the full tip of the condom, firmly attached to his still mostly hard dick.

"I need to go use the bathroom," he excused as he tucked it away and zipped up his pants.

Nodding my head, I didn't ask what he would do with it. He was always intelligent. I'm sure he knew how to get rid of it and lessen the chance of my parents finding it. Alone in the pantry, I looked down at myself. All but naked, I smiled, the sensations still circulating through my body. Clipping my bra closed, I quickly pulled up my pants and buttoned my blouse.

Using a metal canister, I checked my reflection and took my band out to finger-comb my hair, so I didn't look like I had just gotten boned by my brother's best friend in the pantry. Taking a deep breath, I exhaled. Going out to the kitchen, I went to the sink and splashed water on my face. Then, with another breath, I turned to face the room.

Standing at the kitchen counter, Barden drained his glass of orange juice. Smacking his lips, Barden came towards me and put his glass on the sink beside where I was standing. "You okay?"

"You keep asking me that."

Turning to face me fully, Barden caressed my jaw as he put his mouth to my ear. "Because you're mine, and I want to make sure you're okay with what's happening between us, that I wasn't too rough and hurt you."

A sigh escaped my mouth as his lips pinched down my neck. "That was very risky. We could have gotten caught."

"It's worth the risk to finally be with you."

"Is it? If my dad caught us..."

Pulling back, Barden stared into my eyes. Taking my hand, he put it to his chest so I could feel his heart beating. "I've wanted you since I first laid eyes on you, Sash. Any way that I get to be with you is worth the risk."

Shaking my head, I felt a tear escape. "I didn't know. You just stared at me like I'd hurt you all the time. How was I to know?" I wasn't even interested in boys until a year ago.

Wiping away my tear, Barden stayed focused on my eyes. He confused me so much. I thought I'd offended him somehow, and he hated me for it. I used to try and be nice to him but gave up after a few months. Now, he'd made his sexual interest in me known, and I felt both elated and spun around in circles and too dizzy to focus.

Until Friday, he'd never touched me or shown any interest. Or, not that I'd noticed. Raisa said it'd been there for years. Maybe I was just blind to it. Either way, I didn't want Barden changing his mind now. Not after the way he got me hot on Saturday night or the way he'd made love to me yesterday and then fucked me in the pantry.

"Get used to this, Sash. Until you are ready to be honest and tell everyone about us, I will steal kisses or more wherever and whenever I can."

Biting my lip, I grabbed Barden's shirt and pulled him down to kiss me. Barden moaned into my mouth, pinching his lips against mine before stepping back and looking down between us. "Keep doing that, and I'll need to raid your brother's room for another condom."

Blushing, I let Barden go. "Sorry."

Smirking, Barden chucked my chin. "Don't be. But I think I should go home. Your dad is awake now, and I don't want you to get in any more trouble."

"What about Savas?"

"I'll tell him you kept asking about my wings, and the temptation to take you upstairs and let you feel me got too much. He'll understand."

"He will?"

Lips twitching, Barden caressed my jaw. "Yeah, Sash. Only you have missed how I feel about you. Trust me, it will not surprise anyone that I adore you. Your family has just been waiting for you to realize it." Not sure how to take that, I chewed my lip.

With a final smile, Barden dropped another kiss on me, then turned around and grabbed his school bag, heading back out. Going to the table, I did my homework, but my mind was on Barden.

When my dad came into the kitchen thirty minutes later, he made a coffee and sat at the table with me. "I thought Barden was here."

"He said he needed to get away from me before he did something he'd get in trouble for." When my dad's brows went up, I huffed and focused back on my books. Barden was right. I was the only idiot here.

"Want to tell me about Mia burying you alive now?"

Blowing out a breath, I put my pen down. "It was scary. The Execrable were chasing us, and they'd changed into these horrific beasts that stunk. I yelled for Mia to open the earth to trap it, and then the ground disappeared beneath me. I had a second to realize I'd gone into the earth, and then it was crushing around me."

"Mia reopened it and got you out?"

Blinking, I looked up at my dad. "No, I called water, turned the earth around me into the mud, and used the water to force me above the surface. Then she grabbed my hand and pulled me out."

Sitting forward, my dad leaned on the table to stare into my eyes. "She left you in there?"

"I'm sure she didn't mean to. She probably panicked and lost control. It's not like we have ever been attacked by Execrable before."

Pursing his lips, Dad considered me for a long moment. "You used your abilities? More than one?"

Nodding, I slouched in my chair. "I used my fire to burn one to ashes, and I created an electric net to catch another who was right on top of me."

Sitting back, my dad eyed me. "So you used fire, water, and electricity in front of the others?" When I nodded, he clenched his jaw. "Damn."

"I'm sorry. I didn't mean to. It was just instinct to protect them."

Getting up, Dad came around and squeezed my shoulders, then dropped a kiss on my head as his phone rang. "It's okay, Sash. You did what you needed to survive." Taking his phone out of his pocket, he looked at the screen and then put it to his ear as he headed for his study.

For the rest of the week, Savas picked me up. I found myself longing to see Barden and dreaming about him every night.

The Diner

THROWING my bag over my shoulder, I headed to the car park where Mum usually waited to pick me up from swim practice. I'd still done my laps, just a little slower due to the cracked ribs.

The other swim club members said goodnight and went to their parents' cars or their cars if they could drive. Frowning, I couldn't see Mum's car anywhere. Checking my phone, I had a message telling me she was still with a client and would be late. That was only ten minutes ago.

Sighing, I pressed the call button. "Hey, I'm with a client."

"I got the message. The car park is a ghost town. Do you mind if I go to the Milkbar and study while I wait for you? It will be safer than sitting out here while the sun sets by myself."

"That's a good idea. I'll let you know when I'm on my way."

"I could just get Dad or Savas to come and get me."

"Your dad will be getting ready to work, and your brother had his rep soccer training here in the city this afternoon. You'll have to wait."

"Fine, I'll be at the Milkbar." Hanging up, I headed for the diner. While the sun was up, I wasn't as worried about the Execrables now, but I didn't want to invite trouble of any sort either.

When I reached the old-fashioned cafe, I pushed through the doors and straight for the table at the back I always sat in to hang out with my friends. Halfway there, I was surprised but happy to see my three besties chillin' in our booth, empty plates and glasses cluttering the table.

Glancing my way, Mia's smile faded when she saw me, and when she forced it back into place and told the others I was there, the laughter and chatter quickly ended. Blinking at the reception, I slowed my approach when I got to the booth. "Hey, are you studying?"

"Just hanging out." Raisa smiled. "We thought you were grounded?"

"Yeah, I am, but Mum got caught up at work, and Savas is at his soccer training, so I thought it would be safer to wait here for my lift home."

"Sounds like a smart move. Don't want to be out after dark by yourself," Raisa chirped happily.

"Hey, Sasha," Falco welcomed as he started collecting the empties from the table. "Need a menu?" No one had moved to make room for me to sit with them. In fact, I got a distinct impression that I wasn't welcome.

"No, I'm just going to grab a caramel milkshake. Thanks, Falco." Spotting that one of the booths halfway back to the front was empty, I turned that way. "I'm going to go do some study while I wait."

Taking the seat with my back to the girls so I could see the front of the shop, I tried to reason through what had just happened. The girls had seemed fine at school all week. I mean, at least in class, they had. Mia had spent her lunches with the cheer squad prepping for the game tomorrow night. Yasmine, with her chess club preparing for a tournament, and Raisa decided to use the break to spend more time on her major artwork, so I went to the library.

Still, until now, I hadn't thought anything of it. We all had our own interests, which occupied our time sometimes. Pulling out my notebook, I set up, ready to utilize my time wisely.

"Everything okay?" Falco murmured as he set my milkshake on the table for me. "I don't think I've ever seen a frostier reception than you just encountered."

Chewing my lip as I put the money for the milkshake on the table, I didn't feel reassured that Falco also picked up on how the girls acted towards me. "Yeah, I just wanted to study, and they're busy having fun."

Furrowing his forehead enough that two lines appeared between his eyebrows, Falco glanced from me to my friends and back again. "Did you bang one of their boyfriends? Because I've only ever seen girls freeze out one of their besties like that when a guy was involved."

Thinking about how I'd admitted to kissing Barden and how the girls had talked about him on Saturday night, I wondered if that was the problem.

"I mean, maybe, but none of them had a claim to him." Mia had said there were family politics involved, and that's why she'd never considered him.

Smirking, Falco slid into the seat opposite me. When our eyes met, I felt dizzy for a second. Then I was captivated by how the pupil seemed to bleed out through various hues of grey until they had an almost white feathering right before the black ring around the iris.

"Which one of the boys did you mess around with? Nash, Vidal, or Athur?" Falco rattled off my brother's friends and the members of the Delta team. Nash was Raisa's older brother, and Vidal was Yasmine's.

Intrigued by the one he didn't mention, I tilted my head. His irises had ribbons of black pleats moving around his pupil like a roulette wheel, reminding me of the only guy I'd ever got hot for. "Barden."

Falco's eyebrows jumped. "Huh, well, yeah, that will do it. I mean, I thought you'd moved in on their turf or something, but Barden is a different kettle of fish. Is it serious between you two, or are you just playing with him until you settle down with someone your family would consider appropriate?"

Surprised by Falco's interest and ideas, I chewed my cheek. "Well, I'm not playing, but it's only new, so I wouldn't say it's serious. I'd like to think it could be, but I'm not sure how it would work with me going away for university next year either."

With his mouth kicking up, Falco looked over my head towards the back. "Interesting. I'll let you get back to your studies."

As Falco shifted sideways, I leaned forward. "Can you not say anything to anyone? The girls only think we kissed once; my family doesn't know yet. My mum will flip out about it and ground me until kingdom comes when she finds out." Realizing I was over-explaining something that wasn't his business, I forced myself to shut up.

Tilting his head, reminding me of an eagle considering a smaller animal and wondering if it could eat it, Falco leaned towards me. "You're really into him, aren't you? It's not just banging a hot guy for you?"

"Well, duh! I've had a major crush on Barden since the day we met. I've never even looked at another guy that way."

Sitting back, mouth hanging a little, Falco stared at me. "Huh. Interesting."

"Not really." I rolled my eyes. "Apparently I'm foolish and never noticed he liked me just as much either until he finally kissed me."

"Huh," Falco repeated again. Standing up, he double-blinked at me. "You're different from them." His head tilted towards the back booth that housed my friends. "I always thought it, but this just proved it." His eyes glanced towards them, and his face fell. "They've been coming here for their lunch breaks without you all week. I'm guessing they hid it from you?" When I swallowed, tears welling in my eyes as I turned my focus on the front door, Falco nodded. "Thought so. Sorry, Sasha." Then giving me a half smile, he returned to cleaning up from the after-school rush.

Unable to focus on my studies, I pulled out my phone and thumbed through my contacts. I didn't have Barden's number, but I had Calliope's for some reason, so I texted and asked her for Barden's number. My phone rang a second later.

"Why do you need Barden's number?" Calliope asked as soon as I answered.

"Ah, well, I..." Seriously, she was fucking my brother. What could she say about me being with hers? "I need to talk to him."

"Why?"

"He kissed me." The phone was silent. "And I really like him and miss him staring and grunting at me."

There was a sound akin to a snicker, but only if it was made by an evil demon in a dark cave just before it ate you. "I'm at work, and something nasty just showed. Let me deal with it, and then I'll text it to you." The line went dead.

Funnily enough, I didn't think she was referring to her work in the Vestigial world. I'd never really ventured beyond this realm to experience the other world. Having just heard that noise, I don't think I'd want to.

A few minutes later, my phone vibrated with a text. Smiling at Barden's number, I sent thanks to Calliope, and then before I could text Barden, his number was calling me. "Hey."

"Sash?" Calliope must have checked first before giving me his number.

"Yeah." Closing my eyes, I searched for the right words.

"Where?" Barden asked.

"The Milkbar. Mum's working late, and Sav is in the city, so I didn't have a ride home."

"Ten minutes."

"You're still at school?"

"No." The sound of him connecting to his bike came through the phone. "I'll be there soon." The line disconnected.

Staring at my phone, I wondered where Barden was and what he'd been doing that he could make it here that quickly. Chewing my lip, I put my phone away and started drinking my milkshake while I read over my notes from class today.

Not even ten minutes later, the door opened, and Barden waltzed in. He wasn't even in his uniform. Jeans, a t-shirt, and a leather jacket. Have I mentioned how hot he was in a pair of jeans? You know the only thing that made Barden hotter? Him in only jeans. I'm not sure how many of the clientele here had seen Barden in less, but they seemed to enjoy watching him walk my way.

Eyes scanning the diner, Barden nodded to Falco, then noted where my friends were at the back before his eyes found me several booths away. Eyebrows lowering, Barden looked from me to the girls again, then sat opposite me. Our gazes met, then his eyes went to the last booth before coming back to me and cocking his head slightly.

Damn, but it was obvious to everyone I was being frozen out by my friends. Confused about why I bit my lip and focused on not crying. Narrowing his eyes, Barden watched me. "Are you okay?"

"Can you take me home? Mum's running really late and the appeal of getting time out from being grounded has been lost."

Glaring over my shoulder, Barden gave me a nod. "Let's go." Getting up, Barden waited for me to pack up my bag, then walked with me out to his bike. "What the hell are you wearing?"

Blinking, I looked down and realized I was in my wide-leg track-pants and a thin, wide-neck baggy shirt. "Oh," pulling my wet braid over my shoulder, I wagged it at Barden. "I just finished squad training. Mum was meant to pick me up immediately, so I changed into my post-swim clothes. Not sexy, I know."

Reaching Barden's bike, I turned to wait for him. Eyeing me up and down, Barden growled and came close as he handed me his helmet. "Sash, you're sexy as fuck, no matter what you wear, but that top is see-through and not even covering one of your shoulders."

Smirking, I yanked the helmet on. "I didn't take you for a prude, Barden. You didn't seem to mind the outfit I wore to your house for dinner."

"That outfit was why I couldn't keep my hands off you anymore." Barden moved closer. "How about we go home via my place?"

God, I wanted to. "Mum might track my phone. I should go straight home." Nostril's flaring, Barden looked away and stepped by me to throw his leg over. Wetting my bottom lip, I climbed on behind him, but instead of sitting back, I cuddled behind him. "But you have wings, right? There's no reason you can't come over later. I mean, my bedroom has a balcony."

Turning his head to not quite look over his shoulder, Barden smirked as he started his bike. "I've never been in your room. I like that idea." Kicking up the stand, he rolled us forward. "I'd like it better if it was a standing invitation."

"Me too." The bike shot forward, and we were weaving our way out of town a second later.

Coming through the mud room, I dropped my bag by the dining room table and texted Mum to let her know I was already home.

"Dinner's ready," Dad greeted, his back to me as he served. Turning around, he spotted Barden with me and gave us a once-over. "I thought your mum was picking you up?"

"She is still with a client in the city. Barden came and got me." Going to the fridge, I filled my water bottle and then skulled half of it.

Wiping his hands on a hand towel, Dad set his eyes on Barden. "Delila called you?"

"A friend."

Looking unhappy with that answer, Dad threw the hand towel on the bench. "Sash, wet gear in the laundry."

Chewing my lip, I grabbed my bag and walked into the laundry, keeping the door open so I could listen. "Why did they call you?" Hanging my swimmers and towel over the drying rack, I kept as quiet as possible to eavesdrop.

"All he said was that I needed to check on her. When I got to the cafe, Sash was sitting away from her friends, and when I asked if she was okay, she looked ready to cry and asked me to bring her home."

"Damn it! All because of the damn Execrable attack." The reminder made me shiver.

Coming back into the kitchen, I eyed the two of them. "Dad, can I run something past you?"

Frowning, he carried two plates to the table and set them down. "Sure. Everything alright?"

Wetting my lips, I met his eyes. "I want to ride to school." When he took a breath, I rushed ahead. "You've been letting Sav ride to school since he was sixteen and got licensed. You know I'm just as good a rider. I promise, if you let me do this, I will go straight to school and back every day while I'm grounded. And I will let you know in advance if I plan to go anywhere else after my grounding finishes. I shouldn't rely on everyone else to get to school and home safely." Did I have my fingers and toes crossed? Yes.

Exhaling, Dad sat down. "I see the benefit, and I know you are capable on that bike. Your mother is going to fight this, though."

"Dad, I'm eighteen. Do you really want me to rebel against you, or are you willing to have some trust?"

Considering me a moment, Dad eyed me. "I'll speak to your mother. Don't get your hopes up. Barden, did you want to stay for dinner?"

"No, thank you, Gannix." With a glance towards me, Barden left.

With a sigh, I started eating.

"Is there something going on with you two?"

Lifting a shoulder, I smirked at my dad. "He's stopped glaring at me."

Taking a deep breath, my dad rolled his eyes. "Eat your dinner."

An hour later, someone knocked at my bedroom door as I came out of my bathroom, ready for bed. "Yeah."

Mum pushed it open and came in. "Your dad told me what happened. Do you want to talk about it?"

Considering my mum, I blew out a breath and started pulling my blankets back. "No."

"Were the girls mean?"

"No."

"Did they say something?"

"Just that they thought I was still grounded. Apparently, you gave them the perfect excuse to not include me."

"So, why didn't you sit with them?"

"Because I can actually read a room, Mum. They didn't want me there. None of them even tried to move their stuff off the seats to allow me to sit with them. They didn't say it outright, but it was there in their behavior. And if you don't believe me, go ask Falco. He watched the whole thing happen and asked me if I was okay. That's how obvious they were about it."

Holding her hands up, Mum tried to take control back. "Whoa, Sash. Why are you so defensive?"

She seriously had to ask? "Because you don't trust me. I told you I didn't want to talk to you about it, and then you cross-examine me as if I were on trial. I don't even know why they don't want me hanging out with them, Mum. I wasn't the only one to use my powers on Saturday night. Mia buried me alive, and Barden sprouted wings, so why am I getting the cold shoulder? You know everything. Tell me, oh prison warden. Tell me why my besties suddenly hate me?"

"Sasha Tormen! You don't get to talk to me like that!"

"I didn't even want to talk to you!"

Mum blinked, considered me, and opened her mouth and closed it again. "I'm sorry, I was just trying to understand what made you think—"

"Not me, Mum. No one there missed the shade the girls were

throwing my way." Walking to my bedroom door, I yanked it open, then wiped a stray tear from my cheek just as Savas wandered up the hall, looking exhausted. "I'm tired. Night, Mum."

Pursing her lips, Mum stepped out and, only pausing long enough to give Savas a kiss on the head, she kept going. Gazing after Mum, Savas looked back at me and lifted a brow. "What'd you do this time?"

Scoffing, I shut the door in his face, catching his second brow joining the first as I did. Switching off my light, I went to the balcony door, unlocked it, then switched on the music that I usually slept to. Climbing into bed, I sent Barden a message the door was open and snuggled down.

Just as I drifted on the edge of sleep, the blanket lifted, and Barden cuddled me from behind. "You okay?"

"Better now that you're here." Rolling to face him, I wrapped my arms around his neck. "Sav is home, so we need to be quiet."

Smirking in the moonlight-lit gloom of my room, Barden rubbed his nose against mine. "I'll try."

The Discovery

UNABLE TO SLEEP MOST of Friday and Saturday night without Barden, I got out of bed early Sunday morning and dressed for my morning run. Typically, I waited for Savas to get home, and we ran together. But he'd been unusually grumpy towards me over the last week. As twins, we'd always been close. I was left behind when Savas turned sixteen and joined the Delta team. Yeah, I'd resented that Savas got to hunt and fight the Execrable because he was a boy. As a girl, I was expected to do well at school and get a good-paying job to provide for my family later in life.

That's how it worked in the Orey. Because the men needed to sleep during the day to hunt and protect innocents at night, the women had to go out to work and be the breadwinners.

My mother was a high-powered attorney. She told me she went into law because she worried that as society changed, her husband or son might be accused and wrongfully arrested. It was the same reason Raisa's mum went into computers. So she could remove any digital evidence if it was ever needed.

Running the path along the canyon wall next to the river today, my breath fogged. It was just dawn, so the few exercise fanatics who liked to come down the river to start their day weren't out yet. My music played through my earbones. My father said it was necessary for a female was always aware of her surroundings, so I had to use bone-conduction headphones when running. It also allowed Savas and I to listen to our own music and be able to talk.

Running was usually when we shared things. Whatever was going on in our lives since we started running together, we spilled it here. But not of late. I couldn't tell Savas I'd slept with his best friend, a guy I'd only two weeks ago claimed gave me the creeps. Even before this week, when Savas joined the Delta team, he'd been withdrawing from me. He'd either give me short answers or change the subject when I tried to talk.

Really, of late, I'd felt the distance growing between my entire family. My mother was more suffocating than ever, Savas avoided being around me, and Dad, well, looked at me with a sadness that made me feel like I'd let him down. Then there was what happened at the Milkbar with the girls on Thursday, and I couldn't help but think there might be a common theme.

Stopping, I leaned on my knees and caught my breath. "Maybe the problem is me?"

Standing up, I took in my surroundings. Not that I hadn't been paying attention. I'd had my eye out for any danger the entire time, but there was the way you looked for any threats and then the way you admired the beauty of the world around you. I wanted to do the latter.

Stretching, I took in the northern end of the canyon. There were no houses because the forest and mountains on either side too steep for construction. This far up was all national park and the city road bridge over the canyon over three hundred meters overhead.

The sun was up. Not entirely, but enough so you could see the opposite side of the river and the trees beyond. Gazing across the water, something right near the rocks of the shoreline caught my attention a bit further up.

Walking the extra ten meters, I tilted my head to consider that something had gotten stuck floating down the river. Pulling out my phone, I snapped a photo and then zoomed in on the picture.

My mouth was suddenly dry. I checked around me as I pressed my dad's speed dial.

"Sasha?" Dad answered. Weekends were his nights off.

The Delta team covered Friday and Saturday nights. The alpha team, our grandfathers, covered Sunday and Monday because very little happened those nights. The beta team, our dads, took Tuesday to Friday, with two teams working a Friday. So, I should have called Savas, but like I said, there was a distance.

"I'm out for my morning run."

"Savas isn't home yet."

"I couldn't sleep."

"Okay, what's wrong."

"Dad, there's a body in the river. It looks like it's washed downstream and got snagged on something."

"I'll call the team and track you. Move away from the body, keep the area in view, and keep an eye out. If anyone approaches you, run and set off your emergency signal."

Hanging up, I ran back down the path fifty meters, then jogged on the spot to keep warm. The buzz of an electric motorbike raced up the path ten minutes later since it was the only access to the river. Pulling up, my father got off his bike and looked at me. I showed him the photo, then pointed to where it could be seen.

Not even approaching the area, my dad called the police. Forty-five minutes later, I was being questioned by a detective. "So, you were on your morning run and saw the body as you passed?" the woman asked.

"I stopped to stretch and was about to head home. I don't normally come this far up, but I was lost in thought and hadn't realized I'd passed the marker we usually use as our goal."

"We?"

"My brother and I usually run together."

"Where is he?"

"He stayed at a friend's last night."

"Okay, so you stopped."

"I was stretching and admiring how beautiful it is. Then I saw something moving in the water by the shore a little further up, so I walked closer and took a photo, so I could zoom in and be sure it wasn't just a bag of garbage, tree, or something." Taking out my phone, I showed the detective the picture and zoomed it in to show what I'd seen.

"That's when I rang my dad." Again, I opened my call log so she could see that I had called him and when. "I told him there was a body in the river. He told me to move away and keep an eye out in case there was danger. When he arrived ten minutes later, I showed him the picture, and he rang the police."

"Did your dad approach the body?"

"No. I just showed him the photo, and he stayed with me and called it in."

"Why did you ring your dad instead of the police?" The detective asked, closing her little notepad.

"I didn't feel safe. Dad could get here in under ten minutes on the bike, and he knew the trail I ran. If there was some threat nearby and I had to run for it, he'd be the most likely to make it in time. Look how long it took the police to get down here. I would have been dead as well."

The police didn't need to know I could use the river to drown someone. Hell, I'm not sure my own family knew the extent of my ability with the water element.

"Okay, thank you, Sasha. I'll call you if I have any other questions. Can you send me that photo you took?" Nodding my head as Barden's mother, who was part of the forensics team, approached, I turned to my mum. She was standing behind me, observing the questioning. "Actually, Sasha, do you know the girl? She's about your age."

Frowning, I looked back at the detective. She was looking at a tablet that Mrs. Assion had just handed her. "She is?" My eyes itched at just the thought. "I couldn't see her face in the photo I took." When the detective showed me the picture of the girl's face on the tablet, I covered my mouth. I took a step back, tears rushing from my eyes immediately, my mother wrapping her arms around me.

"I'll take that as a yes?" The detective lowered the tablet so I couldn't see the face anymore.

"It's Sophie Thinehart. We go to school together. She's one of Elisha Vincent's best friends." My eyes tracked up the river, mapping its path in my head, my eyes going wide.

"Sasha, you look like you saw a ghost. What are you thinking?"

"Um." My eyes returned to the detective, Barden's mum, and then to my mum.

"If you know something about this girl that you think might help, you should tell the detective," Mum urged.

"There was a party last night at Blindman's Corner Beach. The girls were talking about it at school on Friday." The tears continued pouring down my cheeks.

"Blindman's Corner Beach? I've never heard of it."

"It's a really isolated part of the canyon. One way in and out, but it's got a sandy shore, and a lot of the teens go swimming there in summer after school," Mrs. Assion filled the detective in. "Unless you grew up here, you wouldn't know about it. It's very much a teenagers' hangout. Parties there at night are rare due to the dangers of getting down to the beach, but they do happen. You are limited in how many people can fit in the space. Maybe twenty kids at most."

"Well, that narrows our suspect range with any luck. Let's send a forensics team to the beach and see what they find," the detective decided.

"At this time of the morning, we'll probably find most of the party-goers still asleep or climbing out of the canyon to make their way home." Mrs. Assion turned to walk away to her team. Pulling out her phone, she typed in a quick message, looked back at me, then to my mother, and left.

"We could hope to be so lucky. If they are, round them up and get names and cheek swabs."

"You'll need parental consent if they are under eighteen for the swabs," Mum lectured. Placing her hand across my shoulder, she turned me around. "I'm taking my daughter home now." Going to where my dad was sitting, Mum hugged me tightly. "Have they finished questioning you?"

"Yes, it only took them five minutes." Looking at me, Dad reached out and wiped my cheek. "What happened?"

"The girl is a classmate from her school. Sophie Thinehart. There was a party at Blindman's Corner Beach last night, apparently. They are now sending a team to determine if it was the murder scene."

"That's usually a safe place for the teens because of the difficult access. The Execrable don't like hard-to-get locations."

"It may not be Execrable. Maybe it's a Vestigial killer, or maybe the girl got drunk or high and went for a swim and drowned in the current. That's for Nelly to determine still." Silence fell between them. "Let's get Sasha home."

The bike parking area was packed when mum pulled her car into the driveway. Not just the delta team, but likely all the Orey teams living locally. Noticing where my attention went, my mother sighed as she parked the car in the garage. "Your Dad will fill them in. Go shower, and I'll have breakfast ready when you finish."

"I don't think I can eat anything."

"You ran a long way this morning and suffered a shock. You need to eat." Getting out of the car, my mum walked inside.

Closing my eyes, I stayed in the car. The tears came faster as I saw Sophie's face in that picture. Covering my face, I started bawling. When the car door opened and my dad pulled me into his arms, I clung to him like a little girl after a nightmare.

Apparently, it was the month of firsts for me. The first kiss, the first make-out session with a boy, the first boy-induced orgasm, the first time, the first body find, and the first time someone I knew died. What if that was the party we'd decided to go to? It could have been one of my friends. What if Barden and the team didn't make it in time last weekend? It would have been.

"Dad, I'm so sorry, I lied. We weren't at Yasmine's place last weekend. We went to Elisha's party. We were going back to Yasmine's when the Execrable netted us in the park. I called the team, but we had to fight them off until the boys arrived. Savas covered for me, but we lied. I'm sorry. I promise too never do it again. I promise."

Holding me, my dad soothed me, rubbing my back and letting me cry and confess everything that happened at the party and with the Execrable. Okay, not everything. I left out the mudroom with Barden, but I sobbed out everything else.

Later that afternoon, I was lying on my bed. My mind flashed between Sophie's dead face and how all the teams watched me as my father walked me inside when I'd finally calmed down.

When I say all the teams, I mean Barden. The way Barden's eyes locked onto mine and the coolness of his gaze followed me until I left the room again.

A knock on the door, then it cracked open, and Dad stepped in. Sitting up, I made room for him to sit beside me. "I've spoken to your mother about what you told me. We've decided not to expand your current grounding even though you lied about your whereabouts. You didn't drink, didn't engage in risky behavior, and probably saved your friends' lives in the end. We feel your current punishment is enough."

Nodding my head, I stared out the window.

Putting his arm around my shoulders, my dad leaned his head against mine. "I spoke to Savas and Barden, and they confirmed what they saw at the party matches with what you told us. Savas apologized for covering for you, but said he also felt that had your mother not been so strict with you these last few years, you probably wouldn't have felt the need to lie and sneak out. I didn't share that with your mother, but I agree with him. I also understand what your mother sees at her work is why she is the way she is with you. After today, I think you might be a little more understanding, too."

Sitting there quietly, I couldn't argue with him. We never discussed my mother's cases. She didn't like to bring her work home with her, plus there was confidentiality. That still didn't entirely excuse trying to keep me a prisoner in my home sometimes.

"Is there anything else you need to tell me about?" Dad urged. "Like if something happened between you and Barden?"

Chewing my lip, I looked at my dad. "You know?"

"That he and Savas had words last week."

Rubbing my lips together, I looked back out the window. "We played seven minutes in heaven together at the party. No one else was playing, but we found ourselves alone, and he put the timer on his phone. When the alarm sounded, he called the team and told me to go home."

"How far did it go?"

My face heated because I couldn't lie to my dad, but I could tell the truth and not answer the question he was asking. "There was tongue."

Lifting his brow, Dad rubbed his lips together, the sides twitching. "I thought he gave you the creeps."

"He did. But at the party, the girls were talking about how hot he was and how they'd love to..." remembering who I was talking to, I skipped that part. "Then Raisa told Mia how Barden's had a thing for me for years, that he's obsessed with me and wants me. I didn't know. I didn't realize that's why he always stared at me. I really thought he hated me, but he kissed me."

At this point, my father was smirking, and I was red like a ripe tomato. Wetting his lips, Dad kissed my head and stood up. "Let's not tell your mother about you and Barden. She's not ready for you to be a young woman yet. I'm not either, but I find your naiveté of Barden's interest in you all these years to be quite endearing."

"You knew?"

Snickering, Dad opened the door. "Honey, everyone knew but you. Even Savas thought it was hilarious. What always interested me was that Barden didn't care that anyone else noticed. He only cared that you failed to. I have no issue with you kissing him. Just keep it PG. If I find out it's become R-rated, I'll make you marry and move in with him. Consider that every time he kisses you with the intent to do more." Cocking an eyebrow at me, Dad chuckled as he closed the door.

Falling back on my bed, I huffed out a long, frustrated breath as the morning in Barden's room, the pantry, and Thursday night in this very bed played through my head. The intelligent thing would be to put the brakes on, but I craved Barden when he wasn't near me. Besides, did it matter now? If no one else found out, Barden and I could do whatever we wanted.

Turning my face to the side, I saw my school year photo. Sophie smiled, her platinum hair and tanned skin healthy and alive. She was never going to get married or have kids, never going to graduate and go to university or have a career.

My eyes filled with tears. I hugged my pillow and cried again.

Monday morning, I got up and did my morning run with Savas. We didn't talk, and we turned back at our usual marker, so we didn't go anywhere near where I found Sophie.

"Are you okay?" Savas asked when we got home.

Meeting his eyes, I shook my head, then went and got ready for school. While having breakfast, I realized nothing was said about me riding my bike to school on the weekend. While permission wasn't given, it also wasn't denied. So, after cleaning up, I got on my bike and went to school. I didn't wait for Savas to ride with me, but I did leave mum a note on the kitchen table.

Went to school as agreed with Dad.
Hope you have a great day. I'll let you know when I'm there safe and when I'm home again.
Love you,
Sasha

The Crow

SITTING on the swing in my backyard, I stared at the trail which climbed the hill behind our house. The black dress I wore to Sophie's funeral dragged in the grass beneath the swing, but I didn't care. In my head, I kept seeing myself walking off up the mountain path, like a yearning in my soul.

Dressed in his school uniform, Savas took the swing beside me. Reaching out, Savas took my hand, and we sat there like that for a long time. It was nearly two weeks since I'd found the body. It took that long for the police to release it. Anyone who wanted to attend was dismissed from school for the day to participate in the funeral.

"Do you want to talk about it?" Savas asked.

"All anyone will say is that she was murdered, but it was an open casket. With a touch of her lifeless hand, I knew what had happened to her. I didn't know that would happen. I've never touched a dead body before."

Gripping my hand tighter, Savas stayed quiet, his eyes glassy as he watched me.

"It wasn't an Execrable. They broke Sophie's neck. Just a quick snap, and her lights went out." The silence dragged out. In my head, I heard their voice as they talked. They were standing behind her, but I knew that voice. I just couldn't pick how. It wasn't familiar in that I heard it every day, but I'd heard it before and knew I knew whoever it was.

My mind kept playing it over in my head.

Savas squeezed my hand gently. "You've had a lot happen the last few weeks. The Execrable attack, the–"

"I didn't know the Execrable could change forms," I interrupted, wanting to chase that thought rather than be stuck in Sophie's last minutes. "To become the things that chased me through the park three weeks ago. Did you?"

Savas stared across the backyard, leaning his head on the swing's chains. "It's rare, but they can change. I'd never seen it before the night they attacked you girls, but Dad warned me. He's only seen it happen once, the night Vidal's mum was killed."

Frowning, I peered at Savas. "Yasmine's mum was killed by an Execrable?"

"Killed would be putting it mildly," Savas muttered.

My mind flashed back to that park. "They changed when they realized we were Orey. We'd used our powers on them, and the ringleader yelled that we were Orey girls. We were running, but after that, they all changed into those disfigured dreadful things."

"We are meant to protect you from all this. You should never have been exposed to them or what happened to Sophie. We are trained to be able to hack this shit psychologically; you aren't."

Looking at my hand in my brother's, I considered his words. "Is that why you don't talk to me anymore? Because of what you see and deal with every weekend?" Savas stared at the woods. Following his gaze, I leaned my head on the swing chain, mirroring his pose. "I enjoyed fighting the Execrable. Even when I got hurt going into the ground. The adrenaline and thrill of the danger, all of it. I loved it just as much as riding my bike fast along the canyon roads."

Squeezing my hand, Savas stood up. "That's not your role. Focus on your studies."

"I'd be dead now," I called as he started back to the house. Twisting the swing to face him, I met my brother's eyes. "If I hadn't mimicked your training growing up. If I hadn't honed my powers and learned how to use them for defense. If I hadn't listened to dad teach you how to fight as a team, then Mia, Yasmine, Raisa, and I would be dead."

Standing up, I faced my twin. "You may be the boy, but the night that five Execrable surrounded my friends and me, they turned to me for leadership, knowing that I'd learned what you boys know, and because of that, they are still alive."

"You sneaked out to a party. Your actions are what put your friends in danger!" Savas yelled at me.

"They were already going! I didn't want to go, but I'm glad I did because if I had stayed home and they went alone, they'd all be dead."

Gritting his teeth, Savas stormed towards me, thunder rumbling overhead as storm clouds swirled into existence from nowhere. "No! If you hadn't been there, Barden would have called the team, and we'd have escorted them home. With you there, Barden couldn't help but play with you by turning it into a game of cat and mouse. Do you think he didn't confess his part in all that? Do you think I don't know what happened between the two of you in the mudroom? Barden tells me everything, especially regarding you and your reckless behavior."

A tear shattered on my cheek as Savas clenched his jaw. "Mum's right. You're acting out and a danger to the rest of us." Storming inside, Savas slammed the back door.

Backing up a step, then another, I felt the electrons firing through my nervous system, torn between shame and hate. Clenching my fists, I yelled my frustration to the storm clouds. Lightning branched through the heavy black clouds, and the rain poured down.

Turning, fired up, and needing to burn off this energy, I started walking towards the forest trail. Picking up speed, I kicked off my ballet flats as my walk shifted into a jog, and then I was running into the trees, turning and pumping my arms hard as I climbed the slope, the path winding its way up the hill. The rain made the track slippery and muddy, but my feet were sure and light.

Reaching a clearing halfway up the hill, I stopped and bent over, panting. The forest track was not a gentle incline, and my leg muscles were burning from racing up here. Making my way over to a fallen log, I sat down and gazed at the view.

Our house was far below but close enough to see anyone coming and going or when the lights were on in different rooms. Across the canyon, I could see the Assion house—higher still than where I sat and too far away to make out details, but I knew that house, even from this distance.

Hugging myself over my thighs, I rested my head on my knees. I burned off the adrenaline and anger in the run, and now I was tired. Too tired to go back home, not that I wanted to yet, anyway. As the rain stopped, the sun started to set.

"Sasha!" My dad's voice echoed up the hillside. "Sasha!" My brother's voice joined my dad's after a few minutes. As darkness descended, they stopped calling for me.

Shivering a little, I hugged myself tighter as night descended. I should go home. I knew I had to. I just couldn't bring myself to stand up and start. A shadow passed overhead as the sound of large wings flapping beat down on me. Lifting my head, I saw the sky was clear.

A drop of water raced down my spine; my hair was still drenched from the storm. Shivering, I huddled in on myself just as there was a thump, like something landing further up the track. Turning that way, a tall, dark figure of a man was striding toward me. Tears shattered on my cheeks as Barden stopped in front of me. "Sasha?"

"I'm not okay. So very *not* okay," I sobbed.

Sitting next to me, Barden pulled me into his lap and held me against his bare chest as I cried next to him. The only times I felt like myself anymore were with Barden. Mia, Raisa, and Yasmine weren't even talking to me unless our parents forced us together for one of the social mingles. That made science really awkward, considering Mia still wouldn't do any of the work.

"Did something happen?" Barden asked when I finally calmed down and just stayed snuggled into his chest.

Blowing out a breath, I hung my head. "I had a fight with Savas and needed to burn off the negative energy, so I ran up here."

"What was the fight about?"

Bowing my head, I licked my lips. "He said it was my fault that we got attacked by the Execrable."

Tightening his arms around me, Barden gave me a squeeze. "What, how?"

"He said had I not been at the party, you wouldn't have played cat and mouse and let us leave the party unescorted."

"That makes it my fault."

"Apparently, I'm reckless."

"You are far from reckless, Sash." Standing up, Barden shifted, and his wings snapped to either side. "Hold tight."

Crouching a little, Barden raised those enormous wings and then jumped into the air as he flapped with a great woosh, and we soared into the sky. Seconds later, we were gliding down from the mountain towards my house. With a flap, Barden changed his trajectory and landed on my bedroom balcony.

Carrying me into my room, Barden set my feet down. "You're shivering from sitting in wet clothes as the sun set. You need a warm shower."

"Stay with me?" Unzipping the black dress, I shoved it free of my body. Unhooking my bra as I stepped free of the dress, I kept my eyes locked with Barden's as I backed towards the bathroom. Dropping the lacy bra, I hooked my fingers on the side of my knickers and shoved them down. Not even hesitating, Barden followed me into the bathroom, shutting the door as he reached for me.

Grabbing Barden's waistband, I made quick work of his fly while his lips nipped and sipped at my neck. "I want you to be my partner for the formal dance," I breathed as Barden stepped free of his jeans.

"Done."

"And I want to see you during the week."

Reaching for the mixer tap, he flicked it up, and cold water poured over us. I didn't care. Barden's body kept me warm. "When I can. I still need to perform my duties."

"Is it scary in that realm?"

Caressing my neck, Barden stared into my eyes. "It all depends on which part you are in. I quite like it there and have lived there for a long time. I only moved to this realm permanently to be close to you, Sash."

"Can you take me there one day?"

Rubbing his nose along mine, Barden smiled. "It would be my pleasure." Then before I could keep talking, Barden went to his knees, lifted one of my legs to his shoulder, and set his mouth against the heat of my sex. His tongue teased my lips, then gave a sudden quick flick to my clit. Cursing, I held on for dear life as Barden french kissed my underworld, making my eyes fold back in my head and pant his name.

An hour later, I stood on my balcony staring at the stars. Initially, I'd stood here to watch Barden fly away. A longing to fly away with him had taken over me, and I'd stayed here dreaming of all the places I wanted to see around the world.

"Sasha?" My mother called as she opened my bedroom door and came into my room without asking. Blowing out my breath, I stepped back into my room. Mum stopped and frowned. "What were you doing out there?"

"Dreaming of impossible things."

Rolling her eyes as if I was ridiculous, she handed me a piece of A4 paper that I recognized as my university preference sheet. "Well, I've been doing something useful and working on your university preferences for next year."

I gritted my teeth when I glanced at the list of six degrees and universities. "They're all law or pre-law. I don't remember saying I wanted to follow in your footsteps or stay in the area."

Scoffing, Mum walked over and picked my wet clothes up off the floor, taking them into the bathroom to hang them up to dry. "Why have you left wet clothes on the floor?" When I didn't answer, she kept on. "They are all great schools, and you can commute daily to and from most of those campuses from here. If you organize your schedule right, you can drive in and home with me each day and intern at my firm."

"Oh, so now I'm specializing in criminal law?" Throwing the sheet of paper on the end of my bed, I pulled back the quilt and climbed into bed.

"It'll be the most useful for the teams."

"And that's all that matters. The boys. We give up everything we want so they can run around dispatching evil souls back to the underworld."

Coming back out of the bathroom, Mum saw me already in bed and checked her watch. "You're going to bed already?"

"I'm tired."

Blinking at me, Mum came to the bed. "How was the funeral?"

"It sucked."

"Why? Did someone do something?" Mum asked, perplexed.

"Yes, Mum. Someone killed a girl I knew. So, forgive me for not wanting to discuss your ideas for my future because today I stood by a grave, knowing Sophie will never have one."

"Sash-"

"Night, Mum." Turning my back to her, I turned out the lamp on the bedside table and snuggled against my pillow.

Clearing her throat, Mum stood silent for a moment, then grabbed the preference list of choices from the end of the bed and took it to my desk. "Well, make sure you give the list to your guidance counselor tomorrow." Going to my bedroom door, there was another beat of silence. "Night, Sasha. I love you."

The door closed, and I squeezed my eyes on the tears coming and going all night. Giving in to them, I cried myself to sleep.

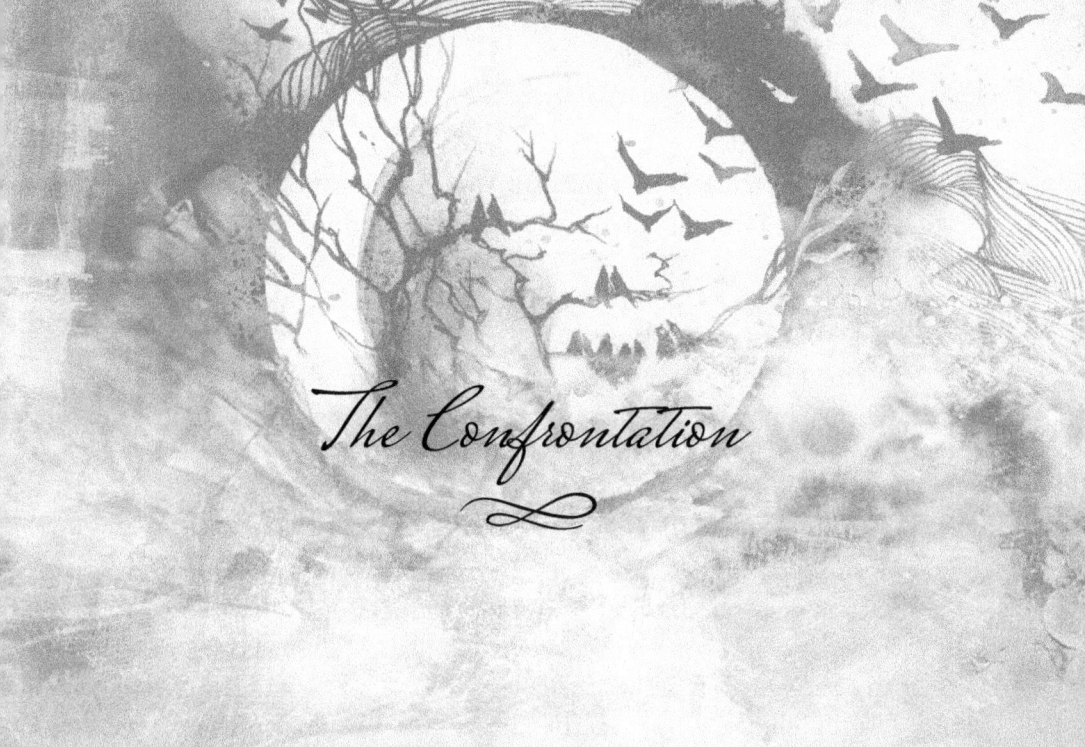

The Confrontation

SINCE THE EXECRABLE attack a few months ago, I'd gone from having a close group of friends to whom I could say anything to Nigel-No-Friends. I hung out in the library every lunch to avoid said ex-friends. If there was something I was grateful for, I only had one class with Mia. While Yasmine ignored me and Raisa gave me sad eyes in the classes we shared, Mia was as blatant as she could be about hating me.

"Hey, Sasha," Elisha greeted when we met by our lockers.

"Hey. How are you?"

Elisha gave me a kind smile. "I'm better." Elisha had taken Sophie's death hard. For a month after I found the body, she always looked like she'd just been crying. "How about you? You seem to have had a lot going on. I noticed you're no longer hanging with Queen Bitch Mia."

"Yeah. We had a falling out after your birthday party, I guess. Not that I was aware of it."

Brows drawing together, Elisha met my eyes. Hers were suddenly intense. The pupil seemed to bleed into the blue of her iris until dark gray striations swirled through the usually clear blue. "Really? Because you made out with Barden Assion?"

How did she know about that? "Um, I don't know. I mean, yeah, I told her about that, but when we were walking home, some guys attacked us, and she injured me while we were fighting them off."

"On purpose?"

Stopping to think about it, I shrugged a shoulder. "I thought it was an accident, but I'm not so sure."

Narrowing her eyes over my shoulder, Elisha considered what I told her. Then slipped her arm through mine to hook my elbow. "Come sit with us for lunch today," she suggested as we headed for the courtyard. She waited until we were sitting down to keep talking. "The Racles are like fanatical naturalists, aren't they? All about keeping things pure?"

"Yeah, but Mia isn't like that. She eats meat when her family isn't around and does a heap of other stuff her parents would disapprove of."

"Doesn't surprise me she's a hypocrite," Darina, Elisha's other bestie, scoffed. "She's a two-faced witch."

Elisha's elbow slipped and knocked into Darina's. "Sorry," she muttered but gave Darina a stern look. "Let's talk about something uplifting. The formal isn't far away yet. Has anyone asked you yet, Sasha? Simon's still free."

"Thanks, but I'm going with Barden Assion," I replied meekly.

"Ooh! Nice." Elisha grinned.

"Damn, he is hot!" Darina feigned, melting into a puddle. "I would have jumped his bones if he even showed an ounce of interest these last two years, but that guy is blind to the opposite sex. Are you sure he's not gay?"

"I'm pretty sure," I chuckled.

"Barden and Sasha hooked up at my birthday party," Elisha gossiped to her bestie. "That's when Mia and the others turned on her."

"Wow! How did you score with Barden? I mean, go you for tapping that fine specimen, but how?"

Mouth full of spit, I shrugged a shoulder. "Ah, Barden actually made the first move. Apparently, I've been blind to his interest for years, but once I turned eighteen, he was done waiting."

"And what about you?" Elisha asked conspiratorially. "Is it just fun before university or a way to rebel against your mum?"

Scrunching my nose at the thought of sleeping with a guy just to annoy my mother—though, honestly, that would work a treat, I knew that wasn't the case. "No, neither. I've had the biggest crush on Barden since we met, but I thought he hated me all these years. My parents don't even know yet." Blowing out a breath, I deflated. "I really like Barden. He's making me rethink my plan to go to university as far away as possible."

Both girls sat, blinking at me. "So, you're in love with Barden?" Elisha asked.

"I think it's a little early to use that term, but it's certainly more than fooling around. Or at least, it is to me. I'm not sure about Barden. He's not the talkative type, and he seems happy with hooking up when he can get me alone, so I'm not sure this is anything more to him."

Arching eyebrows at each other, Elisha and Darina had a silent conversation before turning their attention back to the formal. When the bell rang, I grabbed my stuff, ready to head to class, but Elisha grabbed my arm.

"Look, I don't know all the details, but I know you. You're too nice to everyone. Don't let Mia walk all over you, okay? You're way more than she'll ever be, and I think she feels threatened by you, in all honesty."

Taking those words as solid advice, I headed to Chemistry, where Mia spent the entire class filing her nails and texting. When class ended, she got up and left without helping pack up. Clenching my jaw, I put everything away, then handed my paper in. Our teacher looked at it and raised a brow.

"You haven't put Mia's name on your lab report again this week."

I hadn't put Mia's name on the report last week, either. "She doesn't do the work, doesn't contribute, and doesn't even help clean up anymore. Why should I put her name on my hard work?"

"Don't think I haven't known that for a long time, but you always seemed happy with that arrangement. I'm actually grateful that you've stopped covering for her. I'm sure Mia only chose this subject so she could bludge while you did the hard work."

Considering her family's stance on all things natural, that would make more sense. "You're probably right." I pulled out my phone and sent a message to Barden before heading out the door.

> Want to meet me at Milkbar for a drink and then ride home together after my swim practice?

Going to the gym, I changed into my swimmers before Barden responded.

BARDEN

> Yes.

In-person, that would have just been one of his affirmative grunts. Opening the thread of messages with Savas, I let him know my plans.

> I'm going to Milkbar after training. I need a time-out from Mum. Barden will meet and escort me home if you're okay with that?

SAVAS

> Fine by me. Is Dad okay with it?

Good point. Better smooth that over too.

> Dad, I'm going to Milkbar after training. I'm going to eat there so don't cook for me. I've organized an escort home with Savas and Barden.

DAD

> Is that how you ask now?

> Asking gives you the option to say no. I'm a legal adult. I've had a stressful week already, and I just want time to myself before Mum launches another one of her future plans for my life attacks.

There had been discussions about my future law career since the university preference list, including trying to set me up on a date with Vidal, Nash, or Athur.

DAD

Home by eight.

A smile pulled at the side of my mouth as I switched back to my thread with my twin.

Dad's copacetic.

SAVAS

He just messaged me to double-check that we were meeting you to bring you home later. I know what you're doing.

Giving you until 8pm to hook up with Calliope?

There was a long pause between messages.

SAVAS

How do you know about that?

I walked in on it months ago at the Assions. A side of you I never wanted to see and certainly more than I ever needed to see of Calliope. Are you complaining about your free time?

SAVAS

Whatever. It's not like my coming and going gets policed.

Ignoring the blatant attempt to rile me about the fact my freedoms were limited, I closed that thread and went back to Barden.

I'll let you know when I finish practice.

Putting my phone away, I headed out to the indoor pool and tuned everything out, focusing on my breathing and stroke.

Two hours later, I was parking down the side of the Milkbar. I was relieved to see the back booth where I'd always sat was free. Sliding into it, I pulled out my study notes from class today and started reviewing them.

"Sasha, hey. What are you up to?" Falco greeted as he came over.

"Studying while I wait for Barden." I smiled. "Can I get my usual?"

"Sure." Giving me a smile, Falco headed back into the kitchen.

Fifteen minutes later, I had my laptop, and my study book opened to rewrite my notes and add further information when the door opened. Three familiar laughs came into the dinner. The laughter shut off suddenly, and I didn't need to look up to know my former besties had just spotted me in our booth.

"Ah, what do you think you're doing?" Mia snarked. Out of the corner of my eye, I could see her cheer skirt and realized the other girls must have hung around after school to watch her practice.

Without even looking up, I answered, "Studying and getting dinner."

"This is my booth. Everyone knows that," Mia snipped.

Lifting a brow, I sat back and met her eyes. "Yours?"

"That's right."

"Hmm, strange, because I was born and grew up here. I've been sitting in this booth since the fifth grade while I waited for my bus home. Hell, Yasmine and Raisa didn't even start coming here with me until high school, and you only moved here three years ago, Mia. So, no, this isn't your booth. It's mine. Find yourself somewhere else to sit from now on. You don't want to be my friend anymore, that's fine, but it means you give up the benefits you gained by being my friend, and this booth is one of them."

Glaring at me, Mia leaned closer and lowered her voice. "You want to watch your back, Sasha."

Laughing in her face, I crossed my arms. "Or what? You'll bury me alive again? You already tried that shit. You going to cause cracks for me to fall and hurt myself?"

"You can't swim with a broken neck, Sasha," Yasmine taunted.

Grinning, Mia threatened. "Wouldn't want you to be the next body someone finds by the river in the canyon, would we?"

Oh, that was a low blow. Slowly, I stood up and leaned on the table so we were almost nose to nose. As I did, I funneled the water out of my open water bottle and had it pool around Mia's feet. "Earth is all you've got, Mia. Tell me, what good is that when you stand in water during a lightning strike?"

Holding my hand between us, I pulled electricity from my body and had it spark between my fingers. Then, I purposefully looked down at Mia's feet and back up. When Mia followed my gaze and realized her predicament, she quickly backed up. "Whatever! Have your stupid booth. It's not like it's going to buy you any friends."

"Are you causing trouble in our restaurant?" Hawk asked, folding his muscular arms over his chest, his eyes on Mia. Getting the attention of everyone else at the dinner.

Falco stood leaning on the wall holding my burger as if he was waiting for this bullshit to finish to deliver it. His brother Hawk had come out of the kitchen and was leaning on the counter. Their pupils were pinpoints with deep striations running into their weird blue-black eyes.

"No." Mia swallowed. "We're good." She tried to give me a glare, but the way her eyes flicked down to the water on the floor and she shivered ruined the effect.

My former three besties retreated to another booth halfway toward the front and slid into it. Exhaling, I grabbed some napkins and tried to clean up the water on the floor.

"Sorry," I murmured to Falco.

He put my dinner on the table and then squatted down. "Don't worry about it," he said, catching my hands and pulling them back before I could get the first napkin wet. "I'll get the mop and bucket. Just take a breath and eat your dinner."

Giving him a sad smile, I climbed back into my seat. "Want me to fill up your water bottle?" Falco offered.

"If you wouldn't mind."

Giving me a wink, Falco grabbed my bottle and said, "I don't."

Watching his brother go, I noticed Hawk still glaring at my ex-besties. Taking a breath, he glanced my way, gave me a nod, then headed back to the kitchen to keep cooking.

Closing my eyes, I took a moment to center myself, then focused back on my studies. Easier said than done, considering how loud my ex-besties were tonight.

The girls discussed where and what they planned to study next year as if they had the place to themselves. Giving up on my studies, I sank into my booth and sucked down what was left of my milkshake. Was this normal? Girls just hit a certain age, and suddenly all their relation-ships changed?

The Confidant

"WE SHOULD HEAD HOME before it gets dark," Raisa said. "I just need to run to the toilet." Getting up, she went out back.

"So, we're good for shopping tomorrow morning?" Yasmine asked as she and Mia stood up, picked up their bags, and headed out.

Once the door shut, Raisa came back and stopped by my booth. "I don't hate you," she murmured. "I get why you never told us. Seeing how they're treating you, how Vidal and Athur treated Savas. They only accepted him and Barden because of the team. It took a while to be comfortable with your kind, but it happened. Maybe the girls will forgive you for hiding it from them eventually."

"My kind?" I frowned, lifting my gaze to hers. What bullshit did they tell themselves to justify ending years of friendship? "What's that supposed to mean? Because I have more than one power? Thank fuck I do, or I'd be dead right now. Mia frigg'n buried me alive. At first, I thought it was a mistake, that she panicked, but she opened the ground under me, then closed it around me, and she didn't even try to reopen it to save me. The Execrable wasn't the danger to me out there that night. It was the person I falsely believed to be my best friend. And you all have the nerve to turn on me? It should've been me angry with her for what happened."

"Wait, you don't know?" Raisa looked horrified.

"That Barden is a crow? Not until the day after the attack. I thought he was Orey like the rest of us. I don't understand why it's a problem, since he helps our brothers."

Hesitating, Raisa gulped. "You really don't know. And we thought we were betrayed."

"No, that was me. I saved your asses. As a thank you, I got buried alive and then shunned for my efforts without explaining what I did wrong. Good luck the next time you run into demons. If the Execrable doesn't kill you, Mia probably will."

Mouth falling open, Raisa gripped the shoulder strap of her bag as tears filled her eyes. "For what it's worth, I'm sorry. I better go." She walked out of the restaurant like Falco was snapping his towel at her bum.

A body slid into the booth opposite me. "That seemed tense?"

I huffed at Falco and rechecked my phone. I'd been here an hour, and no sign of Barden yet. "Raisa's okay. I just don't get what I did."

"Who said you did anything?" When I just shrugged, Falco leaned in. "Did Mia threaten that you would be the next body they find in the ravine?"

"She did." I winced. "And Yasmine threatened to break my neck. That was really low. There is nothing funny or acceptable about saying stuff like that when it's only been a few weeks since Sophie died. I can still see her body on those rocks." My eyes filled with tears.

Placing his hand over mine, Falco squeezed it. "Finding her can't have been easy. Are you scared those girls will act on their threats?"

Shaking my head, I wiped my eyes. "No. Raisa isn't that callus. Yasmine is all talk. Her abilities are so pathetic—"

"Abilities?" Falco raised a brow.

Realizing what I had said, I tensed and pulled back. "Yeah, you know, her physical prowess? She's a chess geek. Doesn't play sports or anything physical, so the chance she could beat me in a fight is pretty low. Hell, I can outrun her with ease."

"And Mia?"

Lifting a shoulder, I dropped hit again. "Mia can try. It's not like she hasn't before."

"Are you regretting hooking up with Barden?" Falco asked intently.

"God, no! I'll choose him every day of the week. I'd choose him over my own mother. Would you believe my Mum's ranked law schools and completed my university nomination sheet with those preferences without asking me if I wanted to do law? I hate law. It's the last thing I want to do for a living. And now she's trying to encourage me to date Yasmine's older brother. Argh! No thanks. None of those guys even hold a candle to Barden. I can't even imagine being with anyone else."

For a moment, Falco fell quiet, then sat back and gave me a calm smile.

"So, what are you thinking of studying?" he asked.

I opened my mouth, ready to tell him I was considering taking a gap year and traveling. Not telling anyone and just getting on a plane out of here. But I barely knew Falco, and hardly spoke to him until my friends pushed me out. "I haven't decided."

"Do you think you'll stay local?" he pressed.

Taking a breath, I assessed the sun starting to set outside. "I don't know. I didn't plan it but leaving means giving up Barden, and I suspect that will be hard to do." Even thinking about it brought me to tears.

"Hey." Falco leaned over the table, covering my hand with one of his and using his thumb to wipe away a tear. "It's sweet how much you care for him."

Dropping my gaze, I nibbled my lip. "You've slept with a lot of girls, right?"

Chuckling, Falco shrugged. "Did you want to jump in line, Sash? I thought you only had eyes for Barden."

"I do. I wasn't—" Chewing my lip, I tried to take that back. My anxiety only made Falco laugh. He squeezed my hand and encouraged me to keep going. "How does a guy let a girl know it's more than fun?" When Falco's eyebrows went up, I lost control of my tongue and just blurted out my worry.

"We don't really talk or hang out. Every moment we get alone, it's all kissing and touching and not talking or just being with each other. I mean, Barden was meant to meet me here, and I told him I was here an hour ago, but he hasn't shown. I thought we'd have time to hang out, but it looks like he will show up in time for us to ride home and make out a bit before I go inside. I told Barden I wanted to spend time with him during the week months ago, but he doesn't organize to meet up and just hang out. I always have to be the one to reach out, and I'm starting to feel like I don't mean as much to him as he does me, so if you could tell me how to figure it out, I'd appreciate it."

I was a bit breathless after spewing that all out, and as I met Falco's eyes, he seemed to be trying not to laugh at me. Which made me deflate in my seat. Before Falco could advise me, the door opened, and Barden came in. His eyes fell straight on me, then to where Falco was holding my hand, and his pupils narrowed on us.

"What's going on?" Barden asked when he got to the booth.

Still humored by my outburst, Falco squeezed my hand and stood up. "Chill, I'm just checking she's okay. Her former friends were here being witches."

Barden's jaw tensed as he looked at me as if checking I was okay, then back to Falco. "Don't play with her. She's not like them."

Lips lifting on one side, Falco nodded his head. "Tell me something I don't already know." Falco grabbed my empty plate from the table and gave me a kind smile. "Next time, Sasha." With a wink, he headed back to the kitchen.

Before Barden could sit down, I grabbed my stuff and left the booth. "I thought we were getting a drink?" Barden asked, frowning at me.

"Yeah, over an hour ago. The sun's setting. I need to be home before it's down." I actually had until eight. "Sorry. I was in a good mood before Mia showed up and threatened me, but now I'm tired, over everything, and just want to go home." With any luck, Mum would already have retreated to a bubble bath with a glass of wine or her home office by the time I got home.

"Mia threatened you?" Barden growled.

"I don't want to talk about it."

Following me, Barden gripped my elbow as I put my helmet on. "Hey," he murmured and stepped closer to me. I chased his lips when they brushed mine, longing for more of him. "I'm sorry I was late. I was on the other side."

He was doing his actual job. I couldn't really be angry with him for that; I just wished we could find time for us. If there even was an us. Barden's words–when he used them–always made it sound like I was his everything. It was his actions that were letting me down. "It's fine," I whispered as he kissed me again.

Regretfully pulling back, I yanked on my helmet before I forgot why I was upset. "We should go."

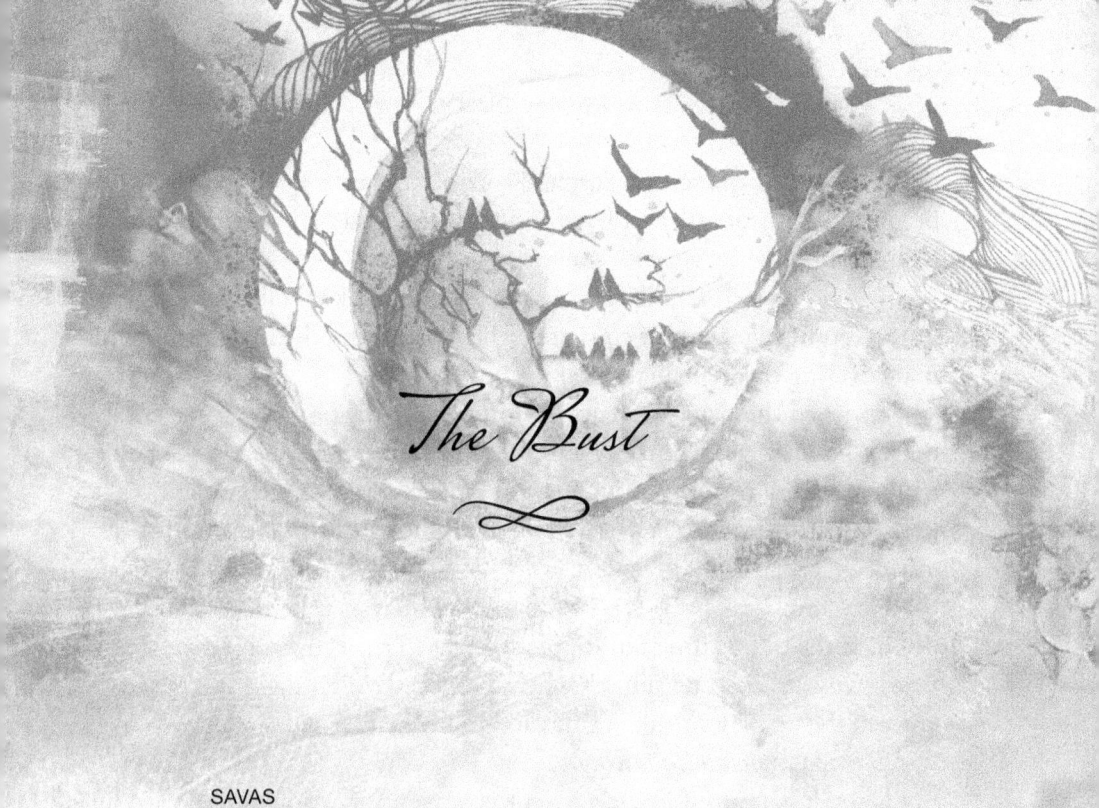

The Bust

SAVAS

Barden will meet you at school and ride
home with you. Tell me where you parked so
he can meet you there.

LOOKING at the message from my brother as I took a break from
studying in my free period, I huffed and put my phone back in my
pocket without answering. My mum probably asked Savas to stick
around and ride home with me. As much as I liked to see Barden, I
desired more than him following me home. I wanted to hold his hand,
kiss and hug him openly in front of my family.

Just having him crawl into my bed late at night twice a week and
leave before sunrise wasn't enough. It hadn't been since the moment it
started. I was also sick of having to be nannied all the time. I was eighteen and could not ride twenty minutes home by myself in broad
daylight. It was ridiculous.

When school finished for the day, I went to the locker rooms to
change and walked to the bike racks. I'd parked my motorbike next to
the bike rack, as they had access to a separate exit from the school
grounds using a cycle path. No, it wasn't meant for motorbikes, but no

one had pulled me up on it yet. Probably because I tended to arrive before most students, and by the time I changed, the foot traffic had cleared out.

The bonus of parking here was that I could take the back roads out of town once I got out of the gate rather than using the main entry and maneuvering through all the traffic.

I opened the navigation app before setting my phone into its cradle on my handlebars. I sent my mother and father a notification so they could track my trip if they wanted to. Donning my helmet and gloves, I pressed the button to start the bike and glided down the empty back exit.

Five minutes away from the school, Savas called. Groaning, I declined the call. It took ten minutes to get to the canyon road and start the downward descent. This is where I enjoyed riding the most. Just as I entered the first curve, my notification in my helmet activated.

'Barden Assion within range.'

Knowing he would have gotten the same notification and learned he was getting closer, I huffed. "Sash?" Barden's voice came through my helmet.

Dropping low to the bike, my lips curled up as I picked up speed, falling back on years of experience to navigate this road at high speeds.

There were a few cars on the road, but I could get past them quickly. Once I hit the river, the road straightened out, and I could open up the throttle until I reached the bridge. On the other side of the river, I accelerated again, heading back down the river toward home. I caught sight of Barden's bike hiking the straight on the other side.

"Slow down, Sasha," Barden growled.

My lips curved up as I went a little faster than usual, but I knew my limitations, and I'd never been out of control of my bike. A few minutes later, I was pulling through our driveway gates and zipped up to the already-opening garage. Pulling up, I backed my bike into the wheel stand, dismounted, and jacked it up.

I removed my gloves and shoved them inside my helmet before I grabbed my phone and closed the navigation app. In the boot room, I set my helmet in my appointed cubby hole, dropped my bag to the bench, unzipped my jacket, then sat down and removed my boots.

By the time I was ready to go inside, Barden was storming into the garage. "Sasha."

Hitting the button to close the garage door, I turned my back on him, grabbed my bag, and went into the kitchen, ignoring my brother's best friend. I grabbed a soda from the fridge and continued to my father's den. "I'm home. Heading upstairs to study."

"Okay, Sash."

"Barden's here," I mentioned as I backed out.

Frowning, my father lifted his eyes from his book. "With you?"

Huffing a laugh, I shook my head. "No. I guess he's meeting Sav here again."

Leaving it at that, I took the stairs as my father got out of his chair and went out to the kitchen.

"Afternoon, Barden. You want something to drink or eat?"

Heading down the hallway to my room, I dumped my bag on my desk, opened it, and took out the bundle of wet clothes from swim practice this morning. I'd left my blazer, kilt, and shoes at school since I'd get dressed there again tomorrow. Only my blouse and socks needed to change daily.

Coming back out of my wardrobe, where I'd changed into shorts and a shirt, my phone pinged.

MUM

> I spoke to your guidance counselor today. Apparently, you haven't put your preference list in yet. The cut-off is only a week away. Make sure you take it tomorrow.

"Argh! For fucks' sake! Leave me alone, you controlling bitch!" I tossed my phone on the bedside table and looked up to find Barden at my door.

Leaning on the jamb with his arms crossed, Barden just wore his uniform and that glare I'd come to consider his resting bitch face.

Annoyed, I went to the door and tried to shut it. "Not today."

Barden put his hand to the wood, and I couldn't even budge it. "Don't." Barden's shirt sleeves were short for the Spring uniform, his arm at my eye height. Frowning, I touched my finger to a chain of minor burns on his skin. It looked like he'd put his arm against a hot wire fence.

"What happened to your arms?" Because now that I was looking, I could see both his arms were healing from the burns.

"Sash," Barden breathed my name as my fingers trailed delicately up his arms. The muscles bunched under my touch, hard beneath the skin.

"Why don't you talk to me?" I asked him, fascinated by how my fingers tingled when touching him. How my entire being seemed to sizzle near him. "We've never really been friends, and you never said we were boyfriend and girlfriend. I just hoped you'd want to actually know me and confide in me like I do you?"

Reaching his shoulders, my hands traveled to his pecs and stopped. "I liked you, you know? When we first met. I tried being friends, but you wouldn't talk to me. After the party, I thought maybe I got it wrong, maybe you did like me, but I'm starting to feel I'm just a way for you to pass the time."

Holding back the tears, I patted his chest and stepped back. "I need more than you sneaking into my room at night and leaving before I wake in the morning."

Before I could close my door, an animalistic snarl ripped from Barden's throat. Turning me around before I knew it, Barden was pressed against my back as he stepped forward and shut my bedroom door.

"Mine!" he snarled in my ear, one of his hands caressing my stomach beneath my shirt, setting off the longing he caused in me to compete with the fear he had just triggered.

Trembling, I shoved away and turned to face him. "No. I'm not yours. Not in any way, shape, or form, and we are not doing this again. Go use someone else to get off. I'm not playing this game with you."

Lifting a brow, Barden stared into my eyes. Taking another step closer, he stood over me, his dark gray-blue irises seeming to pulse as the black abyss-like channels pushed open. "Mine," he whispered this time.

Falling into his eyes, I felt a tugging in my soul, a familiarity that felt like home. As Barden caressed my face, I blinked free of his gaze, a tear tracking down my cheek as I realized he was right. I'd been his from the moment my soul crossed to be born into this world. I was always his, and he'd known it from the moment we'd met—but it took until this moment for me to recognize what I'd been feeling.

"Wow!" I breathed as the understanding hit home.

Barden's lips against mine were new life to my being. My lips tingled with the delicate brush, then fireworks exploded behind my eyelids as he pressed my lips more firmly. Wrapping my arms around Barden's neck, I kissed him back with everything in me, my entire being wanting to crawl out of my mouth into his.

Picking me up, Barden carried me to my bed, then set me down on the ground. His hands lifted my shirt, and I raised my arms, the thin fabric falling to the floor. My hands worked the buttons of his shirt as our lips melded, tongues tasted, and Barden's hands pushed my shorts over my hips.

When his shirt was open, my hands moved over the velvet-like skin of his pecs and abs. The muscles flexed beneath my hands as we kissed breathlessly. Once his trousers were open and pooled around his bare feet, Barden wrapped me in his strong arms, pulling me tight against him. I wasn't short, but Barden made me feel vulnerable and delicate in his arms.

With just our underwear between us, Barden laid me under him on my bed. His mouth pinched and sucked at my neck as he snuggled his hips between my legs, pressing the prominent bulge in his underwear against me until we both moaned.

"Sash-"

My door opened, and Barden and I quickly pulled back to find my dad standing in my doorway, his eyes wide and holding a large envelope. Face shutting down in barely restrained rage, Dad glared at Barden. "Both of you dressed and in my den, now!" Stepping back, he shut the door and stormed away.

Swallowing hard, I glanced up to Barden as he backed away and quickly started getting his clothes back on to a string of curses beneath his breath. It was the most words I'd ever heard leave his mouth in an hour.

Grabbing my shirt and shorts, I hurried to cover myself and try to tame my hair so it didn't just look like Barden had been fisting it while we dry-humped. As I went for the door, Barden grabbed my wrist and pulled me back to drop a delicate kiss on my lips. Hovering close enough to feel his breath, he gazed into my eyes. "Mine."

Double blinking, I wet my lips. "Officially?"

An approving grunt as Barden circled his nose around mine.

"So, we're boyfriend and girlfriend now?"

Another grunt confirming.

Chewing my lip, I stared into his eyes. "Are you going to act like a boyfriend or just stare at me like I kicked your dog and try to get in my pants when no one is looking?"

Barden loosened his grip on my wrist, blowing out a breath, then slid it down to twine our fingers together as he took hold of my hand. I guess that was a pretty strong answer for Barden.

"SASHA TORMEN, GET YOUR BUTT DOWN HERE NOW!"

Jumping at my dad, yelling loud enough to hear him in the kids' wing, I grabbed the door and pulled it open. Barden chuckled as I jogged down the hall to the stairs and the lower level with his hand still clasped in mine.

The Fight

OUTSIDE MY FATHER'S OFFICE, I suddenly became very timid. Squeezing my hand, Barden walked us into the den. Three walls were full of books, a table for tactical planning at one end, and a comfy reading area with lounges at this end.

"Sit!" Dad ordered from where he stood with his butt leaning on the table. My legs dropped from under me, and I sat on the floor where I was.

Pressing his lips together, Barden tried to hide his chuckle. Rubbing his forehead, my father bowed his head to try and hide his need to laugh as well.

"On the lounge, Sash," he snickered.

"Oh." I got up, my face and neck hot as I quickly scurried to the lounge and sat down.

Still smirking, Barden sat beside me and took my hand. "Gannix, I know it looked terrible, but—"

Standing straight, my father glared at Barden. "No! You know the rules. They were very clear. You don't fraternize with Sasha until she is eighteen. You can be friends, and you can flirt, but nothing else until the day an Orey girl turns eighteen. No sex before graduation. I know you kissed her at the party she snuck out to. I let it go since she turned eighteen the next day. Has she graduated high school?"

Jaw tense beside me, Barden glared at my father. "No."

"I told Sasha that it needed to stay PG-rated. Was that what you consider to be PG?" My father shifted his eyes between us.

Bowing my head, I winced at the memory of my father's threat to what was acceptable. "No," both Barden and I answered. While I was remorseful, Barden looked pissed. "But it wasn't R-rated either," I quickly added. "More like mature audiences."

Pressing his lips, Barden bowed his head as his shoulders shook beside me.

Eyeing me, Dad noted how we were holding hands and exhaled. "How far has it gone?"

"Dad, we were arguing, and things got heated, and... we got carried away."

Barden's hand tightened on mine, probably worried about my father's ability to detect lies. Still, it was the truth, and if he thought I was admitting to fucking him to my father, then he was wrong.

Watching us both, dad shifted his stance to cross his arms, legs slightly apart. "Don't get me wrong, I was a teenager too once. I understand how you can lose control too easily when those hormones are new. The high of intimacy is very addictive, but that doesn't excuse the rules. Sasha's graduation is only months away. Resist the temptation to be alone together until then."

When my father's eyes flicked to the doorway, I turned and spotted Savas leaning there, arms crossed and glaring at me. "From now on, Barden, you are barred from the upstairs area of this house. You boys can study at the kitchen table."

"Permanently barred, or just until Sasha graduates?"

Huffing, Dad dropped his arms. "Until you are married. I've warned Sasha what happens if I catch you doing more than kissing. She knows the penalty."

"You said R-rated," I clarified, but shut up and lowered my head when my father pierced me with one look.

"Does this mean they can't ride home together?" Savas asked from the doorway. "Because I can't babysit her every afternoon, and I don't think Barden wants her going to the Milkbar alone to wait for me anymore."

"Wait, why can't I go to the Milkbar?" I asked Barden with a raised brow.

Savas stepped into the room, scowling at me. "Come on, Sash. Do you think Falco was getting all touch-feely with you because he just wants to ensure you're okay? The guy has banged everything with a–"

"Savas!" My dad cut him off.

"I don't know why she's getting pissed off–"

Reefing my hand free of Barden's, I stood up, fingers already sparking. "I'm pissed because apparently, I'm an imposition to you even though I never asked to be nannied. In fact, I'm sick of it. I'm pissed because you both think that I'm so easy I'd fall for Falco's charm even though Barden is the only guy I have ever even looked at like that. And maybe I'm pissed because I just don't want my boyfriend telling my brother all of my business."

"Why? What does his telling me that Falco was holding your hand matter?"

"Because Falco wasn't hitting on me! My ex-best friends had literally just threatened to kill me! They made enough of a scene that Hawk came out of the kitchen and told them to back off. I was upset, and Falco sat there and listened to me. Something that no one in this house has bothered to do in a long time. I have a right to have friends who aren't Orey, who have nothing to do with this family. I'm entitled to live my life how I want to live it. Because, while I know this is a strange concept to the Orey, not every fucking thing I do is about you guys!"

"Hey! Language!" My dad scolded, getting between Savas and me but being careful not to touch me. "Sasha, calm down. If you start a fire in this house, I'll ground you until you are thirty."

Turning away from my brother and his shocked expression, I focused on breathing. Inhaling through my nose, I exhaled twice as long, trying to shake the excess adrenalin off while swiping at my tears. Barden went to wrap me in his arms, but I flinched as I shocked him with my electricity, and he backed up.

"Savas, your sister is right. Your comments are out of line. I have no issue with Barden and Sasha riding home together as long as it is straight home and they stay downstairs when they get here. Now, I need to talk to Sasha privately."

Watching me for a moment, Barden waited for me to meet his eyes, his jaw tense as he observed me, then he followed my brother out, closing the door as he did. Going back to the table, my father blew out a controlling breath.

As the door closed, I shut my eyes and focused on controlling my emotions. "Dad, I'm sorry. I had no intention of that happening with Barden. We were fighting, and then he was kissing me, and it got a little out of control."

Coming back towards me carrying the envelope from earlier, Dad handed it to me. "Barden is discussed. Now, let's talk about what I actually came up there to discuss in the first place."

Taking the envelope, I noted the school name and insignia on the envelope. I swallowed around the lump suddenly in my throat. "It's just the prospectus."

"For a university very far away from home."

Licking my lips, I lifted my eyes to meet my dad's. "Hence the appeal."

Sitting in his reading chair, Dad watched me. "I thought you and your mother already picked your universities, and you submitted your preference list."

Clenching my jaw, I looked down at the envelope. "Mum picked the universities and the courses and filled out the list. I wasn't asked or given a choice in what I wanted. Like I just said, no one listens to me. Especially not Mum." I wasn't telling him I'd thrown the preference list out instead of submitting it.

Considering me, my dad sighed. "We need Barden here, Sash. The team needs him."

Frowning, I shook my head. "This isn't about Barden."

"Yes, it is, Sash. You've just started a committed relationship with him. He will want you to stay close. He'll go if you go; it will get the rest of us killed."

Eyes filling with tears, I glared at my dad. "So, once again, it's not about what I want, but what everyone else wants. Thanks, Dad. So good to know someone here actually gives a shit about me."

"I do, but I have to put the team above all else. We are Orey. We have to do our duty."

"Who says?!" I challenged. "What great power made it our job to be the otherworld border patrol? Or did one of our ancestors just take on the mantel and burden all future generations because he liked to hunt Execrables?"

"We are Orey. It's our duty."

Pissed off, I looked down at the envelope in my hand. "No, it's *your* duty." Glaring back at my father, I didn't hold back the hurt. "I'm just a girl, remember?" Storming to the door, I yanked it open and went back to my room. Getting changed, I skipped downstairs and grabbed my mountain bike from the garage. I needed to burn energy to suffuse my frustration, both sexual and emotional.

Before nightfall, I rode into the backyard, my legs and bike covered in mud from the mountain trail. I could see Dad cooking dinner through the glass back doors, Barden and Savas sitting at the kitchen table talking to him. The sensor light lit up the backyard when I came within range, alerting them to my presence. Ignoring them, I dismounted, set my bike against the wall, and started hosing it down.

Despite having my back to them, I knew it was Barden who came out to talk to me. Coming up behind me, he cupped my shoulders in his palms and kissed my nape. "You okay?"

"Define okay?"

"Sash," Barden murmured as he wrapped his arms around me and hugged my back to his chest, resting his chin on my head for a moment. "Talk to me."

Closing my eyes, I bowed my head. "I can't do this anymore," I admitted.

Tensing behind me, Barden hugged me tighter, a growl leaving his throat. Patting his arm where it bound me over my chest, I kissed his forearm.

"Not you. I mean them," I clarified as I flung my hand out towards the house. "I can't handle them controlling every aspect of my life. Making everything about the teams and their duty. I can't breathe here anymore, and it's killing me. Being with you is the only time I feel free, and they won't allow it."

Turning my cheek into the curl of Barden's bicep, I rested my face as the tears fell. "I just want the space to breathe and be me."

"You want space from me?" Barden murmured.

"No, but..." Staring at the hose on the bike, I sighed. "My Mum never used to be this strict, you know. Up until a few years ago, she let me be me. I realized tonight that she started trying to control me not long after you became friends with Savas. I remembered the first time you came over and hung out with Savas, and I tried to join in. Mum called me to come to help her in her lab. She told me to stay away from you boys. Before that, she never had an issue with me hanging out with the boys. It's because you're a crow, wasn't it?"

An affirmative grunt vibrated through my back. More tears fell. Nuzzling my hair, Barden breathed me in. I probably smelled like crap after riding the hell out of my bike and wearing a helmet.

"You blame me, don't you?" he finally asked.

Honesty was the best policy. "Part of me does. The rational part of my mind knows her bias caused it." My bike was clean now, but I didn't want to move out of Barden's arms, so staying where I was, I lifted one of my legs to the frame and started hosing the mud off me.

"It doesn't matter now, though," I told Barden. "The damage is already done. Her bias has driven a wedge between us that I don't think we can ever fix, and I don't regret being with you, nor do I plan to give you up on the off chance she'll back off. I know my mum. She won't."

A grunt of agreement this time.

Closing my eyes, I hated what I was about to say. Swapping my legs, I told Barden my dilemma. "Dad wants me to stay because he's scared if I go, you'll leave. He claims that if you do, they'll be killed. They need you here. They don't need me, Barden. They only want me because they want you."

Dropping my leg back to the ground, I turned the hose off and threw it aside so I could cling to Barden's strong arms. The scabs of his burns were rough against my palms.

"I want to tell you that it's not me who has to choose to stay or leave at the end of summer; it's you, because I'm going no matter what. But if

I do that, if I give you that ultimatum and you choose me, and they die..."

Barden tightened his arms around me as the sob wracked my body. "Shh," he crooned. "That's not going to happen. It's okay, Sash. It'll all work out, okay? If you need to leave, you go. I'll hate every minute you are not here, but I'd rather see you free and happy than for you to hate me for keeping you here."

It was a good answer, but it wasn't what I wanted to hear. I needed Barden to tell me they would be fine without him and that he'd follow me to the ends of the earth. But it wasn't just the Orey he'd be leaving behind. I'd be asking him to leave his family. Turning in his arms, I buried my face in his chest as I tried to get my crying under control.

Holding me to him, Barden kissed the top of my head. "Apply to the universities you want to, Sash. Plan the life you want. We'll make it work. I promise. Just don't run away without talking to me first."

I loved that answer, and as I clung to him, I acknowledged that I was falling in love with the man who muttered it. "Thank you."

The Preformal

A FEW WEEKS LATER, the preformal was upon us. Saint Christopher's boys and our school seniors came together to prepare for the formal. Some were working on the theme and decorations, and others the dancing. It wasn't so much dancing lessons as having one leading coordinated dance that most seniors participated in.

Despite my objections to being nannied, I'd meet the boys after school most afternoons and ride home together. Wednesday afternoon, Barden met me after swim practice to ride home. Then I sat at the dining room table, watching the teams do their training drills in the backyard while I studied.

There was no further fraternization between Barden and me during daylight hours, but whenever he looked at me, I felt his lips on me and couldn't help but heat up. But most weeknights now, he snuck into my bed and held me while I slept, and none of that was PG-rated.

"So, you're going with Barden?" Elisha asked with a cheeky grin. It was good to see her smiling again. I thought she'd lost the ability for a while after what happened to Sophie.

"Yep."

"Are you more than just formal partners?" She waggled her brow.

I'm sure the heat rushing to my cheeks was answer enough, but I nodded a little just the same. Elisha and her friends gave a little cheer, then gushed about my hot boyfriend before talking about their dates.

Resisting joining in, I just rolled my eyes. "Did you go dress shopping yet?"

"Are you kidding? I've had my dress for weeks," Elisha pulled out her phone and showed me a picture. "Pretty hot, huh?"

It definitely was a very sexy formal gown. There was no way I'd get away with wearing something so revealing while my mother was still alive. I wasn't not sure I'd want to.

Swiping to the left, Elisha showed me pictures from every angle. Across the room, my former best friends were laughing, and when I glanced over, Yasmine and Mia were looking at me. When they saw me looking, they started laughing again. Ignoring them, I turned my attention back to Elisha.

Swallowing, I forced a smile. "It's lovely and will really suit you."

"Show me your dress?" Elisha asked.

"I don't have one yet. Mum was meant to take me looking for one, but that never eventuated. At this rate, I'll just be stealing something from her closest." When Elisha winced at that idea, I shrugged. "She goes to many formal events with her firm, galas, and stuff. She has a whole room dedicated to designer dresses she's bought over the years."

Elisha's smile was warm. "I guess that's not so bad then."

When Mia and Yasmine started with the cackling again, I gestured over my shoulder. "I'm going to go use the bathroom."

Walking away, I bypassed the ladies' bathroom and slipped through a fire exit to get outside. Chocking it open with the piece of brick there, I sat down on the stair, hugged myself, and stared up at the night sky, taking steadying breaths.

The door behind me opened and a cold chill followed by liquid warmth raced down my spine. Squatting beside me, Barden waited until I turned my head to look at him.

"It's lonely, being different." How he knew what I was thinking, I didn't know, but he nailed it. Wetting his lips, Barden turned his eyes skyward. "Until you find your people, anyway."

My eyes grew itchy, and I had to take a breath to control them. "I don't understand why. When did it all change?"

"The execrable attack. Your friends hadn't seen you fight like that before. They didn't know you had those other powers, did they?"

When I chewed my cheek and shook my head, eyes glassy, as I considered my own family didn't know half of what I could do.

Barden looked my way again. "The Orey community has always been judgmental and suspicious. Plus, I think those girls are a little jealous."

"You know this from experience?"

Shaking his head, Barden smirked. "No. Those girls are never careful about who might be listening when talking. They only look out for Vestigials; they forget we might be listening too."

I considered how my brother used his different abilities in training. "The team did this to Savas?"

Dropping his gaze to the cement, Barden grunted. I worried he'd go back to not talking. It was amazing how much I longed to hear his soulful and deep voice.

Reaching out a hand, I wrapped it around his. "Did they do it to you?"

"I have always been an outsider to them. I will always be one, and I'm okay with that. I know who my people are. Your brother and father are the only ones who have readily accepted me on the team. Your mother is like all other Orey, but my longing for you makes it harder for her."

"Why didn't you speak to me like this before we got together?"

Tilting his head to meet my eyes, Barden moved closer, his lips pinching mine tenderly, then pulled back. "You didn't need me to." Rising up, Barden offered me his hand. "They are about to start dance choreography."

"Do you care?"

"Yes. I like to dance. I'm going to like it even more with you."

Loving that answer, I took his hand and dusted off my jeans. Stifling a yawn, I leaned into Barden. "I missed you last night." Barden had to work helping souls cross the boundary and got home late, so he didn't come over.

Kissing the top of my head, Barden squeezed my hand a little. "I missed you too."

Going back inside, Barden kicked the brick out and closed the door properly. Walking hand in hand, we emerged back into the function hall just as the choreographer called everyone into the center of the dance floor.

When we stopped amongst the gathered, Barden stepped partly behind me, using one arm wrapped around my waist to hug me in front of him. Eyes latched onto us as if we were under a spotlight, and then the whispers started. Even the Oreys threw us surprised looks.

When Raisa murmured something to Savas, he looked our way, then shrugged a shoulder in answer. My resentment towards my brother dropped a notch.

Nose in my hair, Barden put his lips right next to my ear. "Ignore them. They'll never understand our connection. They are not like us."

Frowning, I turned my head to see Barden's face, but his eyes were on the choreographer, who was starting to show us his vision. Facing forward, I wondered what he meant by that.

After three hours and the choreographer satisfied that we'd learned our parts, I grabbed my stuff and headed out to the car park and my bike. Savas was parked next to me, Barden on the other side. Nash, Vidal, and Athur were waiting there for us.

"We'll ride as a team, get the girls home safe," Savas decided.

"I'll head home," I answered.

"You'll ride with the rest of us," Savas lectured.

"Sav, I understand you want us all safe, but I'm beyond exhausted. I've been up early all week to run, competed at state championships all day yesterday, and we just did three hours of dancing. If I take the time to ride all over town, I will come off my bike on the canyon roads. I need to go home while I have the energy to do so."

I don't know if it was because I wasn't powering up for a fight or the giant bags I was lugging under my eyes, but Savas looked me over and grimaced. "Barden will ride with you. Talk to him if you feel your attention waning. Don't come off the bike and keep your tracking app live."

"I will. Thank you."

The others mounted up and rode out while I took some energizing breaths, then buckled my helmet into place. Activating the tracking app, I notified Dad, Mum, and Savas.

"You okay?" Barden asked, his voice coming through the helmet.

"Just tired." Ready to go, I started the engine on the bike. No noise, quiet as a mouse.

"Is my staying over disturbing your sleep?"

"I get less sleep, but I sleep better in your arms. It's the nights you're not there that I have nightmares."

"Am I the cause of the nightmares? Knowing I'm a Gelus?"

Turning to Barden as I backed my bike out of its park, I frowned. "Gelus?"

"The Corvus Gelus. That's our species. The soul transporters. We refer to ourselves as Gelus, but the Orey call us Crows."

Taking a moment, I nodded my head. "Sometimes it's the Execrable in their mutated forms chasing me, but mostly, it's Sophie and what happened to her." I saw and felt it all as if it's me, and then I saw her body on the shore again.

Holding a moment, I took a few deep breaths and turned my thoughts elsewhere. "Sorry, I'm too tired. I can't think about that now, or I'll definitely get distracted and come off."

"Can I help?"

"I have a physics exam tomorrow. Can you quiz me as we ride home? Savas told me you scored well in that class."

Smirking, Barden knocked down his visor. "Sure."

Riding out of the car park, Barden took the lead. The town was still fairly busy, with it being dinner time and late-night shopping. Avoiding the main roads, we stuck to the back roads to avoid most of the traffic and get to the canyon faster. As we turned onto the road out of town, an SUV that had been following further back for the last few blocks caught up and passed us.

"You okay?" Barden asked.

How he knew the car had spooked me, I didn't know, but it did. "Yeah, the car just gave me chills when it caught up to us. I don't know why."

"You don't normally ride after dark."

He had a point. As an Orey female, I avoided being out after dark if I could. The Execrable only came out at night.

Returning to the physics formulae Barden was throwing at me, I kept my mind busy but focused on the road.

Rounding the next corner, we came to the bridge that crossed the canyon and gave us access to the canyon road or took us to the next town and city beyond. Halfway across the bridge, I was blinded by headlights pointed straight at us, the SUV facing toward us as if it had skidded and spun. Hitting the brakes the same as Barden, I shielded my eyes from the sudden light.

Standing in front of the car on the bridge were six men. Moving forward towards us, the laughter of one of them sent chills through me.

"Execrable," Barden murmured in my helmet, neither of us taking our eyes off the approaching danger. "You can call lightning?"

"I generate it. How do you know that?"

Barden didn't answer. Kicking his bike stand down, he didn't turn off his bike. "Build it, then take the three on the right. Tell me when."

Staying on my bike, I built up my power, pulling electrical charges from the air around us, then my muscles and nerves. Then I tapped the motorcycle as well. As practiced as I was, it took as long as it did for Barden to dismount, remove his jacket and face our oncoming enemy.

"Ready," I whispered.

"Your time has come, Orey!" one of the Execrable called, getting closer. Opening his visor, Barden glared their way. The black channels in his irises grew more profound and broader. If they'd had any sense, they'd have run just with Barden giving them that look.

"I doubt that," Barden answered.

"Oh, yeah. Why's that?" They were near to us now.

Barden grinned. "Because we're not Orey. Now, Sash!" Throwing his hands into the air, bright sunlight filled the sky, making the Execrable scream.

Directing my arms to aim, lightning branched across the bridge to hit my three targets. The branches grew more vigorous, pulling more energy from the bike until the bodies of the Execrable burst into flames. By the time I dropped my arms, breathing heavily, Barden was near the other three fallen Execrable with a sword made of light in his hand. Three beheaded bodies disintegrating, the other three man-shaped ash shells.

A gunshot rang out behind us. A body wrapped around me, giant wings folded to shield us.

"Gelus!" someone spoke in awe behind us, then the sound of running feet.

Staring wide-eyed at Barden as he released me from his hold, I gaped when he crouched and leaped into the air, his enormous black feathered wings spread wide.

Barden shoot towards the Execrable who'd been hiding behind us. In one swing, he took the enemy's head with the sword of light, their body disintegrating as it fell to the road.

It was hard to breathe. My brain and body were beyond its limit.

"They weren't Orey," a man panicked, his footsteps sounding as he ran out of the bushes by the bridge and down the road towards town. "We attacked Gelus. They were two Gelus on bikes. Everyone's de–" His voice cut off as his head lifted into the air as an arc of light separated it from the body.

Struggling to breathe, my head was swimming in exhaustion. I pressed the button to shut off the engine. Throwing my leg over, I lowered my bike and myself to the ground.

Barden pulled his wings back in as if they'd never existed and pulled out his phone, his voice still coming through my helmet. "It's me. We were ambushed. Eight Execrable on the canyon bridge. We're safe now, but Sash overextended herself and is about to pass out. We need to clean the scene quickly before anyone happens upon us. I'll get Sash home and then come back for the clean-up."

My ears were buzzing, lights flashing behind my eyes. Feeling like I was suffocating, I quickly unbuckled my helmet and threw it off, then my eyelids closed, and I was done.

The Unfurling

SAVAS KNOCKED ON MY DOOR. He was dressed and ready for school. "You didn't run this morning?"

Still, in my pajamas and slouching against my bedhead, I returned to staring out the window. "No. I'm too tired. I drained my energy right down last night."

Lifting his brow, Savas dropped to the end of my bed. "I heard it was quite the light show." His eyes came to me. "How are you feeling?"

"Confused."

"About Barden?" Bending towards me when I kept staring out the window, Savas put his hand on my wrist; whether in comfort or to get my attention, I wasn't sure. "You are meant for him, Sash. These last few months have been the first time I've ever seen Barden smile. He couldn't wipe the grin off his face after he got busted with you. Not because he got busted, but because you finally agreed to be his."

Face filling with heat, I chewed my lip. "Barden said we're different. Not Orey?"

Grimacing, Savas looked at the garment bags hanging from my wardrobe door. "Formal dress?"

"And tonight's party dress."

"You finally got to go shopping with Mum." Savas smiled.

"Nope." Scowling, I avoided looking at the bags.

"No?"

"She just came in last night and hung them there, chirping about having gone and picked up my dresses after one of her work meetings."

Furrowing his forehead, Savas turned his eyes to me. "Wait, did she at least send you pictures or show you a catalog or something?"

Glancing at my brother, I met his eyes with a clear 'what do you think?'

His adam's apple bobbing, Savas eyed the garment bags. "What did she get you?"

"I don't know. I haven't bothered to look."

Getting up off the bed, Savas unzipped the first bag and looked inside. I caught a glimpse of pastel florals and lace frills. What was I, eight? Grimacing, Savas zipped it closed and did the same with the second bag. He didn't even get it open before he winced and zipped it back up. "Okay, let's go."

"Where?"

"Mum's wardrobe. There is no way you are wearing either of those dresses."

Smirking, I let Savas pull me down the hall to the other side of the house and sneak into my mother's wardrobe. She had an entire room dedicated to her designer formal and cocktail dresses she wore to fundraisers and firm events. Her casual and work clothes were in the wardrobe attached to their bedroom.

Savas searched one side of mum's wardrobe, and I half-heartedly searched the other.

"Oh, perfect!" Savas grinned, pulling a deep magenta velvet fall of fabric from the rail. "Barden will lose his shit when he sees you in this."

As he held up the formal gown for me to see, I resisted grinning at how perfect it was. Taking it from Savas, I admired it. The velvet was so soft and rich. "I don't even remember mum wearing this."

"Me neither. It's probably from when we were young or before we were born." Moving to my side of the wardrobe, Savas kept looking. Grabbing out a rich blue cocktail dress, he held it up, looked at me, considered the halter, shook his head, and put it back before pulling out a lilac ombre with a wide neckline. "Perfect."

Handing me the tea dress, Savas gestured we get out of here. "This one is more family-friendly for tonight, but still going to make Barden regret getting barred from going upstairs." The way he chuckled lightened my heart. I'd missed this side of my brother.

Back at the center of the house, Savas stopped by the stairs. "Now, hide the formal dress for now. I need to get to school. You rest up and recharge."

"Sav?" I waited until he turned to look at me. "Thanks."

Giving me a wink, Savas skipped down the stairs. In my room, I put both dresses away for later. Going back to bed, I put my music on and fell into a restless sleep of nightmares.

When I woke in the early afternoon, I wandered downstairs, still half asleep.

"Sash?" My dad called from his den. "What are you doing home?"

"Couldn't human today. Need food," I grunted as I kept the momentum to the kitchen.

Opening the fridge door, I stood staring at the contents blankly, my brain not processing the possibilities while my stomach growled loudly.

My dad's hands fell on my shoulders and directed me to the meal table, forcing me into a seat.

"I'll fix you something, Miss Zombie."

Setting my cheek on the table, I closed my eyes while Dad got out a pan. The next thing I knew, he rubbed my back and put a plate with an omelet beside my head.

"Eat up, Sash."

Forcing myself to sit up, I moaned appreciatively at the smell of food and started eating.

"Barden said you bottomed out last night, but I didn't expect it was this bad. I better call the school and tell them you are unwell. Didn't you have an exam today?"

"Crap!" I mourned.

"I'll call them." Getting up, dad made his way back to his den while I finished eating. When he returned, I drank the large glass of juice he had left me.

"All taken care of. You'll get a resit next week." Collecting my plate, he rinsed it and set it in the dishwasher.

"Thanks, Dad."

"Did you want to talk about last night?"

Thinking about it, there was one question burning my brain out.

"Why did Barden tell them I wasn't Orey?"

Wetting his lips, my father stepped forward and gripped the bench taking a deep breath.

"Okay. It's about time you heard this story. I never knew my father. He was a boy..." Dad frowned and shook his head, eyes darting to me. "A *man* who lived in the same town as my mother. He didn't go to school, but quite often, they encountered each other. At a party one night, they had sex. For a few months, they had an affair, but then it was time for my mother to go to university. He'd moved on by the time she realized she was pregnant and came home to tell him."

"With another Orey girl?"

"Towns. He'd left town after she left for university. She never saw him again. Because she was pregnant, none of the Orey men would have her, so my mother left me with her parents to be raised. At the same time, she finished her university studies, then applied for work in the city and moved away."

I frowned. I'd never heard of an Orey girl leaving her clan. Usually, families clustered together to raise their children. "Why would she leave?"

Adam's apple bobbing, Dad pulled his shirt over his head. Rolling his shoulders forward, huge mottled grey and white wings unfolded, black lines angling through the beautiful velvet-looking feathers. "Because of this."

My glass cluttered to the floor and smashed as I stood up and backed away, my brain not accepting what I saw. "You're a crow?"

"Strigidae," Dad corrected. "We are not the keepers of souls but the guardians of the border between the worlds. Your grandfather was Strigidae Gelus.

"My mother's clan, like many Orey, did not interact with the other inhabitants who crossed between worlds. When my wings unfurled for the first time, her clan made it clear I would never be accepted. Her parents encouraged her to give me up to my father or another, but give me up and find an Orey husband to make things right. My mother left that night. She moved here to the city and raised me as Orey."

"Does Mum know?"

Bowing his head, Dad nodded. "I was cruel and didn't show her until we were married, and you and your brother grew in her belly. She hated me. Could barely bear to be in the same house as me until you were born. She forgave me when I gave her two beautiful babies, but we didn't tell the others.

"None suspected until you and your brother started to really come into your powers. You, I could hide and protect, but your brother was exposed as soon as he started training with the team. They didn't shun us, but they endured us more than they accepted us. When the Assions moved here, it was the first time your brother and I met others like us."

Dad huffed under his breath. "Well, we thought that was the case." For some reason, it made my father smirk. My eyes focused on my father's wings.

"Savas has wings too."

Licking his lips, Dad met my eyes, sympathy swimming in his gaze. "Yes."

Betrayal burned down my throat. "How old was Savas when they unfurled?"

"Five."

My mouth fell open, and I stared at my father, sure he must be joking. My brother and I were inseparable until we turned sixteen, and he started hunting with the team. "He's hidden them from me all our lives?"

"We told him he had to, Sash. You didn't have them." Stepping forward, my father cupped my shoulders. "I'm sorry. But Savas was jealous of you. Your friends didn't turn on you because you weren't so obviously different."

Stepping back, I shook my head. "Just because it took longer doesn't mean I had it easier. Savas was my best friend, and he started pushing me away two years ago, and now I find out he's been lying to me all our lives. You all have been. Maybe had you told me, I could have been the one person Savas didn't feel isolated from, but I didn't understand why he changed because none of you told me."

Blinking twice, Dad stepped back and snapped his wings away. "You're not upset about the wings?"

Gritting my teeth, I was torn between crying and raging. "The girls knew. This is why they turned on me. Everyone knew but me."

"I'm sorry."

"That I don't have wings or because you kept me in the dark?"

"We weren't being malicious, Sash. Your mother thought that you had a better chance of fitting in with the other Orey kids without knowing you were different."

"Mother knows best," I scoffed. "I can't believe any of you. You demand honesty and obedience from me at all times but are content to lie and hide who I really am from me my entire life."

Dad didn't reply.

Shaking my head, I headed for the stairs.

"You used protection, didn't you?"

Turning around, I frowned at my father. "For what?"

Coming closer, Dad met my eyes. "You expect me to believe that you were alone with Barden for nearly two hours on your birthday and all you did was drink tea? You couldn't keep your clothes on for twenty minutes last week, so don't try to play me for some naive idiot, Sash."

"I have never treated anyone like an idiot. That's how you all treat me. Even asking me that question, you assume I would be too stupid to know better."

"Sash-"

"Forget it. Just do the usual and assume whatever. No one bothers to ask me; you just assume you know and tell me. Why stop now?" Storming towards the stairs, I ignored my mother coming through the mud room door.

"What happened?" she asked as I reached the stairs.

"Barden revealed she wasn't Orey."

"Did they...?"

"I don't know, Delila. Sasha's a mess emotionally, so I can't get a read on her for any one thing. She knows we lied to her about what she is, about Savas having wings. She's too angry and hurt for the usual indicators to be there."

Reaching the top of the steps, I headed to my bedroom and shut the door. Cursing not having a lock on my room, I dragged over the reading chair and propped it to block the door from opening quickly.

Once I was sure no one could just let themselves into my room, I went to my bed and started punching the shit out of my pillow, taking all my frustrations out. When I was exhausted again, I collapsed on my bed, hugged the pillow to my chest, and cried.

The Orey Gathering

A FEW HOURS LATER, I was showered, dressed, and standing out on my balcony, staring at the river waters, when there was a polite knock on my door. I'd moved the chair after my shower, so I didn't bother going to open it or even giving permission for them to enter. My family would just let themselves in any way.

"Sasha," Mum called from my balcony door. "Can we talk?" she came out beside me, eyes scanning the lilac dress. "That's not what I bought you for tonight."

"It's the dress Savas and I picked out." Standing straight, I turned to face my mother. "What did you want to talk about?"

Taking in how the dress flattered my bust and cinched around my waist, my mother pressed her lips into a severe line. "You went shopping with Savas?"

"Well, you couldn't make the time for me like you promised, and my friends have dumped me, so who else was I meant to go shopping with?"

Pursing her mouth, mum turned to look out over the river. "I'd like to talk to you about Barden and your relationship with him. It appears you're no longer creeped out by him."

"No, I'm not. After my friends turned on me for being different and

145

me having no idea why, Barden was the one who noticed and explained why. As of last week, we are boyfriend and girlfriend."

"I don't think that's a good idea."

"Why?"

Eyes bulging, my mother stepped forward. "He's a crow!" she whispered harshly.

"He's a Corvinus Gelus. Dad is a Gelus, Savas is, and so am I."

"You are more Orey. You don't even have wings."

"Neither does Calliope, and she is full-blooded Gelus."

Licking her lips, Mum shook her head. "You don't understand. If you marry Barden, the Orey community will never accept you. They only accept your father because of me and because he's a good warrior. You and Barden will be shunned."

Nodding, I met my mother's eyes. "I already am." Stepping past her, I went back into my room, grabbed my phone, and sent a text.

"What are you doing?"

"Telling Barden where to find me."

"What? Why?"

"Because I'm not attending your party. The Orey has already decided I'm not one of them; tonight is an Orey team's party. What's the point in pretending anymore?"

"You have this long."

Turning to face my mother, I shook my head. "No. You have. I never knew the truth to know better because you lied to me."

"Sasha, you can't just decide not to show up to this party."

Turning my back on my mother, I finished undressing, then pulled on a pair of jeans and a t-shirt. "Watch me." Picking up the dress, I put it back on its hanger.

"Hey." Savas leaned into my doorway. "Has the party been canceled? Vidal just messaged that you canceled it."

Huh. They were all linked to my calendar reminder of the party; when I canceled it for me, it must have sent them a notification.

Throwing her hands in the air, Mum stormed towards the door. "No. Sasha is just chucking a tantrum and refusing to go. I'm going to go talk to the caterers. You get your sister to see reason."

Picking up my phone when it buzzed, I read Mia's message.

. . .

MIA—> FRIENDS GROUP

Is the party canceled? Why? Vidal hasn't
heard anything about it being canceled?

Huffing, I went to the settings and removed myself from the group chat
and them from my calendar. They weren't my friends anymore; I had no
business in the group chat.

Getting a notification, Savas looked at his phone and frowned.

"What's going on?" Savas asked, assessing me.

"I'm sick of being lied to, and I'm not going to pretend everything is
alright for everyone at this party when it isn't." Grabbing my backpack, I
shoved a warm jacket, the book I was reading, and my headphones
inside. Sitting on the bed, I pulled on a pair of socks and then my Docs.

Raising an eyebrow, Savas crossed his arms. "What did Mum lie to
you about?"

"Not just Mum. You did too." Getting up, I pushed past Savas to get
out my door and headed down the hall while he was still frowning at
what I said.

"What is that supposed to mean?" he called after me.

"Ask Dad."

Skipping downstairs, I went into the garage and pulled out the
camping supplies box, grabbing a hammock and the fire pack. After
raiding the pantry for snacks and a big bottle of water, I went out
through the back door, none of the caterers paying me any attention as
they went about setting up for the party. As I hit the mountain trail, my
phone buzzed again.

RAISA

What's going on? Why did you leave the
group chat?

Turning off my notifications, I started hiking up the mountainside.
When I reached the plateau clearing where I'd run to last time, I

dropped my bag and looked around. The view over the canyon below and the mountain pass on the other side were fantastic.

A fire pit was already dug out in the ground, and the cleared area around it told me someone regularly came here to get away and chill out. Probably my dad and Savas. Connecting the hammock between two trees, I collected some fallen branches and twigs for kindling and set it all up in the fire pit. I didn't light it yet. I just wanted it ready in case it got cold before I went home.

Putting my headphones on, I climbed into the hammock and started reading my book. An hour later, the smell of the food from the party drifted up the mountain making my stomach growl. Closing my book, I swung my legs out to the side to sit up in the hammock. A light breeze blew through the canyon, making the air chilly.

Dropping to the ground, I grabbed the fire starter and got the fire pit going. I was just settling into the hammock with a pack of veggie chips when footsteps reached me from the path below. Swinging my legs over again, I sat up and waited to see who was an asshole enough not to get the hint that I wanted to be alone.

Carrying two plates covered in foil, Barden stalked into the clearing. Noting the fire, he came to the hammock and handed me a plate before retrieving some cutlery from his jeans pocket. Pressing my lips together, I admired how his body filled the dress shirt and dark blue denim.

Dropping a backpack I recognized as my brother's on the ground, Barden scooted up next to me on the hammock and took the foil off his plate. "You promised not to run away without talking to me."

"Technically, this is our land, so I'm still home." Taking the foil off the plate he'd handed me, I felt my heart skip a little that he'd known all my favorite foods. "I couldn't stay there and pretend nothing had changed."

"I get it."

We ate in silence, the sounds of the party below just background noise for the most part when the wind allowed it to reach us. Once we'd finished eating, Barden threw our empty plates on the fire, then grabbed a blanket out of Sav's backpack.

Getting back up on the hammock, Barden encouraged me to lie down with him, then spread the blanket over us. When I was snuggled against him, he grabbed my thigh and pulled it across his lap, pulling me as close to him as possible. "Better."

Smirking, I rubbed my hand across his pecs, then lifted my face to admire his face. "Did my dad say anything to you?"

"No."

"He asked me if we used protection. I deflected."

"Your mother is even more unhappy with me than usual."

"I told her we were dating. She warned me if I chose you instead of an Orey, I'd be shunned from the community."

Fingers tensing where he held me, Barden kissed my temple. "She's right. I'd like to think they aren't as narrow-minded as they used to be. Still, their acceptance of Gannix and Savas is circumstantial, and I am barely tolerated. Your mother fails to realize that I'm only here for you."

Frowning, I played with the button on Barden's shirt. "What do you mean?"

"I came here to find you. When I told your father you were mine, he told me he'd permit me in your life if I taught Savas and him about their Gelus side, and it would be expected that I help the Orey. Those were the terms. Even after we marry, I can't just up and abandon them. I was smart enough to set my terms as helping Gannix and not abandoning him to fight this fight alone. I would not tie my fate to the Orey witches. My duty is here for now. I will no longer be held here when your father abandons the witches."

Dropping my head, I had all the buttons of Barden's shirt open. "He won't do that."

"Gannix made his home among the Orey because they were all he knew. Now, he knows my family. He has a choice, Sash, just as Savas does."

"But you are different types of Gelus."

Moaning as I rubbed my hand over his bare flesh, Barden slipped his hand beneath my top and found my breast causing me to bite my lip. "We are different, but you are still the soul meant for me, Sash."

Finding Barden's belt, I tugged the buckle open. "I don't want to talk anymore," I murmured between kisses to his chest. "I want you inside me."

Fisting my hair, Barden tilted my head back and then pressed his mouth to mine. The heat rose quickly in my blood as we got rid of our clothing, then Barden shifted, settling on top of me and pressing inside me. Clinging to him, I gasped. A cock his size probably always required foreplay. The hammock probably didn't help.

"Hold on," Barden murmured, then adjusted us to be more on an angle in the hammock with my leg around his waist. Suddenly, it felt so much more intense. A noise in the forest above us made Barden tense and turn his eyes skyward.

"What is it?" I whispered. His body blocked my view of anything but him above me.

Shaking his head, Barden looked down at me. Caressing my cheek, he lowered his mouth and kissed me heatedly, then his hips matched the urgency of our mouths, and I'd never felt anything so good in my life. Moments later, I was panting Barden's name, and Barden had to smother my mouth with a hard kiss when I cried out as my body fell apart.

Grunting his own delicious agony, Barden stilled as tremors passed through his muscles, then he relaxed and dropped his head to my neck while we both tried to catch our breath.

"Are you okay?" Barden finally asked as he dropped pecks up and down my neck.

Smiling up at the dappled light coming through the trees as the hammock still swung from our exertions, I hmm'd a reply and nibbled his ear. "I want to do it again."

Chuckling, Barden shook his head. "I would happily appease you, but I only brought the one condom with me."

Caressing my face, Barden kissed me again. "Let's stay up here until the party is over. Then I want you to come home with me."

Staring into Barden's eyes, I found myself smiling at the mischief in them. "You're a little naughty, you know that?"

Chuckling, Barden pulled back, leaving me gasping anew as he withdrew. "Only for you, Sasha. Only for you."

The Confession

THE SUN WAS NEARLY SET as we emerged into the
backyard, hand in hand. Savas saw us first from where he sat around the
fire pit with the Orey our age. "Hey. How was the hike? Did you clear
your head? I see Barden found you." Getting up, Savas came our way
and met us by the swings, well out of earshot of the rest. "Are you
okay?"

Glaring at Savas, I went to step past him, but he got in my way.
"Okay, you're still pissed, but Grandma is inside, so maybe cover the love
bite on your neck before you go in. She doesn't know about you and
Barden, so you should go in alone."

Sweeping my hair to cover one side of my neck, Savas tucked it into
my jacket to make it look natural that it sat that way. Electricity sizzled
in the air around us. Closing my eyes, I took a breath to calm my
emotions.

Blowing out a breath, Savas stepped back. "She refused to leave until
she saw her granddaughter."

When my eyes flicked to the gathering around the fire pit, Savas
glanced over his shoulder and then back to me. "I'm hanging with my
team. Their sisters are hanging with them."

Handing my brother the hammock, I looked up to Barden. "I need to go pack my things. I'll bring my bike. I could use a race around the canyon roads tonight."

Eyes going to the roof of the house, Barden grunted. "Not too long." He didn't have to tell me he was worried about us getting ambushed again; I could feel it in the weight of his bearing.

"I'll do my best. It will all depend on Grandma."

"Pack your things for what?" Savas asked, grabbing my arm to stop me from walking away. When I glared at him and shrugged him off, Savas let me go, but he turned on Barden immediately. "Why is she packing her things?"

"Sasha is coming home with me."

"No," Savas growled. "Just no."

"It was Sasha's decision."

"You're taking advantage of her emotions and this situation."

"I'm taking what I came here for. I've waited patiently. I've abided by your father's rules-"

"Barely."

"It's not permanent. Not yet."

Looking over my shoulder at them as I moved out of earshot, I could feel Barden's eyes on me, but seeing the intent and focused look on his face got me instantly wet. Just the thought of sleeping in his bed tonight, or not sleeping, as the case may be.

Everyone watched me as I came near the fire pit, but that's all they did. Gritting my teeth, I ignored them and kept walking towards the house. In my peripheral vision, Raisa stood up, but Yasmine grabbed her hand and yanked her down. "Don't. She didn't even want us to come to the party."

"No, she canceled it in her diary. That's not the same."

"Who spends their Friday evening hiking instead of at a party?" Mia snarked.

"The girl who survived another Execrable attack last night and just needed space from it all," Savas answered as he and Barden joined the others. "What do you care anyway? You've made it clear you're not her friend anymore. Since you feel that strongly about our kind, I'm surprised you came tonight. Isn't it beneath you? Or were you hoping for another opportunity to bury my sister alive again?"

The fire crackled in the sudden silence.

"What's going on with you and Sasha?" Nash asked Barden.

"He's being the friend she needs," Savas answered harshly, but he threw a glare Barden's way just the same.

Stepping into the kitchen, I tried to control my emotions when I saw my mother sitting with my Grandmother at the meal table. My father's mother, not hers.

My mother's family stopped coming around when we were just kids. I thought it was because they didn't like traveling into the canyon. After all, Mum still took me to see them in the city. I suspect she only ever took me to see them because they rejected my father and brother when their secret came out.

"Sasha. You finally decided to show your face?" Mum rose from the table, trying to look composed but equally stern.

"I was hoping everyone would have left by now."

Pursing her lips, Mum indicated the other person in the room. "Your Grandma has been waiting hours to see you."

"Delila, enough," Grandma huffed. "The girl is so emotional she's charging the air, causing the hair to stand up on my arms, and you're going to be the reason lightning hits this house."

Standing up, Grandma headed further into the house. "Come now, sweet girl. Give your grandma five minutes of your time before I leave." Striding into the house, Grandma didn't look back. "Call my car, will you, Delila? I'll be ready to go by the time it gets here."

Ignoring my mother, I followed my grandmother. Striding into my father's den, she cleared her throat. On the lounge were my father and Barden's parents. "Gannix, I'd like to talk to my granddaughter in private, please."

"And you couldn't seconder any of the other many rooms in the house, Mother?" Dad asked, standing up, his eyes coming to me.

"This is the only one downstairs with a thick door to prevent overeager ears from prying," Grandma answered, then tilted her head towards the kitchen.

The Assions snickered as they got up to follow my dad. "Evening, Sasha," Nelly Assion greeted me, then hugged me. "Hmm, you smell like Barden. Guess it was a good party," she whispered before pulling back.

Giving me a wink, she chuckled and headed out, leaving me slightly panicked that my Grandma could smell the sex on me too.

My father took my hand and squeezed it once as he passed. "Thank you for coming home," he murmured as he stepped by me.

Eyes filling with tears, I took my hand back and stepped out of his reach. With a sigh, Dad stepped out into the hall.

Shutting the door, I dropped my backpack and went to sit opposite my grandma. "Sorry, I wasn't here, Grandma. I just needed to be by myself today."

"You needed to get away from your controlling mother and try and sort out how much of your life has been a lie," Grandma responded. She waved my reaction away when I stared at her with my mouth open. "Your father told me what happened this afternoon. The discovery you made as a result of the attack last. Your mother may try to keep everyone in the dark, but Gannix has always kept me informed. Especially with regards to my grandchildren."

"When you say he keeps you informed...?"

"About the Gelus, too, yes."

Hanging my head, I swallowed hard. "Oh."

"I've known about them since they turned up here, Sasha. Gannix told me the moment he met others like him. He's been looking for his father all his life." Her eyes became glassy and distant. "He's not the only one."

"You loved him. The Gelus that seduced you?"

Gifting me a tender smile, Grandma looked twenty years younger for a moment, and I almost saw myself another twenty years from now. "Yes. We loved each other."

When I frowned, Grandma licked her lips and took a deep breath. "I lied to my son, a little. I told him I went away to university, and when I discovered I was pregnant, I came home and found his father had left. I didn't tell Gannix that I told his father to go."

Surprised and confused, I frowned at her. "Why would you do that?"

Stiffening her back, Grandma met my eyes. "I loved him, but I knew if I married him, my family would cast me out, and he would never be accepted. So, I ended it and told him to leave and never come back.

Then I went away to university and hoped when I came home, I could move on with an Orey man."

"But then you found yourself pregnant."

"Yes, and Lorka had left by the time I got back to tell him. He'd mentioned he came from here. So, when I finished university and Gannix's wings unfurled, I came east looking for him. There are Gelus all around if you know what to look for. I tried asking them if they knew him and if they could get a message to him. Eventually, I got a response. I'd made my choice and chose the Orey. We were done."

As a tear slid free of my grandmother's eye, one slid free of mine. "He didn't want to know his son?"

Swallowing, her voice cracked. "I never told them." She sniffled, dabbing at her eyes and nose with her handkerchief. "If Lorka didn't want me back, I wasn't letting him take my son. Gannix was all I had left." Pressing her lips together, Grandma took a deep breath. "I tell you this in confidence, Sasha. Please, don't tell your father."

"Why?"

"Because I disagreed with them keeping that part of your heritage from you. When that Gelus showed up claiming you as his and your family kept it from you and forced him to keep his distance, I argued against it."

Leaning forward, Grandma reached out and brushed a tear from my cheek with her thumb, then she got up and took the seat beside me. Clasping my hand, Grandma looked me in the eye. "Gannix wanted you to know, but Delila was sure you were Orey and should be raised her way." Sighing, Grandma patted my hand as she shook her head.

"Those two fought badly in those early days after she discovered his truth. She hated him for a long time and kept threatening to leave him. Gannix told her if she did, he'd be taking Savas with him, and since it would be cruel to separate twins, she'd lose you too. That's the only reason she stayed, in the end. They moved here, hoping to be accepted despite what he was. Even amongst the other outcasts, it was hard for them."

"Other outcasts?"

Grandma raised a brow. "These are the borderlands, my dear. There are more Gelus here than in the other Orey areas. It's where the Orey who are shunned by their family tend to find themselves drawn to." Her eyes searched the windowless wall. "Anywhere there is a gate, there are always more otherworld or edge-walking creatures. Execrable, Gelus, Witches, and others you are too young to have to worry about yet.

"The Orey clans tend to keep back from the boundary to create a buffer zone, but the outcasts are drawn to the borderlands by nature. They form new clans, but the bonds between them are never as strong as they were in their old family clans. They exist together here more like soldiers in a war."

Grandma smiled gently and drew her thumb over my eyebrow, bringing her focus back to me. "I understand you are angry for what they kept from you. For letting you think you were Orey only to now experience the suspicion of the other families. You have every right to feel betrayed. That doesn't mean your family doesn't love you."

"Mum doesn't want me with Barden. She said if I marry him, I'll be shunned by all the Orey families. She believes my only chance of acceptance is to marry one of them, but I think she's wrong. My friends have been shutting me out since we got attacked a few months back. Once they saw my power, they knew I wasn't like them, but I didn't. I thought they just hadn't been trained to fight. Barden doesn't care. He's there for me. He makes me feel wanted, and he does it without judgment. He seems to understand what I'm thinking and feeling without me even having to tell him."

My Grandmother's brows rose. "Ah, so you are intimate with him." When my mouth fell open, Grandma held up her hand. "I'm not going to judge you, Sasha. I fell in love with Lorka before I was eighteen. From the moment you first kiss, first start to desire one of them, a connection forms. It has to be reciprocated for the bond to grow, but if it is, it only takes a kiss for the seed to be sewn. Everything after that just makes the bond stronger and harder to break."

"So, if we have sex...?"

Nodding her head sadly, Grandma patted my hand. "He will be your best friend, Sasha, and he will always know what you need. If you love that Gelus, you should never give him up. If you do, you'll spend the rest of your life searching the horizon for him."

Tears fell from my eyes. "Will Dad and Savas hate me if I marry Barden?"

"What?" Grandma laughed, shaking her head at me. "Oh, my sweet girl. Do you think Gannix would have let that Gelus into your life and have developed friendships with his clan if he objected to something forming between you? He merely put rules in place to make sure you were legal and ready for such a commitment before he allowed the boy to make his feelings for you known."

"Daddy is okay with this?"

"Of course! That poor boy has had to keep his feelings and hands to himself for over two years as part of their pact. I hear he used to stare at you all the time because he couldn't talk to you without wanting to tell you that you were his." Grandma laughed. "And it creeped you out and made you keep away from him. Oh, the poor boy. He must feel relieved that he can finally express his feelings for you."

She chucked my chin. "And you must be so confused. Your feelings were always there for him, too, you know. From the moment you met. It panicked your father how keen you were to have his attention. You used to always try to get him to talk to you and spend time with you. Even before you were interested in boys that way, you were immediately drawn to the Gelus. So, yes, your father knew what that boy claimed was true. You were meant for him. He just wanted you to be an adult before he seduced you away."

Kissing my cheek, Grandma stood up. "My car should be here. Don't fight your heart, Sasha. You are where you are meant to be. And don't worry about your mum. She can threaten all she wants. She will not shun you for falling in love with your own kind. Her family will, but they are not that great a loss."

"Does she still hate my dad for lying to her?"

Inhaling, Grandma shrugged a shoulder. "She forgave him long ago, and they fell in love all over again. Seeing her children struggle to exist as part of the Orey and watching them get hurt by their friends' rejections of them stings that old wound."

"Maybe we need to stop trying to be part of the Orey and just live alongside them like the Assions," I suggested.

Gifting me a smile beaming with pride, Grandma nodded. "It's worth a try. Good night, sweet girl."

"Grandma. Thank you for waiting for me. I needed this talk."

Giving me a wink, Grandma opened the door and stepped out. "Gannix," she called. A moment later, my father's shadow was outside the door. "I'm heading home. You have a brilliant and beautiful soul for a daughter. I expect she will want to start spending more time with her boyfriend. The bond has formed. Don't choke it, or she'll fight you, and you'll be the one to lose. She's more headstrong than I ever was, so she's not going to let you bully her out of following her heart. Walk me out. We need to discuss some other things."

I grabbed my bag and headed for the stairs as they walked away. Grandma knew what I was planning, and she'd just paved the way.

"Sasha, you look calmer." Nelly Assion came out of the kitchen to appraise me. She was always so lovely, such a warm personality, despite her eyes having that same serial killer chill as Barden's.

"Um, Barden offered for me to stay over a few nights. Are you okay with that?"

Smiling kindly, Nelly put her hand on my shoulder. "I expected that would come very quickly once you came of age. You will always be welcome, but I will insist you come home for the weekends. Barden has duties that keep him away from home just as often as ours do. So, as long as you understand that even some weeknights, Barden will have to ask you to come home, for now, I think it will be fine."

Swallowing, I kept my voice low. "What if I'm not welcome here after I stay there?"

Nelly frowned, then looked over my head. Turning, I saw my dad standing there. "You will always be welcome in my home. This is your home, too."

As the tears escaped, I hugged my dad tight, unable to say how relieved I was that he would allow this. "You only have a few months left of school. Don't let this arrangement affect your grades, okay? That would be the only way you could disappoint me by choosing this path."

Nodding my head, I hugged my dad tighter. He'd always been the voice of reason when Mum and I clashed. Now, I just had to hope he could talk Mum around.

The Wings

BLINKING my eyes open in the grey morning light, I waited for my eyes to focus. Looking at the clock, I yawned and turned my head to the gorgeous man lying next to me. Barden still slept, lying on his stomach with one of his arms draped across my middle. This had been my morning wake-up for the last three weeks, except for the nights I stayed home so Barden could work.

Rolling towards Barden, I caressed his face, admiring how handsome he was. The arm across me tensed and dragged me across the bed until I was underneath Barden. As he settled between my legs, his lazy smile and glassy eyes filled my heart completely.

"Morning," I murmured, leaning up to brush his lips with the barest kiss. "Sleep well?"

Grunting an affirmative, Barden slid the hard head of his cock through my slit and niched it at my entrance. As he leaned forward to kiss me, he pushed inside me. Gasping at the delicious sensation of him stretching me open, I bowed back and dragged my fingers down his spine, forcing the covers to pool above his ass.

Wrapping my legs around him, I ravaged Barden's mouth with my hunger, moaning my need for him in words and sounds as he plundered my depths.

The first week staying with Barden cured me of the blushing innocence. The following weeks introduced me to many other ways he could pleasure me. Foreplay, different positions, and making it last longer to reach an even more mind-blowing climax had all been experienced in excess. But the mornings were my favorite.

Nothing beat being freshly woken, with him hard as hell and both of us so hungry for each other that we screwed each other brainless. Some mornings were a little more hurried because of school, but on others, we woke early and could lie in each other's arms for a bit afterward before starting our day.

Growling with his need, Barden picked up speed. It felt so good, like the world disappeared and just became our two bodies merging. Even when I'd masturbated, I had never imagined sex ever feeling like this. It was so much more than I'd counted on.

"Barden," I panted, my eyes wide as I realized we weren't using protection. Typically he wrapped up before starting, so I'd forgotten about it until this moment.

Eyes glancing to the bedside table, Barden snarled and pumped his hips harder and faster. His face scrunching like he was in pain. "Sasha, it feels too good."

He was right. It felt even better than it had before now. I imagined this is what being high on drugs felt like. An out-of-body experience where sensation is everything. Smashing his mouth to mine, Barden kissed me hard, shoved hard twice more, and then rolled us to put me on top.

Breathless, I stared down at him, both of us lying there panting. "Marry me," Barden panted.

"What?"

He stopped me from pulling away, hugging me tight to him. "Not the ceremony thing. For Gelus, when you both love each other and then you have sex, that is marriage. We mate for life. We haven't mated yet because we use condoms, so it's prevented the bond from cementing. I've been playing it safe with you until you can comprehend the commitment we would be making, but Sasha, I need to mate with you. It's an urge deep in my soul to make you mine and never let you go."

"I'm not ready."

Barden's arms loosened, and I drew my legs up and sat straddling him, which did nothing to deter my body's neediness when his cock pressed deep inside me and made my eyes roll back a little.

"Don't think it's the commitment; it's not. I have never wanted anyone else, Barden, and I know it's not through lack of exposure. I've been around all the other Orey guys, around the Vestigials, and I've never been attracted to them. It was you I fantasized about when I started to become interested. It's why it annoyed me so much that you wouldn't even talk to me."

Frowning, Barden propped himself up on his elbows. I gasped as the angle change pressed that already overly sensitive trigger. "Then why?"

Licking my lips, I pressed a hand to his chest and wiggled my hips, biting my lip a little and whimpering. "I'm scared of getting pregnant."

Face softening, Barden reached out to caress my face as he sat up and pulled me close. "Sasha, I'm bare inside of you right now, and I've already nearly come twice. You must have felt the weave of our souls start to knit already?"

When I chewed my lip and nodded, Barden brushed his lips across my mouth. "You've done sex ed, Sasha. You know it might already be too late."

Closing my eyes, I dropped my head. "I didn't realize. I was so hungry for you that by the time I thought about the condom, you were already twitching inside of me."

"I know. It was the same for me too, and then I just couldn't stop." Caressing my face, Barden urged me to look at him. "Marry me. We can use protection every time after until you are ready but mate with me now. If a child comes from this, we will be blessed, and if not, we can be more cautious going forward. Please, Sasha. We need to finish the weave."

Staring into Barden's eyes, I knew he was right. It had already started, and it wasn't going to get pulled undone by us adding protection now. Plus, I knew in my heart he would be the only one for me. Grandma had never loved another, and if my suspicions were correct, I doubt Lorka ever moved on, either. I'd prefer to find myself pregnant next week than think of ever living without Barden.

Kissing Barden's lips hesitantly, I rocked my hips. Gods! This position kept him so deep, his cock flicking back and forth against my cervix, building that amazing orgasm from deep within my core and leaving me paralyzed for moments afterward. A new experience that Barden introduced me to only last week.

Assisting my hips, Barden kissed all around my neck, his hands tugging me harder against him, building that euphoria faster. Closing my eyes, I lifted my face to the ceiling and let go of my fears, of everything other than being here with Barden.

As soon as I did, my body opened to him, and my entire being exploded in sensation. Crying out my name, Barden thrust hard. The jerk of his cock inside me opened my eyes wide, my head hung back, and I lost control.

My soul yanked forward, Barden pulling me tight in his arms as we weaved around each other until there was no delineation in the fabric of our being. Closing my eyes, my blood rushed through my body, tingles raced up my spine, and then burst from my back in a wet slap.

When I opened my eyes, Barden stared up at me in awe. Staring at him wide-eyed, I hesitantly peeked over my shoulder and swallowed hard.

"It's okay," he urged.

"I know, I just... It's kind of got pins and needles."

Nodding his head, Barden slid his hands up the sides of my back to reach where the wing bones were still folded on themselves. Slowly, he helped them unfurl by rolling them out between his thumb and index finger until they were stretched out behind me.

Gently easing one forward, Barden caressed my underwing, and I got the first good look at them. Still dripping blood, the white velvet feathers were decorated with black slashes just like my father's. Still, as I shook their birthing blood off, and the morning light shined through the window, a forest green tinge shone over them just like Barden's. "Green?"

Smirking, Barden cupped my face in his hands. "Your mother's bloodline is not as pedigree as they like to think. There is Corvus on that side."

"How do you know it's my mother's?"

Smirking, Barden kissed me heatedly. He was right; it didn't matter how he knew; he did. What was more exciting for him right now was that he was going to get to teach me to fly. I could feel it like the marrow in my bones. Pulling back, I stared down at Barden. "Maybe Calliope does have wings, and she just needs to find her mate."

"Ah, yeah. Let's not tell Calliope, or she will rape your brother to get her wings."

I'm sure my eyes were wide as saucers. "They're mates?"

"I did tell you we mate for life, and I remember you finding out some months ago they have been banging since your brother was sixteen. You didn't put it together?" The smirk on Barden's face was full of teasing.

"Come on. You've had your dick in me since telling me about the mating-for-life thing. I have not been thinking about my brother or your sister in any way, shape, or form."

"Good point." Lifting me up, Barden put me on my back beneath him, his cock already hard again inside me. "And today is the first day you are here where we don't have to rush to school."

School finished up for spring break yesterday. Our formal was in three weeks, and our exams started a week later. "True."

Barden's wings unfurled over us, then stretched out to the side and swept forward to touch the tips of his to mine. His wings were much more enormous than mine, but he was also a head taller than me and much bulkier. As Barden's feathered fingers caressed my wings, a shiver passed through my body, funneled down to my core, and coiled tight like a cobra ready to strike. "Fuck!" I moaned loudly. "That's amazing."

Chuckling, Barden pumped his hips forward. "You're amazing."

As the pleasure built, I clung to Barden, my legs still wrapped around him as he drove me to that higher state. As I reached the precipice, I threw back my head, caught the flash of large wings flapping in my peripheral, and turned my head to look out the window. Then the orgasm picked me up and threw me off the edge of the cliff of ecstasy, and my mind shattered into blissed-out nothingness.

In the afternoon, Barden needed to sleep before his night patrol, so I packed my study papers and readied to head home. "You could sleep with me," Barden whined as he walked me out to my bike.

"I need to do more studying, and you know we won't get any sleep if I come to bed with you," I excused with a smile as I threw my leg over my bike. I grabbed Barden's shirt and pulled him down for a long, teasing kiss. "I'll miss you tonight."

"I could be there when you wake up?"

Barden's mischievous smile always made me want him. "Can you?"

With one more deep, toe-curling kiss, Barden winked and stepped back. "I love you."

Biting my lip, I met his sparkling homicidal eyes and felt those words resonate in my core. "I love you too." Putting my helmet on, I pressed start on my bike and headed home. As soon as I was inside, I messaged Barden that I was home safe and headed up to my room to return to my studies.

When it was dinner time, my dad called me down. He slept most of the morning to do the parent thing of an afternoon before he worked. It worked better since Mum was always in the city and was often home late.

"Hey, Sash, how has your week been?" Dad asked as I came into the kitchen and started helping serve up.

"Pretty good."

"What did you get up to today?"

"Studied mostly. I was going crosseyed when you called me down, actually," I chuckled.

"Good answer," Dad smirked.

"I also unfurled my wings this morning."

A loud smash sounded as Dad dropped the plate on which he'd been about to serve my dinner. "You what?"

Biting my lip, I checked to ensure we were still alone and turned to face him as I took a deep breath. "Barden and I, ah... you know, mated for the first time this morning." I couldn't say unprotected sex to my dad. No way.

His mouth fell open, and he stared at me. "Only this morning?"

"And when we did, they just burst out of my back." I started cleaning up the smashed plate on the floor. "Barden wants me to keep it quiet until I learn to use them so Calliope doesn't rush to mate with Savas."

Dad just blinked at me with his mouth still hanging open. Letting him take it in, I grabbed another plate and started serving up.

"Okay." Dad finally recovered, his eyebrows lifting. "Can I see them?"

"Um, it took me the better part of an hour to furl them this morning. Barden had to help as I really have no control over them."

"They probably have atrophied after not being used all these years. But I checked your spine when you were five. You didn't have the ridges."

"I'm pretty sure they only developed today," I replied as I cleaned up.

Blinking some more, Dad looked around. "Um, are they white like mine?"

"Pretty much exactly the same, the markings are a little different, and mine have a dark green shine in the sunlight."

Dad's brow furrowed. "Like the crows?"

Leaning forward, I smiled at my dad. "Barden said it's from mum's bloodline, that they are not as pure Orey as they'd have you believe. I reckon she knows that too. That's why she's been so dead set against me being with Barden and why she was so angry when you revealed you were Gelus to her."

When Dad's eyebrows jumped into his hairline, I set his plate in front of him. "Barden's going to come home from hunting with you in the morning."

"What?" That snapped his attention back from wherever it had gone.

"Well, he's my mate. I want to wake up with him beside me. It feels right having him there. Plus, it means I see he's okay and not hurt after encountering an Execrable."

Huffing, my dad stabbed a piece of meat. "Barden has never been hurt yet. With all of his centuries of experience, that's not surprising. The crows can be vicious fighters."

My butt dropped in my chair, my eyes staring at my plate. "Centuries?"

Dad's face fell. "Crap. He hasn't told you yet?" When I just stared at the plate, Dad dropped his fork and took my hand. "Sash, most of the Gelus out there have been around for a long time. Your brother and I are some of the youngest born by centuries. I guess it makes you the youngest now. They rarely breed."

"So, you'll live a long time?"

Tipping his head, Dad lifted a shoulder. "Barden says as long as I avoid any fatal wounds, I'll have as much a chance at eternity as him and his clan. He was worried about you. Calliope is a full-blooded Gelus; that's the only reason she's lived a long life. Barden worried you would live an Orey's lifespan. With the development of your wings, he will be celebrating, knowing he will have eternity with you."

"Wings?" Savas asked from the doorway. "Sash, you've got wings?"

Still shell-shocked about my husband's age, I stood up. "You know, I didn't get my run in this morning. I've still got an hour until sundown. I think I'll do a quick run now."

Getting up, I grabbed my sneakers and headed out. I needed the cool air of the coming spring night to unravel my brain. Taking deep breaths as I ran the river, I breathed in the scents of the canyon. The crystal clear running waters, the wild thyme that grew along the rocky edge, the night blooming jasmine that was up above along the road edge. I cleared out my mind and ran, and breathed.

Centuries.

Shaking my head, I ran harder and then harder again.

Centuries.

Rarely breed.

Centuries.

The trail was growing cold, the sun no longer in the canyon, hidden by the mountains on either side. The squee of a falcon, the scream of a girl, the traffic on the bridge. Wait!

Stopping, I looked up and locked on the shadow plummeting to earth from beneath the canyon bridge over three hundred meters overhead. My eyes widened as the body descended to earth, a flash of a shadowed wing from beneath the overpass, and then the scream stopped short as the girl hit the rocky shore of the river.

"Oh, God, not again." Jumping the railing, I sprinted across the rocky shore to where the girl lay prone with her limbs at weird angles.

My phone started ringing; pulling it out, I panted, "Barden."

"Sash, why are you freaking out. I can feel your fear."

"A girl just fell from the overpass. I saw a wing." I yelled as I reached the girl. My eyes widened, my knees crumpled, and I didn't even wince as the rocks stabbed into my knees.

"A wing?"

"Gray." A sob escaped. "It's Yasmine. Oh, God, Barden. The girl who fell was Yasmine."

"Fuck! Sasha, run. Run now!"

Staring down at my friend, I stared into her eyes, which stared off into nowhere.

"Yasmine," I reached out to touch her and closed her eyes. Flashes of images paralyzed me as I lived her last moments.

"Sasha, run, get out of there!" Barden sounded far away, the air coming through the receiver.

There was a swoosh of air, I turned, and a gray wing clobbered me. My entire body swung around, and my head hit the rocks. Everything went black. Another gust of air and the sound of two bodies colliding.

"She is Gelus!" A voice I'd never heard before called as it stood over me. "She is my blood and not part of this war!"

A falcon squawked, and wings flapped into the air away from me. Tears poured forth, my vision watery as I forced my eyes open. My field of vision was filled with snow-white wings. "Dad?"

Kneeling over me, he checked my head, then picked me up in his arms. "Shh, you're safe."

My vision cleared enough to see that the Gelus holding me was not my dad, but they looked alike. "Lorka?"

My mind tumbled, my head pulling to the left, Yasmine's body bleeding into the ground and burning into my retinas as the sun went down. Another cry filled the night.

"No!" my favorite soulful deep voice roared.

"Barden," I whispered, and then darkness filled my world.

PART TWO

Edge Gelus

The Bruise

"DID YOU DO IT, *or were you just running your mouth?"*

"What?" Squinting into the darkness, I tried to make out the face hovering before me, but everything was blurry. I stumbled again, catching myself on the metal brace under the bridge. My heart raced in my chest as the wind buffeted against me. That was a long way down.

"Sophie? Did you do it?" the hollow voice asked again. My hearing was as distorted as the rest of me, and I couldn't even tell if they were male or female. I stumbled, trying to get to the wall and away from the edge, but I tripped.

"Did you do it?" they snapped, getting in my face, pain ripping at the back of my head where they grabbed my hair.

"No. Of course not," I cried. "All I know is the stupid slut got what she deserved."

They let me go. Climbing to my feet, I tried to dust off my knees. The world spun, and I stumbled towards the edge, grabbing the rail as the ravine below swirled in my vision.

Two hands latched onto my shoulders, yanking me back, making me lose my grip, and then hurled me sideways. "I guess that makes two of you."

The realization hit me that I was falling. I screamed and scrambled for anything to catch me, but there was nothing. No one. Just the wind deafening me, and then...

"Sasha."

Opening my eyes, I stared into dark grey-blue eyes. Blinking, Barden's face became focused, and I remembered who and where I was. Licking my lip, I released my white-knuckle grip on the blankets beside my hips.

"Hey," I cleared my throat and relaxed. "I thought Dad was picking me up?"

Sliding off the hospital bed, I went to grab my bag, but Barden snatched it out of my reach before I could. "Your mother insisted you wait for her to finish work, and she'd pick you up on the way home, so Gannix called me and suggested I bring you home instead. That way, you're not left waiting here all day."

"I prefer this anyway," I murmured, cuddling into his side as we left my hospital room. Passing the nurses' desk, I waved and said thank you for taking care of me the last four days, and then we pushed through the doors of the Head and Brain Injury ward.

A grey wing came out of nowhere, and I spun as I fell, and then my head cracked against the rocks.

I jolted.

"Sash?" Barden stopped and assessed me.

"Just a flashback. The doctor said it's normal," I assured him. When Barden didn't look convinced, I combed his messy dark brown hair out of his face, loving the feel of silk between my fingers. "I'm fine. They wouldn't let me come home if I wasn't."

Grunting as if that was doubtful, Barden wrapped a protective arm around my shoulders and led me outside to where his mother's car was parked. "What happened to the bike?" I asked.

"Not today."

Accepting that answer, I dropped into the car and waited for Barden to get in and start the engine. "Please tell me you're taking me to your place? I don't want to deal with my mum right now."

"Your place. We need to talk first."

Frowning, I eased away as Barden started heading from the city where I'd been flown in the medivac–I'd been unconscious and missed the whole ordeal–back to our small town and the canyon we called home. "Okay, what's going on?"

"Yasmine's family wants to ask you questions. They're coming over this afternoon to 'see how you are', but really, they want to interrogate you about what you saw. It's why your mum wanted to pick you up, so she could prep you for their questioning," Barden explained. His hands clenched on the wheels. "I hate to ask this of you, but I need you to lie."

Double blinking at the request, I studied Barden's face. He was stressed. "What am I lying about?"

"You said on the call to me you saw a wing. I didn't tell anyone. I need you to leave that out of your story, just like you did for the police. In fact, we need you to stick to the same story you told the police."

I considered the request and drew away from Barden a little. "Is there something I should know?"

Rubbing his lips together, Barden kept his eyes straight ahead. "A lot of Gelus live around the gorge. People you know and never realized are Gelus. Sophie Thinehart was one of them."

My throat closed at the mention of Sophie's name, but then the last moments of her life flashed behind my eyes, and it somehow made sense.

Barden stayed quiet while I processed that bomb. "The Gelus suspected one of the Orey killed Sophie," he added softly.

My mouth opened and closed, and that voice that was familiar and yet undefinable for me whispered in my ear just as it did Sophie's, *"Stupid wingless bitch,"* right before they snapped her neck.

Flinching, I massaged my neck to make the feeling go away. It wasn't the neck-breaking, but the tingle against my skin, almost as if the murderer had something in his hands or was channeling magic when they did it.

"Why do they think that?" I asked, instead of admitting they might be right.

"The way she was killed. No human has the strength to harm a Gelus like that. So, her killer had to be another edge walker."

Edge walkers resided between the living and the land of the dead or Underworld. I'd grown up believing I was an Orey Witch, one type of edge walker, only to find out I was another type entirely. Talk about having an identity crisis. I wasn't sure what I was anymore.

"But why Orey? They only kill Execrable," I challenged. My bruised temple pulsed with pain, and I winced, closing my eyes and hovering my hand over the pain. It was still too sore to touch.

When I opened my eyes, Barden was watching me. Slowly, he turned his focus back to the road. His concern I was coming home too soon was a caress down my spine. Our mating made it easy for us to sense each other's emotions now, but it was still a weird sensation for me.

When Barden didn't answer my concern, I frowned. "There's a war, isn't there? Between the Gelus and Orey?"

Barden side-eyed me, his emotions a shiver across my shoulders. "What makes you think that?"

"When the Gelus knocked me down, Lorka told them I was Gelus and that I wasn't part of this war."

Inhaling, Barden rolled his shoulders back. "I didn't know you knew Lorka."

"I don't. My grandmother told me about him. When I saw him, I thought it was my dad, but then my vision cleared for a moment, and I realized they were very similar but not the same. It was a guess that the Gelus who saved me was my grandfather." I watched Barden for another moment. "Is there a war between the Gelus and Orey?"

Blowing out a breath, Barden's resignation stirred my stomach. "There is now."

"How is this going to affect us?" I asked, realizing that Barden was clearly on the Gelus side of things, but my family straddled the two.

Taking my hand, Barden squeezed it. "It won't. Your family and mine, we're not involved. That's why I need you not to tell anyone about the Gelus who knocked you down, or what you heard Lorka say. No one knows Lorka got to you first. Stick to what you told the police. You need to stay impartial here. Grieve your friend, but don't take sides."

"She wasn't my friend. Not in the end."

Squeezing my hand, Barden returned to his quiet as we exited the freeway and swung around onto the road to town. Before the bridge across the canyon, we turned onto the gorge road and descended down the winding road to the river and the small village here.

Ten minutes later, we were climbing the driveway to my family home. When we hit the flat of the front yard, Barden pulled to the side and parked in front of the front door instead of in front of the garage like usual.

"You're not staying?" I asked as the front door opened, and my dad came out.

A negative grunt was my answer, and Barden got out and handed my dad my bag. "I'm staying over tonight," Barden told Gannix. "I know your rules, but you know it's too late. She's my mate. So I either sleep in her bed or take her home, and she sleeps in mine."

My dad's eyes came to me. It's not like my family hadn't been to see me every day at the hospital, but Dad always looked sad when he saw the bruising on my temple. "I expected as much. Should I make dinner for you?"

"No. I shouldn't be here while your visitors are. They have never really liked me, and my being here might be seen as interfering," Barden explained. "Call me when they are gone, and I'll come over when I've finished work for the day."

He meant soul transporting. That was Barden's real job. He moved here and enrolled as a high school student to be in my life. I still hadn't worked up the guts to ask how old he really was yet.

When dad agreed, Barden hugged me and gently kissed the top of my head. "I'll be back tonight. Rest up. If having visitors gets too much, excuse yourself and go rest. Don't strain yourself to be polite. Your health is more important."

Releasing me, Barden basically placed me in my father's arms. "Don't let them twist her words, Gannix."

"I won't," he assured Barden as he put an arm around me. "Come on. Let's go inside."

Instead of going to my room, Dad led me to his study and sat me on the sofa. "I want you to stay near me for now. You rest. I'll get you some water and food, then you can curl up and sleep if needed."

"Dad?" I waited until I had his full attention. "How bad is it?"

Sighing, he dropped into the seat beside me. "Right now, none of the families have an issue with us. We hope it will stay that way, but your mother is the only person they consider Orey in this house now. If things get worse, being on the team may not be enough to convince them where our loyalty lies."

"Would the Gelus consider us traitors for still working with the Orey?"

Shaking his head, my dad clenched his hands together. "Barden assures me they don't. That they now know about you being Gelus as well improves their perception of us."

"Why?"

"Because you're nice to everyone, Sash. You've never hated or liked anyone because they were or weren't Orey, even when you thought you were," Dad explained.

"It's not like I knew they were anything other than Vestigial. I always thought Sophie was." My mind drifted to her last moments again.

Wrapping his arm around me, Dad hugged me tight and kissed the temple that wasn't black and shiny. "It doesn't matter. They consider you and this family neutral. Let's keep it that way."

As he got up to leave, I wet my lips. "I met Granddad."

Freezing, my dad turned wide eyes my way. "What? When?"

Barden hadn't told him. "When I found Yasmine's body, a Gelus who looks a lot like you came and fought off whoever attacked me. He told them I was Gelus, his blood, and not part of this war. I'm pretty sure it was Lorka."

Blinking at me, Dad ruffled his hair. "That doesn't make sense. For him to say you're his blood means he knows I'm his son. Why wouldn't he approach Savas or me? Why did he come to you?"

That's why Barden hadn't told him. He didn't want to hurt him. "Honestly, I think he's been watching us for a while. Maybe he only showed himself because I was in danger."

Grinding his teeth, Dad nodded. "Let's not tell anyone. Especially not your grandmother. Not yet, anyway." He waited until I nodded agreement, then headed for the door. "I'll get you something to eat, then you should rest."

The Interrogation

"THE REIDS ARE HERE," my mother called as she walked to the front door. She was pissed that Barden picked me up instead of waiting for her. But when she came in and found me curled up on Dad's sofa with tears in my eyes, she'd kept her annoyance to herself.

Instead, she'd got my painkillers and left me to rest. Frankly, I would have welcomed the lecture. It could have kept my mind from the vision of Yasmine and Sophie's last moments replaying in my head.

"The Gelus suspected one of the Orey killed Sophie."

That couldn't be true. Could it?

Sitting up, I groaned with the effort moving took. My head smashing into a rock might have nearly killed me, but the clobbering I took from that wing had also left me sore. Thankfully, not as severely bruised.

As I got to my feet, the earth tilted a little, and my dad caught and steadied me. "I've got you," he assured me, then helped me to the formal lounge where Mum had set up for our guests. The Reids came through the door as we exited Dad's study, so they saw me needing his support.

"Sasha, you look very pale. Should you be out of the hospital yet?" Helena Reid, Yasmine's mother, asked with concern.

"The doctors said that Sasha just needed to rest and heal," Mum

183

told Helena. "The fracture to her skull was one thing, but the concussion and how long she was unconscious really worried them. We've got a few key things we need to keep our eye on, but the prescription is rest."

We made it to the lounge, and Dad sat me down beside him while Mum fussed with offering drinks and finger food. Tired, I rested my head on my dad's shoulder. "I'm very sorry for your loss," I murmured, tears filling my eyes as I saw Yasmine's body falling before me again. Her scream pierced my head.

"Thank you," Helena choked out, her eyes also growing wet.

"Hey, you're home." Savas came in, followed by Vidal. He came over and kissed my head before taking the sofa on my other side. Mum took the single-seater at the end of the coffee table, and the Reids took the other three-seater.

"Have you heard anything from the police?" my mum asked.

Sipping on his whiskey, Jebidiah grunted. "They've got nothing. They keep asking about her mental health. Was she depressed? Was she on drugs? It's not half obvious that they just want to write it off as a suicide."

"Are you sure it wasn't?" my mother asked with a sympathetic tone.

Jebidiah snapped his eyes her way. "Yasmine was happy. She left no note, nothing to suggest it was self-inflicted. Ask your daughter. She was there. Did it look like suicide to you, Sasha?"

Lifting my head off my dad's shoulder, I blinked at Yasmine's parents. "I... I don't know."

"Please, Sasha. You were her friend for a long time," Helena appealed. Interesting that she knew to use the past tense. "What happened that day? What did you see?"

Staring into Helena's eyes, my own filled with tears again. "I heard a scream. I looked up, and a girl was falling from under the bridge. I saw her..." Closing my eyes, the tears ran free.

"It's okay, Sasha. What happened next?" Helena pursued.

"I jumped the rail and ran across the rocks. When I got there, I saw it was Yasmine. God, she looked so..." Dead. Her eyes stared at nothing, and her limbs weren't sitting how they were designed. A sob racked my chest. "I turned to get help and must have slipped on the wet rocks, because I fell and hit my head. I woke up a day later in the hospital and prayed it had all been a bad dream."

"Are you sure you slipped?" Vidal asked. "You weren't pushed?"

Frowning at the college-aged boy, I wondered if he'd been there. If he saw it too. "What could have pushed me? It was just me and Yasmine out there."

"You didn't see or hear anything?" Jebidiah pressed, bringing my attention to him. "Anyone yelling? Sounds of a struggle? Anything that doesn't fit?"

Shaking my head, I closed my eyes. Liquid splashed on my face. "Wake up!" Jebidiah yelled. "I asked you a question!" He stood over me, breathing heavily, his now empty glass in his hand.

My brother and dad were shoving him away while Vidal tried to back him up. "Dad, what the hell? She's got a concussion and can barely sit upright," Vidal scolded.

"Sasha, I'm so sorry," Helena was crying. "We should go. I'm so sorry. We should go."

Mum handed me a napkin, and Savas sat next to me, helping wipe my face.

"Alcohol," I muttered as the Reids ushered their angry patriarch out of the room. Everyone froze.

"What was that?" Vidal asked.

Blinking, I lifted the napkin to my nose and inhaled, scrunched my nose, and then stared at the napkin. "Yasmine smelled like this when I got to her."

The Reids were suddenly very quiet, looking between each other and refusing to meet our eyes. Blowing out a breath, I relaxed back in the seat. "Raisa, Mia, and Yasmine go to parties all the time. They drink, and" – my eyes flicked to her parents, then to Vidal – "was there a party under the bridge that night?"

Vidal licked his lips and shook his head. "No, but not far from the bridge." Vidal stepped closer, studying me. "Mia and Raisa both said they didn't see her all day. They were meant to meet at the Milkbar for dinner, and Yasmine never showed."

Leaning my head on Savas' shoulder, I sighed. "Honestly, I wouldn't know. The girls haven't spoken to me since the Execrable attack. Could it be connected to Sophie's murder?" I propped my head up and assessed the Reids. "Could the same guy have killed them both?"

Everyone was quiet momentarily, then Vidal asked, "What makes you sure it's a guy?"

"Stupid wingless bitch."

Scratching at my head as my brain tried to identify that voice, I hissed and winced as my wound throbbed. Pain spiked through the front of my brain from that minor touch. Cringing into a ball, I sobbed and held my head without touching the left side.

"Sasha." My dad and brother were there with arms around me. "I think that's enough for tonight. I know you are hurting at the loss of your child, but Sasha nearly died out there, too," Dad scolded them while comforting me.

Rising from her seat, Mum headed for the door. "I'll show you out," she told the Reids, and they followed her. Vidal hung back long enough to watch my dad lift me into his arms.

"Savas, get an icepack for your sister's head and the painkillers on the kitchen counter," Dad directed.

As we approached the door, Vidal reached out and caressed my face. "I'm sorry you got hurt, Sash, and for how Yasmine treated you the last few months."

Weirded out by his sudden affection, I just stared at him. Vidal licked his lips, bowed his head, and followed his parents out. As we started up the stairs, I looked at my father. "That was weird."

"Yasmine had turned on you, and you still raced out there to try and help her and nearly died in the process," Dad explained quietly as we headed for my room. "Vidal has never been quick to judge or take sides. He assesses and gathers the facts."

Dad sat me down on my bed when we got to my room. "I'll let Barden know it's safe to visit." Pausing, Dad considered me. "Do you need help with the shower? I can ask your mum to come and–"

"I'll manage," I cut him off.

Pursing his lips, Dad didn't argue. I know he hated the tension between Mum and me, but it was what it was. "Let's not mention Barden staying over to your mother unless she finds him here, okay?"

"She won't hear it from me," I guaranteed.

My mother barely said anything since I started staying at Barden's. There was no more discussion about my future and university. Apparently, since I'd chosen Barden, my future wasn't worth considering anymore. Even when I was in the hospital, she would stand in the room and talk to the doctor and nurses, but never actually said a word to me.

Sighing, Dad kissed the top of my head, taking care to avoid the wound or bruising, and then left me alone. Once the door clicked, I ensured I was stable and then went and turned on the bath to run.

I unpacked my hospital bag while the tub filled. I put all the clothes in the dirty clothes basket and toiletries away. Once the bath was ready, I stripped and eased myself into the water. I washed and sat there with my legs hugged to my chest, the uninjured side of my face resting on my knees.

My bedroom door opened. I couldn't be bothered moving. "Sash, you okay?" Savas asked from where the bathroom door was ajar.

"Yeah," I muttered back.

"I was hoping we could talk?"

"Not tonight, Sav. My head is killing me."

There was a moment's silence. "I have the ice pack and your painkillers."

Hating having to move because the heat of the water was soothing the muscle tightness from the hit I took, I also really wanted that ice pack. My head was throbbing. "Give me a minute," I replied.

Pulling the plug out, I waited for the water to drain, then pulled my towel into the bath and wrapped it around me. "Can you give me a hand?" I knew without trying that if I tried to stand up, I'd end up right back in the hospital tonight.

Hesitantly entering the bathroom, Savas saw me trying to push up on the edge of the bath and quickly came over, basically hauling me out of the tub and then plopping me down on the rim.

He turned his back while I pulled my shorts and pajama top on, then I dumped my towel back in the tub because it was drenched.

"Do you need to do your skincare?" Savas asked, turning to assess me. My hair had been in a bun, so at least that wasn't wet.

The last thing I cared about right now was face cream. I didn't want to risk accidentally touching the bruised area again. "Just help me to bed, please."

Wrapping a strong arm around me, Savas eased me up and slowly walked me out to my bed. He tucked me in, made sure I was comfortable, then handed me my pills and water bottle. Once I'd taken my painkillers, he helped place the ice pack on my head, then sat on the end of my bed and watched me.

"What?" I asked.

My brother's eyes got glassy momentarily, and I swallowed my attitude. "I'm okay, Sav."

"No, you're not, but you'll lie and say you are. The nurses told Dad you were screaming with nightmares every time you slept. That's why they have those painkillers for you at night. They have a sedative in them as well."

"Oh, thank god! I'm sick of the nightmares."

"You told me when you touched Sophie, you saw her last moments..."

"Stupid wingless bitch."

"Did you touch Yasmine when you found her?"

"Did you do it, or were you just running your mouth?"

Tears fell from my eyes. "Yes," I whispered.

Savas swallowed. "So you know if she fell or if she was..." He couldn't say it. I wish I hadn't seen it.

"I didn't lie to them. Yasmine was drunk or on drugs. She was stumbling around under the bridge but wasn't alone. I can't say she fell, but I can't say they pushed her, either. Maybe she did fall, and they tried to grab her, maybe–"

"They murdered her," Savas finished for me. More tears fell across my pillow. "Do you know who was with her?"

"She was too drunk. I couldn't even tell you if the voice was male or female. All I know is..." Licking my lips, I tasted the salt of my tears.

"What, Sash? What do you know?"

"They asked if she killed Sophie."

Savas sat back, his shoulders tense as I met his eyes. I saw the understanding bouncing around in his eyes, but I voiced it for him. "Yasmine threatened to break my neck when we had that run-in at the Milkbar. Just like Sophie. If it was murder, it was because of that."

"Maybe. Did you tell the girls how Sophie died?"

"No. We haven't been on speaking terms. I've not told anyone but you that I even saw it."

Blowing out a breath, Savas peered at me. "That's a problem then, Sash, because it hasn't been released that Sophie had her neck broken. I didn't even know how she was killed until just now."

Blinking rapidly, I stared at my brother. Taking my hand, he gave it a squeeze. "This isn't our fight. Do you understand?"

"But Mia threatened me too, and they might go after her–"

Firming his grip on my hand, Savas leaned closer, his eyes more severe than I'd ever seen them. "This isn't our fight. If you share what you saw, it could put this family in danger. We need to stay neutral."

Swallowing, I eyed my brother. "I won't lie to Barden."

Sitting back, Savas smirked. "You couldn't now if you wanted to." Getting to his feet, Savas shoved his hands in his pockets. "Barden will tell you the same thing I just did. Get some rest. I'm next door if you need me."

The Touch of Death

THE SHIFTING of the blankets and applying a new ice pack to my head stirred me from nightmares of falling.

"Hey." I winced at the weight of the ice pack and blinked open blurry eyes as Barden shuffled in next to me, being careful not to jostle me too much.

"You were whimpering in your sleep. The last ice pack had thawed, so I went downstairs and got you a new one," Barden whispered.

"Mum didn't see you, did she?"

Caressing my jaw on the good side, Barden kissed my nose. "She's already in bed." Settling onto his pillow, Barden sighed. "She knows we are sleeping together, Sash. We've been living together for over a month."

"She doesn't know we've been sleeping together here," I clarified. "Dad would prefer her to remain ignorant of that. Especially if you came in via the balcony."

"Because then she'll suspect I've been doing that for a while?"

"You were."

Smirking, Barden kissed my lips gently, careful of where his face bumped mine. "I'm here. You can sleep safely now."

Smoothing my hand up his naked chest, I covered his heart and felt it beat through the flesh and bone. "Have you ever touched a dead body?"

Fitting his hand over mine, Barden slotted his fingers between mine on his chest. "Collection is Nelly and Calliope's departments. It's why they work in the human world in jobs that provide them access to their bodies. Nelly deals with violent deaths as a medical examiner and Calliope the natural deaths through her role at the mortuary. Gavel and I ferry the souls to be born. It's more dangerous. Why?"

"You said I have some Crow in my genes. Would that give me a special power with the dead?"

Breathing out a sigh, Barden snuggled a little closer. "Like being able to see their last moments?"

Chewing my lip, I met his eyes. "You know?"

His thumb tenderly wiped beneath my eye, catching a few tears. "I'm bonded to you. I know everything that pains you now."

"I can't get it to stop repeatedly playing in my head," I whimpered.

"It takes practice to learn to block it out. Nelly can help, but your closeness to Yasmine strengthens it."

"They both are just dying over and over in my head."

"They?"

"I touched Sophie after she died. At her funeral."

The space between Barden's eyebrows furrowed. "That doesn't make sense. Her soul had already been collected. For you to see her last moments means you were pulling it from the body, not the soul."

"Does it matter?"

Watching me, Barden shook his head slightly. "I'll speak to Nelly. She knows more about this. For now, let me hold you and convince your mind you are safe." Wiping away the last of my tears, Barden held me. Our hands entwined over his chest, the beat of his heart lulling me to the best sleep I'd had since Yasmine fell from the bridge. No dreams about her or Sophie. Only the deep resounding nothingness of sleep.

Brilliant sunlight filled my room, and an empty bed greeted me when I woke up. It'd been my best sleep since I hit my head. Well, since I regained consciousness. The cold pack on my head was still somewhat frozen, so I assumed another had been applied while I slept.

Getting up, I slowly entered the bathroom and freshened up. There was no point dressing since I wasn't going anywhere, so I just stayed in my PJs and then took a slow and careful trip downstairs. When I entered the kitchen, I was surprised to see my dad sitting and talking with Barden and Savas.

"Hey, how are you feeling this morning?" Dad asked.

Barden was already up and wrapping an arm around my waist to help me to the table. "Better. My head is still a little woozy."

"Well, let's get some food into you. That should help," Dad decided as he started pulling out ingredients.

"You don't have to cook. I know you must be tired."

Ignoring me, Dad started cooking. My side ached when I sat down. Flinching, I tried to stretch it out.

"After you've eaten, I'm taking you outside, and you are going to unfurl and furl your wings until it's second nature," Barden informed me as he poured me a glass of juice.

"I don't know if I'm up to that right now."

"It will help," Barden assured.

"How?"

"It speeds up healing," Savas answered, watching me over the table. "Just a little. Just enough to take the sting out of any injury."

"You've done this?" I asked my brother.

He scoffed. "Many times."

"Plus, before you can learn to fly, you need to be able to control your wings," Barden continued, putting the juice in front of me. "That way, the next time I tell you to run and get out of a dangerous situation, you can fly out of there and not put yourself at risk."

"To be fair, she would need to know how to fight while flying for that to have saved her," Savas argued.

"If Sasha had unfurled her wings and flown away, they wouldn't have attacked her," Barden answered defensively. "Or at least I hope whoever it was wouldn't have if they knew she was one of us."

"On the flip side, if someone saw Sasha flying away from the scene, they might think she killed Yasmine," Dad weighed in as he flipped a pancake. The scent of cinnamon wafted toward me, making me hungry.

"She needs to learn how to use her wings." Barden gritted his teeth, my chair creaking where he held the back of it.

"I'm not saying she doesn't," Dad placated. "Just that she'll need to be careful about where and when she uses them. The Orey don't know that Sasha has wings or that you mated. I think, for now, we keep them ignorant. I don't want them targeting my daughter next."

"I think they already did," Barden grumbled under his breath.

Frowning, I lifted my eyes to meet his, but trying to look up made my head spin, and I barely caught myself before I face-planted the table.

"You mean when Mia put her in the ground?" Savas asked instead.

Barden held me back by my shoulder, his free hand caressing my jaw while my head leaned back against his body. "I don't believe it was an accident. She was opportunistic."

Savas gripped his head, elbows on the table as he cursed.

"Language," Dad warned from the kitchen. Walking over he put the pancake stack in front of me and took the seat beside me. "I thought much the same when Sasha finally revealed what happened that night to me."

"So you think Mia–" Savas cut himself off, his eyes sliding to me. I was still trying to get my brain to stop moving behind my eyes.

"I have suspected since it happened that Sasha used her powers, and Mia immediately acted upon her suspicions. That the girls ostracised your sister immediately after that only proved my theory," Dad clarified.

"I was right; she tried to kill me," I whispered. "Damn. I was only venting when I suggested that to Raisa."

Placing his hand over mine, Dad gave it a squeeze. "If she had immediately reopened the ground and used the earth to pull you out, I would never have thought twice about her claim it was an accident. That she closed the ground and left you there only left me with one possibility. Disturbing as it is."

Barden took the seat beside me. "Mia probably didn't think your water element was strong because you only regularly used fire."

"She didn't know I had water," I murmured.

"None of us did," Dad huffed. "Considering how well you used it, I gather you've been honing your gifts for a while."

"Yeah."

"There was a reason she watched us train. Right, Sash?" Barden commented off-handedly before posing the question to me. "I noticed how intently Sasha watched our sessions and how she disappeared when it was raining regularly. I'm guessing storms were a good cover for you?"

When Savas and Dad blinked at Barden and then me, I chewed my lip, cut a mouthful of pancakes, and sank into my seat a little under the scrutiny. "Yeah. I was doing it from the time Savas started training. Bonus, he regularly caused storms by accident when training. I could use fire and not worry about it getting out of control or seen before the rain put it out, or generate lighting, and no one thought twice about it. And water, well, it was all around me. Puddles, the river, falling from the sky."

Placing his hand on my bare thigh, Barden's eyes glimmered as a smile pulled up the side of his gorgeous mouth. The way I suddenly yearned for those lips, reveled in the simple touch of his hand to my bare flesh, had me leaning into him.

Smile growing just before my lips touched his, Barden gently captured my face with his free hand, turned it to place a lingering kiss on my uninjured temple, and then eased my face to his shoulder as if I'd been planning to hug him the entire time.

Clearing his throat, Dad leaned his elbows on the table. "What I don't understand is why? Yes, the Orey are uncomfortable with the Gelus. Still, they know we are on the same side regarding keeping the Execrable and even worse creatures from this plane of existence."

"If Mia tried to kill Sash, I think it would be fair to consider that her parents may have impressed those views on her," Barden suggested.

"Maybe something happened in their hometown?" Savas offered. "I mean, they told us they were overrun with Execrable, and it wiped their clan out, and they were lucky to escape. Maybe they think the Gelus should have helped them, and their son would still be alive."

Nodding his head in agreement, Dad rubbed his chin as he considered the possibility. "Maybe it's just Mia. What happened to her clan probably traumatized her and influenced her perceptions as a young girl."

"I can reach out to my kin down south. See if they know why the Racles would turn on the Gelus," Barden offered.

There was a beat of silence. "Should we let her sleep?" Savas asked. That's when I realized my eyes were closed, and I'd snuggled right into Barden to the point I may as well have been sitting on his lap.

"She's awake. Just listening and resting," Barden replied. Easing me back, Barden waited for me to meet his eyes. "Eat up, Sash."

The smile on my face was probably loopy as hell, but I didn't care. It made Barden happy just that I was here and still alive. Feeling his eagerness to train me to use my wings, I ate a few more mouthfuls of my pancake before I got to my feet. Wobbling, but not passing out. My head was still a bowling ball of agony on my shoulders, and the movement made my brain slosh around in my skull. Or at least it felt like it was floating in a bowl of soup.

"Have you got a backless top?" Barden asked as he looked over my pajama shorts and top. "You need something that leaves your spine exposed from the top of your shoulder blade to the small of your back." Barden gestured by placing his hand between my shoulders and sliding it down to sit in the curve.

Imagining the type of top I needed, I pictured a halter top slung low in the back to hang loosely above my butt. Once I had a clear image, I tapped opposite shoulders with my index fingers, then hips. Knocked my ankles together and clicked my fingers. A blink later, I stood in yoga pants and the activewear top I'd imagined in a teal blue.

"Holy shit!" Savas gawped. "How did you do that?"

Dad had much the same look on his face. It was Barden who grinned. "That is an Orey power. To change your appearance with magic. Though the hand gestures are unnecessary."

"It's how I worked it out, so I just kept doing it as a controlled method," I defended. "I rarely use it. Just when going and changing is inconvenient. I don't like to abuse my access to magic."

Brushing my good cheek with the back of his knuckles, Barden's eyes glimmered again, his pride shining at me. "Sash, you are magic."

My skin tingled with excitement, his love for me filling me to the brim, chasing away the crippling agony of my injuries until I was only aware of them on the periphery of consciousness.

Taking my hand, Barden slid open the door to the back patio and led me out into the bright light of spring as he murmured, "Let's see those beautiful wings of yours in the sun."

The Unfurling

"JUST BREATHE," Barden counseled.

With my eyes closed, I stood in my backyard, focusing on my breath and trying to feel my wings shift along my spine with every inhale. So far, not so good.

Blowing out a huff, I opened my eyes. "I can't feel them there," I whined to Barden.

Stepping closer, Barden grabbed my hips and met my eyes. "It's okay. They're there. You just have to learn to recognize them. Now close your eyes and breathe."

Inhaling deeply, I did as I was told, closed my eyes, and focused on my breaths. After five exhales, Barden shifted his hold on me, moving his hands to my back and tenderly caressing each side of my spine.

"We know the wings are there, Sash. We just have to get you to a point where you can control them at will, and the first step is knowing they are there." Barden placed a kiss on my uninjured temple. "Just relax and let yourself feel."

Barden lightly tickled my spine by kissing a chain down the good side of my face. As his lips demarked my jawline and then back to my ear, a zing passed down my spine to my core, like lightning branching away from my centre line and sending tingles along all my neural pathways between Barden's mouth and my sex.

"Oh," I moaned as his tongue traced my jugular, my back arching, chest pressing into his where he curled over me. My fingers gripped his shoulders, kneading as those spikes of need spread through every limb. And as his tongue dipped into that gap behind my collarbones, something shifted and shivered in my back.

"Barden!" My dad's voice rang through the back yard making us pull back sharply, sending a ripple of pain through me. Dad's tone was hard and unyielding, echoing off the mountains behind the house when he demanded, "A word!"

Inhaling sharply through his nose, Barden eyed the back deck where I knew my dad stood, then his eyes came to me. He caressed my good cheek and gave me a smile. "Keep breathing and focus on what you just felt. Your wings are another pair of limbs, so treat them like any other limb when you have pins and needles."

With a chuck under my chin, Barden shoved his hands in his pockets and sauntered back to the house, no doubt to cop a lecture about what my dad just witnessed between us. Honestly, it's not like he thought I was still a virgin.

Throwing that thought out of my head, I turned my focus to that sensation I'd caught before my father interrupted. Just another limb.

A shadow passed overhead, too fast to be a cloud. Tilting my head up, I tried to catch what it was, but the sky was clear. A bird, maybe? A shiver raced up my spine like someone walked over my grave.

"Or someone else," I muttered. Another shiver, but the shifting beneath my skin caught my attention. Ignoring what could be out there, I focused on that sensation. I twitched my back muscles like I did when I'd been sitting studying for an extended period. Another shift. There was definitely something there.

Thinking about my body after long periods of study, how I always stretched, I raised my arms overhead, reaching high, going up on my toes, fingers splayed and strained as I arched slightly. As I flexed and extended my toes and fingers, I pushed the same sensation into the memory of the wings I'd found nearly a week ago. Imagined spreading them out to their full extent and shivering to release the tension and allow the blood to flow into them.

As the sensation built, the tension in my back grew tighter, and just as I thought I could feel the tips of the wings, sharp pain radiated through the injured side of my head. "Argh!" I curled over myself, raising my hands, ready to try and hold the explosion in my head.

"Sash!" Barden called with worry, a whoosh of air, but it was too late. The ground rushed up to meet me a moment before blackness encompassed me.

Brilliant afternoon sunlight filled my room. The cold pack on my head was still cold but no longer frozen, so I had no doubt I'd been out for some time.

Getting up, I slowly entered the bathroom and freshened up for the second time today. I still wore the yoga pants and backless top I'd conjured this morning. Feeling like hell, I took the frustratingly slow and careful trip downstairs.

When I entered the kitchen this time, only Savas sat at the table, his books spread around him for study. He looked up and, with relief, dropped his pen and rushed over to help me to my chair.

"I stayed upstairs with you for a while, but after three hours and your breathing steady, I came down for lunch and kept studying down here," Savas explained as he got me to the chair.

Once I was in the seat, he went to the fridge, pulled out bread and cheese, and slapped a sandwich together before putting it in the sandwich press for me.

"Dad's sleeping, and Barden had to go to work. He told me to call him when you woke up. I'll send him a message while you eat."

"Thanks." Eyeing his books, I groaned. "I need to get some study done before school goes back. I've lost five days now." Savas set a cup of tea before me, then went back to check the press. "I tried studying at the hospital, but the words would blur, and I'd get dizzy just reading a sentence and black out."

Sliding a plate with the sandwich in front of me, Savas put his hand on my shoulder. "Focus on healing first. You'll feel a lot better after a few goes of unfurling." Returning to his seat, Savas picked up the cup of tea he'd made himself. "A few years ago, before Barden joined us, I copped a bad knock to the head during training."

"I remember. Athur supposedly lost control of his power and slammed you into one of the boulders near the treeline."

Savas raised a brow. "Supposedly?"

"I'm not inclined to believe any acts of violence towards us from the Orey were accidents these days. Athur has exceptional control. Always has."

Clearing his throat, Savas rubbed the back of his neck. "Right. Well, my vision was blurry for a full day after. Since I couldn't focus on riding my bike, I went out the back and practiced some fighting moves using my wings. You were at school, so it was one of the few times I could have my wings out in the sun. After unfurling them, my vision improved, and the sharp pain in my head became a dull thud. So, I furled and unfurled a few more times, and each time I improved."

Frowning, which hurt like hell, I met Savas's eyes. "But you still had the bruises for the rest of the week."

The side of Savas's mouth turned up. "Dad came out and asked what I was doing. When I explained, he made me stop once I wasn't hurting unless I smiled or something. He didn't want the Orey to know we could heal faster. Dad said it was better to still have something to cause me to wince and the bruising so that they thought we were still hurt. They can't heal like us. They already hate us enough for being different."

"Plus, if they know you can heal quickly, they'd be more likely to try something else next time. Like a broken limb or neck."

When the words left my mouth, Sophie's death played behind my eyes. Tears escaped before I could stop them. "Sash?" Savas worried. Leaving his chair, he sat beside me, encompassing my hand. "Sophie?"

"Yeah." Swallowing, I cleared my throat. "They used magic to break her neck, so they didn't physically touch her. I feel that magic as if it touched me whenever I see it." Squeezing my eyes to clear the tears caused the spike to slam into my temple and wipe away all thoughts of Sophie. "Ouch!" I groaned. "Have you got those painkillers handy?"

Getting out of his chair, Savas retrieved one of the two bottles from the counter, checked the prescription, then brought them to me. "These are the daytime ones. Not as likely to make you sleep, but still not allowed to operate heavy machinery."

Taking two, I sagged in my chair. "Catch me up on the gossip and other shit," I asked.

Returning to his chair, Savas told me what had happened during my convalescence while I munched on my toastie.

"Raisa, Vidal, and Nash have been messaging me daily to ask how you are. Raisa hasn't stopped crying for you or Yasmine. Nash is really worried about her. He asked if she could visit to see if you were okay, but Vidal suggested waiting a bit based on how you were yesterday. He thinks if you pass out on Raisa, she will get worse," Savas revealed once he'd finished discussing all the drama of Yasmine's death and how it affected her family.

"What about Mia?" I asked.

"Haven't heard from her. I gather she's getting updates from Raisa. She's been lying low. Claiming she's too upset to go out after what happened to Yasmine."

"Probably terrified she's next," I mumbled, but Sav heard it and nodded.

"Probably. Especially if Mia connected it to the threat against you in the Milkbar," Savas agreed. "Though, it may not be."

Considering what I heard, I was pretty sure it was. I just didn't know if the killer was there and heard Yasmine and Mia directly or if it got back to them through gossip, and they decided to find out the truth. Sophie was an only child, so it couldn't be a sibling seeking revenge. "Could one of Sophie's parents have done it?" I asked. "They are Gelus as well. Maybe they went looking for answers. Are you okay?"

Savas coughed a few times, then took a mouthful of his tea to try and ease the reaction. "Fine." Gaining his composure, Savas met my eyes. "Sophie's parents aren't topside. I'm not even sure they know she's dead. With how long they—we—live," Savas corrected himself, "those who are topside spend a few decades at most here. They go to school, fit in with teenagers, university, and work for a while. Then, when their lack of aging might get questioned, they go travel or go home for a decade or so, then come topside again as the next generation in their family and start the cycle over."

"Oh." Taking a moment to absorb that information, I finished my tea. "So, there is no one who might want to avenge her?"

"Sure there is," Savas grumped. "The entire Gelus community."

"Right. And how many of those live here?"

Licking his lips, Savas rubbed the back of his neck. "That I know of? About a quarter of the town. The borderlands always have a greater population of Gelus."

My mouth fell open as I stared at Savas. He gave me a shy apologetic shrug, then his eyes went over my head. Turning, I watched Barden land in our backyard, shirtless, with only his jeans hanging from his hips and boots on. Sliding open the back door, he looked me over, then gave me an easy smile.

"Shall we try again before your mum gets home?"

Accepting Barden's assistance to stand, I fell into his arms for a moment, just breathing in his scent mixed with sunlight and ash.

"Did you run into trouble while working?" I asked.

"Just the usual soul eater," he answered casually.

A shiver passed through me. I didn't even know what one of those looked like or how dangerous they were. Still, I imagined something like the demonic vampires with soulless eyes that Vestigials called the Nosferatu. When they opened their mouths, it was like looking into a cavernous black hole of pain and anguish.

Another shiver tremored my spine, and the shift of my wings on either side made me suddenly keen to try again. "I nearly got there last time," I told Barden and Savas.

"Well, let's make it this time," Barden cooed, then wrapped his arm around my good side and walked out to the backyard.

Trying the same method as last time, I raised my arms overhead, reaching high, going up on my toes, fingers splayed and strained as I arched slightly. As I flexed and stretched my toes and fingers, I imagined my wings spreading out behind me and how good it would feel to extend them as far as possible.

As my muscles tightened, and a tingle of pins and needles revealed the tips of the wings, I curled my body forward—before overdoing it again—and pushed out through the center of my back.

Like it was in slow motion, my skin shifted, and the weight of my wings became physical as they ever so slowly unfurled. I controlled it like uncurling my fist one joint at a time.

The wind caressed them and tickled the sensitive underside as they came all the way open. They snapped out to the side without me trying, shaking the pins and needles away with a heavy shiver.

The weight surprised me, pulling me back and throwing me off balance. Pain spiked my temple as I started to tip, only pulsing and radiating around my head and down my neck when Barden quickly grabbed me into his arms, keeping me upright.

With a sigh, I met Barden's smiling eyes, his grin spreading across his face. "Very graceful and controlled," he praised. "We'll work on building your back muscle strength over the next few weeks, ready for when you learn to fly." His eyes fell to my lips, then he captured my chin between his thumb and index finger before his mouth smashed against mine.

I expected the sting of my busted lip. Instead, there was only a minor niggle, but not enough to deter me from meeting the passion of my mate's kiss as I wrapped my arms around his neck.

"What in the hell!"

Yanking back and turning suddenly made my head spin and ache. Only Barden's hands grabbing my hips stopped me from toppling over again. Savas stared in awe as my vision focused through the pain and behind him, my mother with tears in her eyes. Her bags dropped to the ground as she stared at me. Her eyes went to Barden and then to my wings.

"Mum—" I wanted to apologize because I could recognize the betrayal in her eyes. Still, I couldn't be sorry about who I was. Taking a step toward her, ready to explain, I winced as my temple throbbed. Her face shut down, rage replacing her hurt.

"I've had enough!" Mum snapped. Her voice was low and threatening. Then she grabbed her work bag, turned, and stormed back to the garage.

Savas sighed. His eyes took me in, observing where Barden had wrapped me in his arms to support me as tears fell down my face. "I better go wake Dad." Then he went inside.

Turning me to his chest, Barden rubbed my back, and it was only then that I realized my wings were gone. I must have furled them. But it didn't matter. I had a feeling that was the last straw for my mother, and she wouldn't want anything to do with her Gelus daughter.

The Love of Family

IT'D BEEN an hour since Mum drove off. Barden kept me outside and told me to let my dad handle it and to focus on furling and unfurling my wings. I wish I could say I put it out of my mind, but tears streamed down my cheeks the entire time. Doubly so when Savas joined us and pointed out the green sheen to the black part of my feathers in the sun.

Once I'd done enough that the spikes of pain had ceased and only the bruising and dull ache remained, Barden and Savas let me quit and go and find Dad. He was in his study looking like shit, clutching his phone as he sat in his reading chair staring into open space.

"Dad—" I tried to apologize.

"Not now, Sash," he muttered, rubbing his head as if he'd inherited my concussion. "Go rest."

Unable to even consider sleeping, I'd joined Savas and Barden in the kitchen. Between us, we'd made dinner and put it on to cook. There was a weighted silence between us, Barden reaching out to run a soothing hand up my arm or down my back whenever I thought it might break me. I'd fallen into that comfort, but the guilt ate me up.

Savas placed a cup of chamomile tea in front of me, where I sat at the kitchen table, then took his cup to his chair. Barden was beside me, rubbing my back. Savas's study books were closed, no longer able to focus. No words were spoken, but exchanged glances said it all. Concern for how this would affect our parents and our family.

Dysfunctional as my relationship with my mother was, I couldn't imagine it getting any worse for me. Still, it was different for Savas and Dad. I didn't want to mess it up for them, too.

Barden's hand slid to the back of my neck, gripping gently as a grunt of disapproval echoed through his chest. I didn't need his words. The sensation of his comfort, of his reminder that I was not at fault, was a constant vibration in my soul. I leaned into his body, resting my head on his shoulder, and sent my twin what must have been my hundredth silent apology.

The mirror of my eyes in his masculine face shifted from anxiousness to sympathy. In that look, I knew he didn't blame me either, not for having wings, but there was disappointment there, probably for how this played out. I hadn't told our mum. I let her get shocked by coming home to find me making out with the boy she disapproved of, and a set of snowy white owl wings attached to my back.

Tears welled and spilled. Barden did his caveman grunt again as I turned my face into his chest, his arm tightening around my shoulders as I barely held back a sob. The large hand at the back of my neck shifted as Barden used his thumb to tip my chin up.

Barden stared into my eyes. "It wouldn't have mattered how. Delila's reaction would have been the same. You are not responsible for her actions or reactions, Sash. You can only control your behavior. Your mother is the adult and parent here. It's up to her to act like it."

Lowering his face, our mouths brushed, Barden hovering to nibble my bottom lip a little. When our eyes met again, they were filled with heat, and the sensations vibrating off him were very much the sort of comfort that required us to go to his place and lock his bedroom door.

"Delila, it's been an hour. Please answer the phone so we can talk," Dad's voice reached us. Coming closer as he approached the kitchen. "I have to start my shift in two hours. Let's talk before I go. Please."

Joining us in the room, Dad went to the kitchen counter, leaned his empty fist on it, and met my eyes as he exhaled. "I swear I didn't know until Sasha told me, either. Sasha planned to tell you tonight over dinner. That's why she was out the back practicing. She'd only unfurled the once and was trying to learn to do it again. Please, come home. Let us explain everything."

Giving up, Dad disconnected the call and placed the phone on the counter, dropping his head and taking a few controlled breaths.

"Dad," I sobbed as I stood to apologize.

Coming around the bench, Dad wrapped me in his arms. "Don't you dare, Sasha. You don't apologize for being the beautiful being you are. And don't you doubt for a second that we love you any less because you turned out to be even more amazing than we already thought you were. Your mother was just surprised. Give her a beat to process it, and she'll tell you the same thing."

Choking on a sob expelled as a laugh, I clung to my dad. "Look at you, fibbing left, right, and center tonight."

My father could tell when others were lying to him. He prided himself on not lying to others if he could help it. Oh, he omitted information like a mob boss pleading the right to remain silent, but he didn't like to outright lie. Yet, we both knew I had no intention of telling my mother about my new feathered limbs, and he knew my mother would think less of me for them. Just like she already did for my choosing Barden instead of a nice Orey boy.

Huffing out his humor at my words, Dad pulled back and sat at the table, dropping his head into his hands and messing up his already mussed bedhead. "I hate doing it, but your mother has a volcanic temper. She erupts as an immediate reaction. If I don't give her enough grovel with the facts immediately, it will be days or weeks before she'll be willing to hear me out."

"Thank god none of us inherited her temper, hey?" Savas chuckled. When we all just blinked at him, Savas looked offended. "What?"

Thankfully, the timer went off, and Barden stood, distracting us from having to answer my incredible twin. "I'll serve. You three strategize." With a comforting squeeze of my shoulder, Barden gave us some space.

Meeting my dad's bloodshot eyes, I told him, "It's okay, Dad. Put the blame on me. Tell her I didn't tell you until this morning. She already hates me anyway."

"Your mother doesn't hate you."

Barden grunted. Dad twisted to look back at him. "She doesn't, Barden."

"That's not what Barden was suggesting," I defended.

"He was saying it was he who mum hated," Savas clarified, understanding Barden's Neanderthal as well as I did now.

Dad's eyes came back to me. "She loves you, Sash. She just struggles to understand you or your motivations." He sighed and messed his hair again. "You never know. Maybe knowing that you are Gelus will help her see why your aspirations differ from the Orey girls."

Barden grunted again. I kept eye contact with Dad and gestured toward my mate. "That was him calling bullshit."

The side of Barden's mouth twitched while Savas and my dad chuckled. Love radiated from the kitchen to me, filling my soul and letting me know I belonged here, no matter my mother's opinion. My mate, brother, and father loved and accepted me. That was more than some people had when they revealed their path diverged from the ones their parents hoped and dreamed for them. For that, I felt fortunate.

Rechecking his phone, Dad sighed. "She's gone to her parent's house."

"She messaged you?" I asked.

Flashing his screen at me, Dad shook his head and said, "I pulled up her tracker."

"Stalker much?" I accused.

Not even bothered by the accusation, Dad shrugged. "My wife works in the city and drives home to the borderlands every night. If you think I wasn't going to be able to locate her should she not turn up one evening, you're wrong."

"No wonder you kept your mouth shut when she bought me GPS earrings for my birthday."

"The only reason Barden doesn't have a tracking device on you is that he can track you through your mate bond," Dad replied.

Barden grunted in the affirmative, causing me to roll my eyes. The side of Barden's mouth tipped up when he caught it. Carrying plates to the table, he pecked my lips as he placed mine down. "Eat up. You start training tomorrow. You'll need your strength."

"Training?" Dad worried.

"Unfurling later in life means your back muscles haven't strengthened to support the wings. Sasha needs to work on strengthening her back muscles before I can teach her to fly, or it will be dangerous for her," Barden informed as he finished serving up and took his seat. "When I'm home, I'll train with her, and she can study while I'm working."

"I'll help," Savas offered. "With the training and studying." Savas ate a mouthful of his dinner, watching me while he did. A moment later, he tilted his head as he addressed Barden. "Do all Gelus girls get wings after they mate?"

"Sasha's the only one I've heard of it happening with, but finding your mate isn't common either. Not all Gelus females are born wingless either. No one is sure why some are born with and others without. I guess we'll find out in a few decades if you decide to marry," Barden answered.

"Sasha's my age, and you decided it was fine for her to marry," Savas challenged. "Or are you worried I plan to marry my current girlfriend?"

Barden lifted a brow. "I'm not against you and my sister marrying, and Calliope would do it in a heartbeat, especially if wings came as part of the deal. Still, I want you to be ready for that commitment."

Savas's eyes came to me. "Were you?"

Chewing my lip, I pushed my food around my plate. "I've never even been attracted to anyone else, and there is no shortage of hot guys around. I've just never been interested in any of them except Barden. And we agreed it wouldn't prevent me from living my life."

"You mean going away to university?" Dad questioned.

"Wait, what?" Savas gaped. "You're not staying local?"

"I haven't decided yet. Barden and I discussed it before we got together. I wanted him to know my plans, and he told me upfront that he made Dad a promise and would abide by that. So, if I go away, I have to leave him behind."

"And you're okay with that?" Dad asked Barden.

A negative grunt from my mate. "But if that's what Sasha needs to do, I won't stop her. We're mated now. I'll always be able to find her and vice versa." Barden nudged me with his shoulder. "Eat."

The fact that the conversation hadn't distracted him from caring for me warmed my core. I wasn't hungry. Too worried about Mum and the fallout of today. So, I'd just been pushing my food around and not eating.

Barden's hand returned to the back of my neck, and he rubbed up and down my spine. It eased my worry, and a moment later, I was hungry.

"Will that always work?" I asked him.

A positive grunt.

"Can I do that to you? Sway your emotions?"

"My life experience makes me a bit more even-keeled, but you can calm me when stressed and ease my worry just as I do yours. Though, since you are who I worry about, just being in the room with me already does that," Barden answered, drifting closer as he spoke until he could kiss the side of my throat.

"Are all mates this sickeningly mushy?" Savas screwed up his face. "Because I'll take a hard pass and just marry a girl the Orey way like Dad did if they are."

This made me frown considering Barden revealed Calliope wasn't just a casual hookup when I'd brought up our siblings. "But—"

Barden squeezed my hand to cut me off. Down the bond I felt Barden's warning not to go there. That my brother wasn't ready. My mouth sort of gaped when I realised Savas didn't know why he was drawn to Calliope and no one else, and I had to quickly shove a forkful of food in it to cover.

I didn't doubt that my brother would be way worse when he and Calliope bonded. He didn't have the whole bad-boy caveman persona to overcome that Barden did. Savas was already a sensitive new-age guy, so he would likely make me sick with his sappiness when he finally let it out.

Letting it go, I focused on eating my dinner. After I finished, I started to get pain in my head again. Not like earlier, but enough to remind me I took a hard hit. Barden got up, took my plate to the kitchen, and helped Savas clean up.

"You okay, Sash?" Dad asked, watching me rub my forehead.

"A bit of a headache creeping back in and suddenly very tired."

"Maybe take your pain meds and lie down," Dad suggested. Getting up, he grabbed the pill bottle and put it in front of me. "I should go get ready for my shift," he announced, rechecking his phone.

"Will you try calling her again?" I asked, taking a tablet.

"No. I've left two messages and pled my case. I'll let your mother cool down, and she'll contact me when she's ready." As he stood up, the buzzer at the gate sounded. Dad checked his phone and frowned. "Vidal is here."

"Why?" Savas asked. "I told him training was canceled this afternoon, and it's way late anyway."

Dad considered his phone, then peered up at Barden, whose eyes were already locked on me. Savas followed their gazes and blew out a breath. "Right."

"What did I miss?" I asked.

Shaking his head, Dad looked at Barden. "Have you got your stuff here so you can justify your presence by studying with Sav?"

A grunt of affirmation, and then Barden went into the mud room to retrieve his school bag. Dad turned his eyes to me.

"Sash, it's probably best you go to bed. You look exhausted, but if you want to lay on the sofa and watch some television until you drift off —" A knock at the door cut Dad off.

"I'll get it," Savas answered, having reopened his books.

"The lounge would be best," Barden told Dad. "That way, we can watch her, and I can take her to bed later."

Accepting the suggestion, I walked across the room and lay on the sofa. Dad covered me with a throw rug while I turned on the television, turning the volume right down before switching to the music channel I loved. From where I lay, I could turn my head and see the dining table and the way Barden was watching me from his seat.

"I'll go get ready to go," Dad told us before he bent and kissed my head just as Savas returned, followed by Vidal. "I love you," he murmured. "And don't worry about your mum. She'll come around."

Standing back up, Dad turned to Vidal, exchanged a few words of greeting, and asked how his family was coping before excusing himself. "Keep it down, okay? She needs to rest."

"We will, Dad," Savas assured. He waited for Dad to leave, then spoke to Vidal. "She doesn't feel safe by herself right now, and she should stay down here rather than try to go up and down the stairs if she needs something."

"Can I talk to her?" Vidal asked.

"Sure, but she might fall asleep on you," Savas warned. "Don't go throwing your drink at her if she does."

"Fuck, I'm sorry about my dad. He's just..." Vidal trailed off.

"I get it," Savas assured. "We'll be over here studying."

Vidal came over and stood where I could see him without moving my head. "Hey, Sasha."

"Hey," I replied, trying to stifle a yawn. "Did you want to ask me more questions?" I started to sit up.

"No. Please, don't get up. I just wanted to see you. Check how you were." When I frowned, Vidal sighed and rubbed the back of his neck. "Can I sit with you for a while?"

Still unsure of his request, I laid my head back. Vidal sat at the end of the corner sofa to see me, the television, and my brother at the table. I squinted against the steady ache in my head, then rubbed the grating annoyance in my chest from the possessive Neanderthal across the room.

After a few moments, it became hard to keep my eyes open. After a little longer of fighting sleep, I gave up and drifted into the darkness.

The Wait

MY EYES OPENED to the best sight in the world. Barden was asleep in bed beside me. It was still early morning, the sun just filling the canyon. With his messy dark brown hair, this gorgeous man was curled around me as if he was protecting me from my nightmares. And he was mine.

My mate and husband. The only person who ever had me think dirty thoughts. Oh, how I'd longed for Barden to like me, for him to find a reason to get me alone and kiss me just once. All those years of longing, and here he was, naked in my bed. Only Barden chased off the ghosts of Sophie and Yasmine from reliving their deaths as if it was my own.

Last night, I'd woken screaming and crying from those haunting dreams. Savas wrapped me in his arms and assured me I was safe while Vidal stared at me, mouth agape and wide-eyed. He'd swallowed with difficulty, his eyes shining with tears as he watched Barden and Sav soothe me.

Not caring that Vidal was there, Barden took me in his arms and sat on the lounge with me across his lap, my cheek pressed against his chest, his heartbeat calming me faster than their words. "We'll stay right here," he murmured, bundling me up like a child.

At that point, the boys gave up on studying, and the three settled with me to watch television and discuss their shift on Friday. I'd barely stirred when Barden carried me to bed and tucked me in against him hours later.

My stomach growled. It was nearly impossible for me to leave the sight of this beautiful man sleeping beside me. Still, when my body told me I had to, I climbed out of bed and headed downstairs for breakfast. I wasn't the only one exhausted. Barden had been burning the candle at both ends to be there with me while fulfilling his duties with the Orey and Gelus.

My dad sat at the kitchen table, a fresh cup of tea in his hands as he stared out the floor-to-ceiling windows to the yard. "Morning."

"Morning, Sash," he replied as his attention turned to me.

"How did the shift go last night?" I asked, the dark circles under my father's eyes telling me Barden wasn't the only one exhausted this morning.

"Thankfully, quiet. Or at least we didn't encounter any Execrable."

Going to the fridge, I removed some eggs, spinach, and cheese. "Did you finally get hold of Mum?"

"Not yet."

Annoyed with her taking her issues with me out on Dad, I slammed the frying pan on the stove.

"Sash—"

"She's such a bitch! Treating you like this when it's not your fault that I'm not the daughter she wanted." I sprayed oil in the pan and cracked the eggs into a bowl.

"I lied to her. Hid what I was from her."

"That was twenty years ago. You told her. You had it out back then; she can't keep hating you for it. Especially not when her blood isn't as pure as she pretends." Grabbing the spinach, I washed it, tore the leaves off then chopped them.

"Sash—"

"Why is it such a big deal? Sav has had wings since he was five, and she has no issue with him. Yet, for years, she's tried to control everything I do. I'm not allowed a moment of privacy. She has to approve every move I make. It's been suffocating. And now that she can't control me, she's punishing you." Grabbing the whisk, I started beating the eggs.

"Oh, it's okay for her to lie to me my entire life about who I am, but I don't tell her I have wings in the five minutes I've known, and she chucks a hissy fit and storms out without even giving us a second to explain. Making you worry about her all night when she knows you have to be focused on what you are doing out there. How dangerous it could be."

The Execrable attack definitely made me appreciate how deadly the job the men in my life had was. Barden's fundamental responsibility to the Gelus was even more so. Pouring the eggs into the pan, I added the spinach and cheese, then put the heat on low and covered it with a lid.

"Sash—"

Turning to face my father, I took in his weary face. "No, Dad. No excuses. No defending her. What if you were distracted last night, and something happened to you? You'd get injured or worse because she did the typical 'everything is about Delila' dance? It happened to me too. I fought those Execrable off, so I know your life's perilous. I found Sophie dead. I watched Yasmine fall to her death. Heard her scream and her body impact the rocks." I flinched as that moment played over, as if I was right back on that running track.

My temple pulsed, and I cringed, almost pressing my hand there but stopping just short of touching. It would only hurt more to touch, but thank the gods, it didn't hurt as much as yesterday. The boys were right about the healing benefit of unfurling our wings.

"The sounds of her crunching will haunt me for the rest of my days. Yet amongst all that, I fell in love and discovered I'm not all Orey, that like you and Sav, I have these beautiful wings. Do you know how good it felt to finally understand why I always felt like an outsider to the other Orey girls? Why can't she just love me for who I am?"

Dad blinked, then turned his attention to the mud room door. Following his gaze, I finally noticed my mother standing there. Her jaw was set, her eyes glaring daggers at me. "You're looking better," she said with no emotion.

Huffing, I put the bowl and whisk in the sink and grabbed some fruit instead. "Only because of the wings. You can thank Dad for the fact I'm still alive because of his half of the genetics."

Turning back to Dad, I ignored my mother like she'd ignored me since I chose Barden. "There's enough frittata for two. Don't let it burn." Not sparing my mother another glance, I headed for the stairs.

"You're home," Dad murmured behind me.

"All my clothes are here, and I'm due in court at ten."

She wasn't home for us. That's all I needed to hear.

A groan came from the bed behind me as Barden rolled over. A few minutes later, Barden appeared at my balcony door, still looking half asleep and sexy as hell.

"Hey, what you doing out here?" he asked, combing his fingers through his bed head.

Moving further onto the balcony, Barden noticed Savas taking up the only other chair on our joined patio. Not missing a beat, Barden dropped a kiss on my cheek as he wrapped an arm around my waist, and a second later, he occupied my seat with me in his lap. Sighing, I curled into him.

"What's going on?" he asked Sav, as his hand ran the length of my spine, soothing me without asking. That he could feel my emotions just as well as I could his was still unnerving.

"Mum came home, but only to get a change of clothes," Sav answered.

"Is Gannix okay?" Barden checked, and I loved him more for worrying about my dad.

"We don't know," I muttered. "Mum only just left five minutes ago. Sav was about to go down under the pretense of breakfast to check."

"I just wanted to give Dad a minute in case he needed it," Sav mourned. With a sigh, he got to his feet. "I'll text if the coast is clear." Then Sav went through his bedroom door.

Tucking hair back behind my ear, Barden frowned. "You are more tense than usual about your mum. Did something happen?"

Cringing, I leaned into Barden's chest. "I may have been ranting about how unfair she was being and how horrible she'd been to me when she came home. I'm unsure how much she overheard, but I would guesstimate a good portion of my bitch session."

Being the great guy he was, Barden combed my hair back and tilted my face to his, booping my nose. "I dare say it was overdue for you to tell her how you feel anyway, Sash. Don't fret. Delila earned your angst. Either the way she's been ignoring you will stay in place, or maybe hearing how you feel about everything will help her wake up to herself."

"I don't understand why she is so prejudiced against the Gelus. She fell in love and married one. Why was she so against me finding love there too?"

Exhaling hard, Barden caressed my ear with his thumb, tracing the cartilage from top to bottom before following the vein in my neck, coming to rest over my pulse.

"Your mother was just trying to protect you from going through what she did. Her family basically ostracised her when it came out that Gannix was Gelus. Her parents only kept in contact with the stipulation that she didn't bring her husband or half-breed son to their home. They had to move out here to the borderlands. I can understand why she was so dead against us being together," Barden sympathized.

Caressing my jaw and ear again, Barden met my eyes. "I can understand her behavior, but I won't forgive her for how she has treated you since you chose me. Especially not since the incident last week."

Huffing, I cuddled back in against him. "You should have seen her at the hospital. She totally ignored me and only spoke to the doctors. I think she wanted me to have amnesia or a personality shift or something."

Barden snickered, and I loved the sound reverberating through his chest cavity, followed immediately by the grumbling of his tummy. It made us both chuckle. I was about to suggest we get some breakfast because the two pieces of fruit I ate barely touched the sides, but then I remembered we were waiting for Savas to give the all-clear.

"Will my dad be alright if she leaves us?"

An affirmative grunt was my answer. It made me lift my head to appraise him. My thoughts took a turn to a dark place, and my stomach clenched at just the idea of going away to university now.

"Will you be okay if I leave at the end of summer?"

Staring into my eyes, Barden hesitated, then grunted again.

There was a subtle difference in the tone, which along with the bond between us, let me know he had just lied. He wouldn't be okay if I left, but he'd let me go because he loved me that much.

As if he knew I'd found his true answer, Barden swept my hair back with both hands, cupping my face in the heat of his palms. "It's different for us, Sash. You're my mate. I will long for you whenever we are apart. I do every day that I leave you just to go to work. But I understand why you need to escape. You're young and need to explore and learn and make your way in life. I'll be here when you are ready to return to me."

Thumb brushing my lower lip, Barden leaned close. "Your parents are not mates. Gannix loves Delila, so it would hurt to lose her, but not even close to how bad it would be if she were his mate."

His lips brushed my forehead, careful to avoid the bruising. "But I would put good money on your mother huffing and puffing but never actually blowing your house down. She loves Gannix too much. If she was going to leave him because of his wings, she would have done it when she first discovered it."

Smiling up at him for those words of wisdom, I lifted my chin to encourage those lips of his to find mine. As they made contact, the gates opened, and a car pulled up the drive. Jumping from Barden's lap, earning a grunt of unhappiness, I moved to the balcony and watched a town car pull up.

"Grandma Tormen's here."

The Torture of Secrets

"OKAY, INTO BED." Barden used my shoulders to direct me inside and to the bed, then tucked me in.

"Why am I having to go back to bed?" I complained. Other than a few aches and pains, which were all bearable for the most part, I felt fine.

Barden leveled his face with mine. "Because yesterday you could barely stand without passing out. Your behavior around those who are not Gelus and don't know about your wings needs to be that of any other Orey girl who nearly died from taking a rock to the temple."

"I think that would require me to play dead," I sassed.

Barden shrugged and kissed my forehead. "If you trust her, tell her about your wings. If you have even a snippet of doubt that she may be horrified, keep it to yourself."

"I'm more worried about blurting about meeting the man she once loved. The same man she's been looking for ever since."

Blowing out a breath, Barden straightened. "Probably don't mention Lorka until he gives you the okay. You don't understand the Gelus world yet, Sash. There are reasons Lorka has watched you from the shadows and never openly approached your family. His declaration that you were his blood was the pebble that will make waves in the Gelus community."

227

Grabbing his clothes from the floor, Barden headed towards the balcony again. "I'll go shower in your brother's room."

I watched Barden leave, but my brain was scrambled, trying to figure out what he was trying to tell me. The tension and concern that pulsed down my bond made me anxious and curious to learn more about my grandfather.

A warning growl came down our bond, letting me know Barden sensed that curiosity. Something told me I wouldn't get answers from him about my grandfather.

A soft knock at the door brought me free from my internal puzzling, and a tender smile on my grandmother's face as she peeked into my room filled me with love. Grandma Tormen always loved me without question. I firmly believed she'd love the revelation of my wings, but I wasn't sure now was the time to reveal them either.

"Oh, good, you're alone." Grandma came over and sat on the side of my bed. "My sweet girl." Putting her index finger under my chin, she turned my face this way and that to get a good look at the bruising. She'd been to see me at the hospital twice. She tsk'd and released my chin. "How are you feeling?"

"Better than I was yesterday, and that was better than the day before that," I answered, not wanting to lie. "What are you doing here on a weekday?"

My grandma was a radiologist and usually worked weekdays. She earned a decent living even as a single mum and still managed to buy her own place. Once Dad left home, it eased the financial burden. Now, she owned her private practice but still worked five days a week.

"I took the day off," Grandma explained. "What's the point in being your own boss if you can't take a day off when it's important?"

"And it was important to come today, not Saturday?"

Grandma pursed her lips. "Your dad called me last night. Told me you need to go to your doctor today for a follow-up. He also said something happened with you and your mother, and she stormed out, and he needed to sleep, so he was worried you'd miss your appointment."

"Did he tell you what happened?" I asked.

Sweeping the hair back from my face on the undamaged side of my head, Grandma gave me a closed-mouth smile. "He said you sealed the mate bond and married your Gelus."

"Anything else?" I asked.

Grandma's hand hesitated near my face, her smile falling as she pulled her hand away. "No. Was there something else?" When I chewed my lip, Grandma blinked wide eyes at me. "Sweet girl, please tell me you're not pregnant?"

"No!" I blurted out, then frowned. "Or at least I don't think so. We only mated the morning of the incident, so I haven't given much thought to it, but I guess we did have unprotected sex, so—" I bit my lip, suddenly stressed. My head pounded, and I whimpered and flinched, though it was not like I could escape the drilling inside my skull. At least it wasn't as bad as the last few days.

Grandma sighed. "Oh, well, we should probably talk about that. Well, your mum should, but we know there is no chance of that happening in a way that won't make you wish that fall had ended you, so I'll fill in. And as luck would have it, I'm taking you to see your doctor today, so let's talk to him about contraception while we are there. First, let's ensure there isn't already a great-grandchild brewing."

"You can do that?" I asked, frowning as she gestured I move my blanket so she could touch my abdomen.

"So can you. Sense and learn." Rubbing her hands together, Grandma placed them over my lower abdomen.

A sensation of ants rushing across my belly made me gasp, then that sensation pushed through my skin and into my abdominal cavity. "Ohh, I don't like this. It feels so—"

"Intrusive?"

"Bad," I clarified. "Like I'm being swarmed by ants and about to be eaten alive."

The ants withdrew as Grandma raised a brow at me. "I've never heard it described like that before. For most Orey women, it's like pouring fizzy soda over them. They don't feel violated by it." Tilting her head, Grandma considered me. "Are you close with your boy's mother or sister?"

"Um, Nelly is lovely, but I wouldn't say we're close. Why?"

"Because I wonder if the Gelus in you will not like a Vestigial intervention. It might be good to ask a female of their kind how they manage birth control and choose that option for yourself."

"Oh. You don't think I'm Orey enough," I murmured.

Taking my hand, she gave it a squeeze. "I'm not saying it's a bad thing. In fact, I'd be sort of jealous."

That made me frown in confusion. "Why?"

"Because while the Orey community is tight, it is also rigid, judgmental, and exclusive. Since I came east, I've become friends with a few Gelus. They are also a tight-knit community, but they understand that everyone is different. They encourage inclusivity and integration. Plus, imagine being able to fly anywhere at any time. That would be so cool. I love that Savas got wings like your father. I hoped you would too. I had all these wonderful little daydreams of you and your brother sprouting wings at bath time and driving your mum nuts fluttering around the room while she tried to wash you."

The imagery made me laugh. "You never liked my mum, did you?"

"Oh, I loved her when they first married. She and Gannix were perfect for each other, and your father loved her wholeheartedly. I ached for her when she discovered Gannix's origins, but I also resented how she treated him after that.

"And then the way she was determined to make sure you were raised Orey and not acknowledge your father's Gelus side really put a burr in my ruff. It made Gannix feel ashamed, especially when he and Savas had to keep it secret from you.

"So, over time, I started not to like Delila as much as I once did, and her treatment of my son drove me to seek out female Gelus and learn about them. It also broke the last of those rigid biases of my upbringing. Then when your boy showed up, and your mother became ridiculous in trying to control you, I struggled to empathize with her."

"I was ranting to Dad about her this morning when she returned to get her clothes. I don't know how she took it, and I don't care now."

When Grandma lifted a doubting manicured eyebrow at me, I huffed and winced at the spike of pain it caused in my brain.

"Okay, I care. I don't want my mum to hate me, but I've had years of her being this way now. I hate how it's impacting Dad and Savas, though. I don't want to be the reason they lose their wife and mother."

"Sweet girl, if anyone is to blame here, it's Delila. Not you. You did nothing wrong. This is your mother's bias, her problem to deal with. Just because her family is so pure blooded Orey—"

I scoffed. I couldn't help it. But it drew Grandma up. Chewing my lip, I averted my gaze, but Grandma was no fool. "Oh, you have some gossip, don't you? Come on. Out with it. What do you know about your mother's family that makes you doubt their claim of pure bloodlines?"

Rolling my bottom lip through my teeth, I considered the risk of giving her this ammunition against my mother. Still, I was sick of Delila's high and mighty, 'Orey is better' attitude. "Well, Barden says there is Gelus in Mum's genes."

Both my grandma's eyebrows lifted. "And he knows this, how?"

"It's sort of the reason Mum stormed out yesterday. You see, she came home to find me in the backyard shaking out my wings, and she flipped."

"Wings?"

Nodding, a smile grew as my grandma's mouth slowly fell wide open with awe. "Yeah, they unfurled the first time I mated with Barden, but we're keeping it secret right now, so please don't tell anyone. Dad, Savas, and Mum are the only ones who know."

"That's amazing!" Grandma cheered. She wrapped me up in a hug, her eyes full of happy tears. "Your boy must be so happy."

"He wasn't upset about it," I chuckled, remembering how Barden ravished me when my wings unfurled the first time.

"But how does that prove your mother's got Gelus in her line?"

"Well, I have wings like Dad and Sav, but the black in my wings has a green tinge to it, like the Corvus Gelus, and Barden said that came from Mum's side, not Dad's."

"Oh, hell. Not just Gelus, but the Corvus. Delila will be devastated." For once, Grandma looked sad for my mum, so I didn't think it was malicious for a moment. She genuinely felt sorry for my mother, knowing it would tear her bullshit opinions of her family and their self-righteousness down on itself.

A knock at the door broke the unplanned pity party for my mother before Barden stuck his head in. "Sorry. I thought I'd see if you were up to coming downstairs for breakfast," he asked as if he'd only just arrived.

Snickering, Grandma got off the bed. "How about I go cook, and you help Sash prepare for the day?" Grandma left me alone with Barden, sending me a wink as she closed the door.

"I think Dad told her you've been staying here," I told Barden.

Nodding his head as if he had realized that, Barden sat beside me and kissed my cheek. "Everything okay?"

"Yeah. But can you go suss Dad out for me? Let me know he's okay before I come downstairs."

The side of Barden's mouth twitched as he rubbed my forearm in comfort, then he headed off. With a sigh, I grabbed my phone and dialed Calliope. Nelly probably would have been nicer about things, but Barden's sister would be direct and truthful, even if it hurt.

"Hey, how's the head?" Calliope answered. It was probably the nicest she'd ever been to me.

"Sore, but better."

"Good. Barden was freaking out, and I dreaded having to reap you on him," Calliope sighed.

"Wouldn't that have been your mum since it was technically from a murder scene?"

"You think she wants the job any more than me?" Calliope huffed. "So, what can I do for you?"

"Um, I was hoping you could tell me how our kind does birth control. I mean, can we use the same stuff as Vestigials or Orey, or is that not as effective?"

"Our kind?" Calliope asked a little nasally.

"Yeah. It turns out I'm more like my dad than my mum. Which means no one in my family can help me with this."

"And I was the first Gelus you thought to call for help?"

"Yeah. Is that okay?"

There was a pregnant pause, then Calliope sniffled. "Yeah. Yeah, it is. Okay. Let's talk girl stuff."

The Blackout

GROANING, I folded my arms on the dinner table and laid the good side of my head on them. My study books were spread around me, Savas sitting opposite me, still studying.

"Hard day?" Dad asked where he cooked in the kitchen.

"Barden made me work for two hours on building my back muscle strength before he left," I grumbled.

"You'll be sore tomorrow, so make sure you stretch and have a bath after dinner to help," Dad directed. "How did the doctors go?"

"He wants weekly checkups until the sharp pains have stopped and the bruising improves. I booked in for Saturday afternoons since I'll return to school in another week."

"That's good. I can take you on a Saturday afternoon," Dad said as he checked his phone.

"Is she coming home tonight?" I asked, knowing exactly who he was hoping would text him.

Sighing, he returned his phone to the counter and grabbed some plates. "I have no idea, Sash."

"I can stay with Barden tonight if she does, so I'm not here to cause issues." I offered.

Savas looked up at me, his pen tapping the table as he watched me. Guilt swarmed me that I was the cause of all this angst in my family.

"I'd prefer you stay here," Dad answered bluntly. "Is Barden coming for dinner?"

Swallowing under my brother's watchful gaze, I sat upright and lowered my gaze to the table. "Barden said he'd be working late unless I needed him," I answered. "I'd prefer not to be here if she's going to come home. It'd be easier for you both, since I'm the problem, if I remove myself so you can patch things up without aggravating her."

"What if Vidal drops by without notice again?" Savas asked. With a shake of his head, Savas kept fidgeting with his pen. "I agree with Dad. You should stay here and maintain appearances." Returning his focus to his books, Savas said nothing more, but I noticed his gaze flicking to me afterward.

Sighing, I got up and grabbed my painkillers, taking a couple of paracetamol to deal with the dull ache in my head and stiffness in my back. "I'm going to go do some stretches before we eat, or I won't be able to stand afterward," I excused myself. I went through the glass walkway to the home gym behind the garage.

While I could read now without getting dizzy and passing out, I struggled to focus. I kept getting distracted by everything around me. That was not great, considering finals were just a few weeks away.

The murmur of distant voices through the open door told me Savas and Dad were talking in the kitchen, but I didn't want to listen. Turning on some tunes, I moved through some light stretches to help release my muscle stiffness. As a twist caught on my bruised ribs, I hissed and had to ease it back.

Yeah, unfurling had helped heal me faster. It would have been weeks before I could move like this without them, and I knew it. Still sucked to be in pain at all.

Worry battered at me down my bond with Barden, and I sighed. Taking a breath, I sat back into child's pose—which wasn't as easy as usual—and sent thoughts that I was safe back to him.

We seriously needed to talk about being able to turn this off and on. I didn't want to spend the rest of my life shifting my emotions so that I didn't worry Barden when he needed to focus on his work.

A growl echoed down the bond. I huffed and fell to my good side. "See, this is exactly why. I can't even have a private thought anymore. That's not cool."

Despite being sure that Barden couldn't hear me, I felt like his hand was rubbing my back and then him withdrawing a little. Giving me space. Closing my eyes, I breathed out in relief and enjoyed a moment of peace. I really wanted to get on my bike and go for a long ride, but besides my helmet most likely causing pain, I knew the three men in my life would lose their shit if I even considered it.

I went to get up, but my head became heavy, pulling me back to the ground. Suddenly, it became impossible to keep my eyes open. Blackness clouded my mind as my body seemed to weigh a ton.

"Sash," Savas' voice cut through the darkness. "Sash, wake up. Dad!"

Groaning, I opened my eyes to see Savas leaning over me, shaking my good shoulder. "Hey," I whispered.

"Are you okay?" Savas asked as Dad rushed into the gym and kneeled on my other side.

"What happened?" he checked as his fingers found the pulse in my neck.

"I tried to get up but felt so heavy, and I couldn't keep my eyes open."

"I'll call Nelly and ask her to come look at you," Dad decided.

"Doesn't she work on dead people?" I frowned.

"Yes, but she had to become a doctor before she could become a medical examiner," Dad clarified.

He and Savas helped me sit up, and I noticed two others standing by the door. Mum and Vidal were there. Both looked pale as if they'd thought the worst seeing me lying on the floor.

"What was she doing in the gym?" Mum shrieked.

"I was aching and thought some light stretches might help. I barely did anything. Even child's pose hurt."

"You can barely stay conscious sitting still, was stretching really the smartest idea?" Mum scolded.

"What do you care?"

Mum stiffened, but before she could open her mouth, Dad snapped, "Sasha!" He gave me a look of warning as he helped me to my feet. "Sav. Vidal. Help Sasha to the sofa; I'll call Nelly. Delila, we'll talk in my study."

Mum moved out of the doorway while the boys guided me back to the living area and over to the sofa. Savas squatted in front of me to meet my eyes.

"I'll get you a water," Vidal said, then crossed to the kitchen.

Savas' phone started playing the intro to Stray Kid's Side Effects. He pulled it out of his pocket, checked the screen, and looked at me. "It's Barden." He touched my shoulder as he put the phone to his ear. "Hey. Now's not a good time. Sash took a turn just as Mum and Vidal arrived."

Listening to Barden, Savas squeezed my shoulder, stood, and moved away. "I don't know. Dad's calling your mum to come to look at Sash. I thought she was dead, man. She was so pale when I found her..." Sav's voice fell away as he shut the door to the mudroom behind him.

Kneeling before the couch, Vidal held a glass of water. "Do you need a hand sitting up?"

Giving him a slight shake of my head, I used the back of the sofa to pull me up, then cuddle against it. Once I was settled, Vidal handed me the glass.

"How are you feeling?" he asked as I sipped the water.

"How do I look like I feel?" I muttered, then huffed and rested my head against the sofa.

"They messed you up, that's for sure. You're lucky you're still alive," Vidal answered.

Frowning, I winced against the ache of moving the bruised tissue around my face. Still, even that was more reactionary than near the pain I was in two days ago. "They?"

"The guys who attacked you and my sister."

Confused, I went to rub my head, but Vidal caught my wrist, stopping me. "You don't want to do that."

Letting him move my hand away, I didn't react to him holding it. My focus was on his words. "Guys? What guys? I watched your sister fall from the bridge. I was on the shore alone. There was no one anywhere near me when it happened."

"Is that what you remember or what you were told when you woke up and couldn't remember?" Vidal pushed.

"Told?" I set my eyes on Vidal. "I wish I couldn't remember. I see your sister falling and hear her screaming over and over whenever I close my eyes. The only way I can sleep is if I take those drugs which knock me out. Even then, I swear they are there. I'm just too deep for them to reach me and make me see them."

"Them?" Vidal pressed his fingers harder against my wrist.

Sorrow flooded my eyes, fell over the rims, and caressed my cheeks. "Sophie and Yas. Both of them are there, on the shore. Their eyes empty, vacant, haunting me. I can't unsee them. They won't let me." I sobbed, wrapping my free arm around my waist. "I wish I could forget your sister's screams. Sometimes, it's me. Stumbling around under the bridge, then falling. Falling and screaming and hitting the ground. I remember the sound of the impact like a song played too often on the radio, and now it's embedded in my brain."

For a moment, we sat there in silence. Vidal still with his fingers on my pulse, his eyes in my peripheral vision laser-focused on me. Tears continued to fall as I stared off into the canyon, the riverbed, the wing striking me. I winced as I remembered the force it hit me with. The caw of a hawk. Then the rocky ground rushed up to meet me, making me jerk where I sat as if I was hit all over again.

"Sash…" Vidal's voice was tender, his thumb caressing the side of my wrist.

"I remember too clearly. I wish I could forget. I wish I could sleep without seeing it happen all over again and again," I murmured.

Vidal tucked a few strands of my hair behind my ear. "Okay, Sash. I believe you. I won't ask anymore."

Wiping away my tears only for fresh ones to fall, I eyed Vidal. "Is that why you are here? To question me more?"

"That's why my parents think I'm here," Vidal muttered. His thumb caressed the vein on my wrist, making me frown at his hand. "Being home sucks. They are angry and hurt and keep going on about how she was meant to marry Athur and how it could mess up the alignments now. It's not even that their daughter died, but the fallout of all their plans for her not coming about. I come here and watch you breathe, which sets me at ease. I hope you don't mind. I know you feel like shit and are going through a lot, but it helps to see you breathe."

Wiping away the last of my tears, I eyed Vidal. What he revealed about his parents, about the way they were carrying on. "I guess everyone grieves in their own way. Maybe your parents find it easier to focus on the logistics than the emotions."

"Maybe," Vidal agreed. "Do you mind me coming here?"

Shaking my head a little, I cuddled back into the sofa and sighed.

"What's going on?" Savas asked, suddenly standing at the end of the sofa, his eyes targeted where Vidal was holding my wrist.

Clearing his throat, Vidal took his hand back and collected the empty glass of water before standing. "Just talking to keep her conscious," Vidal answered. "What did Barden want?"

"Organising to study together tomorrow," Savas answered without hesitation. "Nelly's on her way. I'll serve up dinner. Vidal, you staying?"

"If that's okay?"

"Sure. Can you go into the garage and get a few cans of drink? We're all out in here," Savas asked as he went to the dining table and started packing our study stuff. I noticed how he packed away mine quickly and piled it up next to his on the buffet table.

Savas returned to me as soon as Vidal went out to the garage. "You okay? Did he say or do something?"

Considering my brother, I shook my head. Vidal was grieving his sister and felt unsafe doing it at home. If I told Savas that Vidal was questioning me, he'd probably ask him to leave. I didn't want to cause more issues around here.

Assessing my tear-streaked face, Savas chewed his cheek but didn't push it. "I'll get dinner on the table. Are you up to eating?"

I wasn't really hungry, but at the same time, I was starving. "Sure."

The Mate

A COOL BREEZE slipped beneath the blankets, making me shiver before something hot filled the space beside me.

"What time is it?" I mumbled, still half asleep as I cuddled into Barden's warmth.

"The sun is about to rise," Barden whispered with a yawn as he huddled under the blankets with me. His fingers tenderly swept the hair back from my face, then brushed across the bruising still around my temple. The lightness of his caress didn't aggravate the injury now. Just the ease of his attention and affection relaxed me.

Nelly's assessment Thursday night was that stretching my back by touching my toes and hanging there for ten seconds was the cause of my collapse. Something about an inverted pose affecting my blood pressure to my bruised brain.

Nelly had been worried enough that she told Barden to ensure he was there while I slept that night. Despite Mum not talking to me, she had me sleep in her room on Friday night. Then Dad took the reading chair in my room last night to watch over me until Barden got home from his Orey watch shift with Savas.

"Did you sleep?"

"The nightmares woke me a few times," I admitted. "I kept waking Dad up with my crying."

Barden's eyes went over my shoulder. I didn't need to look to know what caught his eye. His hand drifted to my ear, fingering the arc of the cartilage. "Are you sure you want to go today?"

"Yes. Yas was my friend for more years than she wasn't."

"Did you do it?" the distorted voice growled in my head.

A lance of pain stabbed through my temple, and I flinched. Barden's hand paused, hovering above my head as his brow pinched as if he felt it too. Blowing out a breath, I relaxed again. "You're coming, right? I think Vidal could use the support."

Caressing my jaw, the bruising there no longer painful, Barden considered me. The sides of his mouth turned down as his thumb traced my chin. "Vidal is not my concern. Unless he tries to question you while you are vulnerable and alone again. Then, I will have words with him," Barden murmured. Savas must have told him what happened while he was on the phone on Thursday.

Placing my hand on my mate's chest, I splayed it across the bare skin where his heartbeat could be felt strongest. "You would do the same if your sister died suspiciously."

Releasing a huff, Barden brushed his thumb over my lips. "I will be there as a team member supporting a fellow team member. Not going would create unrest, and Athur is already being difficult about what we are."

"Athur's a prick," I muttered. "And a bully. He's never liked that Savas was more powerful, and that is just comparing their Orey abilities."

"My point remains. I'm going." Taking a beat, Barden observed me. "I know we've been keeping our relationship quiet from the Orey, but that doesn't mean you can't stand with me or look to me for support when they are around. It would be good for them to see something developing between us."

"I thought they've known we were crushing on each other for years?"

"My interest was always known. Yours will be the shift in our dynamic. Plus, I think you will need a shoulder on each side of you to get through the day."

"Thank you." Before Barden could change the topic, I opened my mouth and wrapped my tongue around his roaming thumb, sucking it into my mouth. My splayed hand passed across his nipple, then wandered south over his defined abs to the band of his boxers.

"Sasha, no," Barden breathed. "You are still fragile." He freed his thumb and then grabbed my hand as it traced just below the elastic of his waistline.

"I feel much better."

Bringing my naughty hand to his lips, Barden kissed it. "You were told you need to rest."

Drawing my hand back down the centre line of his torso, I met Barden's eyes with a wicked smile. "I was well enough to do those back-strengthening exercises every day."

"This is a different sort of exertion," Barden protested. Still, his eyes had narrowed. His nipples were hard, and as my hand brushed over his boxers, there was no argument from his cock, which jerked at my attention.

Slipping my hands around Barden's neck, I rubbed my nose against his. "Then you do all the work."

"I need to sleep," Barden argued, but his voice was breathy with want.

Keeping hold of him, I rolled onto my back, forcing Barden to move with me or potentially hurt me. "I don't need a marathon, just a few minutes out of my head."

"Sash—"

"Please! When I wasn't dreaming of them, I was dreaming of you. I need you. Touch me, and you'll know it's true." Taking his hand, I guided it down my body, between my thighs, and under my nightdress. A growl reverberated through Barden's chest as his fingers found my slick desire. "Please," I whispered.

"Damn it!" Barden muttered. "That was too darn hot."

"What, how wet I am?"

"No. I mean, yes, but you begging me to fuck you... Sash, it got me so damn hard. I think I just discovered my kink."

My eyes opened wide, then a laugh escaped me suddenly as his words sunk in. A twitch of a smirk at the side of Barden's mouth told me he'd been playing with me. Maybe. Just a little. Because as Barden settled between my thighs, I got to feel that his words were actual.

Barden had never been small; in fact, his size had scared me our first time, but I swear my brain injury was still affecting me, 'cause it felt bigger and heavier where it pressed against my pubis. Blinking my shock away, I closed my mouth and slipped my hand between us to touch him through his boxer shorts.

"Holy shit," I gasped. "You really liked me begging." I swallowed a barely restrained smile as I half closed my eyes and gazed shyly through my lashes at him. "Please, Barden. I need you inside me. I need to feel you stretching me, claiming me, making me come all over your huge—"

Barden cursed and dove forward to kiss me as his cock throbbed in my palm. Grunting, Barden kept his weight off my torso and shifted to hold himself with one hand as he started shoving his boxers out of the way. I was only too happy to help, getting them over his hips and using my feet to drag them down his legs before Barden kicked them off.

His free hand shoved my nightie out of the way, then guided his seeping tip through my folds. Grabbing one of my knees, Barden curled my leg over his hip and then slammed into me. All my air escaped my lungs from the sudden intrusion. My core stretched to its limits as Barden held us like that, with him buried deep inside me while we kissed furiously. It felt so good.

"Do you have any condoms here?" Barden asked, both of us breathing heavily. He'd promised me we'd always use protection after we wed until I was ready for babies. Being the honorable guy he was, Barden was looking to keep his word. I loved him even more for it.

Caressing his face, I stared into his eyes. "It's okay. I'm on birth control."

Cringing, Barden started to pull out. "Sash, Vestigial birth control doesn't work for Gelus females."

Digging my nails into his ass to keep him where I needed him, I shook my head. "I know. I spoke to Calliope. She told me how things work for us. Your mum dropped off a jar of the gel for me on Friday, and I've been using it since Friday night."

246

"Are you sure?"

"Hell, yes!" I dug my nails in a little deeper. "Did you miss me pleading and admitting how much I need you? Please, fuck me."

With a curse, Barden captured my mouth in a fiery kiss that zapped straight to my core, making me moan as he simultaneously shoved deep into my body.

"Please, please, Barden, please," I pleaded.

Unable to resist, Barden pulled out, then thrust back in savagely. A spike of pain seared at my opening, but it was instantly muted by the sheer pleasure of him scratching that needy itch in my channel.

Over and over, Barden answered my pleas with savage possession. It was like that time in the pantry all over again. Quick and dirty wantonness rendering all sense of the outside world mute. My body tightened without warning, and Barden cursed as he covered my mouth with his palm just before I screamed my orgasm. He grunted hard, and his cock pulsed his own release as my body milked it from him.

Groaning, Barden dropped his head to my shoulder, both of us breathing hard and his hand falling away to help keep his weight off me.

"So good. Thank you," I murmured against Barden's neck, my fingertips slicking along his sweat-drenched back. "Oh, God. That was so good."

Barden tensed, his head jerking back, his black eyes glaring at me. Right. He hated the word God for some reason.

"Sorry," I breathed, combing his hair back. "It just comes out of habit."

Relaxing, Barden shook his head, his eyes softening. He kissed me gently before falling beside me, his arm draped across my belly.

"Why do you get so angry when I say that word? Is it only when we are having sex you find it offensive or in general?"

Barden glared at the ceiling, massaging my hip, using my perspiration like a massage oil. "A god is not quite what the Vestigial believe it to be. And there is certainly more than one of them."

"So, they aren't some omnipresent power that presides over us and ignores us simultaneously?" The Orey weren't religious. We believed the Vestigial theology to be stories to guide their morality as if they needed some threat of eternal damnation and a perfect afterlife to make them act with common decency.

It seemed insane to us that it was even warranted. Then you heard of the horrible atrocities humans visit upon each other. I sort of understood why they held their theologies so precious. Some wielded religion as a shield to protect them, others as a moral compass, while those with power manipulated it as a weapon to control.

"No. They are more like spirits or ghosts with capabilities, like Orey and Gelus. But where our powers are born of nature, theirs are more biological," Barden explained. "They can turn your body inside out, crush your organs, melt your brain, tie your intestines in knots, shatter your bones, and all that sort of stuff. They don't wield magic or control natural forces, but they can turn your body against you if you give them access. They can also heal any ailment. The key being you have to let them in for them to do either, and praying to them is what draws them to you."

Well, that was unsettling. I could see why Barden didn't want me calling one of them to me. "So, like an extremely sociopathic mage?"

"Mages are usually benevolent, and they wield nature as equally as they can heal, but sociopaths, yes. In our world, we call them Narsitees, but they've learned the Vestigial term for them and answer it if they are nearby and hear someone praying to them. How they engage with you, all comes back to their vanity. How you worship and adore them impacts whether they help or harm you."

Totally freaked out enough to never scream 'God' again during sex, I turned my eyes to Barden. "How common are they?"

"Not very." A slow grin filled Barden's face as he eased up to lean over me and trace my cheekbone with his thumb. "Gelus have a tendency to kill them if they cross our path. They can cause us some pretty bad damage in a fight, but we are skilled and tough enough to usually take them out before it gets fatal or take them with us. Either way, we dwindled their numbers enough a millennium ago that they tend to avoid us like a bad smell. You rarely find them lingering near a Gelus stronghold."

Lowering his face, Barden kissed my eyebrows, my cheekbone, and my jaw, then proceeded to nip and kiss down my neck, making me moan and shift closer as his hand found my breast.

My heart rate picked up as I susurrated, "You have sufficiently convinced me never to use the 'G' word again. I'll have to think of an alternative."

"When we are together, my name works wonders," Barden whispered, his breath hot against my ear, making me squirm with need.

"And when I'm cursing?"

Barden shifted his hand lower, drawing delicate circles that spiraled downward, finding my clit and teasing the sensitive bud into instant pre-climax awareness. "'Damn' or 'blast' work well in negative situations. 'Yes' is a great word to yell when I do something you like and want me to keep going."

"Yes?" I gasped, my body creeping toward orgasm.

"Oh, yes." Barden chuckled in my ear, his finger circling faster. "Do you need me inside you again, Sash?"

"Please!" I wasn't too proud to beg.

Barden, the generous man he was, was only too happy to accommodate my needs. Rolling over me, he eased between my folds, using his cock to tease my pearl for a moment before he slipped through the gully and eased into me. He tracked my lips with a finger and lifted my chin as he passed his mouth over mine.

"For the record," Barden breathed against me. "We've never just had sex. There has never been a time where you were just a way for me to get off, or vice versa. I have loved you since your soul called to me as I carried you to this world to be born, and I will love you until another carries us to rest before our rebirth. And even then, I will seek you out and love you again."

"You've fucked me," I argued.

The side of Barden's mouth tipped up in the most devilish of grins. "Yes. And I will fuck and make love to you every chance I get for eternity. But even when our lust drives us hard, when I let my possessiveness reign like we just did, it will always be a matter of my love for you expressed intensely physically."

Dragging my thumb across his plump bottom lip, I sighed. "I love you."

"And I, you, Sash."

Our lips connected, our bodies rocking in time to the unhurried pace. Having possessed me so thoroughly before, Barden was gentle and undemanding in his desire for me this time, drawing me through several more orgasms before he gave into his body's release.

The Funeral

THE THING about electric cars is that they are quiet. Which I usually love. But it's too silent when no one in the vehicle is on talking terms.

Touching the music app on the console, I tried to turn some music on for the third time. I hated studying in silence. Examination rooms were rarely quiet. Once again, Mum immediately turned it off.

"If the silence bothers you, you could talk," she huffed.

"I have nothing to talk to you about."

"I think there is a lot for us to discuss. Your wings, for starters."

"Sure, we can discuss my wings once you stop acting like a hypocrite with your elitist Orey bullshit and stop being a bitch to Dad and let him sleep in his bed again," I replied politely.

"Elitist Orey bullshit?"

Rolling my eyes, I angled my body to the car door. "If you prefer silence, I can make do." Taking out my earbuds, I put them in and pressed play on my phone music app.

Mum's knuckles went white on the steering wheel, but she didn't respond.

I was stuck riding with Mum because the guys were all on their bikes, arriving with their teams, and there was no chance any of them would let me ride my bike or even ride with one of them.

If Barden's family were going, I would have begged for a ride with them rather than have to be trapped in an enclosed space with my mother. Especially since the crematorium was over an hour's drive away. Still, I came prepared with my earbuds and study notes, so I used the trip productively.

When we pulled into the parking lot, I disconnected the music, put my earbuds back in my purse, and took a deep breath. Mum didn't rush to get out of the car either. We both just sat there, watching the building where Yasmine would be laid to rest.

"Not many people here yet," Mum murmured, looking between the Orey teams and the Orey females. "I'm sure more will come. Nearly your entire year at both schools showed up for Sophie."

We were early, but not that early. With a sigh, I released my seat belt. "Other than the chess team, don't expect many more. Yasmine wasn't that popular."

"I guess Sophie was a cheerleader."

"She was also fairly nice, you know. Mia and Yas always acted like they were better than everyone. And honestly, if this was Mia's funeral, you could halve the number again. I wouldn't show up for her, that's for sure. Even if she had the decency to swan dive off the bridge in front of me like Yas did."

Staring at me, her mouth and eyes wide open, Mum took a moment to regain her composure. "You don't mean that—"

"Yes. I do. The bitch tried to bury me alive. Seriously, Mum. You have your head so far up your ass holding the Orey above all else despite how they've treated your husband and kids. They only let Dad and Savas on the teams because they're desperate and know without them and Barden, they'd all be dead by now. Yet, the Assions accepted not only us but you as well. It took my so-called friends turning on me for me to realize the truth. How is it that your family turned on you, and you still haven't figured it out?"

Opening the door, I climbed out of the car and headed for the chapel. Dad broke away from his team and came to meet me halfway. "You okay?" he murmured.

"Yeah. Just a long drive," I muttered, hugging him tight before pulling back. "I'm going to go stand with Savas."

Dad glanced back at the groupings and noticed Mia standing with Raisa and their mums. "Probably a good idea."

Letting him wait for Mum, I headed towards the boys, but Mia broke away from her group to cut me off. "Why are you here?"

"For Yasmine," I answered shortly.

"She didn't even like you."

Blowing out a breath, I met Mia's eyes. "I'm not here for the Yasmine you turned into your puppet mean girl. I'm here for the bubbly, fun, and nerdy girl I met in middle school. The girl I was friends with."

Scowling, Mia leaned closer and shoved me in my bruised shoulder. I flinched on reflex more than pain, but by how her eyes lit up, it seemed like the latter. "No one wants you here, birdy."

"Mia, back off." Vidal put a hand on Mia's shoulder and forced her back a step as he approached me.

"She's one of them," Mia seethed at Vidal.

"Really? Because she grew up hanging out and playing with the other Orey girls. I've never even heard of her saying a bad word about us or being mean to us, and even after my sister died, Sash has been kind and respectful toward us. So, since this is my sister's funeral, I'll have a say in who stays, and I want Sasha here." Not inviting room for comment, Vidal swept me away from Mia and passed me straight into Savas' waiting arms.

"There's a time and a place to be a bitch, Mia. Funerals are never that place," Vidal scolded her and followed as Savas led me back to the circle of their team.

Barden stood waiting, his arms crossed as he glared back toward Mia. He opened those arms, and I stepped into them, accepting the hug as we grew near. "You okay?"

"Yeah." Stepping back, I smiled up at him, then blew out a breath and moved closer to Savas. Barden stayed tight to my other side, Vidal eyeing us while he spoke to the others.

Raisa approached as everyone started to file inside, her face already streaked with tears as she offered me her hand. "Can I sit with you?"

Chewing my lip, I eyed Mia, who glared at Raisa's back.

"She had no right to speak to you that way," Raisa said with conviction. "You were our friend for most of our lives. You watched her die. You deserve to be here, to put her to rest, just as much as anyone else."

When I swallowed a lump over her words, Raisa stepped closer, her free hand going to my good shoulder to give it a comforting squeeze. "Vidal told Nash about the nightmares you have. Maybe being here today will help in a way that gives you relief too."

Since attending Sophie's funeral hadn't made her quit haunting my dreams, I doubted it. Still, Sophie only started up again after Yasmine died before me. Maybe it was a cumulative trauma thing. Either way, I wouldn't turn Raisa away just because of the last few months. She'd already been kind to me when the others weren't looking and hadn't shunned me in classes where Mia and Yasmine weren't with us.

Squeezing her hand, I gave her a bitter smile and walked into the chapel for the service. We found a pew near the front, but away from Mia, and took our seats.

Delta team escorted the coffin. Yasmine's mother and father led it in. Once they deposited Yasmine where she needed to be, Savas and Barden joined us, sitting on my other side.

The service was short and sweet, and as the coffin rolled into the back area of the chapel and the curtain closed, I said a final goodbye to my one-time friend. Wishing her peace and happiness in her afterlife. I imagined her playing chess against some of the greats in the game who had passed long ago.

"What's that smile for?" Savas asked as we walked outside.

"Just imagining Yasmine now playing chess with some of those old dudes she was always raving about."

Standing beside my brother, Vidal smirked. "God, you're right. She'd nag them until they played to the point they'd all be asking for reincarnation by the end of her first month dead."

It gave us all a little chuckle.

"Are you coming to the wake?" Raisa asked as we stepped outside, and the bright sun made me squint and wince as a spike of residual pain stabbed my temple.

"Sasha has probably overdone it for today," Savas replied, quickly taking my elbow and steadying me. "I might take her home."

"But your bike is here?" I worried.

Barden stepped forward. "Take your mum's car. I'll ride your bike back for you and return for mine."

"It's probably a good idea to avoid the wake. Once Athur gets a few drinks in him, he'll start shit," Vidal muttered, glaring at their teammate. "We don't want him getting Sash alone either. He'll make Mia look like a Care Bear."

Eyeing Athur where he was talking with Mia, Raisa sighed, gave me a gentle hug, and then headed off.

"Barden, if you see Sasha over to the parking lot, I'll go tell Mum we need the car," Savas directed and followed Raisa since our mothers were talking.

"Thank you for coming," Vidal said to Barden and me. "No one will blame you for ditching before the wake, considering the icy welcome you both received."

Frowning, I glanced at Barden, but his mask of indifference was in place, and his only response was a grunt before he steered me toward the car.

"What did I miss?" I whispered.

A negative grunt was my only reply. I understood the 'not here' and 'not now' implication and simply swooned into my mate's hold. My energy was low, and I wanted to go home and sleep. The fact the move only reinforced everyone's understanding of the injuries I'd suffered was just a bonus. If I hadn't healed myself to a certain level, I probably wouldn't have been up to attending at all. Let everyone think I'd reached my limit because the truth was, I had.

The need to uphold appearances, hide my truth and love, and defend myself against others' perceptions and biases was exhausting. Add a severe head injury that was not yet fully healed, and I was wiped.

At my mum's car, I leaned against it and rested my head on Barden's shoulder. Where our arms connected, Barden intertwined his fingers with mine. We'd decided to show slight signs of our developing relationship around the Orey, so when it came out, it wasn't a surprise to anyone, or we weren't accused of hiding it for some sinister reason.

"Okay, let's roll." Savas used his phone to unlock the car. I could have done it since we were both set up for it, but the opportunity to let people see Barden and me holding hands like this couldn't be passed up.

Once we were strapped in, I glanced to where Mum was standing talking to Dad, albeit it was apparent there was some disagreement taking place. "What's up Mum's butt now?"

Savas turned to assess them and put the car in reverse before turning his attention to the cameras and pulling out of the park. "Dad's following us home. The Reids subtly hinted the wake was for Orey and Yasmine's friends from school only. Mum thinks he should go and that we both should have stayed. He told her that she can call him when she's ready to come home."

Changing gears, we left the car park, Dad pulling in behind us even though he could have raced past us and made it home faster.

"Did you and Mum talk?" Savas asked.

"Not really. Why?"

"Don't know. Usually, when the Orey make subtle digs at Dad and me, she just lets it wash over her. Yet, when I went to tell her we were leaving, Jebidiah all but accused us of being Gelus spies. Mum was actually listening for once and had that sourpuss face she gets when making decisions about her cases," Savas informed.

Huh. Maybe Mum did hear me for once.

"I might have called her out on having the same elitist behavior as the other Orey," I admitted.

"Oof!" Savas cringed. "You're not even trying to mend those bridges, are you?"

Shrugging, I stared out the window. "She lit them on fire with her bias. I'm happy on this side of the river. If she doesn't like it, that's her problem." I tried not to sound pathetically woeful, but I don't think I hid it as well as I had hoped.

Clearing my throat, I looked at my twin. "What are you applying for at University?"

Flicking his eyes to meet mine, Savas didn't hide his annoyance. "Doesn't really matter. I'll be a rider the rest of my life anyway."

"Vidal and Nash are going to college. Dad went."

Lifting a shoulder, Savas dropped it again. "Seems like a waste of money to me."

"But what if things change? What if this war drives a split between our family and the Orey, and we are no longer held to their way of things?" I asked. "You could leave, study abroad, see the world instead of being stuck here hunting Execrable."

"Come on, Sash. They may not like what we are, but the Orey won't risk losing us from the teams."

"That may not always be the case," I cautioned. "So, don't blow up your possible future for them. Change is inevitable. You should safeguard yourself." Then without asking, I hit play on the console, and old-school grunge started playing, seeing us through the rest of the drive home.

The Weight Bench

CLOSING THE BOOK, I groaned and lay my head on it.

"Finished studying?" Savas asked from his place on the other side of the table.

"No. But I need a break, or my eyes will start bleeding."'

Shutting his books, Barden stood up. "Come on then. We can get a core strengthening session while you rest your eyes."

I half-cried and groaned. Barden continued to make me do strength training every day this week. At least when Vidal came over each evening, I didn't have to fake being sore or tired.

Barden was pulling out my chair for me before I could protest, and my unsympathetic ass of a twin brother was snickering at me. Bemoaning the misfortune of unfurling late in life, I followed Barden into the gym, where he initiated a workout that would have made the SAS proud.

For the next hour, I did every type of abdominal workout known to mankind, plus some I'm sure were used as torture in the Underworld. Back crunches, obliques, the one where you lie on the weight bench face down clutching weights to your chest and pulling up till your body is straight. Every muscle in my core and back was worked until I cried,

"Oh, my God." And then Barden made me do three more because I said the G-word.

"Okay. Up you get," Barden finally said. Though he had to be crazy to think I could even move at this point.

Chuckling at me, Barden helped me up, sweeping sweat-soaked strands of my hair back from my face as he did. "One more exercise, and then we are done."

"Are you angry with me?" I groaned. "Why are you punishing me?"

Moving closer, Barden swept his hands down my body, resting under my breasts. "Sash, baby, if I was going to punish you, it wouldn't be to make you stronger. It'd be like this." His thumb brushed across my breasts, grazing my nipples and instantly switching my brain from dying to randy.

As Barden pinched and teased my peaks through my top, I hung my head back and moaned. "Okay. Punish me."

Taking his hands away, Barden chuckled. "You haven't earned it. But if you do this last thing for me, I'll lay you on the weight bench naked and feast on your beautiful pussy until you come all over my face."

Putting his mouth to my ear, Barden whispered, "And if you do it without complaint, after you come on the mouth, I'll let you come all over my cock."

The evil man returned to groping and teasing my breasts while he murmured those tempting words. But knowing how much better I'd feel after two orgasms, I could not resist them either. Sighing, I knocked Barden's hands away and met his eyes. "What do I have to do?"

A smug smirk filled Barden's face. "All you have to do is piggyback me around the room once."

My eyes widened. Barden was head and shoulders taller than me and probably twice as heavy in muscle mass.

"Wings are usually about one and a half times your body weight in flight. If you can carry me around this room, then you are ready to start learning to fly." Barden explained.

"I know you are super keen to get me airborne, but it's only been two weeks of strength training."

"Two weeks on top of your lifetime of swimming and two years handling your bike at speed." Barden defended. "You were already halfway there. Let's see if two weeks made the difference."

Exhaling hard, I turned my back to him. "If I fall and get hurt, you get to tell my dad you did it riding me like a pony."

Barden snorted a laugh and jumped on my back, making me stumble forward as I grabbed under his thighs and tried to regain my balance. "The sooner you get around this room, the sooner you can be riding me," Barden whispered.

No further words of encouragement were needed. Making sure I had a good hold on him, I all but ran a lap of the room. When I returned to the start, I dropped his legs and stumbled to the weight bench, panting.

The door closed behind me as I sat my ass down. I checked, and sure enough, Barden had shut it and was coming back towards me. The gym wasn't large, just the size of our garage and set behind it. So no one inside would hear us in here.

Peeling my yoga pants down my legs, I got them out of the way before pulling my gym top over my head. Barden's eyes fell on my naked breasts and then lower as I lifted one leg over the bench to straddle it.

"No underwear?" Barden asked as he lifted his muscle shirt over his head. Shrugging my good shoulder, I didn't clarify. I never wore panties under my workout gear. I was usually crawling out of bed to go running in the morning. It seemed pointless to put on clean panties just to come home and shower an hour later and use a second pair of panties for the day. As for the top, it had built-in boob support. Not enough to run with, but enough for weights and yoga.

Kneeling at the end of the beach, Barden jutted his chin at me. Being a good girl, I laid back, stretching out my naked body along the bench for him to pleasure.

"You earned three orgasms with that workout. I'm proud of you for giving it your all." Before I could respond, Barden dropped his face between my thighs and licked straight through my folds.

"Yes!" I hissed as the tip of his tongue flicked my chit. "Please, don't stop." I pleaded.

"I won't," Barden assured, then he used his fingers to open me and rewarded me for my hard work. Licks, squiggles, sucks, and flicks until my back arched, and I came with a curse.

Before I could come down from that high. Barden slipped a finger through my folds and eased it into my still-clenching core. "You're so beautiful, Sash. Body, heart, and soul." The pad of his calloused finger found my internal pleasure center and stroked it lovingly. "Everything about you leaves me in awe, Sash. I can't believe you are finally mine. Some days I still wake up and think it's all a dream. That you'll still be underage or not interested in me. I'd imagined it all, and I'll have to wait still."

My body was quickly fuelling for another climax. Caressing Barden's neck, I urged his mouth close to mine as I panted. "I'm terrified I'll wake up, and you'll go back to not talking or telling me you are done with me."

"Never going to happen," Barden assured, then kissed me with the same sensual slowness of his finger stroking my go button.

Pulling away, Barden licked and sucked down my neck and chest before latching onto a nipple. His free hand came up to tease the other. "Are you ready?" Barden asked as my breath became uneven, and my body tightened again.

"Yes. So ready."

Giving me a smile, Barden exhaled across the top of my hardened peak. I was coming two seconds later. Writhing and twisting as my body fell apart to his expert touch.

Standing up, Barden dropped his jeans to the floor, then stepped a leg on either side of the bench before he sat down. Spreading my thighs on either side of him. Barden shifted closer until my butt was in his lap and his cock pressed against my sex.

With one of his Neanderthal grunts, Barden shoved into me. I cried out his name as the sensation of him stretching me open for him so suddenly walked that fine line of pleasure and pain. I loved it. I loved him and the way he always knew what I needed from him.

A growl rumbled up Barden's throat as he slowly pulled back, then slammed in again. Over and over, he fucked me like that, making me cry out his name as a moan and a plea.

The bench was drenched with my exertion, allowing Barden to slide me back and forth on the leather while he pounded me. The next time Barden slammed to my core, he gripped my hips tight, shivered, and bent over me to mouth my breasts.

"Tell me you're close?" he begged.

"So, very close. If you fuck me hard, I'll come over your big cock in seconds."

Barden lifted his head and stared at me. His cock jolted hard inside me. "Fuck. Sash."

Grabbing the bench, Barden lifted to lean over me, my legs spreading wide as his body forced them up near my chest, and then he was pounding the life out of me.

As promised, I came hard. So hard pins and needles exploded through my fingers and toes, my legs shook, and I could barely breathe.

With a curse, Barden slammed balls deep inside me and finished. He panted in my ear as he caught his breath. Then dropping his head to my shoulder, Barden gave me a satisfied grunt. He lifted me with him and carried me to the bathroom, where we showered.

A knock on the bathroom door jarred us from a passionate post-coital kiss. My heart rate skyrocketed, and my dad would bust us again. Especially since we hadn't shut the bathroom door. But when we looked, no one was standing there.

"I'd ask if you two were decent, but your clothes were out here, so there would be no point," Savas said from outside the door before chucking the heap of said clothing into the bathroom. "You obviously lost track of time, so heads up that Dad's up and cooking dinner, and Vidal just buzzed the gate. Hurry up and get back inside." Savas yanked the bathroom door shut before he departed.

Barden grunted and turned off the taps. Grabbing a towel, he handed it to me, then took another for himself. Once we were dry and dressed, Barden pulled out his phone and sent a text while he said to me, "Change your top. We don't need him to know you are exercising."

Using my Orey powers, I changed into a summer maxi dress with a lightweight cardigan.

Looking me over, Barden kissed me sweetly, smiled, and took my hand. "Come on. We'll use the side door. I told your brother to tell Vidal I'd taken you for a walk as the doctor wanted you to start moving more.

It will also help release lactic acid build up in your muscles after the workout."

"I think that last orgasm released anything built up," I simpered.

Running his hand over his face as he walked us through the gym to the door outside, Barden halted. "I shouldn't have done that. I tried not to work you up too much as there is still a danger of you dislodging a blood clot or something if you exert yourself."

"You worked my ass off like I was training for the Olympics and made me haul you around the room, but you're worried the best orgasm of my life was too much exertion?"

"The effect of weight training is not the same as cardio. There is a reason we don't let you run again yet," Barden defended as we strolled hand in hand through the backyard, still hidden from the house by landscaping.

Stopping, I turned to face Barden, my hand on his chest. "I'm okay. The injury is all superficial now. Just bruising and stiffness. I'm not in danger."

Caressing my jaw, Barden stared into my eyes with utter love and devotion, making me melt a little more for him. "Don't think I don't notice you wince or feel your pain when it lances your head. You're not as healed as you want us to believe."

Opening my mouth, ready to reply, the sound of someone rounding the corner of the fire pit held my tongue.

"Oh, sorry," Vidal stammered. "I didn't mean to interrupt." He cleared his throat as Barden stepped back, removing his hand from my neck as he did.

Dropping my hand from Barden's chest, I turned to see Vidal eyeing the way we'd been standing. It probably looked like Barden was about to kiss me. "It's fine. Barden was just asking about my head and the doctor's concerns," I told Vidal. "He thinks I overexerted myself just now, but I'm sick of being pent up and feeling weak and pathetic."

Assessing Barden, Vidal nodded. "Yeah, I can see both sides to that. I'd hate to feel that way, but I think all of us are just so glad you are alive, Sash. No one wants you to get hurt again."

Taking Barden's elbow when he offered it, we walked to meet Vidal and continued back towards the house. "Trust me, the last thing I want is more pain or another trip to the hospital, but I want some normalcy in my life too. I'm not allowed to run, swim, or ride my bike. Or even if I could, I can't because my injuries prevented the last two. Walks outside are about all I can get away with."

Walks and orgasms, actually. Still, even the latter was a point of contention. Barden was reluctant at first on Monday. I thought I'd convinced him sex was okay. But after the funeral, Barden grew resistant again, and anytime I'd tried to start something, the most he would allow was a gently coerced orgasm with his fingers. I dare say what just happened in the gym resulted from four days of pent-up need on his part.

"Sash?" Barden stopped walking and turned my face to peer into my eyes.

"What?" I tried to step back, but Vidal was there frowning at me.

"Vidal asked how you were today and if you thought you'll be fine to return to school on Monday," Barden explained.

"Oh, sorry." I forced a half-smile for Vidal, but by the way his frown grew more severe, it failed to land.

"I think Barden is right, and you've overdone it today," Vidal sighed. "Which probably answers my question as well. Let's get you inside so you can rest."

Chewing my lip, I followed the guys in and sank onto the lounge, suddenly bone weary. Barden got me water while Vidal took his usual seat to watch and talk to me. When I had the water, Barden told me he should get some work done and left.

I finished the drink and cuddled up with a throw rug, cringing at the ache in my muscles as I got comfortable.

"How's your mum and dad coping?" I asked Vidal. He didn't really like to talk about them or the fallout of Yasmine's death.

"We're all taking it day by day," Vidal answered. "I guess everyone grieves differently."

Exhaling, I closed my eyes. "That's true."

Faintly, I heard Vidal ask about Barden, but I didn't quite catch it as the blackness surrounded me, dragging me into the hellscape of Yasmine stumbling around the blur of her surroundings as that voice asked, *"Did you do it?"*

The Quick Descent

ON FRIDAY MORNING, I was again dressed in my backless top and yoga pants as Barden and I came downstairs for breakfast.

"I gather by that outfit choice that you are unfurling again today?" My mum asked from where she was making herself coffee. "To do some more" – she glanced at my father and frowned – "healing?"

"Actually, Barden's teaching me to fly today." I countered, enjoying how my mum's throat worked as if the bogeyman had just crawled out from under her bed, and she was trying hard to keep a brave face.

Barden's warm palm covered my lower back as he directed me into a chair at the table. "It will also do a little more healing. Hopefully, by the end of the weekend, Sasha will have done enough to be up to going back to school on Monday."

"Is that a good idea with Vidal coming every day?" Mum challenged.

"We'll keep it subtle. Sash will only unfurl once daily; the improvement, while slightly faster than humans, is still acceptable. If you also made a point of having Sash take a tincture to assist with healing the bruising, something with Arnica, then your skills as an alchemist could also provide a plausible excuse," Barden suggested amicably.

Eyeing Barden and my mother, Dad put an omelet in front of me before focusing on Mum. "That sounds like a good solution. What do you think, Delia?"

Mum cleared her throat by swallowing the coffee she'd just taken. "I can do that. I'll have something for you at dinner tonight."

When Mum agreed. Dad gave me a pointed look before putting Barden's breakfast down for him. I noted his omelet came with a side of bacon and sausage. I snatched a piece of crispy bacon and said to Mum, "Thank you."

Joining us at the table, my parents ate with us. Once we'd finished eating. Barden and I stood to go outside. My father slipped his hand over my mother's where she sat beside him, and gave it a tender squeeze. I noted she'd turned her face away and was trying to subtly wipe a tear away. Inhaling deeply, I took Barden's hand for extra support just in case Mum shot me down.

"Would you like to see my wings? Up close?" I offered hesitantly. "They're a little different from Dad's and Sav's. Especially when the sun is out like today."

Blinking wide eyes at me, Mum stood up. "I... I'd like that."

Yeah, she says that now. Just wait until she sees the evidence of the Corvus in our genetics, and Barden points out it's from her bloodline. Then this uneasy truce would be over before it started.

My stomach fell out at the idea of my mum reacting badly, but at the same time, I'd had a few years of her disapproval and disappointment now. As soon as we were outside, I looked for that tingle along my spine, so when Barden gave me the nod, my white downy wings slowly uncurled. I loved the feel of uncurling them one joint at a time—having control and stretching them as I went.

When my wings unfurled the last digit and straightened out, a shiver of release swept up from my thighs, through my belly, ribs, and chest, and then down my arms and over my wings. The feathers all shook as the tremor reached the tips before fading.

Stretching my arms high over my head, I twisted my body one way and another as my wings swept back together and then forward to wrap around me until the tips touched a few times. Then, with a long sigh, my wings folded to hang along my back as I dropped my arms.

"Go—"

Barden's eyes flashed to mine as I started to say that forbidden word.

"—oh that feels so good." Suddenly all happy, I bounced as I turned my back a little and grinned at Barden. "Look! They're not dragging."

Barden's entire face morphed into a full-blown laugh as he grabbed my wrist and tugged me against him. Cupping my face, he kissed me. Before we could get carried away, my dad cleared his throat, reminding us not only that we were under parental guidance restrictions, but with a tilt of his head, Dad also indicated my mother was lurking to get a better look at my feathers.

Pressing my lips together, I met Barden's eyes and suppressed a laugh as I spread my wings wide for inspection. Stepping forward, Barden took my hands, and I automatically matched my breathing to his, calming down. At the same time, I waited for my mother's assessment.

A shiver raced through me when a hand brushed over the soft feathers. "Sorry," my mum apologized, whipping her hand back.

"It's okay. Just sensitive still," I explained.

"That will calm down after some use," Dad assured. "You know, you're almost pure white on top. Just a thin black line in each of your remiges."

"My what?" I balked, trying to look over my shoulder to see what he meant.

Scoffing, Barden took his phone from his pocket and stepped around behind me, snapping a picture. At the same time, Dad ran his finger along the long, sleeker-looking feathers that made up the curve of my wing. "The long spindly bones or feathers that make up the width and spread wide open or narrow to control how you ride the air currents. Think of a plane wing. They're your flaps."

Barden choked as he took a photo of the underside of my wing. My mother asked. "Let's not call them that!" she muttered. Her hand caressed the black line while Barden handed me his phone to see what my wings looked like.

"Wow!" I gawped at the phone. "They are really different from Dad and Sav's. Very plain."

Smirking, Barden stepped closer, tucking a stray strand of my hair behind my ear. "Like with all birds, the male of the species tend to have more elaborate designs and brighter color feathers."

"So, Sav is a pretty boy," I teased as my twin joined us.

Rolling his eyes, Savas flicked his eyes to Barden. "So is your husband. You should hear the Gelus girls go on about his huge wing-span and the shimmer of his feathers."

"Are you saying his size is above average?" I asked, my eyes dropping to Barden's groin. To his credit, Barden merely winked at me.

Groaning, my father covered his face with a hand, then slowly dragged it away. "Let's not compare our wingspans around the girls, okay, boys?"

What they all seemed to miss in our play was how my mother's hand pulled away when Savas used the term 'husband'. It was weird that I could tell the difference between my mother's and father's hands on my feathers. Size, texture, and even strength were picked up by nerve endings, translated, and understood by my brain.

In fact, with every slight shift of air around my wings, a flash of my surroundings as shadows came to me, like my brain was taking infrared snapshots. Telling me the size and proximity of my surroundings. What was weird was that I didn't even recognize that as unusual until I focused on why Mum had stopped touching me and caught a snapshot of her glaring at Barden over my shoulder.

"Why does the black in Sasha's wings shine green in the sunlight?" Mum asked suddenly. "Is that a mating claim or something so Gelus know she's with you?"

"No. It's the Corvus in her DNA."

Mum blinked at Barden, then considered my father. "But neither Savas nor Gannix has that."

There was a pregnant pause. Barden and my mother exchanged a significant look before Barden answered, "Until Gannix was born, his father's bloodline was pure Strigias."

"Oh, so your mother wasn't the first in her family to be lured by a Gelus," Mum snipped. If she even realized that by criticizing Grandma, she was insulting herself and me, it didn't show.

Snapping my wings closed behind me, I stepped by Barden, keeping my back to the woman who gave birth to me. Taking my hand, Barden stopped me from walking away, but gave it a squeeze of support as he sighed and corrected Delila's hypocrisy.

"No, Grandma Tormen is pure Orey. Us Gelus can sense another of our kind once attuned to it. You cross-breed don't really pick up on it when you are young. But later, you realize that those kids you were drawn to hang out with at school or the Orey girl that you couldn't keep away from carry Gelus blood, and that's what attracted you." Barden's eyes drifted between my parents.

"Delila," my dad started.

"Wait. You think I have Gelus blood?" Mum laughed. She was the only one, and I think it took longer than it should have for her to realize she was the only one who found it humorous. "No!" she said sternly. "There is not a chance."

Barden exhaled and looked at my father. Then he stepped back, wrapped an arm around my waist, and pulled me in tight, kissing my cheek as he did.

Taking my mother's hand, Dad kept his voice low as he explained, "Nelly and Gavel sensed it in you when we first met. They didn't say anything, but when Nelly came over the other night to check on Sash, she mentioned she was surprised by your attitude towards Sasha and Barden's relationship, considering you descend from a rather significant Crow bloodline. I told her I didn't think you knew. I was certainly surprised when Barden revealed it to Sasha."

Gritting her teeth, Mum glared at Barden and the rest of us. "Do you think I'm stupid and don't see what this is? How you are trying to manipulate and trick me?" With fury raging in her eyes, Mum turned and stormed inside.

Dad squeezed Barden's shoulder. "Thank you. I'll take it from here." That Dad had organized this with Barden surprised me. Still, as I watched my father chase after my mother, I understood why they'd taken a risk that I would extend the olive branch by inviting her to look closer at my feathers.

They must have come up with this approach on the off-chance.

"Shit," Savas muttered, then yanked his shirt over his head, exposing his fit body to the sun. "Mind if I stay out here and help demonstrate?"

Lifting his shirt over his head, Barden shook his head with a grunt just as his wing bloomed and spread out enough to shadow me from the sun. Unlike my brother, who was shirtless, Barden's defined and ripped torso immediately impacted the state of my panties. We'd had a lovely gentle wake-up together. Barden used his hand to coax me lovingly into the shattered delight of waking. But I longed for him to take me like he did before my injury or in the gym again. Maybe after he saw me fly, he'd get over his worry about my chance of suffering an aneurysm.

"Okay then. What's first?" I asked.

"Wing positions," Barden answered.

For the next hour, Barden would have Savas demonstrate different wing positions for varying maneuvers. Then for an hour after that, Barden and Sav took turns calling out the name of one, and I had to fold or shift my wings to suit. I'm pretty sure neither of these boys stood around for hours in the sun memorizing wing positions before they were allowed to fly.

Finally, after two hours and two big glasses of water, Savas and Barden agreed I was ready. Standing before me, Barden held my hands and stared into my eyes. I could feel his nerves and excitement through the bond as he flapped his wings, once and twice hard, to lift off the ground, then kept them extended to gently drop back to the ground. I'd like to say the float, but it was more of a decelerated fall.

"Your turn, Sash," Barden instructed. "No higher than the garage roof."

Chewing my lip, I spread my wings and drove down with force. The first one was enough to take me well above the roof. I sucked in a breath, and my eyes widened because Barden had to quickly take another two beats to keep up with me.

Right, I'm half the size of Barden. I don't need as much to get off the ground.

Still holding mine, Barden kept his eyes on mine, his calm gripping me through the bond as we slowly returned to the ground. Again, he dropped faster while I almost glided.

Once my feet were steady, I looked from Barden to my brother and back. "Shit! I didn't expect to go that high. Sorry." I stumbled into him and wrapped my arms around his muscular torso, gripping his back just below the join to his wings. A tremor raced through Barden's body at the same time. An avalanche of lust hit me down the bond, flooding my core and making me moan in need.

"Sash, it's fine," Barden assured, quickly grabbing my wrists and moving my hands to his hips as he pushed back on that wantonness. "I should have remembered how quick and light Nelly is and that, as a female, you'd be much swifter than us."

"I'm actually relieved she can lift that high with one beat of her wings," Savas said. "She'll get off the ground and to safety faster than us. It makes me feel better about all of this."

Barden grunted in the affirmative, then stepped back so he was just holding my hands again. "Don't use so much force this time. Let's learn control now. Guess how much you need to use to lift just your feet off the ground. We can try going higher once you can control your liftoff and landing."

So, for the next hour, I learned to judge how much force to put into a beat of my wings to lift to a certain height and how to control my descent and bend my knees to absorb the shock of landing from differing heights. Once Barden and Savas were happy, they allowed me to shoot as high as possible with one beat.

Closing my eyes, I took a deep breath, lifted my wings high, and then, with a quick exhale, swept them down as hard and fast as I could. I opened my eyes and soared into the air, high above the garage roof and the second story, slowing about four stories tall.

The view was spectacular, and I didn't want to drop straight away, so I fluttered my wings on instinct and hovered while Barden and Savas shot up to meet me, taking three beats to my one to do so. When the boys were even with me, they smiled and hovered with me.

"That's awesome," Savas cheered as he clapped his hands. "I'm going to do a lap, then head straight to my room. Take my shirt in for me?" Then he tilted to the side, turned, and flew away, climbing higher in a spiral as he did.

Pride poured down my bond with Barden, a trickle of lust behind it as he shifted closer. "Concentrate and control the descent," he murmured. "We're going to fall together, so account for my weight in the descent." His hands cupped my jaw, and then his mouth was on mine.

My wings stopped fluttering, but I kept them wide and splayed to act like a parachute. I could also feel how Barden was pulling me forward and down faster. Shifting my body mid-air, I wrapped my thighs around his waist, hooked under his arms to grab his shoulders, and lifted my wings a little higher to counteract the drag.

Pulling back, Barden stared at me as he felt my wings bounce us up. As we landed, Barden bent his knees to absorb the impact, and as he straightened, his hands shifted to my butt to hold me.

High on the adrenaline of my first technical flight, I ran my hand across Barden's wing and clung to him. He cursed as he stared into my eyes, that avalanche of desire sweeping through me from him. "Furl," he growled as he tucked his wings away, and I did the same.

Keeping hold of me, Barden snatched up his and Savas' shirts and strode straight for the back door to the gym. Five seconds after we got inside, my leggings were torn and on the floor, and my panties were shoved aside. Barden was slamming me into the wall as he thrust inside me, and there was nothing slow or gentle about how he fucked me. Three times.

Then he took me upstairs and made love to me as we showered before we curled into my bed together so he could sleep before his Orey shift tonight.

Heaven. I was in heaven.

Later that evening, as I sat eating dinner, Vidal looked me over. "You're looking a lot better today, Sash."

"I feel better. Mum made me a tincture, and I slept well this afternoon." Followed by a vigorous wake-up from Barden. The sum of all his lust frenzy today left me sore but sated.

"What sort of tincture?" Vidal asked.

"It had Arnica and other stuff good for bruising and muscle soreness," Dad answered. "Sash couldn't have it until now because of the chance of a blood clot or brain bleed, but the doctor feels that she's out of the woods now, and it's just a matter of the hematomas breaking down. Now that she can take this tincture, we should see Sash improve much faster and maybe even be okay to go to school next week."

As if to make a show of it, Dad put a small dropper bottle on the table in front of me. "Your mum said to have another mil at dinner and then again before bed. Tomorrow onwards will just be twice a day."

Unscrewing the lid, I filled the dropper and deposited the oil under my tongue for faster absorption.

"So, you'll be at school on Monday?" Vidal asked.

"No, I have a follow-up medical appointment on Monday, but if the scans come back clear from this week, I should be right to go back on Tuesday. I just have to figure out transport until I can ride my bike again."

"I can drive you up," Dad offered.

"No, Dad. You'll be tired on Tuesday morning, and I don't want to worry about you crashing on the way home again," I argued.

"What about your mum? Didn't she used to take you?" Vidal asked.

"Delila's got a big case in the city this week and is expecting lots of late nights, so she'll be staying in town rather than driving home only to get a few hours of sleep before having to go back again," Dad explained.

It was a good enough excuse and covered the real reason she wasn't coming home. Me.

"My dad will be out of town for work this week," Barden said, his voice slow and low, like the energy to speak was offensive. He was like that around the other Orey. "I'll use his car, take you to and from school until you return to riding."

"Can't you drive, Sasha?" Vidal asked, a growl almost in his voice. "Maybe you could just lend Sasha your dad's car?"

"I'm not cleared to drive either," I murmured, but Vidal heard me. The table fell quiet for a moment. "I'd like that, Barden, if you're okay with it, Dad?"

Give me a damn Oscar! Because I kept a straight face, managed to pull off a hint of blush as I spoke to Barden, and somehow made it a little more when Dad said he was happy with Barden taking me to and from school.

The way Vidal looked from me to Barden and the way his fists clenched around his cutlery when Barden sat there staring at me like he had the last few years told me he bought the act of our emerging relationship, hook, line, and sinker. And for some reason, which surprised me because none of the Orey boys had shown interest in me before, Vidal hated it. I just couldn't fathom what had changed.

The Selus You Know

WRAPPED up in Barden was my bliss. Staring up at the ceiling while he kissed my collarbones and we both caught our breaths, I decided this was my heaven, right here and now.

Gently, Barden released my legs until I took my weight and stood still, leaning on the shower wall for support. Caressing my jaw, Barden met my eyes and smiled. "We should finish getting ready."

Sighing, I grabbed my body buff. "Okay. Though, I'd much rather stay with you all day than go to school."

Shampooing his hair, Barden smirked. "There are only a few weeks left of school, then we'll have the entire summer to ourselves."

"And we'll go back to living at your place?" I asked hesitantly. I loved the freedom of living with Barden, but I missed my brother and Dad at the same time.

Rinsing his hair, Barden wiped his face with his hands, then leaned in to kiss my lips. Pure love and devotion filtered down the bond, relaxing my tense muscles. "Like before. You'll come home while I work," Barden murmured to my lips. "I know you like being here, but I like it when you don't have to try and be quiet."

Since the last fuck-frenzy after my first flight, Barden hadn't held back with me. It meant the last three days had been a whirlwind of

281

passion between flying lessons and studying while Barden slept off his work shifts.

"And," Barden began teasingly as he lifted me to his waist again. "If there are no issues with your first night flight tonight, there is no reason we can't sleep at my place most nights, and you can flit across the canyon every morning to have breakfast with your family."

So far, I'd only been allowed to soar above our property due to the risk of being seen by Vestigials. However, tonight would be my first time flying after dark. Savas and Barden were going to pass the river with me. I bit my lip as Barden opened me to him, stretching me in the most delicious way.

"We're going to be late," I moaned.

Slipping a hand between us, Barden found my go button. "Nah, I know how to make you sing quickly." And he did.

"Sasha," Elisha called as I grabbed the stuff I needed for my following classes from my locker. As I turned to say hello, her weight impacted me and threw me back against the locker as she barreled into me with a hug, surprising the hell out of me. I cringed at the memory.

"Hey, Elisha," I muttered against her shoulder.

"Gosh, I'm so glad you're okay. Simon told me what happened to Yasmin and you. Savas updated us on your recovery but wouldn't let us come visit." Pulling back, Elisha held my shoulders as she assessed me. "Are you okay? Your pupils are blown out. You're not scared of me, are you?"

Clearing my throat. I checked around us and realized my breathing was a little off. My heart was pounding in my chest.

"Sasha?" Elisha whispered my name, her hands dropping to take mine to comfort me.

Blinking several times, I cleared the river, and that wing slammed into me from my mind and focused back on the school hall and the weird looks I was getting from some of the other students. Clearing my throat, I concentrated on Elisha. "Sorry. You sort of surprised me."

"Shit," Elisha backed up a step. "I'm sorry. Do you need to answer your phone?"

Frowning, I realized my phone was vibrating in my pocket. Taking it out, I answered the call from Barden. "Hey."

"What happened?" Barden asked straight away.

"Um, nothing... I just got surprised, and it caused a flashback, that's all. I'm okay."

Hearing a breath down the line, Barden murmured, "She's okay" to someone on his end, then refocused on me. "Are you sure you're ready to be back? You could stay home and just come in for the finals."

This had been a constant discussion since the doctors yesterday. I'd been cleared to return to school but advised I should take more time for the psychological trauma. Dad had told Barden and Savas when they got home yesterday, which led to the option to take more time being raised every time my return today came up, including at breakfast again this morning.

Exhaling in annoyance, I lowered my face. "I'm fine. I'll meet you after school." I hung up before Barden could argue with me. Taking a breath, I turned to face Elisha again. "Sorry."

Face softening, Elisha cupped my bicep. "You have nothing to apologize for. Trauma is a bitch. I should have been more careful."

Elisha sounded mature beyond her years in that statement. It was so unlike the ditsy cheerleader she usually portrayed for a moment. I wondered if, like Barden, she was older than she seemed. But then I remembered Elisha and her brother in elementary school with Savas and me and shook the thought away. "I should get to class," I excused myself as the bell rang.

"Of course. Sit with us at lunch today. We can chat then," Elisha said as she linked her arm with mine and walked me to my classroom door.

By lunch, I was exhausted. Instead of going to the cafeteria, I went to the nurse's clinic and begged to use one of the bays to nap. The school knew about the incident and my resulting hospitalization, so the nurse didn't hesitate to let me second a recliner. I stuck my earphones in and all but passed out.

All our classes for the next two weeks were exam prep or in-class assessments. While everyone else wasn't worried about me missing them, I knew many hints were given in these classes, and attending was better.

Since I didn't even know what I wanted to do for my career yet, getting good grades was imperative to ensure that I had the best chance of getting into it when I did figure it out. So, if it meant spending my lunch break in the clinic sleeping to push through each day, I would.

"What happened at lunch?" Elisha asked as we both reached our lockers at the end of the school day.

"I was about to fall over, so I spent lunch napping in the clinic. Sorry."

Eyeing the bruising at my temple, Elisha swallowed with difficulty. "It was pretty bad, huh?"

Closing my locker, I huffed. "Yeah, it was pretty bad. I'll see you tomorrow."

As I went to walk away, Elisha grabbed my wrist. "Can we talk? Like, walk to the Milkbar and get shakes or something? I know you're probably exhausted, but I think it's time we talked."

Frowning, I took out my phone and checked for messages from Barden. There weren't any, so I sent him one.

ME.

> Is it cool if you get me from the Milkbar?
> Elisha wants a chat.

BARDEN.

> Sure. I'll run some errands to give you two
> some time.

"Looks like I have some time until my lift home," I told Elisha. "Let's go."

Hoisting our bags, we headed out the back exit to wander down the road. "Is your mum picking you up?" Elisha asked.

"No. Mum is stuck in the city on a big case. So, Barden is my ride to school and home each day."

"You two make a cute couple. How Barden looked at you at the dance workshop got us all a little jealous that you're the one who caught his eye. But now that you're mated, it makes sense why that was," Elisha sighed dreamily.

"Wait, what?" I stopped walking and stared at Elisha.

She smiled and tilted her head to keep walking. "I didn't think you knew. I told Sophie that I was sure you didn't. You were always careful not to mention the Orey or Gelus to us."

When my eyes widened, and I struggled to keep my feet under me, Elisha caught and steadied me to prevent me from stumbling. "You're—"

"Gelus? Yes."

"But we grew up together. We're the same age, and Barden told me Savas and I are the youngest for a while."

The color that filled Elisha's cheeks could have been an embarrassment for getting caught in a lie, but I think it was more than that.

"Gelus babies raised in the Underworld grow slower than topside. It's why a lot of families come here to raise their young. The faster we mature, the faster we can get working and the less danger we are in. Our parents didn't want to live in the Vestigial world, but a Baba Yaga found their nest. They barely managed to save us, so they decided to move here so we would grow up faster," Elisha explained. "It's why our birthday party was unsupervised. We're a bit older than eighteen."

"How much older?" I asked, trying to quantify all those years of knowing her.

Elisha smiled. "Simon and I turned twenty-eight at that last party."

My breath whooshed from my lungs. My eyes were wide as I made the connections. Elisha's iris could change from crystal blue to striated with grey lines. "So, Darina is Gelus as well?" I already knew Sophie was thanks to Barden.

"And Melina, and..." Elisha proceeded to list off a handful of other students in our year. It took me a moment to process she'd named all the girls in the cheer squad.

"Wait, so Mia is the only non-Gelus on the squad?"

"Yes!" Elisha groaned. "None of us cared until she became captain, and her grudge towards our kind became obvious. But she made hard and fast friends with you, so we figured she wasn't so bad. Most of the Orey here are chill about us. They don't want us hanging around them, but they never made trouble with us either. Until Sophie."

"How do you know it was Orey?"

"The stench of magic was still on her at the viewing," Elisha explained.

We walked silently for a moment, then reached the Milkbar and went inside. On autopilot, I just sat at my usual booth at the back. It wasn't until I looked up expecting to see Elisha opposite me that I noticed Falco sitting there, chewing a bite he'd just taken of his burger.

Elisha was covering her mouth, laughing as Falco gave me a humored grin. "Sorry, I didn't realize—" I tried apologizing and getting up, but Falco gestured I stay, and Elisha sat beside him.

"You're fine, Sasha. How's the head?" Falco asked.

"It was a terrible hit," Elisha answered. "He nearly killed her."

My eyes widened as Falco's weird blue-black eyes connected with the other Gelus I knew. All of their gazes almost seemed predatory. The black ring around his pupil bled out through various hues of grey until his eyes had an almost white feathering right before the outer edge of the iris with swirls of blue in between. It'd been right in front of me all this time, but because my dad, Savas, Barden, and I had weird eyes, I'd never made the connection.

Falco frowned. "It wasn't intentional, Sasha. He was angry and misjudged his landing."

"Who did?" I asked, interested that they knew who hit me. Did that mean they knew who pushed Yasmine to her death?

Shaking his head, Falco made a hand gesture to say it didn't matter. "The point is, it was an accident. He's already had to answer to Lorka for it." Falco turned his attention to Elisha. "How'd she take it?"

Elisha's eyes were focused on me. "Still processing it. We discussed Sophie's murder and how we knew it was Orey."

"The stench of magic," Falco muttered, then took another bite of his burger.

"You know, you were one of our suspects until the funeral," Elisha told me.

"Me?" I asked, insulted.

"You found her," Falco said. "It seemed convenient to some. I personally never considered you a prospect. The way you reacted at the funeral confirmed it for everyone. Though, Barden had already told us you were badly shaken by it."

"The funeral?" When I saw her death.

'Wingless Bitch!'

"You touched Sophie and looked horrified. We figured you sensed the magic on her and realized one of the Orey killed her. How you looked like you'd seen a ghost as you walked away pretty much confirmed your innocence to all of us. That the Orey had recently turned on you too..." Elisha let her words fall away. "Are you okay? You went really pale."

Swallowing the horror of Sophie's last memory, I cleared my throat. "I'm still having nightmares about her. Finding her. Sophie and Yasmine."

"Vivid?" Elisha asked. When I nodded, Elisha licked her lips and went to talk again, but Falco cut her off.

"Don't. Sasha can offer you no justice. Let her be."

Elisha glared at Falco. "You presume too much."

"She is Strigias, the watchers. They do not gossip or enjoy idle assumptions," Falco lectured Elisha.

"Oh, I assume stuff all the time, and while we are on the topic, I'm assuming neither of you is Corvus or Strigias?" I inquired.

Falco pointed to Elisha. "Elisha is Aguilas, and I'm Peregrinus. Corvus and Strigias are actually on the small population side of things. The Assions are the only Corvus in the area. Just like, until you moved here, Lorka was the only Strigias. Even then, none of us picked you as his kin."

Finishing his drink, Falco nudged Elisha to let him out of the booth. "I should get back to work. If your mate catches me 'lurking' around you again, he'll drag me into the Underworld and beat me to a pulp." Giving me a wink, Falco disappeared into the kitchen, leaving me stunned and unsure what to say.

"Don't worry," Elisha chuckled. "Gelus males won't touch a girl once they know she's mated. Once Barden put Falco on notice, his interest in you shifted to friends only."

"Put him on notice? Did Barden bully Falco?" I worried.

Elisha shrugged. "Probably just told him he didn't like him flirting with you. They're good friends, so don't stress. Barden would have told Falco you mated, and everything would have been fine again."

"Wait. So, everyone knows I'm with Barden."

"The Gelus close to you do. Why? Don't the Orey?"

When I shook my head slowly, Elisha gaped a little like a fish, then double-blinked. "But you're going to formal together?"

"Yeah, but the only other Orey male still at school is my brother, so they assumed it was just convenient. We are slowly making it obvious that something is blooming between us. Still, the Orey outside my immediate family aren't aware yet."

"Huh." Elisha just stared at me for a minute.

The bell on the door rang, and Barden strode in, still in his uniform, looking as gorgeous as he did naked in my bed.

"Sorry it took so long. You ready?" he asked.

"Yeah." I grabbed my gear and slid out of the booth, returning my attention to Elisha. "I'll see you tomorrow."

As we moved down the street to the car, Barden eyed me. "She told you."

"Yes."

"You okay?"

I considered his question and asked one of my own. "Why do you all know I'm Gelus, but l can't pick them?"

Stopping at the door to the car, Barden faced me. "I think your perception of your own kind was disrupted by not knowing Gelus existed and that they differed from Vestigials." Caressing my cheek, Barden looked into my eyes. "Even once you knew, it didn't occur to you to suspect those differences you perceive were something you should notice. Now that it's been pointed out, I hope you'll assess those around you a bit differently."

"Should I?" I asked.

Barden dropped his hand. "Yes, Sash, you should." Opening the car door, Barden stepped back. "Let's get you home. You look exhausted."

The Hunting Party

"ARE YOU GOING TO BE OKAY?" Barden checked for the umpteenth time as he pulled his jacket on.

"This is not my first time being home alone," I assured him as I rose on my toes and kissed his lips.

Barden caught me with an arm around my waist, my fingers curling into the leather of his jacket while he made the kiss more. A throat cleared behind us, and I pulled back as Dad and Savas moved to their bikes in the garage.

"Your mum shouldn't be too late," Dad told me as he settled on his motorcycle.

"It's fine. I'm going to study and then watch a movie or something." There was plenty of revision from today to keep me busy until I couldn't stay awake any longer.

With a thumb brush over my cheek, Barden threw a leg over, pulled on his helmet, and pressed the button to start his bike. The garage door closed as my three most important men rode down the driveway to do their Friday night shift with the Orey teams.

Sighing, I returned to the dining room and the pile of revisions. Next week was the final week of attending classes, with the formal on Saturday evening. Then we'd get a week of home study before the exams started. Three different letters of early offers arrived in the mail this week. All of them were my preferences, and all three are far from home.

At the beginning of the school year, I would have been thrilled to get these offers and be starting my argument with my parents to let me traipse across the country to attend them. Now, they filled me with anxiety, because leaving Barden behind for three or more years felt like an impossible task.

After four hours of study, I closed my books and stretched. Going to the fridge, I refilled my water glass and drank it all. I considered the television as I stood in the kitchen. Still, my eyes kept being drawn to the darkness of our backyard.

Setting the glass down, I ran upstairs and changed into my flight training outfit. A quick practice flight around the property wouldn't hurt. My flying improved over the week, with Barden and Savas practicing maneuvers with me nightly. Double bonus, my bruises were now an icky yellow-brown instead of a blue-black-purple.

Instead of going into the backyard to take off, which would get picked up by the cameras, I stepped out onto my balcony. Getting up on the table, I put one foot on the railing and then unfurled my wings slowly to avoid hitting the wall. Opening my feathered limbs out wide, I put the weight into my forward foot, then leaned with my body. As I fell, my feathers caught the wind, and I smiled as I was swept away, gliding over the front gardens and the property boundary.

I didn't mean to leave our land; I was there one moment and over the river the next. Knowing that Barden would be unhappy with me crossing the river alone, I turned and headed back the way I came, flapping to gain height so I could soar high over the house and the hillside behind it. Circling the property a couple of times increased my confidence. Checking the time on my smartwatch, I decided to fly the river like I had every night with the boys this week.

Sweeping across the apex of the ridge behind our house, I kept an eye on my surroundings, staying low to the treetops as I flew north. Approaching the bridge to the city, I swooped down over the national park into the canyon. I turned again to pass along the river, though I kept my height at the ridge line to avoid being seen and recognized. It was a relatively quick flight considering how long it took to run. I landed on my balcony feeling refreshed but tired.

Making my way downstairs, I went to the gym to grab an electrolyte drink. Flying was just as great a workout as the runs I did in the morning — or I would get back to doing soon. I found that having a sports drink instead of water replenished me faster than just water. Barden told me he always craved sugar after a long flight, and most Gelus drank a honey and brown sugar mixture in tonic water after long flights or battles in the Underworld.

Reentering the house, I was walking through the glass-walled annex that joined the gym to the house when a sense of being watched hit me. Frowning, I looked out into the yard, wondering if it was a wild animal, but if something was near the house, it would have set the sensor lights off. So I'd either suddenly become paranoid, or my stalker was standing just out of range in the pitch dark.

Chewing my lip, I quickly went to my dad's study. Almost immediately, my phone rang. "Sash, what's wrong?" Barden asked quietly.

"It could be nothing—"

"I can feel your fear. What is it?"

"I think someone is watching me from the backyard. Standing just out of range of the sensors."

Voice muffled, Barden said to someone else, "Check your cameras for the backyard."

"What's wrong?" Savas asked back.

"You have an unannounced visitor."

The reason my dad's office was soundproof also made it the safest room in the house. The door was reinforced, and there were no windows. Dad's office also contained a security system.

"Sash, Savas is going to deal with it. Just stay inside. He'll let you know when he's checked it out," Barden assured. "I'll stay on the line."

"The others will wonder!"

"We're separated, watching different areas tonight. We'll call only if a backup is needed."

"What? Teams are meant to stay together."

Barden sighed. "Things are tense, and Athur pushed all your brother's buttons tonight."

"Athur's making trouble?"

"He is."

I chewed my lip while I opened the closet, turned on the monitor, and clicked to bring up the cameras for the backyard. Our security system had night vision, so you could see without the light turning on, potentially alerting anyone to them being caught before they entered the sensor field.

I saw a man staring at the house on the monitor halfway up the yard. A shiver raced down my spine. "Sash?" Barden worried.

"I could feel him out there. Even though I couldn't see him, I knew someone was out there watching me," I murmured.

"You can see him?"

"On the cameras. I'm in Dad's office." As I watched, two other men came to stand with the first. "Barden, he's not alone. There are at least two others."

Barden cursed, and then I could hear tapping on the phone screen. "Sasha, I have to hang up. Stay where you are; we'll be there soon." The line went dead before I could reply.

Setting my phone down, I stayed in the closet watching the monitors. The three men showing gray and white against the darkness stood talking and looking around. They didn't make a move toward the house and didn't seem interested in coming in here, but I was still nervous.

Barden had said the teams had split. What if the Orey decided to end what Mia tried to start with me back at the Execrable attack? They couldn't get through the gates without setting off the security system, but they could have hiked from the national park and come down from the mountain. There was a gate at the back of the yard, but we rarely locked it, and the boys knew it.

As I watched, one of the men left the group and walked further back on the property. Shortly after, a man fell out of the sky and landed perfectly before them. I knew it was my twin from his build before the night vision brought him into focus. Words were exchanged, Savas taking a defensive posture immediately.

One of the other men held up his hand, trying to placate Savas, then gestured toward the man who stood with his arms folded, watching the house. As if the wind had changed, Savas stepped back, his tension shifting from attack to uncertainty.

Two more bodies landed next to my brother. My Dad and Barden. My mate instantly stepped between the stranger and my dad, holding his hands up to prevent Dad from attacking. Savas put his hand on Dad's shoulder—reassuring or holding him back, I wasn't sure.

Nervousness and worry flooded the bond with Barden as whatever was happening out there had him on edge while heated words were exchanged. Eventually, another one of the strangers left, and Barden stepped out from between the man still staring at the house and my kin. The tension in Barden was still pretty high, but I understood there was no danger now.

Grabbing my phone, I headed out to the kitchen, staying in the darkness, and stepped around behind the bench to duck and hide quickly if needed. The fact there wasn't a sudden storm pouring down told me whatever was happening hadn't shaken my brother too much.

I only had to wait a few more minutes before the sensor lights triggered, and Barden and Savas were approaching the house while they talked. Barden was relaxed now, but the bond still had a thread of concern. Getting to the kitchen's glass doors, Savas rapped his knuckles against them, probably aware I was watching them.

Going to the door, I unlocked it, and they stepped inside. "Where's Dad?"

"He had to get back to his team," Savas answered. "Are you okay?"

"Yes. Why?"

"You went flying on your own?" he asked, his eyes taking in my outfit and realizing he didn't need to ask that.

"Just around the property, up the range, and down the river like we've been doing," I assured. "I was unsettled and thought it would help wear me out for sleep."

Savas looked towards the garage. "Is mum in bed?"

Swallowing, I stepped away. "Mum didn't come home." Going to the bin, I put my sports drink bottle into the recycling, not wanting to see the accusation of it being my fault on my brother's face. "Who was out there?"

"Our grandfather and Falco," Savas answered, glancing quickly to

Barden as if he wouldn't be happy about Falco's presence. I could have told Savas there wasn't an ounce of jealousy in Barden over this. He was nervous but resigned. "They apparently saw you flying alone and followed you to keep you safe."

"They won't hurt your sister," Barden grumbled in a way that said it wasn't the first time he'd told Savas this. "Situation what it is, they were doing us a favor."

"What do you mean by that?" I asked.

Clearing his throat, Savas went to the fridge and got a glass of juice, pouring one for Barden. "They know we are all on patrol on a Friday night. That you are here unprotected."

"That hasn't been an issue before," I challenged.

Savas exchanged a look with Barden. Barden nodded, causing Savas to sigh. "It wasn't a problem when the Orey thought you were like mum and that you would marry Vidal. That changed after the Execrable attack. Our grandfather has been protecting you from a distance since the attack. Tonight, Hawk and Falco saw your wings. They patrolled for Lorka, making sure no Orey came to the house while we were out, and they saw you flying. That's what the mother's meeting in the yard was about. They know Mia has already targeted you. Falco worried if the Orey found out you are Gelus through and through, whoever killed Sophie would come for you next."

Whoa! There was a lot to unpack from that. First off, "I was meant to marry Vidal?"

Savas rubbed his temple. "Mum lined you up when we were ten. None of the families would consider me for their daughters once they knew I had wings, but you were Orey. We all thought that."

Blinking at my brother, I looked from him to Barden. "And you both knew this? That I was promised?"

Barden grunted, not looking happy about it despite confirming it. Savas shrugged a shoulder. I slumped against the pantry cupboard. "Are there any other secrets I should know? You have wings, we're Gelus, Barden's my soul-mate, I was in an arranged marriage. Anything else kind of big that you think I should know already?"

Savas closed his eyes. "Vidal still thinks you'll be married. It's why he's been coming around, but he's caught onto the growing relationship between you and Barden. He's not happy. Not with Barden, anyway. It shouldn't have surprised him. Barden never hid why he was here, but I don't think Vidal considered him competition until now."

The side of Barden's mouth pulled up in a smirk as he leaned back against the meals table and crossed his arms. He knew the truth. There never was any competition. It was Barden from the moment I met him. Pointing the finger at my mate, I scowled, "That smugness is not attractive."

The sarcastic grunt Barden released was accompanied by a sexy-AF wink calling bullshit on my lecture. *Damn, if my brother wasn't here right now...*

Focusing on Savas to keep distracted from my husband's appeal, I glanced to the dark yard. "You and Dad met Lorka tonight."

My brother considered me. "You've met him?"

Shit! I'd forgotten he didn't know. "Yeah. Just once, and only briefly. I thought he was a Dad at first glance."

"When? And why didn't you tell us?" Savas was standing straighter now. Barden gave me a look, but without it, I could feel the warning growl down the bond.

"You mean like you told me you had wings?" I scoffed back at my twin. Exhaling my annoyance, I met Savas's eyes and remembered Mum was why he kept it secret from me all those years. "I told Dad," I admitted. "He asked me to keep it quiet for now. He was upset that Lorka had never sought him out."

Messing his hair, Savas huffed. "Yeah, he said as much tonight."

"What happened?" I pressed, wanting to know.

"Dad told him if he wanted to be part of our lives and get to know us, he was more than welcome to buzz the gate and join us for breakfast in the morning. Otherwise, he should get lost and leave you alone."

Ouch! That was direct. "What did Lorka say?"

The side of Savas's mouth twitched with a hint of humor. "He said he looked forward to meeting us all in the morning."

The Legacy

BACON SIZZLED IN ONE PAN, mini pancakes bubbled in a second, and eggs scrambled with cheese and cream cooked in the last. The toaster popped with more toast. Flipping the pancakes, I then buttered the toast and set more to cook before. Transferring everything but the eggs to a tray, I put it all in the oven to keep warm, then poured five large glasses of juice and made coffee.

The doorbell rang.

Pausing, I looked at the empty table and chewed my lip. Going to the intercom, I saw the man who could have been my dad, except for a few minor differences. While my dad's eyes were lavender fading to grey like mine and Savas's, Lorka's were entirely lavender with dark gray striations. His cheekbones were more angular than Dad's, and his lips were thinner. That was about all the difference. Even the age difference wasn't evident. They could have been twins.

"Just a minute," I answered, then went to the front door. My phone rang just as I reached it. "Morning," I greeted Barden. "Everything is fine."

"Your anxiety says differently," Barden replied.

Of course, I was anxious. A big-deal Gelus was at my door, and I was home alone. I was only willing to answer because he'd saved me.

"Lorka just arrived. He's fine to let in, right?"

A pulse of concern came throughout the bond. "Yes."

"Are you sure? Because that's not what the bond is saying."

"Lorka won't hurt you. We're on our way home now. You won't be alone too long."

Relieved by that news, I put my handle on the door. "Okay. I'll see you soon. I love you."

"Love you too, Sash."

Hanging up, I swung the door wide and met my grandfather's eyes. "Lorka, right?"

The smile he gave me didn't quite reach his eyes. "Melisanda told you about me, I gather?"

"She did." Stepping back, I let the man who would have been my grandfather into our home, shut the door, and led the way to the kitchen. "She told me the truth of what happened. That she caved to the pressure of her family and ended things with you, only to discover she was pregnant with Dad. When his wings unfurled at age five, she left and came looking for you, and you told her you wanted nothing to do with her."

"She never mentioned your father in her messages," Lorka defended.

Entering the kitchen, I turned to look at him. "And you didn't love her enough to meet her and discover why she chased you across the country."

The striations in Lorka's eyes widened and spun. I shifted my gaze before they made me dizzy. "It was more complicated than that," Lorka grumbled.

"Not really. Coffee?" Before Lorka could argue, I poured the first coffee pod, then set a second to run while I took it to the table and set the cream and sugar down with it. "You should know my father thinks you left his mother behind when she went to university. He doesn't know that she told you to go."

Lorka inhaled as he sat taller, his entire demeanor tensing as he realized my father didn't have the whole story and might turn hostile toward him.

Returning to the coffee machine, I switched the pod to a hot chocolate to pour into the same cup, poured coconut milk into the steamer, and turned it on.

"You don't have questions for me?" Lorka asked.

Checking on the eggs, the heat was on low and the lid on, but I gave them a stir to ensure they didn't burn. "I'd like to know why you stalked me," I answered. Putting the lid back on the eggs, I looked Lorka's way.

Stirring his coffee, Lorka watched me. "Yes."

Pouring the milk into my mocha, I joined him at the table. "Kind of pervy, watching us like that. Is that why you were stalking me? Because you're a perv?"

The side of Lorka's mouth turned up. "No, I wasn't perving. I've checked in on your family over the years since your father first moved you out here. Like everyone else, I thought you took after your mother, but then word of the Execrable attack got back to me. That the Tormen girl called lightning, fire, and water all within a few minutes. No Orey witch has that much power or that many elements.

"Then I heard something more disturbing from that night. That one of the Orey tried to kill you and make it look like an accident. I started 'stalking' you to protect you. Your family couldn't see the danger. Barden did. He worried."

"Barden told you about the attack?"

"He did. Any Gelus in this area reports to me. Barden came to me when he first arrived, told me he'd tracked his mate to this area and would stay until securing her."

"Did he tell you it was me?"

"No. I didn't care who she was until I saw you together up the mountain here. Before that, I'd assumed Barden's involvement with your family was as your brother's friend."

"Why did you come to his house and spy on us?"

Setting the spoon on the spoon holder, Lorka frowned, sat back, and sipped his coffee. "You make a good brew," he complimented before taking another sip and setting the cup down. "I'm not sure what you mean."

"The morning Yasmine was killed. When I got hit," I clarified.

The creases in Lorka's forehead deepened as he assessed me, a slight shake of his head. "What those witches said to you in the Milkbar got back to me, and I'd asked an inquisitor to look into it. That morning, I was going to tell Barden to warn you that the Gelus handling things would want to talk to you. Since you were unaware of the Gelus you had surrounded yourself with, the inquisitor may not take the normal approach. But I never got to the house because I heard that poor girl scream and worried it was you."

Tensing, I wondered what I saw outside Barden's bedroom that morning, if not Lorka.

Sitting forward, Lorka reached across the table. "Your injuries were an accident. My inquisitor was following you, trying to find a way to approach you when your friend fell. Knowing the danger, he intended to get you out of there, but as he landed, he slipped on the moss and struck you instead. I wasn't aware of his motives. I was heading to your house, heard the scream, and by the time I caught sight of you, all I saw was him diving towards you and you falling. I assumed he attacked you —but later, on asking, I realized it was all an accident. It didn't change that you nearly died as a result. Barden was livid." Patting my hand, Lorka sat back.

"How can you be sure he wasn't lying?" I asked.

The side of Lorka's mouth twitched. "Your father's ability to sense a falsehood is genetic. My family has carried that ability for many centuries. I wouldn't be surprised if your brother has it too."

Well, damn. That's why Barden couldn't hide what happened the night of the Execrable attack from him. "That would explain a lot." I huffed. Lorka chuckled. "Does your inquisitor still need to talk to me?"

"Ah," Lorka said, then grimaced. "As I said, Barden was livid. My inquisitor is lying low right now. Despite the proof it was an accident, he nearly killed you, and your husband and family... needed an outlet for their rage."

Frowning, I studied Lorka, then sat back, my mouth falling open. "They attacked him? Even knowing it was an accident?"

"It was before I was able to investigate. Your father and brother did pull Barden off him once they realized the truth of his words, but understandably, he's kept his distance." Cocking his head, Lorka lifted a brow. "Speaking of your family..."

The garage door opened, and the three important men in my life came in. They looked tired, and my brother and father looked wary of seeing Lorka at the table with me.

Getting up, I started serving breakfast. Dad joined me in the kitchen. "You okay?"

"Yes. The coffee should be ready." Where I liked my pods, the guys preferred drip. Dropping a kiss on my head, Dad took the coffee pot to the table while Barden came to help me with the plates.

"Morning," he whispered to my ear, pressing against my back as his arms wrapped around me. "Good talk, so far?"

"So far," I answered. "You beat the guy who hurt me?"

Cursing under his breath, Barden grunted a resigned confirmation. He didn't excuse his actions or make any show of regret. I couldn't be sure if I loved him for it or was a little unsettled by it. That Barden loved me enough to do that. Exhaling, I shook my head and used my ass to bump him away. "Here, take these." I handed him two plates, then put one in the crook of my elbow and one in each hand so I could carry the other three.

"If you ever need a job, Hawk will hire you," Lorka teased as I set a plate before him.

"Not the career path I'm after," I answered.

"I figured," Lorka chuckled. "I heard you are very driven. So what are you planning to study next year?"

Everyone looked my way, but I ignored them and sat beside Barden. "Not law." I started eating, cutting off that conversation. Barden placed his hand on my thigh and gave it a gentle squeeze. He knew I was torn. Barden probably knew about the offers, too, even though I hadn't mentioned them. Still, I doubt it was a topic he wanted to raise.

Considering me with his eyebrow cocked, Lorka looked to Savas. "And what about you, Savas?"

"I have a few offers," Savas answered between mouthfuls.

That raised Lorka's second brow. "I guess that's the problem with endless possibility, too much choice."

"Sasha and Savas aren't restricted by a Vestigial lifetime. They have the time to try everything," Barden defended our lack of future direction. "With everything that's happened this year, the twins now have opportunities they never considered."

Lorka's gaze came back to me. "I guess so." Turning his focus to my father, Lorka took a breath. "I understand you believe I abandoned your mother. I expect you to seek the truth from her for her part, but you should know Melisanda told me to go. She chose her Orey family over me when she left for university. It wasn't easy for her. I knew she loved me, but the sneaking around and knowing we would never be accepted made up her mind. I never knew you existed until you moved here with your young family."

To give my father credit, he listened and made no accusations. "Why didn't you introduce yourself back then?"

"Three reasons. First, you obviously didn't know I was here, and I wasn't sure, after twenty years, that you would want to know me. Even if your mother told you the truth about why I left her behind, I doubted she lied about my rejecting her pleas to speak to me five years later. The second was that you came here with an Orey wife and integrated with the Orey without trying to build connections with the Gelus. That spoke volumes about who you identify with and who you want your children to be around. I suspected I wouldn't be very welcome by you, and definitely not your wife."

Tapping his coffee mug with a finger, Dad ground his jaw. "The third?"

Considering us, Lorka met Barden's gaze for a moment, then cleared his throat, dropping his eyes to his coffee. "The third is that I'm not your average Gelus, and the revelation that I was involved with an Orey witch and had a child and grandchild of questionable lineage would have caused unnecessary drama. Considering the angst between you and your wife when you moved here, I decided more drama was the last thing you needed. As time passed, finding a reason why we should meet became harder."

Meeting my father's eyes, Lorka appeared humble. "I'm sorry it took the danger to your daughter for me to make myself known."

Picking up his mug, Dad took a big drink, then set it down. "Me too. I would have liked to have known you. I had a thousand questions about who I was. Questions that Barden ended up answering for both Savas and me in your absence. Still, I would like that opportunity now, if you're willing?"

"I am. I have been for a great many years now."

Barden pushed his chair back and stood up, collecting the empty plates. "I'm going to get some sleep."

Dad also stood up. "I'm afraid we will all need that, but you're welcome to come back for dinner tonight if you like?"

"Sadly, I have an engagement in the Underworld and won't make it back for dinner, but might I suggest Sasha has a sleepover at Barden's or Elisha Vincent's?"

"You truly think the Orey might try to hurt Sasha?" Savas asked.

"Yes," Lorka answered simply. "As far as they are concerned, Sasha is Gelus now, and she's the easiest for them to get to in payback for their dead girl."

"Do you know who killed Yas or Sophie?" I asked.

Gritting his jaw, Lorka shook his head minutely, almost as a subconscious answer. "No. But so far, we haven't identified any Gelus who were involved."

"Meaning what?" Savas asked.

"It means I don't think a Gelus killed the Orey girl. Which means someone is trying to make it look like we did to start this war."

The Sight

"THANKS FOR LETTING me stay while Barden isn't here," I said into my cup of tea.

A finger tapped under my chin, forcing me to look up and meet Nelly's eyes. "You're welcome. Try not to look so down in the dumps about it."

"Sorry. I just know you don't like me being here without Barden."

Sighing, Nelly came around the kitchen island bench and sat beside me. "That wasn't about you personally, Sasha. I get called out all hours for work, Gavel spends more time in the Underworld than he does here, and Calliope has her own life. We discussed what you and Barden would look like if you accepted him and decided that you would be safer under your parent's roof while he's working if things progressed the way he hoped."

Wondering why they were worried back then, a thought came into my mind. "Because of Sophie?"

Nelly nodded. "We couldn't be sure if she was targeted because she was Gelus, the pregnancy, or some other reason. All we knew was that someone used magic to snap her neck, which rules out Vestigial, Execrable, and other Gelus. True, it didn't mean it was an Orey, but here in the borderlands, you don't have many other suspects."

Considering that information, I frowned. "Sophie was pregnant?"

Nelly's eyes widened a little. "Yeah. Sorry, I forgot that wasn't common knowledge. She was only in her first trimester. The police spoke to Elisha and Darina to see if they knew who she was seeing, but other than the fact she was seeing someone, they didn't know who."

"Not Hawk or Falco?" I asked, sure that Sophie had been involved with them like most of her friends. Hell, even the Orey girls were sleeping with them.

Sophie was Gelus.

"No. They both hadn't been intimate with Sophie for most of this year. Since she took up with her lover." Nelly looked sad as she drank her tea. Putting her cup down, she shook it off and focused on me again. "Speaking of Sophie, Barden asked me about absorbing the memories of the newly dead. He said you saw Sophie and your friend die?"

My eyes filled with tears as I chewed my lip. Nelly put her hand over mine. "Tell me what you saw, what you did and felt when those memories passed to you."

My bottom lip caught between my teeth, and I swiped away the single drop that escaped my eye. "With Sophie, it was at her funeral. I touched her hand at the open casket. There was a tingle, and then it was like I'd seen it and could remember it. But it wasn't a clear picture, and the voice of her killer was familiar, yet at the same time, I couldn't recognize it. I'm unsure if that was because it was familiar to her or me. It's like I know it and don't simultaneously, if that makes sense?"

"Maybe it's a voice you've heard often enough that you've met them regularly but not enough to know them personally?"

I perked up at the understanding. "Yes. That's exactly what it's like."

"You didn't see the killer?"

"No. They were standing behind her. The memory is like a flash of those last moments. I feel like she was walking away from them when they struck. In fact, it's more a sense with Sophie than a visual thing. I couldn't see her surroundings, but she was moving, and then the creep of the magic, the sound of her neck—" Bile rose in my throat as it sounded all over in my head.

'Stupid wingless bitch.'

"Then it cuts off," I said, taking a big gulp of my tea to prevent drowning in the memory.

"Is your experience with your friend the same?"

Shaking my head, I wrung my hands. "There's way more. It's fuzzy because she was drunk, so I can't tell if the person with her was male or female. I heard their conversation; I felt and saw her surroundings as she stumbled around under the bridge. I fall and scream with her every time."

Hands grabbed mine, stabilizing me, bringing me back to the here and now. I opened my eyes and met Nelly's; the black channels in her gray eyes fanned open, nearly obliterating the color of her iris and melding with her pupil. "Easy. Stay here with me, Sasha. Deep breaths."

Following her instruction, I mimicked her deep breathing, and once I was firmly present again, Nelly pulled back. She stared at me for a long moment, then blinked, and the otherworldly abyss of her eyes snapped shut, leaving striated gray irises again. "When I touch the newly dead, I free their souls to be escorted to their place of rest until reincarnation," Nelly explained as if tutoring me.

"I see their last memories. Because people aren't necessarily focused on their present when they die, that doesn't necessarily mean I see how they die. The woman I collected this morning wondered why she never left her abusive husband at the first red flag. It was the memory of that first bad sign that I saw. The man last night was playing the argument he had with his son over and over in his head, and then the train tracks were rushing towards him. He didn't know he was about to be pushed in front of a train, so his memories were elsewhere until that last second."

"That makes sense. I was focused on what I'd just seen in Yasmine's death when the inquisitor knocked into me. So, if I had died, you would have probably seen Yasmine's death the way I did, and then snapped back to me and the glimpse of the wing, and then—" I exploded my hands as if to indicate nothing.

"Right," Nelly agreed. "But when I collected Sophie and Yasmine, I didn't see their deaths as you described. For Sophie, I saw her memory of telling her lover she carried his child, how happy he'd been, how he'd caressed her flat belly from where he stood behind her. At the same time, they talked about if it was a boy or a girl. I didn't see or hear her neck break. She was lost in happy thoughts one moment and gone the next."

That was reassuring that it wasn't horrible for her. "What about Yasmine?" I asked, suddenly anxious. If this wasn't a Corvus ability, was it Orey?

Nelly's face fell. "I saw her lust for the forbidden, her jealousy of you, and her suspicion of her brother. Then she was looking back up at the bridge and screaming. But Sasha, when I saw her fall, I didn't fall with her. It was like watching a movie from the antagonist's point of view."

"She was suspicious of Vidal?" I asked. Surprised. "I know they weren't close, but Vidal loved his sister. The grief when he's been at our place of late couldn't be faked."

Nodding, Nelly licked her lips. "After you exposed yourself as Gelus, and Mia explained to Yasmine why what you did was not Orey, Yasmine started paying closer attention to her brother. I never got what happened from the memory, just that she doubted him."

Pondering that, I tried to think back to all those days of training I'd watched and if Vidal ever showed any exceptional ability. The problem was, I never really watched the other boys. Just my father and twin until Barden came along. Staring at my empty teacup, I returned to what Nelly had revealed. "So, this isn't a Corvus ability?"

Inhaling, Nelly sat taller. "I never said that. Even amongst the Corvus, our abilities vary, yet not so much that you could be anything other than a collector or deliverer." Tapping her nails on the bench, Nelly met my eyes. "But something else makes your ability stand aside from the average Corvus, Sasha. Collectors can only see those memories at the time of collection. Once the soul has left the body, it's an empty vessel. There is nothing for us to absorb. I collected Sophie's soul beside the river, yet nearly two weeks later, you absorbed her death from that empty vessel. And the same with Yasmine. You got her last moments before I saw the body, but her soul was still there for me to collect. So, whatever ability these tragedies have revealed, I don't think it is purely a Corvus one."

"So, you can't help me turn it off?"

"Well, perhaps," Nelly answered vaguely. "Your Corvus bloodline is unique. They are the only ones to absorb the last moments of the collection. I assume that's where your ability stems from, but it has evolved in you. One of your distant kin might be able to help you."

"And how would I find them? My mother didn't even know her Orey genes weren't as pristine as she believed."

Smirking, Nelly stood and took our empty mugs to the sink. "Well, it just happens, I know your great-uncle resides in the city. If you're up for an excursion this evening?"

Nervous but excited by the prospect of getting rid of this ability that caused me to be haunted, I nodded and followed Nelly to her car.

The conversation heading to the city was light around my exam prep and how I planned to cover any residual bruising before the formal next Friday. Honestly, I'd given the formal no thought these few weeks. Everything that had happened over the last three months made it hard to consider a dance important. Instead, my mind was lost to all the random information coming at me from different sources.

Sophie was pregnant.

This is how the hour's drive to the city flew by, and I found myself standing beside Nelly as she knocked on an apartment door. I wasn't prepared for when the door opened, and a man who was the spitting image of my maternal grandfather stood looking at us.

"Nellimniah," my grandfather's doppelgänger greeted Nelly before his eyes came to me and narrowed a touch before they returned to Nelly. "What can I do for you?"

"This is Sasha. Your great-niece through the Orey line."

"Orey line? Don't take me for a fool; she's as Gelus as you or I," the man argued.

"Yes. With Gelus grandfathers on both sides of the family, it seems the twins are both as Gelus as they are Orey." Nelly turned her focus to me. "Sasha, this is your great-uncle, Billeizum."

"You look just like my mother's father," I told him.

"I'm not interested in knowing my father's random spawn." Billeizum huffed and looked me over before glaring at Nelly. "Why did you bring her here?"

"Sasha recently encountered the dead, and it turns out the power of your bloodline is strong in her, but not as a collector," Nelly explained.

Billeizum frowned. "That's not possible. We have to collect the soul to see the last moments."

"Sasha didn't. In fact, she could absorb the last moments from the body after the soul was collected," Nelly stepped forward, taking my shoulder and pulling me closer to the man blocking the door. "She needs your help, Billy. Those deaths are haunting her. You know how the juveniles are vulnerable to their power."

Eyeing me, Billeizum released his grip on the door to cup my face in his hands and stare into my eyes. His presence pushed into me, something dark and cold, and I jolted back on instinct. Nelly's arm over my shoulders kept me there with her. "It's okay, Sasha. Let him sense you."

Staring into those familiar indigo eyes, I felt a push. My instinct was to push back, but on Nelly's urging, I relaxed. Sophie's last moments and then Yasmine's raced through my mind, dragging me with her as she fell over the canyon's edge.

Jolting, I found myself back at the apartment door of a man with a familiar face but was in every way a stranger. "Hmm," Billeizum muttered, then released me and stepped back, opening his door wide to grab his jacket and keys, then pulled his door shut as he stepped out and walked down the hall. "Come, little niece. Let's see what we can do to tame your ability."

The Bloodline

I WAS dead on my feet as I climbed out of Nelly's car the following day. Barden's irritation niggled below my sternum, and my eyes struggled to stay open as I shuffled towards the internal garage door.

"I've got you." Nelly took my arm to prevent me from walking into a wall and guided me.

"Barden's cranky," I warned.

"It won't be at you," Nelly assured.

Leading me around the corner, we entered the open living area where Barden sat at the Kitchen bench, three steaming cups in front of him. His damp hair and the sweatpants sitting low on his hips suggested he'd already showered and was waiting for me to get here to go to bed. It was a sign of how tired I was that the sight of him shirtless didn't have me yearning for him like my crazed hormones usually did.

As soon as he saw me, Barden shot out of his seat and took me in his arms, guiding me the rest of the way to the island bench. Barden growled at his mother in his Neanderthal style.

"You asked me to help her," Nelly argued back.

With the snarl he replied with, I could almost hear the words, 'Did that have to involve an all-nighter exposing her to the newly dead?'

"We made sure none of them were traumatic for her."

I'm pretty sure the next grunt was, 'Who's we?' I was becoming fluent in Neander-Barden, though I'm sure being able to feel his irritation with his mother helped.

"Billeizum was helping Sasha control that side of her blood's power."

Sitting me at the table, Barden wrapped my cold hands around one of the warm mugs before focusing on Nelly, who took a seat on the other side of me and drew one of the steaming cups to herself.

"So, it was the Corvus in her?" Barden finally used his words.

"Yes and no. Yes, the power comes from Sasha's Corvus genes, but the ability is different. Sasha is not a collector. From what Billy and I could determine, Sasha takes the memories from the physical body. The longer it's been dead, the less of an impression she takes. Hence, Sasha took so little from Sophie, but the Orey girl is almost like she personally experiences her death."

"A mutation of their ability?"

"A side effect of breeding an Eyal Corvus with a Strigias," Nelly countered.

"A watcher who can witness last moments," Barden considered. His focus locked on me. "If you went into law enforcement, that could be a handy gift."

A laugh sputtered from my lips. "You want me to be a cop?" When Barden shrugged, I shook my head. "Let's consider the number of times that gift might prove useful and divide it by how often police find themselves in dangerous situations. You'll find that positive and negative cancel each other out."

Nelly smirked in my peripheral vision. "You could study medicine and come work for me."

I cringed. "I think I've had my fill of dead bodies already." Finishing the hot chocolate, I stood up. "I'm exhausted. I'm going to have a shower and go to bed for a few hours."

"I'll be up in a moment," Barden said, taking my empty mug to the sink with his.

Understanding he wanted to talk to his mother, I wished Nelly goodnight and headed to Barden's room. I'd showered and curled up under the covers before Barden joined me. Slipping into bed behind me, Barden wrapped me in his arms and kissed the top of my head. "I know you need to learn, but adding to your trauma is not how to do it," he murmured once we were settled.

Exhaling, I relaxed in his arms. "I agree."

"You do?"

"But at least I know how and why it happens now," I muttered. "I know to not touch the dead anymore."

Barden was quiet for a moment, and by the time he whispered my name, I was too far down the sleep tunnel to drag myself back.

Waking at lunchtime, I left Barden asleep, ate with Nelly, then got a lift home. I wanted to study and preferred the comfort of my house rather than imposing on Barden's family, who were all home for a change.

I'd been home for an hour when the front gate chimed. I answered it quickly to prevent it from waking Dad and Savas, sighing when I saw it was Vidal. Going to the front door, I opened it and let him in. "Hey, you're early today."

"I wasn't in the mood for my dad's carry-on today and thought I could kill some time and check on you simultaneously," Vidal answered as we made our way to the kitchen. "Is everyone still asleep?"

"So far. They usually wake up soon." I stopped by the dining table and considered my study notes but felt bad ignoring a guest. "I might make some coffee. You want some?"

"Thanks." Vidal followed me to the kitchen bench. "How have you been?"

"I'm better. The bruising should hopefully be gone by the end of this week. The headaches are minimal as long as I take regular breaks from studying."

"How was your first week back at school?"

Setting the pot on, I turned to face Vidal. "I coped. I spent lunch resting in the clinic to get through."

"Maybe you should have waited to go back," Vidal suggested.

Rolling my eyes, I huffed. "Don't you start. I have heard enough of that from everyone else this week."

Vidal lifted a brow. "Maybe they have a point."

Sighing, I grabbed a couple of mugs from the cupboard. "I didn't want to miss anything to help prepare for the exams." The kitchen fell silent, just the dripping of the coffee filtering into the pot.

"It turned out to be a really nice day," Vidal said. "Did you want to go for a walk?"

Blinking at the request, I turned to consider Vidal. He met my eyes, then looked away. "I'd like to talk to you about what's been happening, but I don't feel comfortable saying this where your brother or father might overhear." Vidal's grey-hazel gaze met mine again. His were more green than his sister's brown.

My hesitation was apparent. All I could think about was everyone worrying that Orey might try to hurt me, that Yasmine didn't trust her brother, and that we had no idea who killed Sophie. "What could you want to tell me that you don't want my family to hear?"

"A lot," Vidal answered as he slid from his seat to stand. "I'm not going to hurt you, Sash. I just want to talk. We can help each other, but I need you to trust me first." Vidal offered me his hand.

Assessing Vidal, I realized something about him lit my senses. Something that stood aside from the other Orey I knew. My focus went to his eyes, and sure enough, despite the Orey multi-chroma iris, there was something predatory in them. Was that what Yasmine realized? That her brother was a hybrid like us.

Inhaling deeply, I grabbed a notepad and left a note that I'd gone for a walk. My father would see Vidal's bike here and come looking. I didn't doubt it. Then, taking a leap of faith, I took Vidal's hand and stepped out into the backyard with him.

He headed for the path into the gardens, the one he found Barden and me on last week. I'd expected him to try and take me up the mountain or down to the river, so his intention to stay near the house helped relax me.

"Did you know we were promised?" Vidal began.

My mouth fell open, surprised that was his starting point. "Ah, not until last week. You never approached me in a way that suggested you were interested, so I didn't think any of you Orey boys were."

Vidal smiled. "Oh, I was interested. Absolutely smitten with you until Barden came to town. He didn't hesitate in declaring that you were his. I laughed at first, but then I saw how you looked at him. So, I decided to step back and let that play out." Vidal gazed at me. "I wasn't sure you were still into him or whether he made a move, but I've seen how you look at each other these last few weeks. You're in love with him, aren't you?"

"Yes," I answered softly.

Nodding, Vidal gave my hand a gentle squeeze. "I don't resent you for it. Don't worry. A little jealous, but not angry." We walked around the corner, which took us out of sight of the house, and Vidal stopped, turning to face me. "It does make what I'm about to do a bit of an asshole move, though, so please forgive me."

Before I could react, Vidal cupped my jaw and pressed his mouth to mine. I tried to pull back, but he was so strong, and as his lips pressed mine, they tasted of the sweetest honey. My resolve to break the kiss faded. My hands, which had been pushing him away, curled into his shirt, tugging him closer. My mouth that had clenched shut, relaxed, and moved against his, lapping at his taste, desiring more of that sweetness.

In a blink, I watched Sophie turn her back on the person who would kill her. Her hands rubbed her flat stomach, and a smile touched her lips as she took that step away, only for the magic of ill intent to fill my senses and the sound of her neck snapping to drag me into darkness.

I was under the bridge. Stumbling around and drunk as questions were asked of me. This time, when I fell, I caught a glimpse of a face. Yasmine's scream transported me. Taking me from her body to mine. Her scream echoed through the canyon. I was running the track by the river and watching her fall. I glimpsed a gray wing under the bridge before I raced toward her over the river rocks.

I was on the phone to Barden, him telling me to run; there was a swoosh of air and then the wing that clobbered me. At first, I saw it as the same grey, but as I fell, the light caught on the wing showing it was actually brown. Nothing like the wing I'd seen under the bridge.

"Oh, God!" I gasped for air as I returned to my body in the now. My back pressed against a tree while Vidal kissed the sanity out of me. "Vidal," I moaned.

He replied in kind, then his mouth moved down my neck, pinching and kissing. His grip on me tightened, and then he bit me hard. I jack-knifed in his hold, my mind flashing to the garden outside Barden's bedroom window.

Inside, Barden and I made love, and as we climaxed, my wings burst free from my back for the first time, wet with blood and weak from disuse. As Barden flipped me and cemented our mating, the me viewing them stepped back, spread our wings, and in one flap was airborne. Jealousy burned in my chest as I accepted that they were indeed mates.

Shock poured through me, as did molten heat. Opening my eyes, Vidal looked down at me. His green-grey irises glowed with gold flecks. My hands shifted over his shoulders and felt along the enormous dark wings that had torn open his shirt. Where the sunlight shined on them, they reflected a metallic gold glint.

"Oh, God!"

Vidal smiled. "I've missed you praying to me," he whispered. "When you first started fucking the Crow, you called to me all the time. I'm guessing he told you to stop using the G word."

Panic rose in my throat, and tears leaked as I nodded.

"Shh," Vidal murmured as he wiped away my tears. "You have nothing to fear from me, Sash. I told you I was smitten from the time we met. I still am. I'd never hurt you."

My hand trembled as it moved to my neck. Vidal caught it before my fingers could touch the bite. "Shh. It's okay. I got caught up in finally having you in my arms and lost control. We'll talk about that, but first, since you have answered my questions, I think I should answer yours."

Caressing my cheek, Vidal pecked my lips once more, that sweet honey filling my senses and relaxing me again. Taking my hand, Vidal walked us over to a bench and eased me beside him. Then still holding my hand, he began to explain.

"My mother didn't meet Jebidiah until I was three. She told him I was the child of her Orey boyfriend and that he'd been killed by an Execrable. She moved away for college and decided not to go back, that she couldn't face the memories of my father," Vidal explained.

"As you may have already discerned, the truth is that my father was a hybrid god. Or, as the Gelus refer to them, a Narsitee."

"Hybrid?"

"He was a Gelus-Narsitee half-breed. Pretty rare, considering Gelus prefer to kill a Narsitee on sight." Vidal chuckled. "I have no idea how he came to be. My real father never told me the story, just how he seduced my mother. She thought he was Gelus and ran away to protect me from her family. It took my real father a while to find her, and when he discovered me, he found ways to get me alone and teach me both how to use my abilities and how to hide them from the Orey and Gelus alike."

"Does Jebidiah know?"

"He thinks I'm like you and Savas. That's why he was happy with the arrangement between our mothers to match us. He figured no real Orey girl would want me, but one who grew up with a hybrid brother and father couldn't be choosey." My face must have said it all because Vidal chuckled. "Yeah, he's an ass. I only call him Dad because it provides cover. Stops people from wondering. But I really can't stand him."

"Why expose yourself to me?" I asked, curious and a little terrified.

Face softening, Vidal caressed my jaw. "You're a hybrid, like me. Orey and two different kinds of Gelus. You know what it's like. I know you'll understand."

Turning his gaze to the view, Vidal sighed. "I wasn't going to approach you. I wanted to tell someone my secret for so long, but when you mated with Barden, I thought you were lost to me, so I'd decided against it. But then Yasmine died, and I was watching Barden, waiting to see if he figured out who was behind Sophie's death. So I overheard when he told his mother about your gift. How you saw their deaths.

"They discussed the dual Gelus bloodline you carry. How the Crow in you comes from a unique family who can see a person's last moments as they collect the soul." Vidal swung his attention back to me. "That's why I started coming around. I hoped you may be honest and tell me, but as I watched those last moments haunt you, I understood it's not that you were hiding their murderers, but you were terrified of what revealing that power would mean. I knew then you'd understand why I've hidden mine."

Holding my hand, Vidal traced the bones from my fingers to my wrist. "I needed to know what you saw, but I knew getting that information would expose me to you. It was only fair that you should know mine if I knew your secret. I hope you respect that and can keep it to yourself."

My hand shifted to my neck and the tender area around his bite. "This might make it hard for me to keep it from Barden. This and the fact he can feel everything I feel. I'm surprised he's not here already."

The side of Vidal's lips twitched. Jumping out of my seat, I turned to face him. "What did you do? If you hurt Barden—"

"Woah!" Vidal stood, holding his hands out to calm me down. "I haven't gone near the Crow. I simply cloaked you from him temporarily when we came on the walk. He's probably still sleeping peacefully, thinking you are happily studying."

Taking a breath, Vidal eyed my neck. "I'm sorry. I lost control. I didn't realize what I was doing until it was done. I did warn you I was smitten. I guess I should have seen that coming."

"That you would bite me?" I asked, unsure why he looked both happy and a little forlorn.

Vidal shrugged. "Biting is how the Narsitees claim their chosen ones. Similar to how the mating between Gelus causes a bond, biting creates one between a Narsitee and his mate."

My eyes probably bugged out of my head. "Tell me you did not just mate with me!"

Vidal scrubbed his hand up the back of his head, messing his hair up.

"Vidal! I'm already mated," I yelled at him.

"I'm aware. I watched it happen," Vidal grumbled.

Blinking at him, I was lost for words for a moment. "We'll circle back to you watching Barden and me together. Right now, how do you expect to explain this to Barden?" I asked, pointing to my neck.

Blowing out a breath, Vidal stepped forward, taking my hand in his. "Delicately."

The Other Hybrid

"COME ON. Let's go back. Barden is awake and trying to feel you down the bond. He'll come looking for you, and if we are out here alone and he has to come to find us, it'll go worse for us than it needs to."

Shaking my head, I walked with Vidal back to the house. "And Barden was worried about Falco."

To my dismay, Vidal actually laughed. "He should be. Falco was eyeing you up from when your boobs came in when you were fourteen. I wanted to punch him every time I saw him talking to you. Then Barden came to town, and Falco was no longer an issue."

Getting back to the yard and within sight of the house, I deviated to lead Vidal to the swings. "Why were you watching Barden to learn about Sophie? Did you have something to do with that?"

Vidal pressed his lips together, watching his shoes imprint the grass as we meandered through the yard. "Yes. I think I'm the reason she's dead."

My legs stopped short. My entire body is rigid. When Vidal casually turned to meet my eyes, there was a sadness in them that surprised me. A grief that I thought was for his sister. I felt Barden reaching for me down the bond, curious about my sudden caution. Forcing myself to relax, I sent him the feeling of being okay. When Barden returned to his workout, while I lifted my brows at the realization that I could sense what he was doing. Then I shifted my focus back to Vidal.

"The baby was yours," I guessed.

Exhaling audibly through his nose, there was almost an undercurrent of an animal growl in the noise as pure rage filtered through Vidal's grief. "I didn't know you knew about the baby. Does everyone know?"

"Just her closest friends. The police were asking if they knew who the boyfriend was."

Vidal rubbed at his forehead, turned, and went to the swings, dropping into one of them and waiting for me to join him. When I did, Vidal composed himself. "It started as a bit of fun, you know. That's how it usually is. The Orey like to fuck the Gelus. It's like dating the bad boy or something. I don't know what it is for the guys, maybe because Orey girls are off limits until they are eighteen, and they don't want to get wrapped up with one until they are ready for marriage and shit."

"Would explain why none of them ever looked twice at me," I considered.

"Pfft. Don't delude yourself, Sash. We were all looking. But until two years ago, you were mine, and they all knew it. I was the most powerful of them until your brother came into his power, so none of them would even consider messing around with my future wife. Then Barden came along, and it made them all wonder if you were truly Orey or not. There was some talk of fucking around with you, but I made sure they all knew if they came near you, they wouldn't have to worry about Barden getting them. I'd beat him to it."

"That's weirdly sweet and endearing in a disturbing way," I muttered, frowning at the protectiveness.

Vidal stared at the ground. "After you were attacked by the Execrable, I was livid. Not because of the attack but the power you showcased that night. None of us knew you were half as capable, and when Mia buried you alive..."

Vidal gritted his teeth, and the swing's chains screamed as if being mangled in his grip. Blowing out a breath, Vidal relaxed his hands. "I went to the Vincent twins' party after your parents got to the hospital. I needed to let off some steam. I had a few drinks, and Sophie was flirting with me. It was just meant to be fun. But I went back the next night, and the next, and before I knew it, we were together every other night."

"Did Sophie know?"

"Eventually. She recognized the difference in my eyes. Sophie told me that a pull between Gelus allows them to identify each other. She said she didn't feel it at first, but once we became intimate, it became clearer. She assumed my Orey blood masked it." Vidal licked his lips. "I never told her what my father was, so she thought I was a hybrid like you and your brother."

Considering Vidal's grief, I studied him. "Did you want the baby?"

Leaning his head against the chain, Vidal stared towards the house. "It wasn't planned, but from the moment I knew it existed, I wanted to be its father. Sophie and I were waiting till the school year finished, then we planned to move in together."

"Would you have married?" I asked, pointing to my neck.

Vidal smirked. "She would have picked what I was instantly, plus that desire was never there for Sophie."

When my hand fell away, Vidal blew out a breath. "I'm sure you know that Gelus can develop a bond through intimacy, mates or not, but it's a yearning, not what you and Barden have. We might have allowed ourselves to feel enough for each other that we built that connection. I'll never know."

We sat silently until I got the nerve to ask what was bugging me. Strangely, I didn't need to.

"I'd only told my parents. I don't think Sophie had told anyone about the baby," Vidal answered my thoughts. I stared at him in fear. "And yes, I can sense where your mind is going. And yes, Barden is probably going to kill me. Firstly, because he knows what sort of creature marks its mate like that, and he's killed his fair share of them; and secondly, because I marked his wife as my chosen."

Swallowing with difficulty, I moved to cover the bite but hesitated to touch it. I couldn't meet Vidal's eyes as I asked my next question. "Are you as evil as those creatures?"

"I'd like to think that the watered-down genetics has minimized the sociopathic tendencies. Honestly, compared to my biological father, who, again, is nowhere near as bad as the stories I've heard, I'm a saint.

I'd like to think I'm more Orey with a good helping of Gelus and a sprinkle of Narsitee."

The fact I could feel the honesty of that answer coming from Vidal like a second pulse should have worried me, but instead, I found it soothing.

"Crap. Barden's going to lose his shit," I muttered. For some reason, it made Vidal chuckle.

Standing up, I turned to face Vidal as he followed suit. Meeting his eyes, I took the risk and asked him one last thing. "Do you know who killed Sophie?"

Vidal moved closer, caressing his knuckles down my cheek to my mouth, his thumb swiping across my bottom lip. "No, your gift was too late."

Catching myself as my lips moved to chase Vidal's thumb, I forced myself to turn to the side and breathe before I met his eyes again. "Yasmine?"

Closing his eyes, Vidal swallowed hard, his Adam's apple showing the difficulty. "Yeah. I'm pretty sure I know who was with her, but the vision is glitchy, so I can't trust it. I know your sensation of it makes it difficult, but I suspect she stumbled to her own death."

"They didn't try and save her, and they could have," I found myself saying, then frowning, wondering about the surety of my own words.

Vidal cuffed the back of my head. "I know. Sash, I need you to let me deal with this. Can you not tell anyone?"

Blinking up at his earnest request, I struggled to resist. "I... I won't keep secrets from Barden. I couldn't if I wanted to."

As if summoning a demon, the pulse of wings fluttered up my spine, and I knew Barden was coming. That something had caught his attention, and he'd abandoned his workout.

Pursing his lips, Vidal studied me, then cursed and backed up a step. "You're right. I'm sorry. I had no right to ask that of you. Give me some time to get ahead of this if you can."

Stepping aside, Vidal started heading for the path around the side of the house. "Wait!" I rushed forward and grabbed his arm. "You're not leaving me here alone to explain this. You need to stay and help talk to Barden. I can't hide this from him."

"Hide what from me?" Barden asked from behind.

Turning, I realized he'd come from the mountain path and must have flown around to make a stealth approach, probably to make sure he wasn't overreacting. He was still shirtless in his sweats, and the slick of sweat on his skin, plus his gorgeous wings standing out behind him, had my hormones exploding like fireworks.

As if a neon arrow pointed to the issue, Barden's eyes fell on my neck. His jaw clenched as his face grew pale with his rage. His eyes simmered with wrath as the roulette wheel in them fanned open and focused on Vidal. "You couldn't be," Barden snarled.

Vidal held his hands up in a gesture of peace. "It was an accident. I didn't know what I was doing until it was done," Vidal tried to appease.

Barden tilted his head like a bird of prey, considering a potential juicy morsel. "I knew you were different, but I thought you were like Delila, a few generations of watered-down Gelus. I would never have picked you were one of them."

"I am Gelus. A hybrid like Sasha and Savas," Vidal stepped back as Barden moved closer to him.

"No. Gelus don't maul their mates. They also don't mark another Gelus's wife!" Barden snapped the last. "There is only one creature who bites to form a bond." Barden clenched his fist, his sun sword filled his palm, and he launched.

"Barden!" I screamed.

Vidal's wings unfurled as he jumped back, and then he was airborne, holding a golden spear he used to defend against Barden's attack. Before I could draw breath, they were a blur of movement in the sky, clashing and being thrown apart by their own force of impact.

"Sasha?" My dad and Savas rushed from the house to my side, taking me in their arms as their eyes were drawn to the sky and the two Gelus fighting high above us. "What happened?"

"Vidal claimed me as his," I sobbed.

"That's Vidal?" Savas asked. "He's Gelus?"

"Hybrid," I murmured. There was no point denying what they could see. But I didn't clarify what sort of hybrid he was.

"Shit!" My father yanked his shirt off, ready to dive into the fray.

"No," I cried, grabbing his arm. "This isn't your fight. It's between the three of us."

As if fate heard me, a sharp pain lashed my bicep. While there was no blood, there was a red mark. Without needing an explanation, I knew Vidal was injured. Damn it! If this continued, I'd feel both their wounds. This was insane. Despite Barden's bias, he needed to assess the situation and realize Vidal wasn't like the pure Narsitees he'd fought. I also knew somehow that Vidal didn't stand a chance of surviving Barden with all his centuries of experience.

Without thinking, I drew myself up, looked to the sky, and acted. Lightning branched across the sky and struck between the dueling Gelus, causing them to be thrown apart. Then they were falling.

My heart leaped into my throat. What had I done? I screamed.

Cursing, my father and brother launched skyward, swooping to either falling body and catching them.

Pain lanced my head. My heart ached. It was difficult to draw breath.

As my kin brought my husband and his competition safely to the ground, my eyelids dropped, darkness engulfed me, and the ground rushed up to meet me.

The Understanding

THE SOFTNESS of the ground was the first thing I became aware of. The rage in Barden's eyes, the sword of sunlight, Vidal's dark wings, his eyes flecked with gold, his spear. The lightning I called out of fear.

Sitting up, I gripped the sofa beneath me. Barden knelt by my side, holding my hand. "Barden," I whisper-cried and threw myself at him, wrapping my arms around him tight.

"It's okay," Barden soothed. "We're okay."

"I'm so sorry. I was scared, and there was pain, and I just wanted you to stop fighting each other and let Vidal explain," I beseeched. "He's not what you think."

Barden grunted in a way that suggested my neck said otherwise, but he didn't argue with me. He just held me, his strong hand rubbing my spine soothingly.

Calming down, I noticed Vidal sitting at the dining table with Savas while my father pottered around in the kitchen. Those otherworldly eyes focused on me in Barden's arms. The other hybrid looked a little mollified but no worse for wear.

"How long was I out?" I asked Barden as I slowly pulled back.

"We regained consciousness about fifteen minutes ago. Your father already had you here on the lounge," Barden informed. His hand found the red mark on my bicep, his jaw clenching as he traced it, but when I didn't flinch or look concerned, he eased up. I didn't miss how Barden's eyes kept flicking to my neck.

My hands and eyes also cataloged his body and any sign he was injured. Taking my palms from his abdomen, Barden held them in his. "I'm fine. A little scorched from the close call with the lightning, but not injured."

Relieved, I sagged a little. "I know you're angry, but please let Vidal explain. Vidal's just like me. Having the Eyal bloodline didn't make me a collector any more than my mother being Orey stopped me from being Gelus at heart. He has the power, but not the traits that make that power evil."

Blowing out a breath, Barden bowed his head. "What sucks about you saying that is as much as I want to believe he's manipulated you to believe that, his bite actually protects you from his lies or ability to make you see him in a different light. You'll see his truth no matter what."

My hand drifted to my neck, but Barden took it gently in his and stopped me from touching it. "It will heal quickly, but his mark is there for good. He had no right claiming my wife as his."

"It was an accident," I murmured.

Tilting his head, Barden used my chin to make me meet his eyes. "Was it?"

Swallowing, I assessed my words, then shook my head slightly, admitting they weren't true. "Giving in to instinct might be a better explanation, but as you said, it protects me from him, and at least I know what he told me is the truth."

Leaning forward, Barden leaned his forehead to mine. "That's the only reason his head is still on his shoulders right now." His lips found mine. The kiss was tame but claimed me as his just the same.

"Come on. I want you with me while Vidal explains this to me. Don't protect him. If he lies to me, call him on it," Barden murmured to my cheek before kissing it. "Promise me."

I didn't even consider lying to Barden. "I promise."

Rising to his feet, Barden helped me to mine and then led the way to the meals table. When Vidal stood to address me, Barden growled and shook his head slightly to suggest he kept his distance, and Vidal smartly dropped back in his seat.

"Gannix, I hate to commandeer your kitchen, but I think Vidal, Sasha, and I need to discuss what happened between them today."

My father considered Barden and Vidal before coming to me. His eyes went to my neck and darkened. "Are you okay?"

Nodding, I didn't trust myself not to crack if I used my words. I really needed to find a mirror and assess the damage. My throat didn't feel torn open, but the bite obviously stood out for some reason.

Squeezing my shoulder in reassurance, Dad eyed Barden. "I'm going to order pizza for dinner. It takes about forty minutes to get here. That's how long you have to sort this out before I start asking questions."

"Understood," Barden answered.

"Use my office." Without further debate, Dad grabbed his phone and opened the app for the pizza place.

The three of us made our way to my dad's study, Vidal shutting the door behind him, then coming to sit opposite Barden and me on the sofas. Barden ensured he was somewhat between Vidal and me. "Start talking," Barden snarled.

Eyeing me, Vidal slumped back in his seat as if he had no cares in the world, licked his lips, and then told Barden the same explanation he told me. Minus, he'd watched Barden and me mate or saw my wings the first time they unfurled. It didn't stop the images he'd shared with me playing in my mind and getting my hormones revved up.

When Vidal finished his story, Barden looked at me and frowned. Probably sensing my need to jump his bones and have him claim me in that primal way he did. Vidal smirked and had to cover his mouth with his hand as he watched me, simultaneously shifting how he was sitting.

A rush of humiliation washed over me as I realized he could feel my randiness or even read my mind. "Oh, hell," I muttered as I covered my face.

"Don't be embarrassed on my part," Vidal snickered. "I just wish it was me you were thinking about claiming you like that. Give me a chance, and I promise to make you scream my name just as loudly."

"Fuck off," Barden snapped, his eyes becoming something hauntingly scary as his focus shifted to Vidal.

Holding his hands up, Vidal gestured peace. "Okay, yeah, this is awkward, but you can't deny the bite has taken. That means there was something there for me to claim. I didn't do it to piss you off. It was sheer instinct. Still, it wouldn't have taken if I didn't have a right to it." Vidal scratched his temple. "At least that's my understanding. So, unless you know of some other reason, you need to accept she's also my mate, and we need to work out how this will happen without you ripping me limb from limb."

"Still an option," Barden growled.

Vidal rolled his eyes but relaxed back in his seat. My mind was a little slow, but I looked between them and finally caught on. "Wait. You can't actually think that anything will happen between us?" I asked Vidal and caught my mouth from dropping wide open when he lifted a shoulder in a shrug as if he actually did believe there was a relationship there.

"Look, I don't understand this whole bite thing. Other than allowing you to calm me down when I wanted to freak out, it did not affect my desires. I don't want to sleep with you," I told Vidal honestly.

"Are you sure? Because you seemed pretty into it when my lips were on you," Vidal countered but shut up quickly when Barden growled at him. "Then you tell her."

Almost snapping at Vidal, Barden huffed off the end of his threat, then massaged the bridge of his nose. "The bond is there. I can't predict how it will affect you or change your desires. I've never known the bond being used in anything but a sexual situation. Vidal obviously has those inclinations towards you" — Vidal raised his hand — "but since you've never had them for him, maybe it will work differently here."

"I'm just going to add that my inclinations towards Sasha, while somewhat sexual, have always been protective first and foremost," Vidal added keenly.

"What the fuck does that mean?" Barden grumbled, his frustration not even hidden.

"It means that if Sasha wants to get intimate, I'm not going to say no, but from when she was little, my desire has been to keep her safe and see her happy. I accepted when you arrived in town that I wouldn't have her romantically, and I was okay with that as long as she was happy—"

"You kissed her. Put your hands on her. Sank your teeth into her flesh," Barden argued, though he kept his voice eerily low and even.

"I kissed her to get the information I needed. There was no sexual overture in that action. It wasn't until the exchange had finished that it shifted to something more primal. Even then, it did so because my instinct to bond with her pushed it there. As soon as the bond formed, we could pull back from it and focus on what needed to be said," Vidal defended. "I'm not inexperienced. I know when it's my cock guiding my decisions. That has never happened with Sasha. My gut instinct is for her to be safe and happy first and foremost. Strangely, whether that's with me or with you doesn't bother me."

When Barden stared at Vidal, the other hybrid huffed and shrugged. "Okay. I'm a little jealous of what you two have, and I'd love to have a piece of it, but only if Sasha wanted that too."

Grinding his jaw, Barden turned his focus back to me and lifted a brow. I shrugged. "It's all true. He's not lying."

Barden watched me a moment longer and hung his head, a curse falling from his lips. Vidal smirked. "She's young and inexperienced. She doesn't even realize the possibilities."

"What do you mean?" I asked. When Vidal just kept grinning at me, I looked to Barden. He was staring at the carpet. Shifting forward, I slipped my hand into my mate's to get his attention. "What does he mean?"

"It means that you should let me kiss you again. See if it does something more than make your secrets spill from your lips." Vidal winked. Barden growled. "I'm not greedy. I'll share."

Barden's growl turned to something more dangerous.

"Or not." Vidal shrugged.

Blinking, not comprehending Vidal's suggestion, I squeezed Barden's hand. For some reason, it made Vidal chuckle. "So fucking innocent. Smitten, I tell you. Absolutely smitten." He winked and stood up. "I'll give you two a moment."

Vidal moved toward the door, then stopped. "I know we need to work this out, but I'd ask that you not share the other part of my heritage with anyone. Sasha won't. I think it's enough for the Tormens to know I'm a hybrid. We don't need to go into specifics."

Sighing, Barden sat back, easing into the sofa, his arm coming around me and pulling me close as he appraised Vidal. "It wouldn't matter to them. But you're right. You'll have enough explaining to do about your wings and your dental impression in Sasha's throat."

Vidal watched as Barden cuddled me to him, his eyes getting those gold flecks to them as my mate rubbed his nose behind my ear and pulled me into his lap. "Thank you. I'll see you at the dinner table."

"This discussion isn't over," Barden warned.

"I know," Vidal replied, then opened the door and left us alone.

"Maybe you should just pee on me," I muttered as Barden wrapped my body in his.

"I'm not a dog," Barden huffed. He held me to him, his fingers kneading my thigh.

"What happens now?" I asked softly.

Sighing, Barden set his mouth by my ear. "The way I see it, we have three choices. I kill him, and the problem disappears."

"Let's make that a last option."

"We acknowledge his claim and work out how that fits between us."

I stayed quiet, still not comprehending how that worked and not liking the sound of Vidal coming between us.

"Or, my preference. We ignore that mark on your neck, treat Vidal like he's another brother of yours, and continue on as if it never happened."

"Brother is a bit of a stretch," I considered, remembering the kiss. "But the rest of that sounds doable." The silence stretched between us for a moment. "Is it?"

Barden leaned his head against mine. "We can try. We can always reassess if you decide it's more complicated."

Lifting my face to Barden's, I studied his eyes. Our bond was a mix of nerves and desire. Caressing my husband's jaw, I remembered he was in nothing but his workout sweats. His chest was bare and so close to my skin with this flimsy little summer dress I was wearing.

When I licked my lips and shifted on his lap, the edge of Barden's mouth turned up. "Pizza will be here any minute."

Smirking, I shifted to straddle the gorgeous man that was mine. "Then best you work your magic and remind me I'm all yours quickly."

A sexy growl leaked between Barden's lips as he lifted and quickly flipped me so he laid over me on the sofa. There was only a momentary concern as I felt Vidal's reaction out in the kitchen, then Barden was smothering my senses and making sure his claim as my husband was all I needed.

The Formal

BARDEN:

SMILING, I finished putting my earrings in and assessed myself in the mirror. The deep magenta velvet clung to my breasts and ribs, then fell to the floor. The luxurious fabric swished around my legs as I walked and framed my collarbones where the cap sleeves wrapped around the top of my arms, leaving my shoulders bare.

My dark hair hung in long waves, pinned on one side of my head with a faux ruby crystal clip. A pair of black three-inch pumps encased my feet, but you only saw them when I walked. My makeup was minimal, with a deep magenta and black framing my lavender-grey eyes. My lips had a subtle magenta gradient.

A knock at my door called my attention to where Savas stood in his tux, hands in his pocket. I smiled at how handsome he looked. "Don't you look dapper?"

Watching me grab my black velvet clutch, Savas lifted a brow. "Damn, Sasha. You look like Mum all done up to the nines."

341

My heart sank at the mention of her. She hadn't been home all week again.

"Barden is going to lose his shit when he sees you," Savas interrupted those negative thoughts. Taking my arm, he turned us to the door. "Ready?"

"Yes."

We took the stairs together, my brother supporting me to ensure I didn't trip and fall. Dad stood at the bottom with his phone taking photos. His gaze was on the side of weepy with a massive dose of adoration. "You look beautiful, Sasha," he murmured when I reached the bottom. His eyes tracked to my neck, and he looked relieved. "You managed to cover it?" he whispered.

"Savas gave me that stuff you use to hide tattoos," I told him.

Dad stopped, looked at Savas, and tilted his head. "Why do you have stuff to cover tattoos?"

Savas's mouth worked, then his eyes went over Dad's shoulder. "Mum, you made it?"

Mum walked through the door from the kitchen. "Of course. I wouldn't miss getting photos of my babies going to their formal."

"Mum!" Savas whined as Mum grabbed his elbow and shifted him to where she always took our photos from our first day at school. Encouraging Savas to pose for her, which he did.

Behind her, Vidal emerged, also dressed in a suit. "Vidal. What are you doing here?" I asked, surprised by his presence.

"I'm a chaperone for the formal. Thought I'd catch a lift with all of you," Vidal told me, a smirk pulling at the side of his mouth as he moved closer. "You are stunning," he murmured as he kissed my cheek.

"Hey!" Savas snapped, shoving Vidal back. "Keep your hands off her, or I'll make it harder for you to heal your lying face next time."

Grimacing, Vidal checked his jaw, moving it to the side. After he'd confessed his hybrid status to my brother and father, Dad demanded to know about the bite. The revelation that Vidal kissed me and tried to steal me from Barden caused Savas to punch Vidal in the face. Twice.

"Savas, let me get a picture with your mum and you, and then we'll get you with your sister," Dad intervened, giving Vidal and me a moment.

"You're not causing trouble, are you?" I asked Vidal quietly.

"I'd signed up to be chaperone months ago. Mum encouraged me to do it," Vidal assured.

"And Barden knows you're coming in the limo with us?" I didn't need Vidal to answer. Besides his humble look, our bond answered clear as day. Shaking my head at him, I went to join the photo shoot.

"Sasha, you look beautiful," Mum complimented as she indicated I stand by my brother and got her camera ready. Her eyes cataloged the dress, but she didn't mention that it wasn't the one she bought me or recognized as hers.

After a ton of photos with Savas and me mucking around, Dad got Vidal to take one of the four of us. The way things had been of late, it might be the last photo of us together.

"The car is here," Savas announced, going to open the gate.

"I'll get the door," Dad smiled.

Mum looked at Vidal and smiled. "Let's get a photo of you and Sasha together."

"Mum," I warned, but Vidal was already stepping beside me and putting his arm around me. Exhaling, I smiled, and as soon as the photo was done, I elbowed Vidal in the ribs.

He chuckled. "Can we get one with Savas too?" When Mum agreed, Sav slipped in between us.

"Barden is going to tear your head off, and I'm going to watch if you don't back off my sister, dude," Savas warned Vidal with a smile.

As if summoned, Barden stepped inside with Darina. There was a moment my heart seemed not to beat before Savas rushed forward and gushed about how lovely she looked, and Barden stepped towards me.

"Breathe, Sash. Your mate has never looked at another girl since the day you were born," Vidal murmured, giving my shoulder a squeeze. "Darina is your brother's date." The fact I could feel the sincerity in his words eased my sudden trepidation.

When Barden stopped in front of us, his eyes were wide with awe as he took me in; I wondered how I even doubted for a second. "Sash, you're..." Barden shook his head as if I was a mirage, and he didn't trust I was real. He didn't need words with that reaction. Stepping into him, I wrapped my arms around his neck and kissed his gorgeous face.

"Don't ruin your lipstick," Mum scolded, but she took a photo just the same.

With his arms still around me, Barden's gaze fell past my shoulder.

"I was merely chaperoning and thought I could catch a ride," Vidal defended the look Barden gave him.

"You live five minutes from the venue," Barden reminded. The silence was his answer, but I felt Vidal's reaction in my gut. Barden must also have because he shook his head and turned his focus back to me. "You look like sin," Barden whispered. "Temptation of the highest quality."

"Yours and yours alone," I assured, getting a smile from Barden in response.

After another fifteen minutes of photos with our partners, and then one of all five of us, Barden held me where I was and looked at my mum. "Can you get one of Vidal and me with Sasha?"

Mum looked just as surprised as me by the request but happily complied, complimenting Vidal the entire time on how handsome he looked.

"She only likes you because she doesn't know about the wings," I told Vidal as we wrapped things up. "Which Dad will probably tell her about as soon as we leave."

"Glad I came and got in while I'm still in someone's good graces then," Vidal snickered. He offered me his arm to walk out to the limo.

When I looked at Barden, he eyed Vidal. "It's okay. No reason we can't both escort you tonight."

Frowning, I allowed them an arm each and farewelled my parents as we headed to the car. Once we were in and moving, I eyed Barden. "I don't want to hide that we're together tonight. So if you're considering using Vidal as a smoke screen, forget it."

The side of Barden's mouth twitched, then he looked at Vidal. "We're not hiding anymore. That's not why I'm okay with his being here."

"Double the protection?" Savas asked. When Barden nodded, Savas met my gaze. "Barden can't keep an eye on you all night. He and Vidal can swap if need be. And if you girls go to the bathroom, you go together."

"Less chance of anyone getting you alone," Vidal agreed.

"In a place full of seniors, I think the Execrable could pick softer targets," I argued.

"It's not the Execrable we're worried about," Vidal said, surprising me. All three guys nodded at each other, and I felt like they were in team mode.

"You know, if you can't work with Athur anymore, you three could always form your own team. I think you'd work well together," I suggested randomly. They all looked at each other.

"That leaves Athur and Nash alone. That's not fair to Nash," Savas countered.

"He might prefer to join us," Vidal considered. "Sasha could replace Athur. She's stronger and a better rider."

I laughed but quickly realized I was the only one who thought it was a joke. The men seemed to be actually thinking it through.

"That would depend on Sasha staying here for university," Savas eventually said, his eyes bouncing between Barden and me.

Swallowing, I relaxed back in my seat, noting how Darina was eyeing us all. "It's a maybe problem for another day. Let's just focus on enjoying ourselves tonight." The others cheered as Barden's hand squeezed mine, nervousness slipping down our bond, not for tonight, but for the decision I would need to make. Turning Barden's chin towards me, I pecked his lips. "Nothing is set in stone," I whispered. "Relax. Let the river flow how it will."

The reassurance worked. Tonight we would just be teenagers celebrating the end of their schooling. Everything else—university, the Orey, our commitments—would be tomorrow's problem.

Living in the canyon, the limo took nearly forty minutes to make its way to the hotel where the formal was being held. That meant it was well and truly started by the time we made it inside. Simon and Elisha Vincent were just inside the doors with their dates waiting for us. As soon as Simon saw me, he made a beeline and pulled me into a tight hug before I realized his intention.

"Thank fuck you're okay," Simon murmured.

A growl beside me had Simon backing up to meet Barden's glare. "Dude, come on."

"Still not forgiven," Barden told him.

Huffing, Simon eyed my face and lifted his hand to sweep my hair back from my temple. Before he could touch me, Barden grabbed his wrist.

"Ah, yeah, okay. Let's stop pawing my sister now, okay?" Savas grumbled, easing Simon back from me. "Seriously, dude. Subtle as a brick."

"Let's go party," Elisha cheered, rolling her eyes at her brother.

Placing his hand in the middle of my back, Barden guided me forward. Vidal stayed on my arm until we reached the ballroom and the formal activity swept over us.

"Have fun," Vidal whispered. Then his gaze drifted to Barden. "Get her to summon me if I'm needed."

Instead of the annoyance I expected to feel down the bond from my mate, Barden nodded once at Vidal before he turned and went to join the other parent-teacher chaperones.

"You are strangely at ease with Vidal tonight," I murmured to Barden as our group moved through the chatting crowd.

"You and your safety are more important than my annoyance with what he did. He hasn't tried to use it to his benefit this week, and as the bond settled, I've been able to pick up on some of what you feel about him through your connection. None of which has caused me concern."

"Really? None of it?" I hissed, disbelieving. There was indeed one thing I was uncomfortable with.

Barden smirked. "Vidal did that to himself. If he didn't want to feel when we are intimate, he should have kept his teeth out of you."

Grumbling beneath my breath, I couldn't believe Barden was comfortable with Vidal knowing our private activity. "Well, let's see if you feel that way when he has sex with someone, and I'm forced to witness that."

That made Barden laugh and put his mouth to my ear. "I'll happily distract you when he does."

Before I could even fathom what that would be like, Elisha and

Darina grabbed my hands. "Let's dance," they laughed and dragged me to the dance floor to shake our booties.

The Escalation

"LET'S GET A DRINK," I gasped to the girls.

They nodded in agreement, and we headed to where the boys kept the refreshment table handy. By the time we arrived, Barden had already held a bottle of water ready for me.

"Thank you." Taking it, I skulled it.

Born Ready by Dove Cameron started playing. A buzz rushed through the hall. Barden took my hand as I set the empty bottle on the table, and we made our way out to the dance floor. The seniors told the others to move out of the way. The non-dancing seniors and juniors made their way to the outer circle of the floor.

"Canyon Falls Boys and Girls Grammar, are you ready to get this party started?" The DJ called. A cheer went up. "Then make some room and clap the beat. Let's do this!"

Tick Tick Boom by Class:y started playing. Giving me a wink, Barden offered his hand, just like every other guy did their partner. The beat hit, and we all started dancing the salsa.

Barden was a fantastic dancer. It wouldn't have mattered if I didn't know the steps as he led me around the floor effortlessly. Spinning me, reeling me in, and swinging those hips like he was born for it. As the music dropped away, we separated, moving to the sides and shifting to get ready for the next stage.

"Canyon Falls Grammar, your cheer squad," The DJ called as Queencard by (G)I-dle came on. Mia, Elisha, and the girls swanned onto the open space and performed their choreographed moves.

"Your volleyball team!"

As the first chorus played, the cheer squad moved to the front and turned, kneeling and cheering as the volleyball team danced the chorus.

"Your la crosse team!"

The boy and girl's la crosse had the slower part of the song.

"Your gymnasts."

Shoeless, the gymnasts took over the dance, and as the music revved up to the next chorus, Karla and a guy from the boy's campus flipped across the floor, drawing extra loud cheers from the others.

"Your swim team!"

Rushing out with the boys and girls from the pool, we took up our places, and as the chorus hit, we danced our hearts out, laughing and smiling as we finished the chorus. At that point, all the teams that previously danced rushed to the floor, and we all joined together to finish the song.

Surprisingly, during rehearsal, Mia, as cheer captain, had been in the center front, taking pride of place. But Elisha and the rest of the team had changed the steps up and somehow forced Mia in amongst the group, stealing her limelight.

The song finished, and we all stopped, laughing and breathing heavily as we moved to the side. Barden was on the far side, waiting for the next part. It shouldn't have surprised me when I got to the side and found Vidal waiting there, giving me a wink as I stayed amongst my group.

"Let's keep this energy up. Your football team."

Bite Me by Enhypen filled the room as the jocks took the floor, loud and boisterous as they messed up their moves more than hit them.

Even the DJ was laughing as he called, "Your mathletes."

We all cheered as the more nerdy guys took the floor and nailed their moves. The fact that Barden was leading that charge probably added to the female volume as he jumped into a handstand and humped the floor as his final move.

"God! He can dance," a girl moaned beside me. "So hot!"

A tingle flickered down my bond, calling my attention to Vidal and how his eyes glittered as he eyed the girl. His focus shifted to me, and the gold flecks in his eyes died away. He shrugged as if it were to be expected, and then his eyes were on the floor where the basketball team was finishing their set.

"Your soccer team!"

The girls went nuts as Simon and my brother sashayed onto the floor with their team, kicking a soccer ball between them with footwork that matched the beat. Flicking the ball to one of the guys, he performed ball tricks while the rest of the team danced to the chorus. While the team left the floor, Savas hung back, pulled at the collar of his shirt, and sang 'kiss me and bite me' as he winked at a group of girls.

Barden ran in with all the dancers for that session and grabbed Savas in a headlock, knuckling his head in jest before they straightened and led all those teams through the final steps. The girls were going wild. Looking to Vidal, I kept my voice low. "My brother is a total flirt!"

Chuckling, Vidal put his mouth to my ear. "He is. Though surprisingly, not the player I expected. I've never even heard of him with any of the girls."

"He's had a girlfriend since he was sixteen," I chuckled.

"Really?" Vidal asked, surprised.

Before I could say more, the DJ called, "Here we go!"

Hall of Fame by Stray Kids started playing. I moved forward with the girls to dance our steps; as the rap came in, the boys merged into us, taking over while we stood and watched. Then as the beat dropped, we were all dancing together.

Barden found me as we shifted places again, then he danced behind me, putting his arms around me and making the moves through the rap parts while I laughed.

As the song ended, the rest of our year joined us on the floor. "Canyon Falls Grammar. Your graduating year of 2023!"

Cheers erupted. Paper streamers and confetti blasted into the air and rained down on us. Wrapping his arms around me, Barden kissed me deeply, then we broke apart laughing. "I'm going to go freshen up," I told him.

Barden sobered, looked to the side, and nodded to someone as he placed his hand on the curve of my spine and led the way. As we got to the bathroom, Darina arrived with Savas. She rolled her eyes and took my hand. "You're not allowed to pee in peace," she muttered, taking me into the bathroom. "Not that I blame them," Darina added once the door shut. "You did nearly die on them. And for a mated Gelus, that's huge. Some mates go insane or become so depressed they kill themselves when their mate dies."

Chewing my lip, I went to the sink and wet a towel, then dabbed the cool towel over my face and neck. I wanted to say I could care for myself, but I'd seen how quickly Sophie and Yasmine died. For all my power, it would mean nothing if someone snuck up on me. As had already been proven down the river.

"What happened with the dance?" I asked instead.

Darina blinked as she wet her own towel to dab behind her neck. "What do you mean?"

"In rehearsals, Mia was front and center. How did you and Elisha end up there?"

Smirking, Darina tossed her towel in the bin. "None of the squad likes her. I need to pee." Slipping into a cubicle, Darina shut the door.

Chuckling, I used a dry towel to pat my face and neck dry. As I did, a wave of desire washed over me, sweeping me away to a hallway near the back of the ballroom. One moment I was kissing Desiree Phillips, her red curly hair tight in my fist as I controlled her head, and then with a masculine groan, a shiver of magic swept through me, and I shifted perspective.

Suddenly I was looking back at Vidal. His eyes were gold-flecked and glassy with lust. "Yes," he murmured as his eyes assessed mine. Then he was thrusting into me hard and fast.

I moaned and bit my lip to prevent crying out as he drove me quickly to climax.

"Sasha!"

Snapping back to my body, my hands gripped the bench, and when I blinked my eyes, I was staring at Barden. He assessed me, his jaw tight.

"I'm okay," I assured. Not as okay as I would have been if given another minute. "Holy hell!" I gasped as euphoria swept down the bond with Vidal.

"I'm going to kill him," Barden murmured.

"What happened?" Savas worried, finally catching my attention that they were standing in the ladies' bathroom with me.

The toilet flushed, and Darina stepped out. "What's going on?" Her eyes swept from the guys to me and back.

"Um, I had a dizzy spell," I covered. "Barden felt it and rushed in to stop me passing out and hurting myself again."

The grunt Barden sounded basically called bullshit without doing so. Whether Darina could translate or not, I had no idea. She washed her hands and asked if I needed water, to which I nodded.

"Stay with Darina," Barden murmured to Savas as she left.

"Fine. But you're telling me what happened to my sister when I return." He glared at Barden as he headed out.

"We should wait outside," I murmured, then followed Savas.

"Sasha."

"I don't want to talk about it," I told him. "He's suffered us plenty this last week."

"Vidal chose that fate. You did not choose to be part of his sexual endeavors," Barden argued as he followed me back towards the dance floor. "You shouldn't have to feel his secondhand lust."

Secondhand? There was nothing diminished about what I had just experienced. I was dragged into Vidal and somehow transferred into the woman he was with, so I felt everything she did as if I was the one he was banging.

"Are you okay?" Elisha was beside me, taking my arm as if I might be about to pass out.

"Here." Darina handed me a fresh bottle of water. Taking it, I skulled it so I wouldn't need to talk for the next few minutes.

Grabbing Barden's arm, Savas pulled him away. "What the hell just happened?" he asked as they moved into the crowd. The girls were with me, so there was no immediate threat.

I spied Mia and Raisa heading our way. Raisa met my eyes and gave me a kind smile. She opened her mouth to say something, just as Mia shoulder barged Elisha, knocking her to the floor.

"What the hell," I scolded and shoved Mia away, my hands touching her bare arms.

"Fuck off," Darina scowled, getting between Mia and me. At the same time, I squatted to help Elisha back up, giving Mia a death look that made her hesitate.

Recovering, Mia turned her focus back to Elisha and hissed, "Stupid wingless bitch." Then she walked off. Raisa looked regretful as she followed her.

Me. I'd frozen as Mia's words echoed around my head. Bouncing around until it collided with my memory of Sophie's last moments.

'Stupid wingless bitch.'

The ballroom spun around me, darkened, and then Sophie stood before me, her mouth moving, but I couldn't hear it over the rage thrumming in my head. This wasn't happening. I thought that Barden, having seduced Sasha, meant Vidal was mine for the taking. But this bitch Gelus was pregnant to him. To the most powerful Orey in our generation, besides that Gelus hybrid Savas. I wasn't losing him to a Gelus whore.

As Sophie turned to walk away, I pulled up my magic to give me the strength of earth as I grabbed her head and twisted it quickly. "Stupid wingless bitch."

The room spun, and I was back in the ballroom, Darina and Elisha bitching about Mia as I stared at the back of my former friend. Then the scene shifted, and Vidal was standing in front of me. His eyes were focused and intent. "Come with me," he urged.

Taking my hand, Vidal moved us quickly through the crowd, leading me to that back hall I'd seen him using while I was in the bathroom. I didn't even resist when he put me against the wall and captured my face in his hands. "Sasha, tell me what that was? What I can feel, I know you're in shock. Tell me what happened."

Blinking at Vidal, I couldn't form the words. Instead, I grabbed his tie and whispered, "Take it away." Then I kissed him.

Vidal's grey-hazel eyes swam and glowed as he closed the distance. I felt his power wash over me. Sophie's death from Mia's perspective played through my head on repeat. The need for retribution became a physical need. Violence whirled through me as I pulled electricity from my immediate surroundings.

A growl and a wash of rage pulled me from Vidal's hold just before Barden grabbed Vidal and threw him against the opposing wall.

Savas appeared and pulled me out of the way. "Don't call lightning," he directed. His power swirled through and around me. "Just calm down and think for a moment."

"It's not me you need to worry about," I reprimanded, my senses returning to me as if the fog in my head had cleared and my gaze connected with Vidal.

Cursing, Savas looked over his shoulder where Elisha and Darina stood watching. "Get Simon. Stay together."

As soon as the girls disappeared, Barden let up on the snarling and lightened the grip he used to pin Vidal to the wall. "You are not vengeance," he hissed.

Vidal glared. "I am worse." The gold motes in his eyes lit up like they glowed from inside.

Huffing, Barden released Vidal. "I'm not stopping you, but this needs to be done right." Barden paused as Simon came into the hall.

Seeing us, Simon turned and checked over his shoulder, gesturing to the girls to go back to the ballroom before he joined us. "What's happening?"

"We know who killed Sophie," Barden explained.

Simon shifted his stance and suddenly seemed old enough to be our father. "Your evidence?"

Three sets of eyes swung to me. The fact that until Savas rubbed my arms soothingly, I didn't even realize I was trembling probably said it all.

"Sasha has Eyal's gift," Barden explained. "But instead of collecting those last moments from the soul, she takes them from the body. She saw Sophie's death when she touched her body at the funeral. When she made skin-to-skin contact with Sophie's murderer, she saw Sophie's death from their perspective."

Considering Barden, Simon licked his lips. "I will need to confirm." There was a pause between them, then a muted growl rumbled down the hall. Stepping closer to Barden, Simon kept his back straight. "Perhaps you should go get your mate a drink. She'll need it."

"Keep Vidal with you," Savas decided. When Vidal bared his teeth at my brother, Savas shrugged. "We don't know how you will react to someone not her mate or family touching her."

Filling his chest with air, Vidal eyed me. Down the bond, I felt him imaging Simon putting his hands on me, and the venom of hatred drew up inside him. Exhaling, Vidal nodded. "You're right."

Vidal went to walk off, but I stepped out and stopped him with a hand on his chest. His mind was already back on his prey. "Wait for Simon."

Vidal glared at me, those golden flecks like starlight as the roulette in his eyes fanned open.

"Draw her to you," I whispered. "She wants you. That's what killing Sophie and trying to kill me was all about. Make eye contact. Flirt from afar. Give her hope. But wait for Simon. Sophie needs justice."

The murderous intent in Vidal's eyes pulled back. The roulette wheel closed in his iris until his eyes were grey-hazel dusted in gold again. Bowing his head, Vidal pressed a kiss to the corner of my mouth, then turned and waited for Barden.

My mate's kiss was far less subtle, stealing my breath as his possessiveness rumbled inside him. Once he'd marked me as his as best he could in the current company, he headed back to the ballroom with Vidal.

With one of his eyebrows lifted Simon considered their backs. "That was bizarre. Why isn't Barden ripping Vidal's head off for putting his lips on you?"

"Vidal's been there through Sasha's recovery. Barden's come to understand that Vidal likes to tease him but poses no threat to his mate," Savas explained.

I mean, if you discount his ability to drag me into his intimacy with another and put me in their body so it's like he's with me instead of them.

Shaking my head free from that experience, I focused on Simon. "What are you going to do to me?"

Squaring up to me, Simon cupped my face in his hands and stared into my eyes. "I am an inquisitor. Do you know what that is, Sasha?"

"I can guess," I answered as Simon's pupil bled into the blue of his iris until dark-gray striations swirled through the usually clear blue.

"Just breathe, Sasha," Simon encouraged. When my breathing steadied, Simon moved closer until our noses were almost touching. "Now, remember what you know about Sophie's death for me."

My vision became blurry, then faded away to Sophie and Mia. When the memory played out, darkness pulled me away.

When I came to, it was to Savas holding me against his chest while tears streamed down my face. "It's okay, Sash. Shh," he cooed. "It's over."

I didn't believe that for a second, but I didn't have the energy to argue. Others joining us made Savas loosen his hold, and then I was in Barden's arms as he cuddled me tight and rubbed my back.

"Sasha, I got you some lemonade," Elisha came up beside us. "Inquisitions can be very draining. The lemonade will help you feel stable again."

Thanking Elisha with a sad smile, I accepted the glass but didn't let go of Barden. Surprisingly, once I'd finished the glass, I did feel more stable and less of a weepy emotional mess.

Lifting my eyes to Barden, I asked, "Where's Vidal?"

Caressing my face, he stared into my eyes. "He did as you suggested and drew his prey to him. Simon met them outside."

Cringing, I worried. "What will happen to Mia?" Not that I felt sorry for her. Having felt her cunning, I had no sympathy. But I wondered how the Gelus dealt with such things.

Pecking my lips, Barden rested his forehead against mine. "She will go before your grandfather, and Sophie will have her justice." Waiting for a breath, Barden lifted his head. "I think I should take you home. People are starting to leave for the after-party, which means Savas and I need to head there too. Your father's team is watching over the car park to ensure the safety of our classmates as they exit."

"Sasha should come to the party," Elisha said without a hint of excitement. "It's at our place. Falco and Hawk are coming, so with so many Gelus there, it will be safer than her going home with only her mother to protect her."

"I think that's a good idea, actually," Savas agreed. "Plus, Sasha asked for a night of teenage normalcy."

"I think that's already been messed up," I grumbled.

Elisha took my hand. "Nah. We can fix it. Let's go!"

The Hall of Guilt

MY PHONE RINGING pulled me from a deep sleep. Yawning, I fumbled around Barden's bedside table until I located the vibrating curse and pulled it under the covers to put it to my ear. "What's up?"

"Sash, it's Raisa. Have you seen or heard from Mia?"

Frowning, I wondered why she was calling me. "No. Why would I have? The last I saw her, she was trying to start a fight with Elisha last night."

Last night. The formal. The after-party. Suddenly wide awake, I understood the question a lot better.

"I know, but she didn't make it to the after-party last night, and her mother just called to ask if she stayed here because she didn't come home," Raisa worried. "Nash and Athur are heading out with our fathers to search for her. Vidal isn't answering his phone."

I turned to wake Barden, but he was already awake and listening. "Did you want me to get Savas and Barden to—?"

"No, it's best not to bring them into it," Raisa cut me off. A breath of silence fell between us. "Sorry, I didn't mean that's how it sounded. I don't have an issue with them, but that team has a definite divide right now."

"Yeah, I know. I don't think you realize that Athur is the divide, and he and Nash are standing by themselves," I told her.

"No, Vidal—"

"Is with us." That's all I told her. I wasn't giving away Vidal's secret, but his alliance would be evident once his involvement in Mia's disappearance became known. Raisa was suddenly very quiet.

Meeting Barden's eyes, I asked quietly if I should tell her. His face serious, Barden nodded, then grabbed his phone and sent a message.

Taking a breath, I told Raisa, "I know about the Gelus now. I didn't know when Mia tried to kill me."

"What are you saying?"

Staring into Barden's eyes, I hesitated, but he swept my hair back from my face and nodded.

"The Gelus know who killed Sophie. It was Mia."

The phone was quiet momentarily, then Raisa whispered, "No. That can't be..."

"Mia and Yasmine knew exactly how Sophie died and threatened the same thing would happen to me. The Gelus overheard. I think Mia telling Yasmine how it happened is what got Yas killed," I expounded.

There was an unmistakable sob on the other end of the call. "You think the Gelus have Mia?"

Again, I met Barden's eyes to check before answering. "Yes."

"Why didn't you tell me any of this last night?" Raisa asked. She'd come to Elisha's for the after-party and hung out with me all night.

"Because I've had months of death and fear, and I just wanted one night of fun," I told her, falling back into the pillows with a sigh.

"I'm sorry for everything you've been through, Sasha."

"That it happened, or you chose not to be my friend through it?" I checked.

"I have to go," Raisa excused and hung up.

Putting my phone aside, I turned my face to Barden. He caressed my cheek. "We should get dressed. The Orey will come for Mia. Who they choose to come after for it, we won't know. It's best if we reach out to them. Lorka will call a meeting and reveal Sophie's killer and the evidence."

"Am I the evidence? Because the Orey might not accept that I saw Sophie's last moments."

"I know, but I honestly have no idea what Lorka has planned. He just told us to be at the hall in an hour."

"The hall?" I queried as I followed Barden into the bathroom.

Turning on the shower, Barden turned back to me. "The old scout hall by the falls. It's the Gelus meeting place and, for lack of a better word, our equivalent of a courthouse." Taking me in his arms, Barden smoothed my hair back from my face. "Remember how I told you Lorka was fairly big in the Gelus world?"

Biting my lip, I nodded, staring into Barden's eyes, curious and terrified I wouldn't like what I heard.

"Your grandfather's importance makes him judge, jury, and executioner for crimes committed by or against the Gelus. Simon took your testimony to him last night along with Mia. If he hasn't already handed down her sentence, he's about to."

Stepping back into the hot water, Barden took me with him, holding me and letting the water fall over us.

"How is Lorka important?"

Caressing my face, Barden moved closer, ready to kiss me. "His family—his bloodline—rule over the Gelus. His father is ruler in the Underworld, and Lorka is his proxy here in the borderlands."

"What? Like a king?" I asked, screwing up my face in disgust. If Barden was about to tell me I was some sort of princess, I would laugh in his face.

Chuckling, Barden combed his fingers through my hair, making sure it was all wet. "No. We don't have royalty. But your grandfather's bloodline is the most powerful amongst the Gelus, so they are our rulers."

As Barden lowered his mouth to mine, he murmured, "But I'll happily call you my queen."

Smirking at his cheek, I pressed against his desire. "Do we have time for this?"

"Always."

When we arrived at the old scout hall, Savas and my dad were waiting outside. Gesturing to a side door, Dad led the way as we furled our wings. "Change your top," he told me. "Let's keep your wings under wraps until all this is done."

Tapping my hips and opposite shoulders and clicking my fingers, I changed into a peasant crop top and skinny jeans. Barden growled and wrapped himself around me, nibbling at my neck, letting me know what he thought of the outfit.

"Is Mia here?" I worried.

"We don't know. Vidal told us to come in the other door. That's all we've heard," Savas answered as we reached the side entrance.

Pulling it open, Dad stepped in first. His shoulders tensed, but he made room for the rest of us to follow. Barden guarding my back as we went in. Once inside, I could see why Vidal told us not to enter the main door. That end of the hall was full of Orey, facing off with the Gelus who filled the opposite side. Using the side door brought us to the middle of the two groups. It also brought all eyes to us. A lot of them were not friendly.

Vidal, who was lurking on the edge of the Orey, immediately separated from his clan and came to me, surprising me by wrapping me up in a hug. What made it more awkward was that Barden didn't release his arm around my waist while he did.

"Lorka is going to try and keep you out of this," Vidal murmured loud enough for my group to hear.

When Vidal stepped back, keeping his arm around me on the other side from Barden, it was to reveal astonished faces on both sides of the hall.

"You should kiss Barden to make this more interesting," Savas snickered. In reply, Savas copped an elbow from Barden, but I felt the humor in both of my bonds.

"Now that everyone is here," Lorka called from the big chair he occupied at the end of the hall.

"Where is my daughter?" Mia's mother, Sallie Racle, demanded.

"Mia has confessed her part in the death of Sophie Thinehart and has faced judgment," Lorka answered.

"Bullshit!" Athur stepped forward angrily.

"That she confessed her part or that she murdered her?" Lorka asked.

"Both!" Athur challenged. "What reason would she have to kill some Gelus whore?"

Vidal tensed and went to step away, but Barden released me and quickly grabbed him and shook his head, warning him not to get involved yet.

"That's an excellent question," Lorka agreed. "What reason would an Orey girl have for wanting a Gelus dead? Then again, this isn't the first time Mia has been involved in the death of a Gelus girl, is it?" Lorka's eyes went to the Racles. "Nor is it the first time your family has found itself on the wrong side of them. Isn't that how you found yourself here, in the borderlands?"

"We moved here after our son was killed," Mia's father argued.

Lorka lifted a brow. "According to my brother, who presides over the area you last lived, your son died protecting his Gelus girlfriend from an Execrable attack. An attack that Mia escaped without injury."

Barden whistled low at the yet unsaid accusation.

"According to the evidence, Mia's actions were suspicious. The Gelus believed Mia purposefully set up the situation to create a condition to imperil the Gelus involved with your son." Lorka watched the Racles squirm and look at each other. "When I heard this, I did a little further investigation into two attacks of Execrable this year. The first involved all your daughters on their way home from a party. Nothing suspicious except that even from the testimony of both Raisa Culloch and Yasmine Reid, those Execrable targeted Sasha Tormen during the attack."

"What?" I gasped, along with Raisa and Yasmine's families.

"I had Simon ask them questions when I suspected Mia tried to bury you," Barden murmured. "I didn't want to scare you."

"Raisa and Yasmine also testified that they thought Sasha was clear of danger when the Delta team arrived, only for Mia to open the ground under Sasha instead of the Execrable, burying Sasha alive," Lorka continued. "Then weeks later, Execrable followed Sasha home and again attacked her. They followed her from the pre-formal, an event that Mia could be sure Sasha would attend."

"Are you suggesting our daughter is in league with the Execrable?" Mia's father hissed.

Gesturing to Simon, Lorka waited for him to produce a note, walk forward to the Orey line, and hold it so everyone could read it. "This note was found in the car of the Execrable who attacked Barden and Sasha on their way home that night," Simon explained. "Do you recognize the writing?"

Raisa gasped when she read it, her eyes filling with tears. "That's Mia's," she murmured. Nash cuffed his sister's shoulders, letting her lean on him for support.

"What does it say?" I whispered to Barden.

"That an Orey witch would be leaving the hotel's location, the date and time, and that she'd be traveling alone over the canyon," Barden revealed quietly. "Mia didn't count on me riding with you."

"Or she did and didn't think you'd be a match for that many," Vidal offered offhandedly.

Leaning back in his seat, Lorka considered the Orey. "So, you see, we have more than enough evidence that Mia has not only been previously involved in a suspicious death of a Gelus, but that she planned and tried on multiple occasions to kill Sasha," Lorka explained. "When Simon questioned Mia last night, she confessed to the murder of Sophie Thinehart. Why would your daughter want Sasha and Sophie out of the way?"

Helena Reid covered her mouth. Her eyes came to her son and where he stood beside me.

"Helena?" Jebidiah asked, massaging her shoulders.

A tear falling from her eyes, Helena lifted her watering eyes to her husband. "Vidal was promised to Sasha. Sophie was pregnant with his child. It was Vidal. Mia wanted Vidal."

Exclamations of shock filled the hall as Helena revealed the motive and Sophie's condition when she was murdered.

The other Orey shifted away from the Racles. Surprisingly, it was Nash's father who turned on the Racles first. "Did you know Mia was plotting against Sasha, and why?"

"No. Of course not," Mia's father rejected the claim.

"But you suspected," Mr. Culloch accused, his eyes on Mia's mother. "When Mia convinced the girls to turn on Sasha, when the boys told us Mia buried her alive and Sasha only survived because she had a powerful water affinity, you suspected it wasn't an accident, didn't you?"

Mr. Racle went to deny it again, but did a double take when he saw the glare his wife was sending to his teammate. "Honey? You didn't know, did you?"

Clearing her throat, Sallie glared at me, then bowed her head. "Know? No. But I worried. Mia wasn't a klutz. I found it hard to believe it was an accident."

"Hmm," Lorka sounded as he stood from his chair. "Forgive me, but I'd like to clarify, Mrs. Racle. Did you know Mia tried to kill Sasha Tormen?"

"I was concerned—"

"Yes or no?" Lorka cut her off.

Swallowing, Sallie stood tall. "No."

My father and brother looked at each other, neither of them happy. Barden cursed, seeing their reaction. "She just lied," Barden whispered. "The witch knew."

My heart beat harder in my chest. Vidal and Barden gripped me tighter while Lorka tilted his head and took another step forward.

"Did you know that Mia killed Sophie Thinehart?" he asked this time.

Jaw tight, Sallie glared. "No."

Once again, my father and brother exchanged glares. On instinct, I put my arm around Vidal, holding him tight. Barden also shifted his hand to rest it on Vidal's shoulder.

"Final question, Mrs. Racle," Lorka told her calmly, standing right before her now. "Did you encourage your daughter to kill her competition for Vidal Reid's affection?"

"Of course not!" Sallie declared, outraged.

"Holy hell!" Savas gaped. My father looked just as stunned.

Lorka smirked at Mia's mum. "Do you know why my bloodline presides over any matter brought before the Gelus?"

When Sallie just glared at him, Lorka chuckled, then he sobered drastically.

"It's because we can sense a falsehood. We know when someone lies to us. And you, Mrs. Racle, not only knew your daughter killed Sophie and attempted to kill Sasha, but you encouraged it. I dare say you were complicit in your daughter's actions, which led to the death of your son while he tried to protect the woman he loved. After all, wiping out the competition is how you caught your husband, right?"

"No." Mr. Racle stared at his wife as Lorka returned to his seat. "Not Patricia?"

What happened next? I don't think anyone saw it coming. I certainly didn't.

Mr. Racle grabbed his wife by the throat, staring into her eyes, rage filling him as he glared her down. "Tell me you didn't kill sweet Patricia!"

My father rushed forward with the others from team beta to try and stop Mia's dad from killing his wife. Helena was squawking, wanting to know if Mia killed Yasmine, which dragged Vidal into the fray as his mother also tried to get her nails into Mia's mum. Barden, my brother, and Nash moved to create a protective shield between the Orey women and the violent turn of events. It was a natural instinct. Part of their training growing up. Because Orey women were meant to stay clean and not be exposed to violence.

This is how, as Sallie's body convulsed, blood streaming from her eyes, nose, ears, and mouth, I was dragged backward, pinned against a body not belonging to one of my mates, with a knife to my throat.

The Fallout

"WHERE'S MIA?" Athur hissed in my ear.

"I don't know," I answered, my hand twisting the skin on the wrist, holding his knife.

"I don't believe you. You're one of them. Where did they take her?"

Enraged that he put his hands on me, that he thought he could threaten me, and his attitude of *'us and them'*, I filled my body with my hatred for this boy. "Hopefully to hell." I scowled, then pushed the fire of my hate into my hand.

Athur screamed and reversed his hold. I used his shock to keep hold of his arm, swing around behind him, and twist that arm up behind his back before I let the fire go.

Simon, Barden, and Vidal were all standing before us, their eyes wide as I shoved Athur away from me with a "Fuck you too."

He fell to the floor, cradling his wrist, which had severe burns.

"Baby!" Vidal looked impressed as he smirked at me. "All those years perving on us training came good." That made Simon laugh.

Barden kicked Athur hard in the gut, then I was in his arms, his lips claiming me while his fingers checked my neck.

"What do you want to do with him?" Simon asked.

"He didn't really commit a crime," Vidal answered.

"Actually, that's assault with a deadly weapon," Lorka decided. "If Sasha is willing to make a statement to the police, we could let the Vestigial law take care of it. As a judge in their system, my statement for witnessing it will carry weight."

"Can't we just beat him up and dump him on the outskirts of town or something?" Vidal asked.

"This isn't the old west," Simon laughed again.

Pulling back from my lips, Barden stared into my eyes, then stepped back to consider the others. "The injury was to Sasha. Let her decide," he told them.

The guys turned their focus to me. "Sasha?" Lorka prompted.

Considering where Athur glared at me from the floor, I shrugged. "He wanted to know where Mia was. If he still loves her that much despite knowing she cared nothing for him, I say take him to her. Let them be together."

That was obviously not the answer anyone expected, especially Athur, who looked excited and confused.

"Bloody hell, baby. You are ruthless," Vidal cheered, grabbing my face and quickly pecking my lips. With his arm around me, he turned to Simon. "I agree."

Lifting his brow, Simon looked to Lorka, who was assessing me as if there was more to see than his eyes could capture. Or maybe it was the way Barden stood with his arms around me, not growling at Vidal for doing the same.

"Hawk. Falco," Lorka called the brothers over. "Take this Orey to see Sophie's killer. We'll clean up here and then decide his fate." Turning his back, Lorka moved to where my father stood by Mr. Racle as he sobbed, kneeling next to his dead wife, but I got the idea those tears were not for her.

Hawk and Falco gave me a wink as they escorted Athur out the side doors, his mother following, demanding to know where they were taking him.

"Bleeding from the orifices," I murmured, studying Mia's mum. "Since when did strangulation cause that?" I turned my eyes to Vidal. The gold motes in his eyes were still full of starlight. He met my gaze, shrugged, and returned to observing the room.

When I turned to Barden, his gaze was also stern on Vidal. Flicking his gaze on me, he shook his head. "Her fate was already determined the moment Lorka learned her truth."

"I believe that covers what brought you here today," Lorka announced, turning his back on the Orey, who were still too shocked to move.

"Wait!" Helena stepped forward. "That's it? All you care about is Sophie and Sasha? What about my daughter?! Where is her justice?"

Head falling, Lorka turned back to face Yasmine's distraught mother. "We haven't determined if the Orey girl fell or was pushed. The Vestigial ruled it an accident occasioning death caused by severe inebriation," Lorka explained.

"So, you just give up?" Helena argued. "You can hear the truth. Ask Sasha what she saw that day. Ask all your Gelus where they were and if they were with my daughter."

Licking his lips, Lorka eyed me before focusing on Vidal's mother. "We did. We asked every local Gelus if they were with Yasmine. No one was lying when they told me no."

Sobbing, Helena collapsed. Jebidiah quickly wrapped her up in his arms.

"Wait!" Vidal stepped forward. "I have information." When he looked at me, I felt my mouth drop open. He wouldn't expose me like this? Vidal met my eyes and pleaded with me to play along.

"It took Sasha a while to remember, and she doesn't trust her mind after the severity of her injury, but in her nightmares, she sees someone under the bridge. It is too far for her to get a clear look, but she was sure she saw someone up there after Yas fell."

Tightening his hold on me as I started to tremble, Barden soothed me. "Shh. Trust the mate bond."

Lorka turned his gaze on me. "Is this true, Sasha?"

Tears streaming down my face, I nodded. "I'm not sure you can trust what I saw, and I worry it would damn the wrong person. That my brain played tricks on me after the hit. Already in the last week, it's changed. I don't trust what my mind thinks it saw that day. Could you tell if it's real or imagined?"

Huffing, Lorka looked lost. "If you don't trust it, then no."

"Use your inquisitor," Barden suggested. "Let them have a look and see if the memory is viable."

Turning to my mates so we were huddled together, I pleaded for them to understand. "It's not," I murmured to Barden. "I thought the person I saw under the bridge was who knocked me down and hurt me. But when Vidal went looking, that changed, and I realized it wasn't the case."

Barden and Vidal listened, but Vidal took my hand in his. "It's cover, Sasha. It's not your memory I need Simon to see, but Yas's last moments. This will give my mother her answers without exposing you."

When I looked to Barden, he wiped my cheek and nodded that I should go along with this. Bowing my head, I sighed. "Best you scram up some lemonade." Turning back to the hall, I nodded.

Considering me, Lorka then eyed the Orey, who were watching with interest. Helena was on her feet, eager. "Inquisitions are sensitive and can be emotional for survivors of trauma. This will be done privately. Helena, your emotions may affect Sasha's experience. Can I ask that you allow Vidal to remain as the representative of your family to witness the outcome?"

Looking at her son, Helena nodded.

"Then I'll ask everyone but Vidal, Barden, Sasha, and the inquisitor to remain," Lorka declared.

"Why Barden?" Jebidiah queried. "Shouldn't it be a member of her family?"

Taking a breath, Vidal answered his father. "Because Barden is Sasha's husband." He took my hand. "We both are."

Murmurs broke out throughout the hall. "Way to let the cat out of the bag," Barden grumbled.

"They had to find out sooner or later. Better before so they don't question what becomes of this," Vidal whispered. Turning back to the shock of his parents, Vidal took a breath. "It's still new for us. It turned out Sasha had two mates. While she and Barden have a physical relationship, an emotional connection between us was cemented earlier this week. We're all still a little confused about it or how to manage it."

"Then how can we trust you have your sister's best interests at heart here?" Jebidiah challenged.

"Because I'm willing to put my mate through an inquisition to gain that truth," Vidal rebuked.

Mouth pressing into a flat line, Jebidiah took Helena in his arm and gestured to the door. "We'll wait outside."

Everyone left the hall. Once it was just the four guys and me, Simon approached. "I'm guessing I'm not looking at Sasha's memory here, but Eyal's gift?"

"It's the only reason I permitted this," Lorka muttered. "It's best the others don't know."

"Remember, this is traumatizing for Sasha. Be gentle," Barden warned.

"Try and slow it down when Yas falls," Vidal suggested. "That's when Sasha is sure she sees something but is unfamiliar."

Taking a breath, Simon placed his hands on either side of my face and leaned in close. "Are you ready?"

"Yes." My words were braver than I felt as Simon's Gelus eyes revealed themselves, and I tumbled into the darkness. Then I was running, and Yasmine's scream rang out.

Strangely, it was like we fast-forwarded through me getting to Yasmine, but as I touched her body and her final moments came to me, it returned to normal speed. Experiencing Yasmine stumbling under the bridge, the questions, and then the fall. And as I turned and fell backward, that face was there again, with the golden eyes, smiling sinisterly at me.

The memory switched back to me on the river, the glimpse of the wing, then the impact. Darkness.

"Fuck!" Simon pulled back.

I stayed wrapped in the blackness for longer this time. Those golden eyes blinked at me from the nothingness, looked to my side, grinned, and disappeared.

Shivering, I returned to myself, held between Barden and Vidal. "He saw me," I barely managed.

"What do you mean?" Vidal asked.

Swallowing the lump in my throat, I met Vidal's eyes. "The Narsitee. He knows I saw him."

"Narsitee?" Lorka growled.

"That's what Sasha saw in Yasmine's final moments. One of them was under the bridge with her," Simon revealed. He shook his head. "But he didn't push her. Not physically."

"Are you satisfied it was real?" Lorka asked.

"Yes. He was there. I also got enough emotion from Yasmine to know why she was with him," Simon explained.

Nodding his head, Lorka gestured the door, then looked to my mates. "Vidal, there is a stockpile of non-perishables in the storeroom out the back. Grab Sasha a can of lemonade."

Vidal whispered his thanks, kissing my temple, then went to get what I needed. Clinging to Barden, I felt drained, and my brain was sloshing around in a bowl of soup.

"How is she?" My father asked nearby.

Barden grunted in response.

"How come when you asked us questions, it didn't affect me like that?" I heard Raisa ask.

"Because I asked. I didn't go into your memories and see them," Simon answered. "Inquisition works in two ways, by hearing or seeing. The latter zaps a lot of energy from the witness, so I don't do it unless needed. Sasha didn't trust what she saw, so her words would have been useless."

"What was it? What did she see?" Helena demanded.

"Wait, Mum. Let me help Sasha, and then Lorka will reveal it," Vidal assured. "Here, baby. Drink this," Vidal placed a can in my hand.

"Stop calling me baby," I garbled. I'm pretty sure from the flutter of humor down both bonds, it made the guys chuckle.

That first sip of lemonade was glorious. This inquisition seemed to take longer and more out of me than the last one. But I felt better when I'd drunk half the can. Standing straight, I nodded to my grandfather, then leaned into Barden again.

"What Sasha saw and the reason she doubted was that she was made to," Lorka explained. "There was a man under the bridge with your daughter when she fell. But he wasn't Gelus, even though he tried to make Sasha see him as such."

"Who was it?" Jebidiah demanded.

"That's the problem," Lorka continued. "Sasha didn't recognize him, but we now have the face to go along with the other evidence Nelly Assion retrieved for us. We think it was your daughter's lover."

"Why do you think lover and not the murderer?" Jebidiah asked.

Scanning the room, Lorka sighed. "Some collectors, Crows, can see a person's last moments. We had one touch your daughter after death. They saw that Yasmine intimately knew the person under the bridge with her. They were arguing about her choice of words while threatening Sasha at the diner publicly a few days earlier. It seemed Yasmine knew the exact method that Mia used to kill Sophie, and it made her lover suspect her involvement. The lover had a vested interest in Sophie and her baby."

"Are you saying Vidal wasn't the father?" Helena worried.

Lorka studied Vidal. "I don't know. That's all the collector could gather."

"Did he push Yas?" Raisa rushed to ask. "Did the Crow at least see that?"

"The Crow's sense is that Yasmine wasn't pushed." Lorka looked my way. "But her lover also didn't try and save her. It could be in the heat of the argument, he turned his back and didn't realize until too late, or he didn't care if she lived or died. I'm sorry, but from our perspective, we can only agree with what the Vestigial found. Yasmine's death was an accident."

The hall was silent, then Helena broke, sobbing into her husband's arms.

Across the room, my eyes met Simon's, and I knew he didn't believe that. Considering the strange look Dad and Savas gave each other, they didn't either.

We waited for the Orey and most of the Gelus to leave, and then I asked my grandfather for the truth. "It wasn't an accident, was it?"

Huffing, Lorka stepped back and gestured to Simon.

"When a Narsitee is involved, it's unlikely," Simon explained. "He was upset about Yasmine's possible involvement in Sophie's death. Not because of Sophie, but the baby she carried. I couldn't tell why, but I could tell that much. Narsitees are fast and deadly. If he wanted to save her, he could have. And the way he smiled at her as she fell..."

"And we have no idea who he is?" I checked. "I mean, there aren't many left. Which is why I thought they avoided the borderlands and the Gelus."

"Very true," Lorka agreed. "But it's a big world, made up of multiple realms. We don't know every creature passing between. That he was staying around here enough to have developed an intimate relationship with one or more females is disturbing."

Simon raised his arm as if he planned to touch my shoulder, but two growls from behind me made him rethink that. He glared at my mates, shook his head, then met my eyes. "We will be looking for him now that we know he was here. I'm sorry, that's all we can offer."

"So, this is over?" When Lorka confirmed it was, I turned back to face my mates and family. "Let's go home."

The Acceptance

SITTING ON MY BALCONY, watching the river sparkling in the spring afternoon, the call connected. "Sasha. What can I do for you?" Delila sounded tired and defeated. I don't think I'd ever heard her sound like that.

"Mum, I need you to come home."

"Sasha—"

"Right, sorry, that sounded like I was asking. I'm not. Tomorrow is our graduation ceremony. Afterward, we'll go out for dinner, which will double as my farewell party."

"Farewell...?"

"I'm leaving for the summer. I won't be here. So, there is no reason for you not to be," I stated plainly.

Sighing, Delila took a beat. "Sasha, there is more to my leaving than just you."

"I'm aware you hold me turning out Gelus against Dad, but if you could accept Savas having wings, there is no reason you can't accept that I do."

"I wish it was that easy," Delila argued.

"It kind of is," I grumbled. "But that's beside the point. A lot has happened, and Dad needs you."

"What do you mean?"

"Mia confessed to Sophie's murder and attempted to kill me. Mr. Racle killed Mia's mum. I have something called Eyal's gift, which I think is a curse. A Narsitee was here and involved in Yasmine's death. Athur held a knife to my throat and threatened me; he's also gone. And Vidal bit me," I rushed the summary.

"What?" Mum gasped.

"Mr. Racle and the Nellafs have packed up and left town. The teams don't exist right now, so what's left of the Beta and Delta teams have joined together temporarily. Dad's father turned up, and we've been getting to know him. He's like a judge and says he knows you from work."

"When did all of this happen?" Delila asked, sounding worried.

"Since the formal," I told her with a shrug. "Anyway, it made settling down to focus on exams hard, but we managed it, and it's all done. You shouldn't miss Savas's graduation just because you can't stand to be around me. That's all I wanted to say. So, come home, Mum. Forgive Dad. He really does love you. And Savas misses you. Dad doesn't play favorites like you. Savas will be getting married and moving out before you know it, so take the time that's left to be here."

When I stopped, and Delila was quiet, I sighed. "I'm staying at Barden's tonight. I hope I'll see you at the ceremony tomorrow. If not, then I guess this is goodbye." Hanging up before she could refuse, I dropped my phone in my lap and prayed to the powers that be that she listened to me for once.

"I don't play favorites, huh?" Dad alerted me to his presence, shoulder leaning into my balcony door.

"Not to Savas's benefit like she did," I replied.

"I thought you were staying here tonight?"

"With all of you out hunting, Calliope thought a girl's night was better than me staying home alone," I told him. "Also, code for they still don't think I'm safe by myself."

"Because of the Narsitee?"

Closing my eyes, his golden irises smirked at me from the darkness. "He saw me. Not by the river, but in Yasmine when she fell. I don't know how, but he did. It wasn't Yasmine he smiled at; it was me."

Coming outside, Dad took a seat at the little patio table Savas and I shared. He placed a large envelope on the table and slid it to me. I looked at the university name and left it untouched. My desire to leave was gone, and I still didn't know what I wanted to do next year.

"Are you scared?" Dad asked.

"Of the envelope? No."

"Of the Narsitee?"

Swallowing, I considered. "Vidal asked Simon to let him hunt it with him."

I gazed at the river. "What if it hunts Vidal back?"

"Do you worry for Vidal or yourself? Because I'm pretty sure Vidal is much more capable than he ever let on. He hid being hybrid pretty damn well." Dad huffed. "I worked with that kid for fifteen years and never once saw any sign he was more than a powerful Orey."

Rubbing my lips together, I avoided meeting my Dad's eyes. "He certainly is more than I ever thought."

"What's it like, having a bond with two men?" Dad asked quietly.

"Argh! Overbearing. Invasive. Weird. Comforting," I revealed, each word falling from my lips a little quieter. "The bond is definitely stronger with Barden. His sort of overrules Vidal's. But Vidal's can push through and make itself known when it wants to." Like, when he was with another girl. It had only happened once so far, but it made an impression.

Dad nodded. "You know, I always knew Vidal was keen on you. I felt bad for him when Barden showed up. I never saw this coming, but at the same time, it didn't surprise me when it did."

Bizarred out by that comment, I gave Dad a look that said as much. He chuckled. "You've always been so different from the Orey and never really fit the Gelus. A few months ago, I learned not to be surprised by anything you threw at me. But I think I'm trying to ask if you're okay with this?"

Frowning as I considered the question, I assessed the last few weeks since Vidal bit me. "I didn't think I would be when it happened. I was sure Barden would kill him."

"Had you not got your lightning on, he may have," Dad snickered.

Nodding, I thought through my words. "I was worried at first it would be awkward because Vidal would want more than I do from it. But he was content straight off just to have that bond. Like it satisfied him in some way at a soul level to have that connection with someone. He's not tried for anything physical, and while he speaks to me as if I'm his girlfriend and likes to hold my hand or have an arm around me, mostly, it's like hanging out with my best friend. What surprised me was how relaxed Barden has been with Vidal, always touching me."

Dad looked to be smothering a laugh. "Trust me, that surprised everyone. The double bond really has the Orey and Gelus talking, considering Vidal's origins are not widely known, and everyone is occasioning it to your hybrid nature. But to add to it, they are okay with each other—but if another man even looks to be about to touch you, that they both growl is hilarious."

I rolled my eyes. They didn't even need to be in the same room. Just last week, Darina, Elisha, Raisa, and I all celebrated at the Milkbar after our final exams. When Raisa hugged me, I felt their growls down the bond. I had to tell them to quit that carry-on as a reply.

"Well, if it gets too much and you need me to put those boys in line, I'm always here for you," Dad promised.

"Are you getting emotional about me going away for the summer?" I asked.

"Yes," Dad observed me. "It is only for the summer, right?"

Grabbing my dad's hand, I squeezed. "Barden made you a vow. While the dust settles with the Orey, I see the Underworld with an experienced guide. And Barden says that travel worldwide is faster and easier via the Underworld, so he made me write him a list of all the places I want to visit. We'll be in the Underworld when Barden needs to work and seeing the world when he's not."

"And Vidal's going with you?" Dad asked.

"Not long term. He's coming with us for the initial trip to Barden's home there and will spend a few days learning the ins and outs of getting between the realms by shadowing Barden while he works. Once he can come back and forth on his own, Vidal will come back and hunt the Narsitee with Simon and come see me when the distance gets too much."

Dad took that in, then said, "Considering how much time he spent here after your injury, I think you should be prepared. He might move there with you and just travel back and forth for the hunt."

Shrugging, having already discussed that possibility with Barden, I didn't negate it. "I think that was more about trying to get me to reveal what I knew about Yasmine's death. But if it happens, Barden's got the space to accommodate him. He mentioned a shack out the back he'd stick Vidal in," I repeated Barden's joke with a smirk. When Barden told it, he kept a straight face and no hint of humor in the bond, so I couldn't be sure it was a joke.

Laughing, Dad stood up. Kissing my head, he murmured, "Love you, Sasha. Thank you for trying with your mother."

"Hopefully, I scared her enough to make her see sense," I mourned.

"Common sense was never your mother's strong point. If it was, she wouldn't have married me." Giving me a wink, Dad headed for the door. "Don't leave without saying goodbye. I need to stockpile the hugs if I don't see you all summer," he called as he passed through my room.

That I could just jump off my balcony and fly across the canyon now was not a good enough excuse for not giving Dad a hug goodbye. He made sure that was clear after the first time I just sent a message and jumped.

My phone buzzed, and I pulled it out, shaking my head at the screen.

VIDAL:

No flying today. I need quality time with my Bae, so I'll pick you up and drive you to your other mate's.

ME:

Or could we go for a flight together?

VIDAL:

Your wings have an effect on me. Probably the same one it does on your mate. All those snowy feathers. If I give you a halo, we could role-play.

Rolling my eyes, I shook my head.

ME:

Fine. Drive me.

VIDAL:

Thought you'd see it my way. Be there in an hour. Just finishing up at the college.

Sighing, I went back to watching the river.

Savas joined me and sat quietly for a bit. Eventually, he looked at the envelope. "I got one of those today."

"City?"

"I decided to follow Nash and Vidal's lead and do my degree online." Handing me a formal letter, Savas showed me the offer.

I was expecting it to be for the degree he wanted. Instead, it was an invitation to try out for one of the professional soccer teams. Not the Premier League, but one just beneath it. "You're going to play pro?"

"It's just an invitation to try out right now. The scouts have been watching me all season, but it's not guaranteed."

When I just stared at him, Savas rubbed the back of his head. "You said to keep my options open and not give up my life for the Orey," Savas reminded me. "With the teams sort of collapsing, I talked about it with Dad and Barden, and we agreed that I should take this opportunity, and we can work around my training and playing. Barden is going away for the summer. Vidal is focusing on the Narsitee who killed his sister, so we've decided to take the summer off patrolling and see what happens. We haven't seen an Execrable since you and Barden wiped out that lot on the bridge. Either you killed the local collective, or they decided to use another border crossing after accidentally attacking two local Gelus."

Again, I just stared at my brother.

"What do you think?"

Swallowing, I blew out a breath. "Firstly, it's not about me. It's your life."

"You're my twin, and you sort of lead the way in not conforming to expectations, so I'm looking for a little support here in my first act of rebellion to our very directed upbringing."

That made me smile, then laugh, which caused the same reaction in my brother. "Well, then!" Jumping up, I fell on my twin, giving him the biggest hug.

Two growls echoed down the bond. 'Oh, it's my brother, for Pete's sake!'

The growls cut off. But I still righted myself and backed up to the railing.

"I think this is a wonderful opportunity, and you should grab onto it with both hands," I told him enthusiastically.

"Now that's the reaction I was looking for," Savas told me with a laugh.

"If you're going pro, what are you doing at university?"

"Sports Management. If I do go pro, I figure it will teach me the business did of things. Still, I'm going to do a minor in sports development and a second in coaching, so I've got options if I don't," Savas revealed. "What about you?"

"Recreational therapy, also online, but I have to attend campus occasionally for workshops. I figured with my love of outdoor activities and my recent interest in therapy and recovery for trauma sufferers, it would be something I'd find interesting," I told Savas.

His eyebrows lifted. "Wow! Okay, did not see that as an option; but yeah, I can see that being something you'd enjoy doing."

"Speaking of outdoor activities," I smirked. "Want to race the canyon with me? I haven't unfurled since we started exams, and I'm itching to be airborne."

Laughing, Savas stood and pulled his shirt over his head. "I know exactly how that feels. All those years, Mum made me hide it from you."

Doing my hip and shoulder tap to change my top, I turned, unfurled, ready.

"I heard you call her, by the way," Savas said as he shook his wings. Turning, he met my gaze and offered me his hand. "Thank you."

Smiling, I took his hand, swiftly kissed his cheek, then yanked him to follow up onto the railing and yelled, "Dive, swoop, glide!"

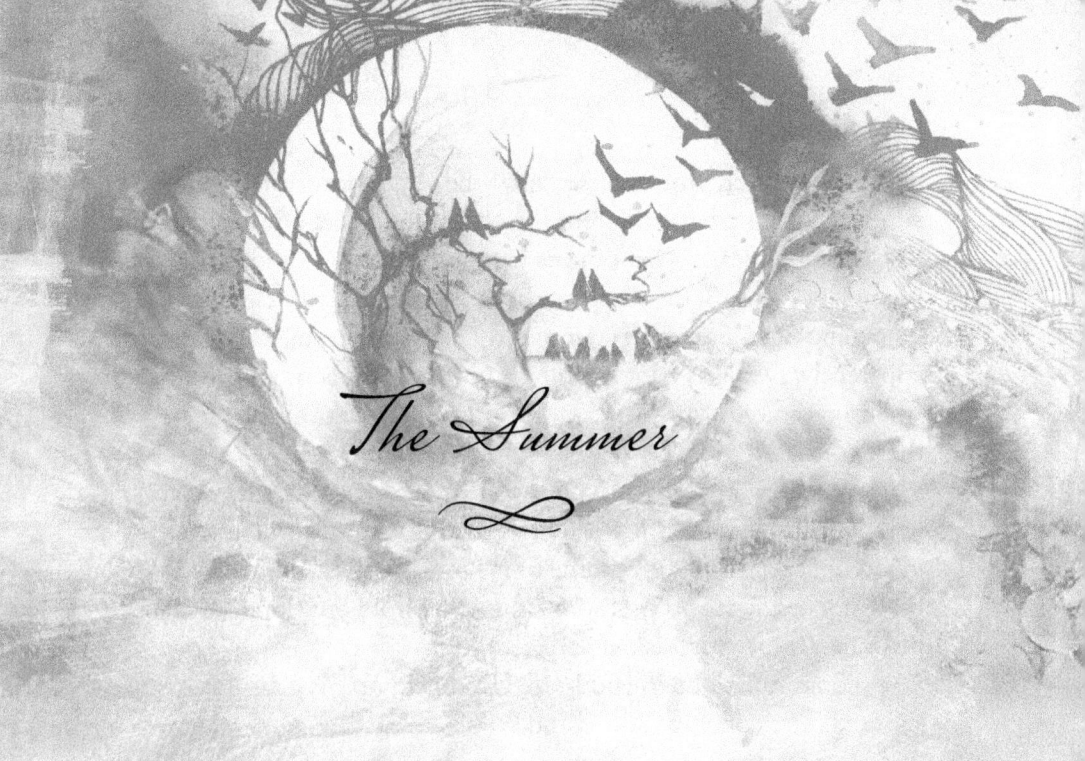

The Summer

"OKAY, A TOAST," my dad called, quieting the chatter at our table in the restaurant for our post-graduation dinner. "To Savas and Sasha. I can't believe you both graduated today for so many reasons. The first is because no parent wants to acknowledge how quickly their kids grow and face the reality that they are ready to leave the nest. The second is mainly directed at Sasha because I've had some serious concerns about you surviving to see this day come from when you were twelve and first took my motorbike for a joyride just so you could ride with your brother. Never more so than the last few months when you've survived some hairy situations."

Barden took my hand under the table. Vidal took my wrist on the other side. Down the bond, I could tell Barden's was to comfort me, and Vidal's was to reassure himself I was there.

"As interesting as this year has been, I think the next few months will be just as interesting in a different way. It will be the first time the twins will be away from each other for an extended period of time," Dad explained to Lorka and the Assions, who came to celebrate with us. "I'm not sure how they are going to cope. Savas has never liked his sister being too far away. And as you just heard, Sasha would steal a bike just to be with her brother. But we'll see how the separation suits you now that you are older and have different interests pulling you out to adventure."

Taking a breath, Dad put his hand on Mum's shoulder. She'd come home last night. Savas told me they'd stayed up late telling her all the news, and then Savas left Mum and Dad alone to talk. This morning, apparently, Dad was a lot happier, and Mum was acting like she used to when he came down to breakfast, so I hoped that meant they'd sorted things out.

"Wherever life leads you now, your mother and I want you to know we are proud of the adults you have become, and we will always be here if you need us." Dad's eyes came to me for that last statement. "Knowing how independent you both can be, I won't hold out hope." Once again, he smiled at me. Surprisingly, so did Mum.

"Congratulations to you both." Dad held up his glass. Everyone else shouted their congratulations and drank.

After dessert, I excused myself to go to the toilet. A man ran into me as I returned, knocking me off balance. His hands grabbed my shoulders and helped stabilize me as our eyes met. He seemed familiar, but I couldn't pick why.

"Sorry about that," he apologized. He smiled, but the smile died when his eyes went to my neck, and he stepped away with a frown.

"Sasha," Mum called as she approached.

The guy walked away, still frowning. Shaking off the weirdness of the encounter, I turned my focus to my mother. "Mum."

Coming to stand before me, she took a breath. "I am proud of you. And I do love you. Your dad and I had a long talk last night, and he made me realize that your independence and my control freak tendencies would always clash. As you got older and started demanding control of your life, I struggled to relinquish it."

When I raised a brow, Delila huffed. "Okay, I refused to let go. You have always been headstrong, but I think, for the most part, you were happy to go with the flow just to keep me happy. When you reached the point where you decided your happiness was more important, I struggled to accept that change.

"I am still struggling to accept some of your decisions. But that's not my job as a parent. It's to support you. And as kids get older, that support changes. I need to trust that I did a good enough job raising you that while your decisions would not be mine, they are what's right for you and your well-being."

"Actually, I think you struggle with me because we are too much alike," I told her. "We both fell in love with the guy our mother hated," I reminded her. "You went into law when your mother wanted you to do computers. And we are both stubborn and unwilling to bend when our minds are made up about something."

Delila considered me. "Hmm. You may have a point."

Smiling, I let my gaze roam back to the table, to the mate I chose. "He loves me and treats me so good, Mum. I wish you could see it."

"I do," Mum whispered. Her eyes filled with tears as she admitted, "I always have. But he wasn't the only one, Sasha."

My eyes shifted to Vidal, and I sighed. "Yeah, I know."

Following my gaze, Delila leaned closer. "Your Dad told me you're sort of married to both of them now, but no one can really work out how Vidal fits into things. When the three of you are together, you're like best friends with a secret language, randomly laughing at some untold joke, teasing, and what have you."

"It's different, but it also feels right." What else could I tell her that Dad wouldn't have already? "We're still figuring it out ourselves."

Barden approached slowly, not wanting to interrupt, but his glance at the window told me time was up. Giving him a nod, I turned to Delila. "We're heading off. Barden wants to go while it's still light, and he really wants my first view of his home to be the early sunset."

"Your dad told me you're spending the summer in the Underworld. I was kind of surprised. Aren't you scared?" Delila trembled as if the very idea terrified her.

Gaze returning to Barden, I smiled. "No. I feel how much Barden misses living there. For him to love it so much, it must be more than Execrables and other scary beings." Focusing back on my mother, I hugged her tight. "I love you. Thank you for coming today. I hope you and Dad can work things out."

"It wouldn't be the first time he's forgiven me for being a stubborn mule," she sobbed. "Please be careful, and let us know you're safe regularly."

"I will." Letting her go, we moved back to the table and made our farewells, then Barden, Vidal, and me headed for the exit.

We rode our bikes to my parents' place, where Vidal had left his bag earlier. We took the long route as it would be my last ride for a while. With backpacks full of our stuff on our chests instead of backs, we unfurled and flew to the crossing, which turned out to be a cave hidden by the falls near the scout hall.

Taking a hand each so we stayed connected, Barden led us deep into the cave, our eyes adjusting when the light vanished. As we approached what appeared to be a dead end, I grew hesitant, but then Barden put his hand to the wall, which shimmered and turned to blackness.

"It can sense you belong," he murmured. "Don't be scared."

Nodding, I followed him through the night curtain to emerge onto a cliff top, high above a sunlit valley. A gentle wind ruffled my feathers as I took in the golden colors of autumn across the ravine ahead of us. Birds and more unusual-looking animals flew through the sky. Much like those in the Vestigial realm, other animals roamed the land.

"Animals can pass the barrier?" I asked, awed by the beauty. It was nothing like I imagined considering the horrible creatures I'd encountered from here.

"This is the... zootopia," Barden struggled. "That's the closest English interpretation. Animal heaven, if you will. All souls return to the origin realm on death. You call it the Underworld because you bury the dead, but we call this realm Elysia."

"The Gelus share this island with the animals roaming all over waiting for their reincarnation. Humans have their own islands. Some are their Nirvana or whatever their personal beliefs inspired. There's basically an island for every religious version. I love visiting Valhalla. It's an endless party with the occasional fight thrown in for fun."

"You have to take me there," Vidal laughed. Barden gave him a wink.

"There are also islands that prescribe to the Vestigial hell. You won't be going there," Barden told me with certainty. "Your white wings make you look like their version of angels, and you'd have them all in a tizzy, and the Sturnias would kick my ass."

"Told you. Halo. Role-play," Vidal snickered.

Barden reached around me and shoved him sideways, causing Vidal to laugh. Still, Barden's mouth was also twisted into a wry grin. "Keep your fantasies to yourself, or at least to the privacy of your sex life."

"And if you could not share that with me, that would be swell," I added.

"Yeah, no. Can't promise that. The heat of the moment and all that," Vidal objected. "So, Mr. Tourguide, are we getting to see your place before the sun goes down?"

Rolling his eyes, Barden tilted his head to the left. "This way." Then he launched from the cliff.

I looked at Vidal, and he gestured to the edge. "After you, Angel."

Doing my eye roll, I leaned forward and fell into a glide, leaning into it so I fell into Barden's slipstream.

Okay, no. Barden wasn't a jet, but he was big enough to cause a channel in the air currents, and I found if I rode those, it used a little less energy.

We flew for maybe an hour, and I hadn't seen a house. In fact, it had all been splotches of heavy forest below us, with regular clearings between.

I was just starting to worry we had to fly across the large body of water on the horizon when Barden waved to his left. Glancing at the cliff face, I saw another Gelus with big brown and white wings jumping from a ledge. That's when I noticed several cave-like openings all up and down the cliff, with other smaller openings throughout. Still, Barden didn't head towards the cliff.

Looking behind me at Vidal, he seemed to have the same curiosity and gave me a shrug. A sensation of calm flowed down the bond from Barden, and I understood it to be reassurance we were nearly there. There was also excitement and the anticipation of being home.

As we approached the waterfront, Barden lost altitude, and I followed. He swept out over a small beach, swung around, and followed the coast north. From this lower perspective, I could see the thick forest contained structures within the trees.

Treehouses!

My awe of the Underworld only grew at this discovery, and my excitement rose when Barden swung back to shore and landed on one of the large balconies of one such structure. I landed beside him, snapping in my wings to make room for Vidal automatically because the jutted-out part of the balcony, which was obviously a landing pad, was really only built for two Gelus to have their wings extended.

Moving forward to the French doors, I peered inside to see a beautiful sitting area all decorated in white, grey, aqua, and teal. Moving along the balcony, I placed my bag on the outdoor lounge and peered in the windows until I found a bedroom with French doors and a stunning canopy bed. It looked like someone had lifted a five-star Caribbean over-water bungalow into the trees. Infinity pool built into the deck of the bedroom and all.

Barden joined me, wrapping his arms around me and pulling my back against his chest as he kissed my neck. "This is my home. I'll show you inside in a minute, but first, I want to show you this."

Turning to face the ocean, I gasped as the sun melted into the sea, purples and pinks washing the sky, the water shifting from aqua, teal to purple, then sapphire.

"Oh, Barden. It's beautiful. How did you ever leave it?"

"Because I love you more," he whispered.

Leaning on the railing, Vidal watched the sunset. Still, I saw the side of his mouth twitch, and a sense of happiness radiated down both bonds that had nothing to do with the serenity the sunset weaved.

As the sun disappeared, Barden showed me that his treehouse was more like a tree-penthouse. Suddenly, I wondered if I'd told my dad the truth about only being gone for the summer, because this place already felt like home.

The Epilogue

WRAPPING A BLANKET AROUND MY SHOULDERS, I dropped onto the lounge on the balcony, watching the sun start to melt into the horizon. The summer in Elysia had been fantastic. We'd visited many of the islands, which all served different afterlives or Elysians.

It was weird to consider that while this was the afterlife for the Vestigial world, it was also the living world for those of this realm. Barden's dad Gavel explained that we were all Elysians, but a war broke out too long ago to recall. The natural inclination of the Vestigials for greed tried to repress the other Elysians. When those of magic rose up, it caused what humans recall as the fall. For Elysians, it was not the fall of magic but the fall of paradise.

In the fallout, Vestigials were forbidden to live out their mortality in Elysia. Narsitees worked together to create another realm where mortals could exist. Corvus were tasked with transporting the souls for life and death. They called that realm Pandemonium for apparent reasons. Vestigials were inherently chaotic.

I learned a lot from Gavel, who regularly visited since Nelly and Gavel Assion owned the Tree-penthouse next door. Gavel being very old, like he joked he had a pet dinosaur once, old—okay, he was only around five thousand Earth years—chose to live here and regularly visit with Nelly. He worked a lot more than Barden, but called in for tea and to share his extensive wisdom every couple of days.

Mainly, I loved the stories of Barden when he was young. You know, like he was a young adult when Alexander the Great was crowned king of Macedonia in 336 BCE. That caused a momentary freakout, but Gavel laughed at me and told me that Nelly was only twenty when Gavel knocked her up with Calliope around the same time Stonehenge was formed in 3000 BCE.

He was trying to ease my mind that a two-thousand-year age gap was barely an issue in the Gelus. Still, all it did was make me ask if what I learned in ancient history was accurate. Queue Gavel visiting regularly to fill my inquisitive mind with all sorts of historical facts.

Considering I'd rarely spoken to Gavel before this, how well we got along amazed me. When Vidal visited, he'd join us for 'accurate history hour', and Barden would use the time to get some work done.

The lounge sank beside me, and Vidal threw his arm over my shoulders. "You going to be able to leave it?" he asked, watching the sunset with me.

"Barden said we can holiday here while I do my degree. Still, I think I'd like to come more regularly. Maybe one weekend a month."

"You're doing your degree online. You could come here for a week every month," Vidal countered.

Giving him a nudge, I smirked. "Trying to get rid of me?"

"No, but I wouldn't want to spend too long away from here, and it's not even my place."

Nodding, I let that settle, then considered. "Hey, if you study online, why are you always on campus during the week?" I asked.

Vidal gave me his 'Solemnly swear I'm up to mischief' smile. "Rizzing." Focusing his eyes on me, Vidal's gaze dropped to my lips. "A lot of girls are keen to ride this pony even if you aren't."

Smirking to try and cover how hot my cheeks suddenly seemed, I shook my head at his tease. Vidal sighed and grew serious. "I've found it's easier not to pull you into my depravity when we aren't in the same realm," Vidal answered honestly.

"I still feel it. But it's a caress rather than an 'I got sucked into a porno' like you did to me at the Formal. And Valhalla," I told him.

I knew Vidal took advantage of his trips home to let off some steam. Considering when he was here, he had to endure feeling Barden and me being intimate down the bond, I thought it was only fair.

"Again, Valhalla was all the fault of the mead and some severe sexual frustration after a week straight of you two at it like rabbits," Vidal excused.

Not that I blamed him. He wasn't the only one having sex in that hall when we visited Valhalla. And he was behaving until the serving girl plopped herself in his lap and whispered how easy the access would be. That's when Vidal gave up trying to be good and gave her a good pony ride. I would know I'd got the transfer body experience again. Something I was sure Vidal could control. At the time, Barden was taking part in an axe-throwing competition and seemed to miss it. Again, something I suspect Vidal might have orchestrated.

Huffing, Vidal cuddled me tighter. "I've always had a voracious appetite. But the bite did change things for me too. The urge is still constant, but it's you I want. When we go home, I'll try not to involve you, but I can't promise."

Exhaling, I relaxed against him. "I know."

"Is it really so bad?"

My elbow in his ribs was all the answer he got. Still, he laughed. Pulling out his phone, he laughed at the screen—cell reception made it to Elysia.

"Savas keeps sending me messages to check you're coming back," Vidal relayed.

"He's been blowing up my phone all week."

"Wasn't he just here last week?"

"Two weeks ago. It's probably the one thing certain to make me leave tomorrow. I need a hug from my brother," I revealed.

Savas and Dad came home with Barden after our third week in Elysia. I'd become mopey and homesick, something shocking. So, after his work, Barden asked Savas to visit with me. Apparently, he'd been temperamental for the week too. Excited about seeing the Underworld, Dad asked if he could tag along, so Barden brought them in, and while Savas used the guest room Vidal normally stayed in, Dad chose to stay next door with Gavel and do sightseeing with his friend. I heard they also went to Valhalla.

"Is the twin connection really that strong?" Vidal asked.

Tilting my head, I watched a silhouette I recognized well by now flying up the coast over the water. "It's not like our bond or anything. And I know it's not the norm for every set of twins, yet it's always been there with Savas and me. We first realized it when Mum started taking me to see her parents and leaving Sav's home when we were six. It's like this elastic band that gets tauter the longer we are apart. As we've gotten older, we can go further for longer, but the tighter the band gets, the more depressed I get, and the angrier Savas gets."

Vidal listened to my words and frowned. "You'll never be able to live away from each other, will you?"

"I've nearly really thought about it," I admitted. "But, I guess you're right. We'll have to live in the same area and see each other regularly."

Nodding, Vidal watched Barden coming in to land at speed. "That explains Barden's suggestions about your living arrangements when you come home."

"What do you mean?" I frowned.

Shaking his head, Vidal smiled. "We'll talk about it over dinner," he assured, then focused on my other mate. "Hurry up! You're missing her last sunset here for a while," Vidal teased.

Continuing to jog forward from his landing, Barden furled his wings and plopped down on my other side.

"Is that blood?" I pointed to a smear across his chest.

Barden shrugged off my concern with a grunt. As long as it wasn't his, I guess it was okay. It wasn't the first time he had come home roughed up. Calliope said the collectors really did get the better part of the job.

Quietly, we watched our last sunset together in Elysia for at least a few weeks. Then we went inside, and I cooked while Barden showered and Vidal worked on an assignment for his summer subject.

Once seated, Vidal looked at Barden and lifted a brow. Rolling his eyes, Barden took a pull of his beer, then turned his focus to me. "We have some news. A surprise is part of it, but you also gave us an idea before everything went to hell before the formal."

Intrigued, I set my cutlery down. "Okay."

"Up for discussion first is our living arrangements when we get home," Barden declared. "This one," he gestured annoyingly at Vidal, "has grown fond of this setup and wishes to continue to sleep over with us. That rules out living with my family. They don't like that he force-mated you any more than I do, but while I have accepted this weird situation, they will not have Vidal staying with us."

"Which means living with my family," I pondered. "Which I wasn't planning to do because Mum has finally moved home, and I don't want to be the trigger for any more issues between my dad and her. I'm pretty sure moving both of you in with us will cause friction."

"Exactly!" Barden agreed. "How would you feel about us getting our own place when we go home?"

Frowning, I considered we didn't have much choice. As much as it was unplanned, I'd also grown fond of Vidal hanging around. "That means moving out of the canyon."

Vidal and Barden exchanged a look. "Maybe not," Vidal optioned.

"Your Dad suggested we build a place like this in the forest towards the ridge above your parents' house. He owns the land and checked when he bought it that he could build anywhere as long as minimal damage is done to the area's ecology. Gavel and I built this place together; he built their house next door and the one in the canyon. He offered to bring this piece of Elysia to Pandemonium for you. As a wedding present."

Blinking at Barden, I couldn't believe that was an option. "Really?"

"If you'd be happy with that?" he checked.

The smile on Vidal's face was there before mine, and Barden's grew just as impressive. "I'd love that!"

"Okay, then. That's great news." Barden seemed relieved. "Second item." Barden nodded to Vidal.

"Remember how you offhandedly commented that if Athur kept causing problems, we should make our own team?" Vidal reminded me. "Well, with the situation what it is, our hand has been forced, and a

Gelus, two hybrids, and an Orey definitely pack more of a punch than what it previously looked like. "

"A lot more power," I agreed.

Vidal nodded. "Remember how I also joked you should replace Athur because you're a stronger rider, and in two encounters, you took out more Execrable than he ever did?"

"I remember you joking about me taking his place, but my body count was never mentioned," I corrected.

Barden quickly stuffed his mouth with food to avoid saying anything. Vidal wasn't so reserved. "I thought your body count was one?" He pointed at Barden.

"Which makes her kill count even more impressive," Barden snickered.

Rolling my eyes, I motioned Vidal to get on with it. "Right," Vidal sobered. "Well, it wasn't a joke. We all agree you'd make a good member of the team. But before you say no, you should know Darina told Elisha, and they asked your dad to train them over the summer."

When I could pick my jaw off the ground, I whispered, "They did?"

"Yes. And while Elisha has much to learn, Darina is a lot older and can kick some serious butt. She's even killed a Narsitee before," Barden offered.

"Dude, way to make me uncomfortable," Vidal grumbled.

The side of his mouth twitching in a smile at Vidal, Barden set his focus on me. "What we need you to consider before saying yes, so we won't accept an answer tonight. We're not just going to be dealing with Execrables anymore. There is a Narsitee in town, or passing through enough he got familiar with an Orey witch. And there are also plenty of other predators to be dealt with. So, it will be more dangerous. Think about it long and hard before committing."

Taking that in, I nodded. "I will." Though, I was pretty sure I already knew my choice. I'd always wanted to join the team with Savas and hated being left out. I remembered telling Savas I'd liked fighting the Execrable and how angry he'd been.

"Are you sure Savas and Dad are okay with me potentially joining the team?"

Barden took my hand and gave it a reassuring squeeze. "It was your brother who suggested it to your dad first."

Inhaling deeply, I picked up my fork to keep eating. "So, will we get plans drawn up for our new place?"

"Back in a sec," Vidal excused and raced to his room. When he came back, he held a roll of A3 paper. Spreading it open, I stared at the plans for our new place. Very much like Barden's place here, but with two extra rooms next to Vidal's, making the future tree-penthouse a little bigger.

"Why the extra rooms?" I asked.

"Well, with us all doing our degrees online, we thought we'd set it up as a shared study space," Vidal explained. "Bookshelves on the empty walls for all your books, and a big table in the middle that we can all sit at and study together like you always do at your place. There will be space for all four of us."

"Four?"

"Savas can study at our place when he wants," Barden informed gently.

It made me smile that they'd included him. "Is that who the fourth room is for?"

"Nah, that's for when you two decide to breed," Vidal said without reserve.

"Not any time soon, Sash. Just future-proofing," Barden assured, though I felt the hope in him to one day be a dad.

Nodding, I looked at the drawings. "Who drew these?"

"Vidal," Barden shot him a look that might have been impressed. "He is studying construction engineering at university. You'd hope he'd know something about drawing house plans."

"It even includes a plunge pool," I pointed out excitedly. After that, I spent a reasonable amount of time pouring over every detail and discussing the plans with the guys until Barden told me we should go to bed because we had an early morning.

Not that I could sleep, but Barden ensured I was thoroughly relaxed by the time he bundled me up in his arms and started snoring lightly in my ear.

The following day, bright and early, we closed up the house and took the trip back to Pandemonium. While Barden and Vidal had come and gone weekly, I hadn't returned to the cliff that was the gate for the borderlands where my family lived. I think I was terrified if I went back, I'd lose the peace I found here. Still, I'd flown to many other gates with Barden while we visited other areas of my birth realm, ticking off most of my bucket list. So, the flight home was easy.

What I wasn't ready for was to approach my parents', and for Barden and Vidal to aim high up on the ridge. There, nestled in the highest trees, was our piece of Elysia.

The sheer joy overflowed my eyes as my feet touched down on the landing deck, designed to fit three Gelus easily this time, as I stared at our beautiful new home.

"Gavel's been working on it all summer for us. That's why he was around for only short visits," Barden explained. "Vidal and I also worked on it when we could. Vidal more so since he had an excuse to be away longer."

"It's not finished yet," Vidal warned. "The kitchen and laundry aren't close to done, and the main bathroom and my ensuite are still only up to waterproofing. But our bedrooms and the master bathroom are finished, so you'll just have to share with me until we can complete the rest."

Leading me to the stacker doors for our bedroom, Barden slid them open. "It's why I was late last night. I was helping your dad and brother prepare our nest," he apologized.

Barden's bed and furnishings filled the room, but everything else was like our place in Elysia. Swiping the tears from my eyes, I wrapped myself around Barden, kissing him deeply before I did the same to Vidal.

When I realized I had kissed him, I pulled back awkwardly. Vidal's eyes were alight with surprise and happiness. Neither of my mates said anything. Deciding to pretend nothing was unusual, I ran and jumped on the bed cheerfully.

The freshness of the paint and timber floors tickled my nose, but with the doors open, it was bearable. Sighing, I sat up. "What about my stuff?"

"Your clothes are in the wardrobe, but we agreed to leave your bedroom still usable in case you have nights you want to stay there," Barden explained.

"Like if you need time out from the two of us," Vidal added.

"Or you need quality time with your brother and the security of your childhood bedroom," Barden finished.

I smiled and laid back. A moment later, I had a handsome Gelus on each side, cuddling into me. "I love it," I told them.

"I love you," Barden answered.

Vidal sighed. "Absolutely smitten."

The End

Glossary

Vestigial - Humans

    Execrable - the detestable, the wretched. Or, in human terms, evil beings that crawled out of the underworld to do horrible things to people. Once Vestigials who were responsible for the fall of Elysia

    Narsitee (Also known as Gods) - Sociopathic spirit/ghost like creatures that can take solid form and appear Vestigial

    Orey - Witches

    Gelus - Winged magical creatures which may be where Vestigial belief in Angels came from. There are many different races of Gelus all with different abilities and proclivities.

    Corvus (Crows) – Transporters of souls. Within the Corvus there are the Collectors who reap the dead, and the deliverers. Not a common bread as they find it hard to procreate.

    Eyal Corvus (Eyal's Gift, Eyal's Child) - A unique bloodline who see last moments instead of last thoughts like the majority of Corvus collectors.

    Strigias (Snow Owls) – Rare. Most were killed in the fall of Elysia and only one very old and powerful bloodline remains. The males of this bloodline are Truth seers – can hear a lie, can tell no lies (but can omit or avoid answering).

Aguilas (Eagles) - Common. Have various capabilities but the most common being their ability to see past someone's words to the heart of the matter. The very powerful are known as Inquisitors and can see into memories and watch them to learn the truth.

Peregrinus (Hawks & Falcons) - Common. Playful tricksters. Soldiers of Elysia. Highly attuned to emotions of those around them. Can use that ability for mischief or to offer support to those who didn't even know they needed it.

Sturnias (Mynas) - Guardians of the Isles of Punishment.

Isles of Perdition - Includes islands dedicated to all the differing religions versions of Perdition. Also the home of Execrable and other demonic beings who were once Vestigials or Orey responsible for the fall of Elysia.

Elysia (Underworld, Heaven, Land of Souls) - The original realm.

Pandemonium - The Vestigial mortal realm. When the fall of Elysia finished, the Narsitees used their magic to create a realm where Vestigials could undertake their mortal lives without inflicting their chaos and greed on Elysia.

Afterword

I really hope you enjoyed the Orey Gelus Duet. I'll admit, this ended far left of where I planned. As usual, the Muse took over and I was left sitting here wondering what the hell just happened. Vidal's bite was never supposed to happen. Yet, once it did, I couldn't take it back off the page. I wanted to explore a mated relationship that wasn't sexual. Where it was more about protection and emotion than physical interaction.

One of the things I was keen to do was showcase a healthy teenage relationship. No abuse, no bullying, no manipulation. Barden was to be the bad boy who wasn't toxic to his love interest. I'm happy to say, I think Barden came through in this for me. Vidal...well he is 1/3 sociopathic god, so I didn't think he did too badly.

Of course, there are some of you who may be keen to see if that unplanned kiss leads somewhere physical in the long run. I wanted to keep Sasha's story FM. Yet, I am planning to have a continuation for Vidal and him tracking the Narsitee who may, or may not have killed Yasmine.

So, if you are hoping that this weird mating might form into a steamy menage, keep your ears peeled for Vidal. There are definitely more secrets to be revealed, including why Vidal's bite took.

Thank you again for reading. I'm so grateful when I hear from readers that they enjoy my stories.

Until next time...

Join the Beautiful and Deadly

Join Ebony's Mischief List

Sign up to Ebony's mailing list for the following perks:

- latest news on new releases
- heads up on upcoming promotions
- exclusive content previews
- first chance at Giveaways
- get a free book

Go to https://ebonyolson.com for more information

Dark Romantasy / Paranormal Romance by Ebony Olson

STANDALONE BOOKS

Of Shadow and Light

Boundary

Silver Rogue

Halos

The Grave Keeper: All Hallows

ANGELIS SERIES

Spectra

Angelis

HIERARCH SERIES (DARK ROMANTASY)

Succumb

Numinous

Masked

Exodus

Burning Immortality

OREY GELUS SERIES

Gelus Hearts (Compilation of Orey Witches & Edge Gelus)

Vidal

CHAOS STAR TRILOGY (SCI-FI ROMANCE)

Praldia

Cyra

Avalonia

ANTHOLOGIES

Booktober: A Halloween PNR Anthology

Romance Suspense by Ebony Olson

Hotel Series

HOLLY CLAIRE TRILOGY

Holly's Trilogy: Books 1-3 Hotel Series

(Compilation of Henderson, Cassidy, & Holmes)

JESS BUTLER TRILOGY

Best Sunset: Books 4-6 Hotel Series

(Compilation of Best Man, Best Layover, & Best Knight)

Black Mark Series

Black Mark: The Complete Saga

(Omnibus of Resistance, Secret, & Heart)

Black Mark X

Standalone Books

Calypso

Rain: A Dark Past Romance

Protective Instinct (On KU as Hunter Enemy & Lover Enemy)

About the Author

Ebony lives in Sydney, Australia, with her husband, daughter, and six rescue cats. She loves to read fantasy, thrillers, and paranormal romance, spending most of her free time with her nose in a book or writing.

Having always possessed an over-active imagination Ebony spent her younger years regaling friends with fantastic stories, holding her audience captive with the passion and suspense of her characters plights. In adulthood, she shows no signs of stopping her imagination from spreading across as many pages as it can find.

Website: http://ebonyolson.com/
Ebony's Mischief & Mayhem Peeps

facebook.com/EbonyOlson.Author
x.com/Ebony_Olson
instagram.com/ebony_olson
amazon.com/author/ebonyolson
bookbub.com/authors/Ebony_Olson
goodreads.com/Ebony_Olson

www.ingramcontent.com/pod-product-compliance
Lightning Source LLC
Chambersburg PA
CBHW060816120726
47909CB00006B/1950